SORCERY
REBORN

ALSO BY STEVE McHUGH

The Hellequin Chronicles

The Avalon Chronicles

SORCERY REBORN

THE REBELLION CHRONICLES

STEVE McHUGH

Text copyright © 2019 by Steve McHugh
All rights reserved.

Published by 47North, Seattle
www.apub.com

Amazon, the Amazon logo, and 47North are trademarks of Amazon.com, Inc., or its affiliates.

ISBN-13: 9781542093125
ISBN-10: 1542093120

Cover design by @blacksheep-uk.com

Cover illustration by Larry Rostant

Printed in the United States of America

For Sarah

LIST OF CHARACTERS

Nate's Story

Clockwork, Oregon

Nathan Garrett: Was once a sorcerer feared by his enemies; now human and believed dead by most. Uses the fake name Nathan Carpenter.

Chris Hopkins: Unknown species. One of the few people who knows who Nate really is. Works for Hades.

Antonio Flores: Human. Ex-Ranger. Lost a leg in battle; now runs a local diner, Duke's.

Donna Kuro: Doctor of ancient history. Married to Daniel Kuro. Grandmother of Jessica and Ava Choi.

Daniel Kuro: Doctor of medicine. Married to Donna Kuro. Grandfather of Jessica and Ava Choi.

Jessica Choi: Mother of Simon Choi. Sister to Ava.

Ava Choi: Sister to Jessica.

Brooke Tobin: Sheriff deputy.

Sheriff Adrian King: Sheriff of Clockwork, Oregon.

Doug Ward: High school friend of Brooke's.

Avalon Members and Allies

Baldr: Sorcerer. Son of Odin. Brother of Thor. High-ranking member of Avalon.

Orestes: Sorcerer. Harbinger team leader.

Apep: Snake-kin. Harbinger team leader.

Adrestia: Daughter of Ares. Empath. Harbinger team leader.

Robert Saunders: Knights of Avalon (KOA) agent. Ex-partner of Jessica Choi.

Bryce Foster: Nazi. Allied to Robert Saunders.

Jackson Miller: Nazi. Allied to Robert Saunders.

Addison Tobin: Nazi. Girlfriend to Bryce and sister to Brooke.

Rebellion Members and Allies

Medusa: Gorgon. Codirector of Elemental Incorporated.

Isis: Sorcerer. Codirector of Elemental Incorporated.

Hades: Necromancer. Married to Persephone. One of the leaders of the Rebellion against Avalon.

Persephone: Earth elemental. Married to Hades. One of the leaders of the Rebellion against Avalon.

Diana: Half-werebear. Considered to be the Roman goddess of the hunt.

Thomas Carpenter: Nate's best friend. Werewolf. Married to Olivia. Father to Kase.

Remy Roax: Foxman hybrid.

Mordred: Sorcerer. Once turned evil by Avalon torture; now trying to atone for his mistakes. Dating Hel.

Selene: Dragon-kin. Love of Nate's life.

Layla's Story

Helheim

Layla Cassidy: Umbra. Able to manipulate metal.

Kase Carpenter: Half-werewolf, half–ice elemental. Daughter of Thomas Carpenter and Olivia. Dating Harry Gao.

Harry Gao: Human. Good with runes. Dating Kase Carpenter.

Tarron: Shadow elf. One of the last of his kind. Searching for the rest of his people.

Zamek: Royal prince. Norse dwarf. Alchemist. Searching for the rest of his people.

Tego: Saber-tooth panther.

Hyperion: Dragon-kin. Able to use ice magic. Father of Selene.

Hel: Necromancer. Leader of Helheim. Dating Mordred.

Seshat: Och. Records the words of every book ever written.

Jotunheim

Fuvos: Giant. High priest.

Jidor: Giant. Guard.

Mimir: Och. Social pariah. Can read people's minds when touching them.

Wedver: Giant. Elder.

Tisor: Giant. Elder.

Goretis: Giant. Warrior.

Surtr: Flame giant. War chief. Enemy of Asgard.

Prologue

Nate Garrett

Two Years Ago
Greenland

I opened my eyes and immediately wished I hadn't. The light caused them pain and forced me to close them again. I went to rub my hand over my face and found myself chained to the bed with thick manacles. There didn't appear to be any runes etched on them, so I tried to use my magic and . . . nothing. No hint of magic.

"Great, another place with runes in the walls," I said. My throat hurt, and I needed a drink. "If anyone is there, I'm awake."

The doors opened, and Hades walked in. He had several weeks' worth of beard growth and looked tired. "Nate, you're finally up." He unlocked the manacles and placed a hand on my shoulder.

"Where am I?" I asked.

"My secret facility in Greenland. You've been in a coma for four months."

I couldn't quite process that as an answer. "What? Four months? But I was . . . Mordred . . . he shot me. Is he okay?"

"We'll bring you up to speed with everyone in a minute. I just need to make sure you're okay. Can you sit up?"

I did as he asked.

"We're going to run some medical tests," he told me.

"Hades, I'm fine. I ache and want a drink, but otherwise I'm good. My nightmare, Erebus . . . he saved me."

Hades nodded. "Let me go get you a drink, and we'll talk. Stay here."

"Hello, Nate," Erebus said from beside me.

Erebus, living embodiment of my magic, was, like everything to do with my life, much more complicated than he first appeared. All sorcerers could commune with the magic inside of them, and to most, these embodiments were considered nightmares—creatures who wanted nothing more than to have sorcerers lose themselves in their magic so that the nightmare could take control. In reality, they were there to help us, to guide us until we were ready to take full control of our power. The world had been lied to about their intent, and a lot of people had died because of it.

"I thought you were going to vanish after I died," I said.

"Apparently not," Erebus said. He looked identical to me, even though he was actually part of the primordial deity who was considered the personification of darkness. It had always been a lot to take in. "The mark on your head unlocked a lot of things, but they're all a jumble at the moment. It'll take some time to sift through it."

"Including who my father was?"

"That's in there, but it's not information I have. Your mind needs time to heal, as does your body. It's been under incredible stress. Your lack of magic will not help things along."

"My magic is gone, full stop, isn't it? I remember Mordred saying something about it."

"Yes, for the next year or thereabouts, you will have no magic. You are essentially just human."

"Anything else?"

Erebus shook his head. "Hopefully when the year is up, you will regain your power. But when you do, it would be wise to be somewhere barren."

"Why?"

I looked up as Mordred entered the room. "He'll explain," Erebus said and vanished.

"Glad you're up and about," Mordred told me.

"I feel like I've been hit by a truck," I said.

"Yeah, it's not a fun experience. You've lost your magic, then."

"I figured that bit out. Erebus said it'll be a year before I can access it again. He also said any info unlocked by the mark will take a while to work through."

"It was the same for me. Took about fifteen months to fully understand everything in my head."

"Did you have messages from your parents in your head too?" I asked.

Mordred shook his head. "No, I had no need. I know who they are, and I've always known who my mother was. Did Erebus say anything about what to do when your power returns?"

"Be somewhere uninhabited."

"Make sure you do that. I didn't realize until it was too late and destroyed a warehouse. When your magic returns, you'll have full use for about a day; then it dies down. You'll need to relearn some stuff. It's not a quick process."

"Untapped, incredible power, but at the cost of a year or more with nothing. Always give with one hand, take with the other with magic, isn't it?"

Mordred laughed. "You need to come with me. There are some things you need to know."

"I'm in a pair of shorts. Can I have a shower and get changed first?"

"Oh, sure. Shower's over there. I think Hades said something about clean clothes for you in the drawer."

I looked over at the door, which presumably led to the shower, and the light-blue chest of drawers. "I'll be twenty minutes."

"Take an hour. Have a long shower. You're going to need it. A lot has happened."

Mordred left me alone, and I went for a shower, making the powerful, high-pressure water as hot as I could bear.

"You feel up to a little company?" Selene asked from the doorway.

I opened the glass door to the shower. "I'm achy, but I'm sure I'll manage."

She dropped her robe to the floor, revealing that she was naked underneath, and stepped into the shower.

An hour later I was clean, dressed, and in need of something to eat. Selene had helped me with my T-shirt, as my body was still incredibly sore and stiff, but the shower and company had done wonders to lift my mood.

"Hades wants to see you," Selene said, kissing me on the lips. "I missed you. Probably not as much as Tommy, but it was a close thing."

I laughed. "I Han Soloed him. I wasn't sure he'd forgive me."

"I think it might be the proudest moment of his life that didn't involve Kasey being born."

I laughed again, and it caused me to wince. "Ribs hurt."

"You want me to kiss them better?"

"I'm not a machine."

Selene smiled. "I'm glad you're back. I was worried. We all were, except Mordred—he kept coming in here playing you his extensive list of video game soundtracks. He said it would help, presumably because he expected you to wake up and tell him to piss off."

"So if I start humming 'Mario,' it's his fault? Good to know."

Selene led me out of my room and down a corridor that wouldn't have looked out of place in a hospital. There was no one around, no one working in any of the rooms we walked past. It was like a clean ghost town.

"What's going on?" I asked as we entered the lift and Selene selected the floor for the main hangar above.

"For the last four months, you have made lightning strike this facility eight hundred thirty-two times. You created a storm that sat just above this facility. People know you're here. People we trust, but Hades, Mordred, and Elaine had an idea to ensure that their knowledge of you wasn't a problem."

"What idea?"

Selene sighed. "Blood curse marks."

The lift doors opened as I was stunned into silence. I looked out across the hangar and saw hundreds of people all watching me as I exited the lift. There was a cheer and round of applause, and I did this weird, uncomfortable wave thing. Because what the hell else were you meant to do when hundreds of people started clapping at you for no known reason?

"What the fuck?" I whispered.

Tommy bounded toward me and picked me up in a bear hug.

"Bones—fragile, human-powered bones," I whispered.

He put me down and grinned. "It's good to see you. Mordred said you were essentially human now. I'm sorry you've lost your magic."

"It'll come back. But it's a little weird knowing it'll be a while."

I looked beyond him to Olivia and Kasey, both of whom waved. Several other young men and women stood beside them, and I knew that they were members of Tommy's ultrasecret task force, which he'd put together before Arthur had taken over.

"How bad is it?" I asked Sky, who kissed me on the cheek.

"It's not good," she said.

"What's going on?" I asked Elaine as she walked toward me with Mordred, Nabu, Irkalla, Hades, and Zamek.

"We need to talk," she told me and motioned for me to follow her into a nearby room. She turned to Mordred as we entered. "Get it finished."

Mordred nodded and walked off.

"Get what finished?" I asked, taking a seat on the table in the middle of the room. "Selene said you were doing something with blood curse marks."

"Everyone here has agreed to take part in a ritual," Hades said from the doorway.

"What kind of ritual?" I asked.

"The kind where we all think you're dead," Irkalla said. "Everyone but Hades, Sky, Mordred, and Elaine, yes."

"Why not those four?"

"Hades and Sky because you need a contact in case something goes wrong during your time of healing, Mordred because he was never going to agree to have anything close to a blood curse mark put on him again, and Elaine because she used to be in charge of everything. This is the kind of thing you'll need someone keeping an eye on you for."

"And where am I going that I need to be kept an eye on?"

"A small town in Oregon," Nabu said. "It's very quaint."

"No," I replied.

"You have *no* powers, and Avalon thinks you're dead," Sky said. "You aren't helpful until you're healed, and if Arthur ever finds out you're alive, he will burn a country down to find you. We need to put you somewhere remote but with people we trust. So you're going to Clockwork, Oregon. Called that because its founder used to make clocks and was really happy about it."

"And do what while I'm there?"

"Read, write, learn how to whittle—I don't think it matters," Irkalla said. "Just stay safe, and don't bring attention to yourself."

"Why there?"

"I have people there I trust," Hades said. "A doctor by the name of Daniel Kuro. I met him in Korea a few decades ago. He's a good man. I've used the town a few times to let friends of mine heal in peace. Or avoid detection."

"Okay, tell me more about this blood curse ritual."

"Mordred, Nabu, and I worked together on this," Zamek said. "Essentially everyone in this facility will think you're dead. We considered just having them forget you existed, but that's too hard. Thinking you died on a field in Wisconsin is a lot easier."

"Essentially we managed to figure out a way to create the blood curse so that everyone affected will believe you dead," Nabu said. "They will believe they've grieved and have moved on. No one here will be caused any pain by your passing. That was integral to our plan. If anyone decided to dig too deep into your death or go after Atlas for revenge, it would break the curse."

"How does the curse break normally?" I asked.

"If any of them see you once the curse has been implemented, they will immediately remember that you didn't die," Elaine explained. "Each of them signed a document stating that they agreed to this. We couldn't do it any other way."

I walked past them all and out into the hangar, where I found Tommy, Olivia, and Selene. "You all agreed to this?" I asked. "All of you?"

"We need to keep you safe," Selene said. "This is the best way."

"Why can't you come with me?" I asked her.

"Because my father and sister would tear the world apart looking for whoever killed me. The smaller the number, the better."

"They offered me and Selene a chance to avoid the curse," Tommy said. "But I couldn't do that to Kasey and Olivia. I couldn't lie like that to any of the people who helped get us here. I'm not a spy anymore. Deception isn't something I want to do."

"What about those who aren't already here?" I asked.

"They already think you're dead," Diana said. "It won't be hard to keep that going."

"So it's sorted? I'll be dead to all of you. What happens now?" I asked.

"Right now we're in no position to fight Avalon," Remy said. "Arthur has started taking control of governments the world over. He's still in the process of removing those who are against him. A lot of ex–Avalon employees are in hiding. We're trying to help them as best we can. That's our main focus at the moment. We can't go after Arthur until we know who is and isn't working with him."

"Saving lives is the best we've got until we can organize some sort of resistance," Olivia said.

"A rebel force, if you will," Tommy said, making me laugh.

"How long have you wanted to use that one?" I asked him.

"Years," Tommy said, hugging me again. "I'm sorry this is a fleeting moment, but you need to go. You need to be safe, and when you're healed, we'll fight Arthur. We could do with finding those other four weapons like you."

"We're fighting a war on several fronts," Diana said. "The Norse and Japanese gods contacted Mordred, asking for help. It looks like the Norse went to the Japanese pantheon a while ago looking for allies. They agreed, but Arthur's forces have broken into Asgard through the dwarven realm. Until we're a united force, we'll always be one step behind. We need you back, Nate."

"But at full strength, not as human Nate," Remy said. "Human Nate sucks."

"Really?" I asked. "It's good that you're so supportive."

"Would you prefer if I gave you a back rub and told you you were a special little boy who just needs to try real hard?"

"That's the creepiest thing you've ever said," Tommy said.

Remy thought for a second. "Yeah, I'm going to pretend I didn't say that."

"We're all going to be doing that," Diana said.

"While you're gone, Wei told me she'll try and help me see if I have any other powers," Remy said, rapidly changing the subject. "Sounds like a plan to me."

Hades placed a hand on my shoulder. "We have to go," he said.

I said my goodbyes to everyone before kissing Selene. "When I'm healed, I'll come find you," I said.

"You'd better," she told me. "I'm going to be particularly angry otherwise. I wish I could come with you. But the fewer who know where you are, the safer you'll be."

I kissed her once again and then left the hangar with Sky, Mordred, Elaine, and Hades.

"Don't you need to perform the ritual?" I asked Mordred as we all climbed into a Black Hawk helicopter.

"Nabu and Zamek will complete it. Anyone in there is going to be affected, so it's best I'm not there."

"What do you plan to do while I'm in the middle of nowhere?"

"What I've always done, Nate. Piss off Avalon and fuck their shit up. Only this time I'll be doing it for the good guys."

The rest of the journey was a chance for Hades and Elaine to explain exactly what Arthur had done since I'd been declared dead. Occasionally I turned to watch the ground fly by at high speed far below us, wondering how far Arthur's corruption had spread across the country, until eventually we landed in the middle of a forest in Clockwork, Oregon.

We all got out of the helicopter, and an elderly Asian man left a Ford Ranger truck and greeted Hades with a hug.

"This is Dr. Kuro," Hades said.

The doctor shook my hand. "You're going to be our guest here."

"I guess that's the plan, yes."

"Your house is ready. We have a beautiful town. You'll like it. It's mostly peaceful."

"Mostly?" I asked with a raised eyebrow.

"We're a small town, not a boring one," Dr. Kuro said with a smile.

I turned back to Sky, Elaine, and Mordred. "I'll be seeing you all soon," I said.

"Take care, Nate," Sky said.

"Have a nice holiday," Mordred said. "Try not to bring attention to yourself. Be a good little human."

"Piss off," I said to him, and he smiled and hugged me.

"I wish this had gone better," Elaine said. "But now we know our true enemy. We know his power and influence. One day soon there will be a reckoning for him."

"Our world has changed," I said. "Humans know of our existence. They know of Avalon; they know they're not the top of the evolutionary ladder. If they don't know now that some of Arthur's allies consider humans nothing more than food, they soon will. Arthur is going to change the world, and we can't stop that. There aren't enough of us, and we're fragmented and broken. But we won't be. Not forever. We'll show Arthur the kinds of people he crossed, and we'll show him just how badly we plan on beating him and those who call him an ally."

I watched them climb back into the helicopter, leaving me alone with Hades.

"Thank you for this," I said.

"No thanks necessary," he told me. "Be safe. Heal, and then we'll deal with what comes next."

"We fight back," I said with complete conviction. "That's what comes next. Rebellion."

Chapter One

NATE GARRETT

Now

A year. I'd been told it would be a year. Gotta be honest: that hadn't turned out so well, had it?

Clockwork was a town of just over seven thousand people, the majority of whom appeared to be quite nice. Acknowledging that being a solitary loner who never spoke to anyone was a pretty good way to screw up your mental health, I'd made sure to make a few friends in my time here. While the last two years had sucked on more than one occasion, having friends was one of the good parts.

I'd introduced myself to Clockwork as Nate Carpenter, Nate Garrett being, for all intents and purposes, officially dead. I'd used the surname of my best friend from my old life. Tommy was one of the people I missed seeing the most.

Duke's Diner was one of three in town and the only one I visited with any frequency. This was partly due to the fact that the owner and chef, Antonio Flores, cooked the best damn food in town and partly because I liked several of the people who worked there.

I parked my blue Mercedes X-Class outside the diner, which was already busy with those who required an early-morning coffee and/or a Mexican breakfast. Antonio served more traditional American food, too, but no matter how good it was, no one came to Duke's for the pancakes.

The snow was a few inches high and crunched under my booted feet. Despite wearing a thick green winter jacket, warm jeans, black boots, and black gloves with a matching hat, I was still cold. The heater in the pickup had spoiled me.

I pushed the glass door of the diner open and enjoyed the warmth and the sounds of eating and chatter that washed over me.

"Is that you, Nate?'" Antonio bellowed from the kitchen, sticking his head out of the serving hatch.

"No, it's Commissioner Gordon. I'm looking for Batman," I shouted back to Antonio.

Antonio smiled. "Are you coming tonight?"

"For the approximately one hundredth time, yes," I said.

Antonio's smile turned into a huge grin. Antonio had been a US Army Ranger. Having served two tours in Afghanistan without so much as a scratch, he'd gone back for a third time and hadn't been so lucky. He'd lost the lower part of his left leg when an improvised explosive device had gone off near his team as they'd been sweeping a village that had been massacred by insurgents. That had been ten years ago, although the loss of a limb didn't appear to have slowed Antonio down. He'd once told me he'd considered it a new challenge to overcome.

Apart from owning Duke's—which, despite me asking, Antonio had never shown any interest in explaining the name of—he also ran the under-fifteen girls' soccer team for the town, with the help of one of the sheriff's deputies, Brooke Tobin.

"Football game tonight," he shouted, using the correct name for the sport.

"I know," I shouted back, gaining a few laughs from the three waitresses and waiter who were working in the diner.

"You are coming, though, right?" Jessica Choi asked me as she led me over to a booth at the far end of the diner. Like all of the waiting staff, the only uniform she wore was a black T-shirt with DUKE'S adorning it in big red letters.

"Yes," I promised.

"Because Ava has been talking about you coming to a game for weeks now," Jessica said. "It's the cup final."

I sat down and sighed. "I promise I'll be there." The match had been postponed for several weeks because of bad weather. Matches were usually played on Thursday nights at the local high school, but the snow had been so bad that playing football in it would have been a special kind of torture. I'd missed a few of Ava's games during the season and always felt bad for doing so, but I avoided traveling to other towns for away games, just in case I got spotted by the wrong person. I was in Clockwork to keep a low profile, so running around the state of Oregon would have been a risk.

Ava was Jessica's younger sister. They had been brought up by their grandparents, Drs. Daniel and Donna Kuro. Ava had been only three and Jessica sixteen when their parents had died in a car crash twelve years earlier.

"How goes the doctorate?" I asked Jessica after she took my order of scrambled eggs and chorizo along with a cup of English tea. An addition to the menu I knew Antonio had only included to stop me complaining about its absence.

"Good," Jessica said. "I feel bad for dropping Simon off at my grandparents' so often, but they don't seem to mind. And Simon loves spending time at their place."

"It'll be worth it when you're Dr. Choi."

Jessica smiled. "Then I just have to find a full-time job."

"That's okay; you can bring Simon here. I'm sure Antonio wouldn't mind him helping out."

Jessica laughed as she walked away to give Antonio my order. She returned a few minutes later with my cup of steaming-hot tea. "Antonio says he hopes you choke on it," Jessica told me, barely keeping a straight face.

"He's really cleaned up his usual language," I replied.

Before Jessica could reply, the door to the diner opened, and she turned to look at the newcomer.

I followed her gaze and watched the man stand in the doorway staring at Jessica. He was over six feet tall, which put him several inches above my own five feet eight, although he wasn't as broad across the shoulders as I was. He removed a red hat and gloves, revealing a bald head and heavily tattooed hands.

I looked up at Jessica and saw the fear in her eyes.

"Jess?" I asked softly.

"It's okay," she said, turning back to me and forcing a smile.

I liked Jessica Choi a lot. She was a smart, kind, and interesting woman. Also, her grandfather, Dr. Daniel Kuro, was one of only two people in town who knew exactly who I was and why I was here. I trusted Daniel with my life and owed him just as much. And while Jessica didn't know the truth about me, she treated me as if I were one of the family, and for that I was eternally grateful.

Jessica walked over to the newcomer. Their conversation was short, and they were too far away from me for any of their whispered words to meet my ears, but I could see that Jessica was upset and angry.

She motioned for the man to wait and went to talk to Antonio in the kitchen before gathering her coat and hat and leaving with the stranger.

A second waitress brought me my food. I was concerned about Jessica and considered following them to check that she was okay. However, Antonio left the kitchen and went out the back door of the diner, making me feel better. If anything was going to happen, I was confident that Antonio could deal with it.

The food looked amazing. The chorizo scrambled egg sat on one half of the plate, while the other half was filled with a mild salsa that Antonio refused to tell me the recipe of. A stack of warm tortillas had been placed on a separate plate, and the whole thing smelled of heaven itself.

I took a bite of the food and sighed in appreciation. Antonio was a grumpy bastard, but he sure as hell knew how to cook. But even the great food couldn't distract me for long; glancing to the rear entrance of the diner, I put my fork down beside my plate.

"Goddamn it." Getting to my feet, I grabbed my warm outdoor clothes and headed toward the rear exit.

"What are you doing?" the waitress who had served me asked.

"I'm going to go see what your boss is doing before anyone gets in trouble," I told her.

The look of relief on her face was reason enough for me to know I was doing the right thing. Everyone else in the diner was either engrossed in their own lives or watching me cautiously. They clearly wondered what was happening but didn't want to be involved in it, just in case it turned out to be something unpleasant.

I pushed open the rear exit and took a face full of cold air before stepping outside and walking down the ramp to the staff parking area at the rear of the property. There were four cars, including Jessica's own black Ford Ranger pickup and Antonio's silver Mitsubishi Evo. There were no signs of either owner, except fresh tracks in the snow that led around to a nearby alleyway, which, in turn, led to a large field behind the diner.

Following the tracks was easy enough, and it didn't take long to hear voices. As I drew closer, the voices became more distinguishable: three men, one of whom was Antonio. The other two were . . . unknowns. I didn't like unknowns; they made me nervous. Exiting the alley into the large field, I spotted Antonio sitting on a bench with the two strangers standing over him.

They looked over at me as I approached, and one of them—a large white man with a bald head and bushy black beard—turned toward me, casually opening his jacket to show the pistol he held. A wordless threat.

"Hey," I said jovially. "It's a bit cold to be having a chat out here."

"Go away," the second man snapped. While his gun-wielding friend stood over six and a half feet tall and probably weighed over twenty-five stone, this one was barely taller than me and considerably less broad. He had military-style short dark hair but no obvious weapons. Like his friend, he was white and wore a thick red jacket, although his was still zipped up. Didn't mean he didn't have a weapon; it just meant if things went bad, he was second on my list of problems.

"I'm just here to tell the chef how good his food is," I said, looking over at Antonio. "How can I possibly repay such an excellent breakfast?"

"It's okay," Antonio said with a forced smile. "I'm good. Go finish your food, Nate."

"Yes, *Nate*," the shorter of the two men said. "Go finish your food."

"Where's Jessica?" I asked, ignoring the man.

"She's just having a nice conversation with our boss," the gun owner told me. "You can see her from here."

He gestured across the field to where Jess stood at the far end defensively. From the amount the man was gesticulating, the conversation looked pretty one sided.

"Now you can fuck off," the shorter man said. "We'll keep Speedy Gonzales company."

I raised my eyebrows. *"Really?"* I asked. "Was that meant to be funny because he only has one leg or because he's Mexican?"

"I don't care what you think," he snapped.

"Did they hurt you?" I asked Antonio in Spanish.

Antonio's surprise showed he hadn't realized I spoke the language, but he shook his head. He looked a little frustrated too. Antonio was used to kicking ass and taking names; I imagined that the two men getting the drop on him had stung. Better to have stung feelings than be dead, though.

"Are you leaving or not?" the smaller man said, taking a step toward me and unzipping his jacket.

"I think I'll sit and wait with my friend for Jessica to finish talking," I told him.

The man shrugged off his jacket, revealing a gun still in its holster. His arms were covered in various tattoos, including a swastika on his bicep that showed from under the blue T-shirt he wore.

"Nazi?" I asked.

He smiled at me. "Not really your business."

"Just making pleasant conversation," I told him. "This doesn't need to go sideways."

"He's right, Bryce," his partner said quietly. "We didn't come here to hurt anyone. The boss will be angry if we do."

Bryce nodded slowly and picked his jacket up off the ground. He was quite wiry and certainly had the appearance of someone who knew how to fight. Maybe he *was* more dangerous than his partner.

Once upon a time, I'd have killed them both without a second thought, but that time had ended two years ago, and I had to remind myself to stay calm. To not allow myself to be drawn into anything that would cause trouble. Even so, I *really* wanted to break Bryce's smug face.

Bryce motioned for me to go sit beside Antonio, but he refused to move aside as I walked toward my friend, and he smacked his shoulder into mine as I stepped around him. A stupid, childish way to tell me he was tougher than me. I sighed, put on my best smile, and sat next to Antonio.

"So are you both Nazis, or are you just freelancing?" I asked.

No one answered.

"Guys, I'm just making conversation," I said.

"Can you not piss off the people with guns?" Antonio asked.

"Ah, they're okay," I told him. "The gun is only so we don't do anything stupid. I just want to know a bit more about our Third Reich–loving friends here."

Bryce punched me in the jaw, knocking me off the bench. "I told you to shut up," he snapped, giving me a kick in the ribs for good measure.

"Enough," the hulking Aryan wannabe snapped. "Damn it, Bryce. Enough."

"He's asking too many questions, Jackson," Bryce said. "He needs to learn to keep his mouth shut."

"Help your friend up," the man called Jackson said to Antonio, who offered me his hand and assisted me in getting back on the bench.

"I meant absolutely no disrespect," I said, with no sincerity. "I just figured talking would be better than awkward silence."

Bryce got into my face. "When the time comes, scum like your friend here will be turned to ash. And those who stand beside the lower born will be right beside them. Got it?"

"Riiight," I said and spotted Jessica walking alone across the field toward us.

Bryce moved away and looked over at her.

"You both got off lucky this time," Jackson warned us. "We might not be so hospitable next time. You need to mind your manners. I thought you Brits were good at that."

"Mostly we just drink tea and live in castles," I told him. "Doesn't leave a lot of time for manners."

The man shook his head as Bryce walked off to intercept Jessica, putting me on edge. "A word of warning," he said. "Don't piss Bryce off again."

"No shit," Antonio said.

"Was I fucking talking to you?" Jackson snapped. "Your kind speak when asked to. Your kind come into *our country*, taking *our jobs* and dirtying *our bloodline*."

His sudden move from calm to rage surprised me. "Okay, no one needs to lose their cool here," I said. "We get it: Nazis hate everyone who isn't a Nazi."

"KOA," he said proudly.

"What?" I asked, confused and wondering whether I'd missed a giant part of the conversation. Before he could answer, Bryce and a worried-looking Jessica returned.

"You okay?" I asked Jessica.

"Yeah, we can go now," she said, not looking up.

"She knows where she stands now," Bryce said smugly. "Hopefully we won't need to have a second conversation. A meeting between you and Robert will be arranged. I advise you not to miss it."

There was a wealth of questions in my mind, but now was not the time or place to ask them.

"You can go," Bryce said. He made a gun from his fingers and pointed it at me. "I'll be seeing you again, *boy*."

I ignored him.

"What's the KOA?" I asked Jackson.

"The Knights of Avalon," Bryce answered. "We're going to take back this country of ours. We're going to make it *pure* again."

I nearly made a smart-ass comment about giving it back to the Native Americans then, but I decided that being a smart-ass wasn't as important as not getting anyone shot. "You're part of Avalon?"

"Let's go," Antonio said from beside me.

"That's right—go on with your friends, boy," Bryce called after us as we walked away.

It took every ounce of self-control not to turn around and beat the ever-loving shit out of the two of them. We stopped in the car park of the diner.

"You want to tell us what that was about?" Antonio asked Jessica.

"Not really," Jessica said, looking miserable. "I'll deal with it; they won't be coming back. I'm sorry for what happened today."

"Take the rest of the day off," Antonio said and rubbed his jaw. "Been a long time since someone threatened me with a gun and I didn't break his arm for it." He looked over at me. "How're the ribs?"

"Sore, but I'll live," I said.

"We should really tell the sheriff," Antonio said.

"No," Jessica snapped. "You can't. It'll just get worse."

"Jess, no offense, but there are literal Nazis with guns in town," I told her. "I'm not sure that's something we should keep from the sheriff."

"Look, I promise I'll sort it out. Please, just give me a few days."

I nodded and looked over at Antonio, who sighed and said yes. Jessica hugged us both and walked over to her car.

"Any idea what the hell that was all about?" Antonio asked. "Nazi fucks."

Jessica drove out of the alleyway and turned onto the road before I spoke again. "Knights of Avalon," I said, almost to myself. "That's not good."

"What's not good? Avalon?" Antonio asked. "Those bastards are taking over the whole world. You see on the news at the demonstrations about them, about the people who are alleged to have gone missing? It's not a conspiracy theory, my friend; it's a fucking fact."

"I know," I said. "Look, I'm sorry about the food, but I need to go see the doc. I think I may have busted a rib." It was an easy lie, but I did need to see someone. I took a ten-dollar bill from my pocket and offered it to Antonio.

He shook his head. "Buy me a beer at the game tonight. Go get checked out."

I smiled, but inside concern gripped me. Avalon was in Clockwork. Were they here for me? Or for someone else?

Chapter Two

NATE GARRETT

The list of people who liked to see Nazis in their town was a short one and consisted of only other Nazis. But my concern wasn't so much with the two Führer-loving bags of dicks but with the knowledge that Avalon had come to town. Avalon was everywhere these days. After Arthur had told the world of the existence of nonhumans two years ago, he'd then set about exterminating everyone who disagreed with him. He'd taken control of most governments on Earth and then started making war on the rest of the realms.

Arthur was meant to have been the hero. The literal knight in shining armor. He'd been comatose for the better part of a thousand years, and everyone had hoped that when he woke up, he'd help build a better world. He hadn't. Instead, it had turned out that Arthur had been born to dark blood magic, and the fact that he'd been comatose had just delayed his plans of ruling over everyone.

I was in Clockwork to hide. Having lost my powers and needing to regain them, I'd been warned to stay out of the limelight and ensure that none of Avalon's many goons saw me, put two and two together, and ended my life before I was back to full strength and could help the resistance fight back.

In the beginning, humanity had accepted Arthur and Avalon with open arms, but the last two years had shown many the truth. Avalon's secret police had hunted and executed anyone who was deemed a threat.

The Inter-species Task Force, or ITF, had been set up, which basically gave the dregs of humanity free rein to hunt not only their own kind but anyone else that Arthur wanted removed. For the most part, the governments of the world were under Avalon's control, and that meant anyone speaking out from the media was soon found with a bullet in the back of their head.

The resistance had gone online, spreading like wildfire to show the cruelty that Avalon was capable of, but the general public, in ostrich-like complicity, still thought it was conspiracy theories, that it wasn't as bad as it was made out to be, or that those attacked had deserved it. At some point there would be a spark, and I hoped to be a part of it when it happened.

So long as Avalon didn't kill me first.

I'd never heard of the KOA and had no idea which branch of Avalon it belonged to, but if Arthur had hired a bunch of Nazi thugs to make up its numbers, then it didn't bode well.

Driving out of the town, I took the main road that led toward Mount Hood for a mile, then left it and continued up a dirt road toward my home. I'd sent a text to a friend of mine, Chris Hopkins, before getting in the car and told him to meet me here. Apart from Dr. Kuro, Chris was the only other person in Clockwork who knew who I was, and Dr. Kuro had told me to trust him with my life.

The dirt road eventually led to a fork, with one way clear and the other with a large wooden gate barring the way. Once I'd negotiated the gate, the drive to my home was relatively short.

I pulled the car up in front of my two-story house. I didn't know who had owned the cabin before I'd come along, but it suited my needs perfectly. It was far enough away from town that, should the need arise, I could get away from people quickly, but it was close enough that I wasn't labeled some weird hermit. It was made of dark wood and steel, with a tiled roof, and did wonders at keeping in the heat. Huge windows sat at the front of the building, letting in large amounts of light, and the solar panels on the roof ensured that it was almost completely off the grid for power. A generator sat in a nearby wooden shed, which helped out if anything went wrong, although nothing had in the two years I'd been there.

Chris Hopkins sat in one of the two chairs on my porch. He was just over six feet tall, lean, and clean shaven, with long dark hair that he kept half–tied up, allowing the rest to spill over his shoulders.

"How the hell did you get here so fast?" I asked, unlocking the house door. Chris had a key, but he'd told me he'd only use it in an emergency.

"I was already on my way here," he said, stepping inside the house, shaking off his large coat, and hanging it next to mine.

"You want a drink?" I asked.

"Coffee, black, please," Chris said, taking a seat on the leather armchair in the living room.

I made the drinks in the good-size kitchen and brought them back. "We have a problem," I told him, passing Chris his coffee. I sat down with a cup of tea, placing it on a coaster on my coffee table, because I'm not a Neanderthal. "So why were you on your way here?" I asked.

"Heard some chatter about Avalon," Chris said. His accent wasn't American, but it was so nondescript that I couldn't place it, and Chris had never shown any interest in telling me where exactly he was from.

"The KOA?" I asked.

"You heard too?"

"Had a run-in with some human Nazis who said they worked for the KOA. The Knights of Avalon. It's why I texted you."

"They're not here for you," Chris said confidently. "Or if they are, my friends in the know don't actually know, and I find that hard to believe. Not sure why they're here, to be honest, which I also find concerning. I've got a few feelers out to try and find more information, but you say they were Nazis?"

I nodded. "Tattoos of swastikas and everything. One of them punched me and gave me a kick to the ribs."

"And he's still alive?" Chris asked.

"Keeping a low profile, remember?"

"So? A lifetime of doing the exact opposite of that isn't exactly easy to change."

"They had guns."

"Ah, yes, well, we don't want you getting shot," Chris said with a smile.

"No, *we* really don't."

"The Nazi connection is unpleasant," Chris said, his smile evaporating. "I assumed they'd all fucked off once they'd lost the war. Doesn't seem to matter how many of them you kill; they just come back."

Chris might have looked like he was in his midforties, but in reality, and based on what he'd told me in the past, he was well over two thousand years old. I wasn't certain exactly *what* Chris was, as he'd never divulged that information, but whatever he was, he was old and powerful. No one lives thousands of years without being the latter.

"I didn't think that Arthur could bring Avalon any lower," Chris continued, "but apparently I was wrong. I never did like the little shit. No one believed me when I said he was a psychotic, power-mad asshole, but hey, guess who was right?"

"I think you might have mentioned that once or twice before," I said with a smirk.

Chris glowered. "It's still true."

"Can't disagree with that," I told him.

"So," Chris said with a grin, "any twinges, signs of impending recovery?"

I shook my head. "*Nothing.* I had a cold a few weeks ago. I fucking hated having a cold."

Chris laughed. "I can imagine. To be fair, Nate, none of us are quite sure what's happening with you with regard to when you'll get your magic back. It's not an exact science, and very few people have ever been in your situation. Unfortunately, it's still a case of just sitting and waiting for something to happen."

"I know," I said, feeling tired. "My friends are fighting and dying for a cause I can't take part in. The woman I love and pretty much all of my friends think I'm dead. There is nothing about this situation that doesn't absolutely suck."

"So to cheer yourself up, you're going to watch Ava play football?" Chris asked.

"I like watching them play; they're a good side. Besides, it feels normal, you know. And precious little about my life these days feels normal." I told Chris about Jessica's involvement with the man at Duke's.

"Have you spoken to Jess about it?" Chris asked.

"I tried to," I admitted. "But she believes she can sort it herself."

"Then I have to ask: Does it involve you?"

"Jessica's my friend. So yes, I'm involved. Besides, I get the feeling that Bryce thinks he can threaten and bully people into submission."

"Don't kill him." Chris paused. "Unless you have to, and then make sure no one can bring it back to you. Your fake background is a hundred percent foolproof, but that doesn't mean you want people checking up on you, and it certainly doesn't mean you want to spend the rest of your recovery time defenseless in a prison cell."

"Don't worry; I'm not planning on killing anyone."

Chris raised an eyebrow. "I've heard stories about you, Nate. From the sounds of it, whether you plan to get in trouble or not, trouble follows you around. Frankly, I'm amazed it's taken two years for it to find you."

So was I, although I had no intention of telling Chris that. He knocked back the rest of his coffee and stood. "I need to get back to the forge. I have an order for something a bit out of the ordinary."

Chris's day job, apart from looking after me, was to make custom bladed weapons. He had a house just outside of town, too, although his was remote because he had a forge attached to it. I'd looked up his creations online; they mostly consisted of strange, fantastical blades that looked to be about as much use in a real combat situation as a rubber chicken. Still, they were pretty, and he seemed to be in high demand.

"I'm going to go see Daniel," I said. "Figure out if he knows something about whoever is hassling Jessica."

"Look, Nate, this isn't *Murder, She Wrote*. If you get involved in something bad, you're not going to be able to charm your way out of it because you look like a harmless old lady. You look like someone who would, and I use this term with all due respect, fuck someone's day up. The short hair, the short beard, and especially the expression of *go screw yourself* that often sits on your face. They don't exactly scream *I'm completely unthreatening*. The fact that you don't have any tattoos of skulls or teardrops is literally your only saving grace. If someone thinks you're going to be a problem, they will try to kill you. Nazis aren't known for their people skills."

"Thanks for the warning, but I don't plan on being involved with this . . . whatever this is," I said, waving my arms around. "I just want to check Jess is okay. That's it. If this is something she really can't handle, the sheriff needs to know. Armed thugs walking around Clockwork isn't good for anyone, especially if they are involved with Avalon."

"Too true," Chris said. "Just be careful. And don't carry a gun."

I kept my expression completely neutral. "I don't like guns."

Chris stared at me for several seconds. "Not *liking* them and not knowing how to *use* them aren't the same thing." Chris's phone went off, and he removed it from his jeans pocket, activated the screen, and shook his head slightly as he took in what was shown. "Switch the TV on," he said. "Any news channel will do."

I switched on the large TV that hung on the wall of my house and turned it to one of the twenty-four-hour news networks. Hera's face filled the screen, and I fought the urge to throw my remote control at it.

Hera was the same woman that most people had heard of from Greek mythology, although the stories and reality didn't always mesh. She had been married to Zeus, although she'd helped her son Ares murder him, and she was an exceptionally powerful sorcerer, maybe one of the most powerful on the planet. She was also one of Arthur's most ardent supporters. She'd been a thorn in the side of good and right for thousands of years, and now that Arthur had ascended to his throne, Hera appeared to have been given carte blanche to do whatever she wanted. Despite the government still officially being in charge of the country, Hera all but ruled London as her own personal territory. It was a city that had been neutral for millennia, and while most of its human occupants didn't appear to have noticed much of a difference, anyone who had gotten in Hera's way soon felt her wrath. She was an exceptionally awful person, and frankly, the day someone killed her would be the day that everyone on Earth became a bit safer.

Hera was sitting beside a news anchor who looked more than a little nervous. He welcomed his "esteemed" guest.

"Thank you, Declan," Hera said, all smiles and sweetness. "I am here today to talk about the demonstrations that you've witnessed online over the last few weeks. I've heard all the conspiracy theories about how we were barbaric to a group of peaceful protesters in Paris. And I'm here to set the record straight." She shook her head sadly, turning the full force of her manipulative personality to the camera.

"Those protesters were *terrorists*. Our ITF forces were maintaining a perimeter to allow the protest to take place. *Peacefully.* However, the protesters had other ideas. Avalon has obtained original footage that shows several of these protesters starting the riot. We found several bombs littered throughout the area, and more than one protester was found with weaponry on them when searched. These people came to Paris, the city of love, with the intention to cause anarchy, to murder innocents."

"Bullshit," Chris snapped.

"I saw the news about it," I said, ignoring Hera's attempt to paint unarmed civilians as terrorists in waiting.

"I knew people who were there," Chris said, looking at the TV in disgust. "They were protesting the treatment of detainees by the ITF. People snatched from their homes never to be seen again. Anyone who speaks out is arrested. And it's not just Paris; it's all across the globe. Since the Paris attack happened, more and more protests are cropping up."

"I saw on the news about the ones in LA and Seattle," I said. "They looked like pretty big crowds."

"You hear about what happened in Denver?"

I shook my head.

"Protest. ITF turned up. Ten dead; about five times that number vanished. But every time one happens, two more protests start. Honestly, I'm not sure what's going to happen next. Avalon can't paint everyone who disagrees with them as terrorists. More and more journalists have gone into hiding, too; they use the internet to get their messages across. I think things will get a lot worse before they get better."

I looked back at Hera, who was wrapping up her little propaganda piece, talking about legislation to protect the people of this country, a fake smile on her face the whole time.

"You know, if she finds out you're alive, she'll risk everything to go after you," Chris said. "You killed her son *and* grandson."

"I know," I said, remembering the deaths of Ares and Deimos. Both had deserved to die, and neither had died an easy death. "Did you want me to see Hera on the news just so you could remind me to behave?"

"Pretty much," Chris said.

"I'm not going to do anything stupid," I promised.

"You know, when Hades told me that you were coming here and asked me to look after you, I assumed it would be a hard job. You're well known for getting into trouble, and for . . . shall we say, speaking your mind. But frankly, you've been the perfect patient. You haven't killed anyone, and if you have, you've disposed of them in a timely and efficient manner so that even I don't know about it, and you haven't drawn attention to yourself. Continue with this, please."

"I haven't killed anyone," I said with a shake of my head.

"Right, so you'll have no problems keeping out of whatever mess Jessica has gotten herself into, won't you?"

"If I say yes, will you believe it?"

"I'll tell you what, Nate—you say yes, and for a little while we'll both live in the blissful ignorance of me believing the lie."

"Then yes. Yes, I will."

"See, that's easy," Chris said. "In the meantime, I'm going to go finish my chores for the day and then go to the football game tonight."

"Antonio said there'll be barbecue food."

"If he's cooking it, at least I know it'll be good barbecue food. Burnt sausages and rock-hard burgers are not my idea of haute cuisine."

I got up to show Chris out, and he paused at the door. "Is there anything else bothering you?"

"Apart from still being here after two years?" I asked. "No, I'm good."

"It's not a science, Nate," Chris said. "I get that you're frustrated, and I can't begin to fathom what you're going through, but you just need to keep going. Eventually it'll work out."

"You hope," I said with a wry smile.

"No, Nate, I know. I know it'll be better, and sooner rather than later Nate Garrett will reveal to the world that he's alive. And then we'll get to see some real goddamn fireworks."

Chapter Three

NATE GARRETT

The rest of the day was a bust. I was too angry about the morning's encounter, and trying to get hold of Jessica or her parents had been a completely fruitless idea, so I settled for working out in the back garden. When I'd punched and kicked away my frustrations, I picked up a book and sat down next to the fireplace and did a few hours of reading. I'd really managed to catch up on my missed books over the last few years, although I couldn't find a particular genre that I enjoyed over the others, so my reading list was quite eclectic.

Changing into jeans, a light-blue T-shirt, and the world's thickest pair of socks, I left the house wearing a large jacket and good boots. If I was going to stay in the field stands while I watched the football game, I was at least going to be warm.

I reached the high school after the sun had set and saw Brooke Tobin, the sheriff's deputy, directing the crowd from the car park through to the seating.

"Nate," she said with a smile as she stopped me.

"Deputy Tobin," I said, returning the smile as she walked with me onto the field. "How's things?"

"Not bad. Looking forward to the game. We had some trouble in the past between Clockwork and Stockton supporters, so the sheriff thought it wise to show our faces."

Brooke was someone I considered a friend. Exactly my height, with shoulder-length dark hair that she often tucked behind her ears, she'd been a deputy for several years and had celebrated her twenty-eighth birthday a few weeks earlier.

I smiled. "Enjoy the evening, Deputy Tobin."

"Behave yourself, Nathan Carpenter."

The majority of spectators had already found their places in the stands that sat on the side of the football pitch just behind the high school's American football field. The field had newly built stands that could easily seat a thousand people. Brooke had told me that the high school had a really popular American football team here, and the principal had decided to renovate the field to accommodate the huge numbers of spectators who wanted to come watch.

Because the football team wasn't allowed to use the American football field, and due to the popularity of the sport in town, the town hall had put another set of stands on the football pitch. It was a bit of a trek from the car park to the football pitch, but I soon reached the stands, shuffling my way past several Clockwork residents and saying hi to those I knew, until I found myself being hailed by Donna Kuro, who waved me over.

Donna was seventy-two years old and barely over five feet in height, and I'd never known her to have anything less than a smile on her face to greet people. Donna had been married to her husband, Daniel, for over fifty years, and rarely had I met two people who were so obviously meant to be together.

"Nate," Donna said. "Good to see you here."

"Yes," Daniel said from beside her. "Ava was worried you weren't coming."

"I wasn't going to miss it," I told him.

Daniel had been born in Los Angeles seventy-eight years ago to Japanese parents, and he'd once told me that when he'd started dating Donna, who was white Irish, it had caused quite a stir within both communities. They'd eloped together to New York the second Daniel had finished at med school, and once there, Donna had gotten a doctorate in ancient history. When their daughter and son-in-law had died in a car crash and they'd had to bring up teenage Jessica and baby Ava, they'd moved to Clockwork to raise them away from the hustle and bustle of New York. I sensed there was more to it than that but hadn't wanted to pry.

"You spoken to Jessica today?" I asked. I didn't care about prying into that.

"She was agitated earlier," Donna said. "She walked off to take a call. Hopefully she'll be back in time." She leaped to her feet, applauding as Ava and her football team, the Hawks, arrived on the pitch, along with the away team, the Bears.

"I hope they give them a good thrashing," Donna said, returning to her seat.

"Now, dear, these aren't professionals," Daniel said with a smile.

"Well, then a good thrashing will teach them the art of humility," Donna said, making me laugh.

Jessica returned a few seconds later, waving at Ava, who was the spitting image of her older sister, except she was already the same height as Jessica and appeared to not want to stop growing.

"I hope Ava's okay," Donna said. "She's been having terrible nightmares."

"She stressed out or something?" I said.

Donna shook her head. "Not at all. She just has them on occasion. They come and go but never last long."

I was about to ask more, but the introductions to the teams happened, and everyone erupted into applause. After the initial checks and handshakes, the two teams took up their positions on the pitch, with Ava as center forward. The referee blew his whistle, and they were off.

It was an exciting opening ten minutes, with Ava forcing the Bears' goalkeeper to make two brilliant saves before she hit the crossbar with a wonderful shot from outside the penalty area. Unfortunately, it was obvious that both teams were fairly equal, with the Bears being a bit more aggressive in their tackling than was probably allowed. Several Hawk parents shouted at the referee to do his job after a particularly nasty tackle on a Hawk midfielder resulted in her having a bloody nose.

Thankfully, soon after, Ava scored the first goal, and the Bears crumbled. By halftime, it was three to zero for the Hawks, and the parents of the Bears were beginning to sound more and more like a hoard of disgruntled morons, with a few of them making comments about Hawk players that turned the atmosphere in the stands into something a bit less pleasant than what I'd expected.

Jessica stood and announced she needed to make a phone call. She walked away as I caught the sheriff and his deputies having a word with a few of the Bear parents.

"Where's Simon?" I asked Donna and Daniel. Simon was Jessica's five-year-old son. He was a good kid: smart, liked to draw, and danced around to whatever music he heard in his head. He also liked to climb everything he saw that was taller than he was, often resulting in him getting stuck and having to be helped out.

"He's got a cold," Daniel said. "We left him back at home with our neighbors. They dote on him, so I'm sure he'll be having a lovely time."

"I'm going to get a pretzel," I said. "You want anything?"

"No, thank you," Daniel said.

"Nothing for me either," Donna told me.

I walked away from the stands, back toward the vendors set up near the car park. The pretzel stand was owned by a baker who lived in Clockwork and made possibly the best cakes I'd had in a long time.

But on game day, she made pretzels. Chocolate and caramel. It was like eating crunchy heaven.

Unfortunately, I wasn't the only person in the queue to get one, and Doug Ward turned toward me, a smile on his face and a pretzel in his hand. "Thanks, darlin'," Doug said to the female vendor, which gained him an eye roll when he looked away.

Doug was a dick. He wasn't *outright* mean or nasty; he was just one of those people who believed, with all their heart, that they deserved respect and love from everyone they met. He thought that his charm offensive made him a Casanova and drove the ladies wild. Thankfully, I'd never actually met a woman who had been taken in by Doug's charm, so I wasn't sure they existed.

Doug also liked to be thought of as the big, tough guy. He was about six four and had the physique of someone who valued being injected with steroids over useful muscle. I was one hundred percent certain that Doug had never met a mirror he couldn't spend twenty minutes posing in front of.

"Nate," Doug said, offering me a handshake that I knew he was going to try to squeeze.

"Just a second, Doug," I said as the pretzel baker asked me what I'd like. I made my order and turned back to Doug. "So how's you?"

"Had a *hot* date last night," he said, having forgotten about the handshake. "Rocked her world."

I felt a little nauseous.

The pretzel vendor coughed into her hand, and I forced myself not to smile. It's my long-held belief that anyone who likes to tell people how much sex they're having is, inevitably, not having any sex.

"Cool," I said with a thumbs-up.

"You seen Brooke?" Doug asked suddenly, seemingly serious.

"Ummm, earlier, yeah," I told him. "She's working."

He looked around as if people were listening and then leaned in to whisper loudly to me. "You know she's a lesbian, right?"

I wasn't a hundred percent sure what answer Doug expected. "Yes, Doug, I do. I'm not really sure why *you're* telling me that, though."

"Well, I just thought you'd like to know. Just in case you decide to hit on her. I think it's only fair that lesbians tell men up front so there's no misunderstanding."

I had the sudden urge to call him a fucking idiot.

The expression on the baker's face pretty much mimicked my own. "Because you can't contain yourself from hitting on her, unless she's a lesbian?" the woman asked in disbelief.

"Sure," Doug said with a nod. "A man needs to know whether that option is off the table; otherwise he might try, and personally, I think it's just information that we should be given. It saves embarrassment for both parties."

"You could just *not* hit on every woman you meet," the baker said. "Or just accept rejection like an adult."

"Just saying, is all," Doug continued.

"Doug, did you hit your head a lot as a kid?" I asked.

"Hey, I'm just doing you a favor," he said and stomped off.

"He's such a *dick*," the baker said vehemently, causing me to smile.

People started to make their way back over to the pitch. About to do the same, I noticed Jessica and Daniel leave the enclosure and walk toward the far end of the car park. I turned back to the baker and asked for a white coffee, one sugar, thinking that I'd wait and see if they returned before going back over to the pitch. Something about the way they both walked concerned me. As if they were worried.

The baker passed me my freshly brewed coffee, and I thanked her again before walking back toward the fence. Pausing, I looked over to where I'd seen Daniel and Jessica heading. I sighed and followed them.

I heard their voices from around the corner of the high school building well before I saw them. I paused and moved behind the nearest car as the voices became clearer. That was definitely Jessica and Daniel. The latter was calm and concise, while the former just sounded upset.

Another voice I recognized as belonging to the Nazi who had hit me earlier, Bryce. No matter what I'd promised Chris, I wasn't going to just stand back and let my friends deal with whatever shit Bryce was dishing out.

Approaching, I saw Jessica crying. Daniel was standing between her and a man I hadn't seen before, as well as the two Nazis, Bryce and Jackson. The other man—the one who'd been talking to Jessica back on the field this morning—was nowhere to be seen.

"Hi," I said with a wave and smile. "What a shock to see you here again."

"What the fuck?" Bryce snapped, placing his hand inside his open jacket.

"No," the newcomer said. "No need for violence here. I only came to talk."

"With Nazis," I pointed out. "Not sure how productive any conversation will be when one half wants the other exterminated."

"Bryce and Jackson are just here to help," the man told me. "Their . . . beliefs do not have anything to do with this. I assure you, despite Jessica and Daniel's Asian ancestry, they won't be harmed."

"Nate, it's okay," Daniel said.

"It's not, though, is it?" I replied.

"This doesn't concern you," the man said.

"You're right," I told him. "And you'd still be right, if Göring and Goebbels here hadn't drawn on me this morning. You see, pointing a gun at my friends, threatening, and hitting them makes me involved. I know—I was surprised, too, but that's how it is."

The man smiled. "Nate, you don't know who I am, but if you don't leave, my friends will become restless and may do something unpleasant."

I returned the smile. "If either of your friends do a *damn* thing, I'm going to feed them their own fingers."

"Ah, you believe yourself to be a tough guy," the man said. "I have experience with people like you. I assure you, no matter how much you think you can bench or whatever you may have done in your martial arts training, you are not a tough guy. We are. Go home."

"Fuck you, fuck your Nazi scumbag friends, and especially fuck you. I know I said that twice, but it really is worth repeating."

The man turned to Jessica and Daniel. "You both wish to stand by your earlier statements?"

"He is *not* your son," Jessica said, her voice firm. "And I will not allow you to see him."

"I think our business is done here," Daniel said.

Jessica and her grandfather turned to walk away, and Bryce stepped toward them, shoving Daniel toward the nearest car before I could intervene. I stepped forward, and Jackson stepped in, throwing a punch my way. I avoided it and hit him in the jaw with one of my own. He staggered back, anger filling his eyes, and charged me.

He was faster than he looked, and he grabbed hold of me around the throat, lifted me off my feet, and slammed me down onto the car bonnet beside me, his strong hands trying to permanently cut off my air supply.

I jabbed my thumb into my assailant's eye socket, causing him to release my neck, screaming in pain. Grabbing his arm, I wrapped my legs around his neck and pulled tightly on the elbow joint until it popped. He dropped to the floor in agony as I rolled off the car bonnet.

The man who hadn't introduced himself to me was already walking away, and Jessica was yelling at Bryce, who had pinned Daniel up against a car. He punched Daniel in the stomach and turned to me just as my fist met his cheek, snapping his head to the side and knocking him to the ground. I dragged him upright as Jackson got back to his feet, a blade in his good hand.

Letting Bryce fall with a thud, I moved back toward my attacker, who swiped at me with his knife, leaving him open to a kick in the balls. A second kick, and he dropped the knife before falling back into a sitting position, whimpering. I drove my knee into the side of his face, knocking him out.

"Enough," a voice commanded. I turned around to see Bryce back on his feet, his gun out, as Brooke stood in a shooter's position ten feet away, her own gun aimed at Bryce.

"You going to arrest me?" Bryce asked with a sneer, looking over at the deputy. "You know what'll happen once I get out, right? You know what I'll do. I'll send you pictures if you like."

I looked over at Brooke and saw the anger and fear on her face.

Bryce laughed viciously. "Yeah, that's what I thought." He got into a nearby Dodge Charger with the mystery man at the wheel, and they screeched out of the car park.

"What the *hell* is going on?" Brooke asked.

"I think this Nazi needs a hospital," I said. "And I could ask you the same thing. Why did you let them go?"

"Just don't kill anyone," she said and walked away to presumably call in what she'd found.

"Nate, you shouldn't have involved yourself," Daniel said, getting back to his feet. "They'll come for you now."

"I tried to keep you out of it," Jessica said with a sigh.

"And what is 'it'?" I asked.

"That was Robert Saunders," Jessica said. "My ex-partner. He thinks he's Simon's father."

"Is he?" I asked.

Jessica shook her head. "But that won't be enough for him. He wants DNA evidence."

"Then give it to him and tell him to do one."

Daniel leaned against the car bonnet. "I don't think he even cares what the result would say; he just wants to hurt us."

"Why?" I asked.

"I left him," Jessica said. "For another man. He didn't take it well. And then I moved back here and forgot all about him while he served time in jail."

"And now he's out and pissed off?" I asked.

Jess nodded. "He wants to be there when the DNA is given, when the test is done, and I don't trust him not to just take Simon."

"Okay, so why Nazis?"

"No idea," Jess said as Brooke returned.

Brooke looked at the semiconscious Nazi and then at me. "You do this?"

"He slipped," I said with a *who, me?* expression on my face. "It's very icy out here."

Chapter Four

NATE GARRETT

There was a rhythmic knocking at my front door. Blinking to remove the sleep from my eyes, I groggily looked over at my clock. It was just after nine a.m. I sighed before swinging out of bed and going to the door.

Ava was standing on my porch.

"Eh?" I asked.

"I want to talk to you," Ava said.

I looked down at my T-shirt and shorts. "Come in. Get coffee or whatever it is you drink while I get dressed."

Throwing on some clean underwear, a pair of jeans, and a black jumper, I returned to find Ava sitting in my kitchen, a cup of coffee in her hands.

"Are you even old enough to drink coffee?" I asked.

"I'm fifteen," she said, rolling her eyes. "Not six."

"The question still stands," I said. "Would your grandparents let you drink coffee?"

Ava glared at me, shaking her head. I removed the coffee mug she held in her hands and made her a cup of green tea instead.

"I have this stuff at home all the time," Ava said with a sigh.

"That's because green tea is nice," I told her. "Also, it won't get me yelled at by your grandmother. Why are you here?"

"There's something wrong with me," Ava said, obviously awkward and looking down at her drink. "I overheard a while ago that you used to work for Avalon. My grandparents were talking about it. I thought maybe you could help."

"This about the not being able to sleep?"

She nodded. "You know about it?"

"Donna mentioned it to me yesterday."

"It's not just being unable to sleep. It's something else."

"Nightmares don't mean there's something wrong with you."

"These aren't nightmares. I dream of people dying. I don't know who they are—I can't see faces or know what gender they are, things like that—I just see the aftermath of the death. I see the body. And after the dream, someone dies. Someone *always* dies."

I had to admit that certainly wasn't usual. "You think you're not human?"

"I think I'm not normal."

"Nothing wrong with not being normal," I said, taking a drink of tea. "Normal is highly overrated. Trust me on this."

"I just want to know. My grandparents, they . . . well, they keep telling me I'm fine, but I don't know if that's to help me or them."

"You ever had a near-death experience?" I asked.

She nodded. "When I was little, barely a few months old, I had meningitis. I died—so people tell me—and then I got better. I've had these dreams on and off since I was a little girl. I know I was only three when my parents died, but I'm certain I saw it. I don't know. My grandfather told me a few months ago that just before the crash I kept talking to people about seeing ghosts when I slept."

That was *definitely* not usual. "There's a test," I said. "But it won't tell me what you are, just if you have power of some kind."

"Let's do it," Ava said, sounding ready.

"Ava, you need to know a few things. If you're not human, I couldn't even begin to know where you'd have gotten your power from. And how are you going to react if it turns out you're not human? There's nothing wrong with not being human."

"Will Avalon come for me?"

"I wouldn't let them," I told her with absolute certainty. "But you would have to keep this to yourself when you're around people you don't trust."

"People at school say that Avalon keeps us safe, but I've seen the videos online. I don't think they do. I think they subjugate us, lull us with a false sense of security while they destroy our freedoms. Granddad said they weren't to be trusted."

"He's right," I told her. "Once I thought they were the good guys, but not anymore. Like I said, if it turns out you're not human, then you'll have to be wary about who you tell."

"Okay, let's do this test."

"Right, well, it'll be easier to do outside," I said. It was partially true. It was easier purely because, depending on her power, she might break parts of my home, and I'd rather she didn't. No need to tell her about that. I could already tell she was nervous and scared.

We both stepped out of the kitchen onto the small part of decking that wasn't covered in snow. The rest of the garden, however, was a blanket of barely disturbed white.

"You're going to need to take your shoes and socks off."

She looked back at me. "Seriously?"

"It needs bare skin to make the connection. I'll draw runes on the snow, and you step onto them."

"My feet will *freeze*."

"Then be fast," I told her. Walking out onto the snowy lawn, I drew a large enough circle that Ava could easily stand in the middle. Once the circle was complete, I drew several runes inside. Then I did the same thing again with a second circle a short distance away.

"How do you know how to do this?" Ava asked.

"A few years ago," I said, "the Norse dwarves put some knowledge of runes in my head. They need power to activate, and as I don't have any, it's completely useless to me."

It was only partly the truth. I'd had the runes in my head since birth, and the dwarves had managed to accidentally recover them, giving me a headful of knowledge into the bargain. While that knowledge had remained when I'd come to Clockwork, I'd had no need to utilize it in the last two years.

I stepped barefoot onto one of the runes inside a circle. Nothing happened. "See? Do you feel better now that I've done this too?"

"What will happen when I do it?" Ava asked, standing on the edge of the decking.

"If there's power inside you, the circle will glow. The more power, the brighter the color. Don't know what color, as it's completely dependent on the person."

She stepped down from the deck and walked across the snow toward me. "Do I just step inside this?"

"I need you to step inside, close your eyes, and concentrate on my voice. I'll ask questions, and you need to focus on what you see in your mind. You remember all of these dreams, yes?"

Ava nodded sadly and stepped into the circle. She turned toward me and closed her eyes.

Ignoring the cold seeping through my soles, I watched Ava. "Right, let's concentrate on your most recent dream. Tell me about it."

"There are two," she said. "The first is a body found in an alleyway in town. One of its arms is missing. Its face is a ruined mess. I can't see details of what the person looks like."

"When did you last have this dream?"

"Two days ago."

"And the second dream?"

"It's in town again. Clockwork is on fire. There are so many dead. Hundreds. Many on the road, most killed in their homes. The school has hundreds of bodies on the field and in the main hall, where the council does meetings."

"How did everyone die? From the fire?"

"Some. Most were killed in other ways. Shot, stabbed—a few were torn apart."

The circle around Ava glowed deep red.

"Can you tell me any more?" I asked.

"I sense power. Not like electricity or anything, but power. I can't explain it."

"Like magic?"

"I don't know what that feels like in dreams."

"Elements?" I asked.

"Apart from the fire? No. I see a snake."

"A snake?"

"A big snake. Bigger than anything I've ever seen. It's dead too."

"How big?"

"Thirty feet long, with a mouth that could take me in one bite."

The red ring grew in intensity, the snow inside the circle melting from the heat of power. "Open your eyes," I told her.

Ava did as she was told and looked down at the grass that showed through the melted snow beneath her feet. The ring of red power pulsed occasionally as it dissipated. "I'm not human," she almost cried.

"No," I said. I led Ava over to the decking.

"What am I?" she asked after several seconds of silence.

"I don't know," I said honestly. "I have a few ideas, though. You said you were sick as a baby and nearly died but that you got better. Obviously."

Ava smiled. "Apparently I was a marvel. I don't get sick now, though. Just the dreams."

"I want you to go back home while I look into it," I said. "I'll come over tonight with answers."

"We're having a dinner party tomorrow," Ava said. "I was supposed to invite you." Her expression became solemn. "Will you really figure out what I am?"

I nodded. "Shouldn't be hard. And it's nothing to be scared of. Leave it to me. I'll sort it out. I'll come over this evening to tell you what I find out." I didn't want to leave her wondering for days on end, especially considering I had a pretty good idea of what she was.

I showed Ava to the front door. "Seriously, though, don't worry. It'll be fine."

"Thank you." Ava put her helmet on, climbed on her bike, and rode away just as the landline phone went.

I cursed their invention and picked it up.

"Nate," Antonio said. "How's things?"

"It's been a weird day. What's up?"

"Can you come down to Duke's? There's something we need to talk about."

"Be there in five," I told him, and he hung up.

I paused. It was a weird phone call, mostly because Antonio had never phoned me at home and never once contacted me to ask if I'd come to the diner to talk. He'd sounded strained. I suspected something unpleasant. I considered phoning the sheriff but wasn't really sure what I'd be able to tell him, so I decided to go find out.

Pulling into the diner car park, I saw that the diner was closed and the lights inside switched off. I'd never known Antonio to not open for lunch and wondered whether I was going to need a gun.

I walked over to the diner's front door and knocked on the glass pane. The door opened, and Bryce stood there with a smile on his face, beckoning me inside.

"Thanks, doorman," I said, receiving a shove to my back as I walked past him.

At the far end of the diner, in one of the booths, sat Antonio. His face was a little bloody, but other than that he looked okay.

"Your friend took some convincing to call you," Bryce said.

There were four other men inside the diner, two of whom sat in the booth next to Antonio, with another one at one of the tables between the booths and front door. He had a cup of coffee in his hands. The last man, Robert Saunders, sat opposite Antonio. He had a pistol on the table in front of him that I recognized as a Smith & Wesson SW1911.

"Do not make me put one in your friend," Robert said, patting the pistol. "Take a seat."

There was no point antagonizing him while he had a gun aimed at Antonio, so I took a seat.

"Where's your big friend?" I asked.

"The one you put in the hospital?" Robert replied. "Busy, I'm afraid."

"Glad to see Bryce is still here; I feel like we've become family. The kind of family you never want to see and don't tell people exist, but family."

"You're very good at pissing people off," Robert said.

"I am," I told him. "It's a natural gift." I turned to Antonio. "You okay?"

Antonio nodded. "Sorry for the call."

"No problem," I said. "It isn't a party if all the guests aren't here." I looked back to Robert. "You want to explain *why* I'm here?"

"I felt that last night you were involving yourself in matters that don't actually have anything to do with you. I wanted a nice face-to-face like this, where I can inform you of what will happen should you continue to stick your nose into matters you shouldn't."

"That might actually be the politest threat I've ever received," I said. "I mean, you can go fuck yourself with a sharp stick, but the politeness is appreciated."

Robert smiled, just before Bryce punched me in the jaw, knocking me off the chair.

"You know, when you have a particularly stubborn animal, you have to break it so that it learns how to behave."

"Ah, the old 'break an animal' bullshit," I said, getting back on the chair. "You don't break an animal by beating it until it behaves. That's how you *create* animals that will one day turn on you." I looked over at Bryce. "Why is Brooke scared of you?"

"Ask her," Bryce said with a chuckle.

"Mr. Carpenter," Robert said. "You genuinely don't seem to understand how badly this situation will go for you." He snapped across the table, cracking the butt of the pistol against Antonio's jaw. Antonio almost spilled out of the booth, but before I could do anything, I found Robert pointing the gun at me.

Antonio was dragged from the booth and punched in the face twice by Bryce. A third punch sent Antonio to the floor, and I readied myself to intervene.

"You do and you both die," Robert said, seemingly aware of my intentions. "We aren't going to kill him. Not now."

Bryce kicked Antonio twice in the ribs and once more in the head.

"Stop it," I said. "You've made your point."

Robert motioned for the attack to stop, and it did. I finally looked down at the semiconscious Antonio and was grateful to see his chest rise and fall.

"He'll need an ambulance," Robert said. "Any witty comebacks?"

I looked up at Robert and had the desire to tear out his throat. "No."

"Next time you involve yourself, both you and Antonio here will die. We'll come back when his waitresses are here, and we'll butcher the whole place. Am I clear?"

I nodded.

"If you see me or Bryce again, you walk the other way. If you think that you're some white knight who gets to fuck Jessica, you're wrong."

"I'm not trying to do anything to Jessica. Is that what this is about? Do you think Jessica and I are together?"

"I think that you only involve yourself in her affairs because you want to get a piece of that ass."

"You're delusional," I snapped. "There's nothing going on, now or ever, with Jess and me. I stepped in because you were all being thuggish dicks."

"And now you know not to," Robert said, punching me in the stomach and pushing me off the chair. "I hope you enjoy the rest of your day. Stay away from me and what is mine, and we won't have to escalate things further."

He kicked me in the head, leaving me lying on the cold diner floor as they all left. My vision went spotty for a short time. The sounds of sirens filled my ears, and I pulled myself upright next to Antonio.

I felt his pulse, and while he still had one, he was drifting in and out of consciousness.

Four paramedics burst into the diner and ran over to Antonio and me as I tried to tell them to look after my friend.

They did their jobs well before taking Antonio out on a gurney, leaving me sitting in a booth at the diner.

Sheriff Adrian King and a deputy walked into the diner and stood in front of me.

"It's turned into a shit day," I said.

"We need you to come with us," the sheriff said.

"Can we do it later? I just want to take some drugs before the headache *really* starts."

"No," the deputy said. "We're going down to the station now." He removed his cuffs from his belt.

"You're arresting me?" I asked, incredulous. "What did I do? I didn't realize getting beaten up in a diner was a criminal offense."

"Not arresting you. We'd prefer you volunteered to come with us."

"Why?" I asked.

"We have some questions about a body that was found this morning," the sheriff said.

Chapter Five

LAYLA CASSIDY

Realm of Helheim

Two weeks ago, Layla Cassidy had fought a dragon. An actual dragon. Big wings, teeth, breathed fire . . . well, a kind of fire that was made of pure magic, but the point was she'd fought and helped kill a dragon. So having spent the time since sitting in a dusty library in the city of Niflhel in the realm of Helheim, Layla was beginning to get cabin fever. It wasn't like she wanted to go fight another dragon. Ever. But the library had countless thousands of books and only six people to go through them.

"I'm *so* bored," Tarron the shadow elf said from across the table. With light-purple skin and a short black beard that matched the long hair on his head, he looked like the kind of person who picked fights in bars. Although Layla was pretty sure that Tarron wouldn't be caught dead anywhere near a bar.

"I humbly request to be refrozen for a few more thousand years," Tarron said. "Because that would be preferable to reading some of the utter rubbish that passes for historically accurate data in these books."

There was the sound of someone being hit somewhere among the rows of books inside the first floor of the library, followed by a sudden exclamation of surprise. The library itself went deep underground, and Layla really hoped that she wasn't going to have to waste the next few years moving slowly down into the catacombs just to find what the group was looking for.

"You fell asleep," Kase shouted.

"I came here to help Layla," Harry tried to whisper, which, considering the acoustics of the room, was nearly impossible. "But it's so boring."

"You know you're both grown men, right?" Layla said, raising her voice. "You can leave at any time."

"Can't," Harry said, walking out from the rows of books, rubbing his arm. "Kase told me I had to stay."

Kase shrugged.

Harry Gao had a brilliant mind. He was a few years older than Layla's own twenty-three and a little taller than her, with unruly dark hair and several days' worth of stubble. He was also someone who got bored quickly. Spending two weeks going through stuffy book after stuffy book was not his idea of a good time. Although Layla was pretty sure there were very few people in the library who were there enjoying themselves.

"Where are the rest of the team?" Harry asked.

"I went for food," Zamek said as he entered the room, the variously colored beads decorating his long brown beard rattling as he walked.

As a Norse dwarf, Zamek carried the traditional large battle-ax on his back and a second, single-headed ax that hung from his hip. Like everyone else, he wore rune-scribed leather armor, designed to stop magical attacks and hopefully slow down teeth, claws, and blades.

He placed a large wicker hamper on a nearby table, opened it, grabbed something that looked like a chicken leg—Layla *really* hoped it was a chicken leg—and set about eating. It didn't take long for everyone else to get the hint.

"So any luck finding my people?" Zamek asked, almost absentmindedly.

The team was in the library to find information about where the remaining Norse dwarves had gone. When the shadow elves had mutated, the first thing they'd done was wage a war on the dwarves that had forced the latter to abandon their own realm to survive. The dwarven realm had been freed of blood elf control, but the majority of the dwarves were still missing.

"No," Kase said, grabbing a platter of sushi.

"Did you go back to *Earth* just to get lunch?" Harry asked.

"Why not?" Zamek asked, as if it were the single best idea anyone had ever had.

Earth was the main realm, with dozens—thousands—of realms all branching off it. Each was connected to the Earth realm via a realm gate, usually dwarven made. The gates connected point A to point B, and for centuries, that was how they'd operated. Recently, Zamek had found a way of enabling the realm gates to change destinations, albeit temporarily. So long as Zamek knew the destination runes, he could change the gate. Apparently for takeout.

"We haven't found anything yet," Layla said, grabbing a bottle of ice-cold water and a chicken-and-bacon sandwich.

"They're out there somewhere," Zamek said.

"We'll find them," Kase told him.

"Does anyone know where Hyperion is?" Layla asked, looking around. "I haven't seen him for a few days. And Tego appears to have absconded too."

"Last time I saw Hyperion, he was heading down to the catacombs." Tarron yawned. "He might still be there."

Layla took a last bite of sandwich. "I'll go find him."

Layla wasn't particularly concerned about Hyperion; he was one of the oldest people she'd ever met at well over seven thousand years. He was also incredibly powerful, having been the leader of the Titans after Cronus and Rhea had been murdered a few years earlier. However, despite his agreement to help find the shadow elves and Zamek's people, Layla got the feeling he had more on his mind than just jumping through realms to find missing civilizations.

It took a few minutes to descend the narrow, winding stairwell to reach the bottom. Layla wondered just how far below the ground they were. She sighed, realizing she would have to walk back *up* the stairs afterward, and wished she'd never bothered with the whole idea in the first place. Still, she was there now, so she stepped through into an enormous cave. It was easily the size of a football stadium, at least in length, although it was still fifty feet high.

"Hello?" Layla called out; she received an echo in return. There were piles of books littered all around, although there didn't seem to be any rhyme or reason for their placement.

Lanterns blazed from the walls of the cave, lending a lot of light to what would have otherwise been complete darkness. Somewhere in the distance a cat growled. It wasn't a warning; she was just letting Layla know she was there.

"Tego," Layla said.

Whenever Layla told someone about her cat, Tego, people always assumed that she meant a moggy. A cute little petting cat that would sit on her lap and purr while she stroked its head. While Tego liked being petted, she was no house cat. Tego was a saber-tooth panther with fur that was a mixture of black and shimmering purple. She was so big that Layla could have ridden her into battle, and even tigers and lions were dwarfed beside her. Layla had . . . acquired her in the dwarven realm of Nidavellir after saving her life; the large cat had stuck by her ever since.

Tego walked out from behind a rock wall and licked Layla's hand, nudging her and purring as Layla scratched her behind the ear. Tego was smart. She could understand human words, and while she couldn't talk herself, she'd found ways to communicate when needed.

The pair continued on, passing half a dozen guards who stood outside a large metal door that appeared to have been carved into the rock of the cave.

"Is Hyperion in there?" Layla asked.

"Went in a few hours ago," one of them told her. "He said you'd be along. Your cat sat with us while we waited."

"You gave her food, didn't you?" Layla asked, raising her eyebrows to look at Tego. The massive cat sort of smiled, showing her huge teeth in the process.

"She likes drake meat," the guard said as he opened the door, referring to the snakelike creatures that lived in the sewers under the city.

Layla stepped into a circular room with a large bed. The bed was about twice the size of a normal king-size bed and contained one occupant: a black woman with long curly hair who appeared to be sound asleep. Silk sheets of various colors covered her body, while Hyperion sat to one side, reading a book.

"Took you long enough," he said, putting the book down.

"Seshat," Layla said, "I presume."

Hyperion nodded. "I came to see her. It's been a long time since our last encounter. She sleeps most of the time these days, her mind constantly absorbing the written words of anything that has ever been put to paper. She's due to wake up soon."

Hyperion looked to be in his midfifties, with a short gray beard and matching hair. He was a dragon-kin, able to change into a dragon-human hybrid that could use ice as a devastating weapon.

Seshat stirred and sat up, the sheets falling to reveal that she was naked from the waist up. She looked down at herself and sighed. "You're still here, Hyperion."

"I did tell you I would be," he said. "I also asked if you wanted to put some clothes on."

"And what did I tell you?" Seshat asked.

"Something about not being ashamed of how you look," he said. "I forget the intricate parts of the conversation."

Seshat stood, revealing that she was, in fact, completely naked.

"Hi," Layla said with a slight nod. "I'm Layla."

"Are you bothered by my nakedness?" she asked, stepping off the bed, taking a jug, and pouring some water into a cup.

"Should I be?" Layla asked.

"Hyperion was alive when the Greeks were fucking one another silly," Seshat said with a slow smile. "I'm sure he attended more than his fair share of orgies, but he sees me naked and wishes to clothe me. You have a metal arm."

Layla looked down at her right arm. It had been cut off at the forearm, and she'd taken the time to learn how to create a new one from steel and titanium. It was stronger than her previous flesh-and-bone arm and could be manipulated by her powers as needed. Layla kept a silver blade in a sheath against her hip that she could transfer into the arm in a moment. The silver made it almost painful to manipulate, but silver could kill most nonhumans, so to her mind, the payoff was worth it.

"Yeah, I'm going for the Edward Elric look," Layla said, smiling at her own joke.

Seshat stared at her. "I don't know what that means."

"It's from *Fullmetal* . . . you know what? I don't think it matters."

Seshat nodded. "I am going for a shower. Can any questions wait until I am done?"

Layla shrugged. "Sure, why not?" She wasn't really certain what was going on.

Seshat exited the room, leaving Hyperion, Tego, and Layla alone.

"She's . . . confident," Layla said.

"She's someone who enjoys seeing others squirm," Hyperion said with a slight sigh.

"Seshat has a point, though; you did look a bit flustered."

Hyperion shook his head. "It is not her nakedness that flusters me. It's being in proximity to her. She remembers everything, and if she wants to show you something, she can just reach out and plant the memory in your head. There's a particular memory of her and me."

"Oh," Layla said with a grin. "You guys had sex."

"Graphically, yes," Hyperion said. "It was a long time ago. She likes to make a point of ensuring people don't forget her."

"That's unlikely, considering . . . ," Layla said as Seshat walked back into the room with a flourish. She wore thin sheets of colored fabric that did nothing to hide what she looked like beneath them. In fact, though Layla wasn't entirely sure how it was possible, she looked even more revealed with clothes on than off.

"You came to ask about the dwarves," Seshat said. "I have a few hours."

"And the shadow elves," Layla said.

Seshat smiled before pouring herself another glass of water. "I can't drink alcohol; it screws around with my head," she said. "It's probably the only thing I miss about my youth."

"You're an och, yes?" Layla asked. "Like Nabu?"

"Yes, and I heard about Nabu. He was a good och. A great one in many respects, and I look forward to seeing him again in a few centuries' time," Seshat said.

Layla nodded. Nabu's death had been recent, and it still hurt.

Seshat raised her glass in a silent toast. "As for me, I dedicated myself to absorbing information and putting it in these books. They write themselves, you know, which I can tell you is a trick *a lot* of authors would enjoy having." She drank the water in one long swig. "So: the dwarves and shadow elves."

"Do you know what happened to them?" Hyperion asked.

"Yes, my dear, of course," Seshat said with a sly smile. "Take a seat."

Layla sat, with Tego lying down beside her.

"You tamed a beast like that," Seshat said. "You must have great power. You're an umbra, yes? You have bonded with your spirits and drenik."

Layla nodded. The spirits and drenik had granted her great knowledge and power, but in doing so they had ceased to be consciously contactable. She had to wait until she went to sleep to see them. It was something she was still getting used to.

"You killed Mammon," Seshat said.

"I helped," Layla corrected.

"Don't be modest," Seshat said with a wink. "I can't abide modesty. It's the same as being fake. Accept your greatness. Revel in it. You killed Mammon the great dragon, yes?"

Layla nodded. "Yes."

Seshat clapped her hands together. "At last someone slew that piece of fetid shit."

"This isn't helping us find anyone," Hyperion reminded her.

Seshat turned to Hyperion. "Shush, you. We shall *talk* more later."

Hyperion actually went red in the face. Layla hadn't even known it was possible to make a several-thousand-year-old person embarrassed.

Seshat returned her attention to Layla. "You ever heard of the land of the giants, or Jotnar?"

"Jotunheim?" Layla asked.

Seshat nodded. "That's the one. That's where you need to go. I can't tell you for sure whether the elves and dwarves are there, but the last time anyone ever wrote something about either of them, it was to do with dwarven prisoners in the realm. Go to the well, find Mimir's writings, or Mimir if he's still alive. He might be able to point you in a better direction. He's an och, like me, although unlike me, he's about as pleasant to be around as a fire ant."

Layla got back to her feet. "Thank you," she said. "That'll help."

"Not really," Seshat said. "There are no realm gates to Jotunheim. The giants destroyed them a long time ago after the war between them and the flame giants. The flame giants escaped to Muspelheim, and the remaining Jotnar shut the gates to prevent their return. If there's an accessible realm gate, I don't know about it."

"What about the elven realm gates?"

Seshat shrugged. "No idea. I can't understand their writing, and understanding their language is next to impossible for anyone who isn't elven."

"A shadow elf merged his mind with hers," Hyperion said. "She can speak the language."

"Now, that *is* interesting," Seshat said with a raised eyebrow. "When you're done, come back and let me catalog the information. It would be fascinating." She paused for a few seconds before walking over to the side of the room. She drew on a piece of parchment with a pencil, then passed the parchment to Layla. "Turns out I do have a little something elven in my head, but I have no idea what the writings mean. This is an elven realm gate destination key. I have no idea where it'll take you inside Jotunheim, but the information has been in my head for centuries, and it'll be nice to make the space for something else."

"Thanks for your help," Layla said to Seshat.

"Hyperion will follow, soon enough," she said. "There are things we need to *discuss*." She looked back over to Hyperion, who gave an embarrassed nod.

Layla made her way back to the rest of the group, who were still tucking into the food that Zamek had brought.

"Ah, there you are," Harry said. "We were considering sending a search party after you."

"I met with Seshat," Layla said. "She's . . . unique."

"What did you learn?" Tarron asked.

"We need to go to Jotunheim," Layla told him. "That's the last known location of the dwarves. Apparently, Mimir might know more."

"Ah, bollocks," Zamek said. "Be careful of him. He's a tricky little bastard."

"Unfortunately, there are no known dwarven realm gates," Layla said, removing the parchment from her pocket and passing it to Tarron. "Seshat gave me this."

Tarron studied the parchment. "Jotunheim," he said softly. "More specifically, it's in Utgard, the capital of the realm. And the stronghold of the giants."

"How happy will they be to see us?" Layla asked.

"Depends on the giant," Tarron said. "Either way, this will take me a few hours to prepare. It's complex and has several security keys inside the writings that mean one wrong move and we'll be wishing we hadn't bothered."

Layla grabbed a bottle of water and drank it in one go. "Right, let's get ready to go to another realm. Where, I assume, we'll be pissing off a whole new bunch of people."

Chapter Six

NATE GARRETT

"I want my lawyer," I said after having been deposited on a chair in an interview room.

"You're not under arrest," the sheriff said.

"Then I'm leaving," I told him, standing up.

The deputy stepped in my way with a glare. "We can always find *something* to arrest you for."

I looked over to the sheriff. "You letting this jackass talk to people like that?"

"Take a step back, Deputy," the sheriff said with a sigh.

The deputy did as he was told.

"You answer our questions, and we'll see about letting you go," the sheriff said.

"I'm pretty sure that isn't legal," I told him.

"You volunteered to come to the station," the deputy said.

"Yes, *volunteered*," I repeated. "Phone call, now. Talk once it's done."

The sheriff stared at me and heaved another sigh. "Fine." He removed my mobile from the bag he'd put it in before I'd been placed in the squad car. "Two minutes."

"Alone," I said. "Or at least stand behind the two-way glass so I feel like I'm alone."

The sheriff and deputy left the interview room, and I looked around. The room was large enough for a gray metal table that was bolted to the concrete floor. Four chairs sat around it. There was a gray metal door and a large window that couldn't have screamed *two-way mirror* any louder than it did.

I called Chris Hopkins, who picked up on the second ring. "What did you do?" he asked me.

I told him everything that happened at Duke's and my current whereabouts.

"Shit," he said.

"Can you come down to the station and make sure I get out? I don't trust the deputy; he seems angry about something. And frankly, I'm not sure that some hick cop won't try to set me up because I'm not from around here."

"Anything else?"

"I'll let you know." I ended the call and sent him a text, asking him to look into Robert Saunders, before I quickly deleted the outgoing messages and locked the phone down. It would take a six-digit number to open it, and I was in no mood to give that number to the sheriff or his people.

"Can I assume you won't be telling us what you did with your phone?" the sheriff asked as he entered the room.

"Yep," I told him. "I'm not under arrest, right?"

"You're a person of interest," the deputy said as he leaned up against the mirror. He was a few inches taller than me, with blond hair and a thick blond beard. Tattoos adorned his forearms, including an Army Rangers badge.

"So why am I here?" I asked, placing my phone on the table.

The sheriff opened a folder in front of him. "Yesterday you were seen arguing with one Jackson Miller."

"Ah, the Nazi? Yes, I did step in and stop the Nazi from hurting anyone."

"You broke his arm," the sheriff said.

"I did."

"You also broke his nose and smashed his face."

"That's true; I did," I said. "He wouldn't take no for an answer."

"So you decided you were a tough guy," the deputy said.

"Not particularly," I said. "I just wanted to stop him being a threat."

"Well, we found his body this morning," the sheriff said.

"What?" I asked.

Sheriff Adrian King removed two color photographs from the folder and put them in front of me. One was a picture of the body in a dumpster in a snowy alleyway. He was missing an arm, although the lack of blood there meant he'd been killed elsewhere. The second photo was a close-up of the ruination that was Jackson's face. It looked like a bear had tried to rip it off and had done a pretty good job.

"Well, he's definitely dead," I said, sitting back in my chair.

"Show some damn respect," the deputy snapped.

"No, he was a Nazi thug. Fuck him."

The deputy took a step toward me.

"You going to beat me with a phone book, Deputy?" I asked.

The sheriff motioned for the deputy to step away, but I could see the anger in the younger man's face.

"You knew Jackson?" I asked him, already knowing the answer.

"We were in the army together," he said. "He was a good man. A good friend."

"And a Nazi," I pointed out.

"Maybe one of your *friends* did it," he snapped. "Maybe some werewolf piece of shit killed him, and you're hiding them."

"What the hell does that mean?" I asked.

"We looked into your background," the sheriff said. "There's nothing there to suggest that you are anything other than human, but maybe you know someone who isn't."

"I'm sorry, what?"

"Maybe that Asian family?" the deputy said. "One of them an animal who looks like a human? Maybe that little boy gets kept in a cage at night, but he got out. Should we go test them all? Are you protecting them? Maybe it's one of the girls. Should we get them in here instead? See if we can't get a confession out of them?"

I stared at the deputy, absolute rage bubbling up inside of me. "I'm going to say this once, slowly, so you both hear me."

There was a knock on the door, and Chris walked in without waiting for it to be opened. "This is my client, and we're leaving," Chris said.

"You're a lawyer too?" the sheriff asked.

"I'm all kinds of things," Chris said, his voice dripping with anger. "Are you charging my client?"

"No," the sheriff said. "But he should hang around in town."

"What were you going to say?" the deputy asked me as the sheriff placed my car keys on the table.

"I was going to say that if I ever hear that bullshit out of your mouth again, I'm going to forget that you wear a badge."

The deputy took a step toward me. "You *threatening* an officer of the law?"

"I heard no threat," Chris said, looking at me with an expression that told me to keep my mouth shut. "I heard only a comment that you shouldn't spout off unsubstantiated shit."

"I bet he's involved with the animal that did this," the deputy said. "Maybe he's eyeing up the Kuros as his next victims. Although I guess if they go, it'll be no great loss to the community."

"Jesus Christ, Deputy," the sheriff said. "I won't have that kind of shit said in my department. Get out, get changed, and go home."

I turned to the sheriff. "Maybe you need to check that the Nazi sacks of shit haven't gotten jobs in your office."

The sheriff waited for the deputy to leave, the latter giving me an evil glare as he walked past. "I'm sorry for his behavior," the sheriff said to me. "I didn't expect him to . . . say anything like that. He's not one of them. But Jackson was his friend, and I think he feels a little upset that he couldn't stop Jackson from sliding toward the beliefs he had when he died."

I stood. "Who called you to tell you where I was? And who told you about the body?"

"Anonymous tip," the sheriff said.

"How is Antonio?"

"He'll be okay," the sheriff said. "We'll look into the attack."

I noticed that the deputy was standing in the hallway beyond. "Well, considering I doubt your deputy could find his cock with both hands and a road map, I assume it'll be a really long investigation."

"The crime rate in town has risen dramatically in recent weeks. People behaving erratically. Violence from people who have never shown any signs of being violent before. I don't know what's happening in Clockwork, but I better not find out that you're involved, Mr. Carpenter."

Chris practically dragged me out of the room before I started a brawl, and we were soon outside. "Fucking hell, Nate," Chris said as we got into his dark-blue Ford Ranger.

"Sorry, but I wasn't expecting to be arrested for some Nazi's murder. I certainly wasn't expecting them to suggest that Jessica and Ava were responsible. Especially all that other stuff about the Kuros."

"They were trying to rile you up, get you to say or do something stupid," Chris said as we pulled out of the car park. "However, I wouldn't be surprised to find that the deputy and your Nazi problem are connected. This is quite the hornet's nest of shit you've managed to involve yourself in."

I shook my head. "I just can't figure out why Avalon would send a KOA agent like Robert just to come here and get involved in a custody issue," I said.

"Ah, the file is in the glove compartment," Chris said.

I opened the compartment, removed the manila envelope inside, unfastened it, and took out the three sheets of paper it contained. "This is a little old school."

"I didn't want to send it to your phone."

The file made for interesting, albeit unpleasant reading. "Robert Saunders is not a nice person," I said eventually.

"No, no, he's not. I haven't read it all, though."

"He was a marine who had multiple citations for assault. And more than one occurrence of the military police having to break up a fight that he appeared to have started. It looks like he was dating Jess, and she left him for another marine, so he took leave, flew to South Korea, where the marine was stationed, found him, and beat him into a coma. Robert was arrested, tried, and jailed for . . . aggravated assault? That's it?"

"I called a military friend of mine," Chris said. "It's not in the file, but essentially the marines got Robert tried and convicted, with a dishonorable discharge, under the agreement that once he'd served his term, he pissed off and never returned. A whole bunch of people didn't do their job, which led to Robert getting to the other marine. No one higher up wanted an international incident and a very public jailing, so it was done quietly. Robert has some powerful and, more importantly, rich parents, so the other family was paid off. The injured marine was given a whole bunch of medals when he woke up. He left the marines a hero who was told to keep his mouth shut."

"And Robert vanished. There's nothing here after that."

"Nope, that's the last official time we heard of him. Apparently, he joined Avalon and the KOA."

"Any joy on finding out who they are?"

"Yeah, and none of it is good." Chris parked the car next to mine outside of Duke's Diner. "The KOA were set up about eighteen months ago to hunt those who stand against Avalon. The KOA go in, get the help of local thugs to cause trouble and stir up civil unrest, and use that to find the people they're looking for. Then the Harbingers come in and kill every living person involved with the rebellion."

I sighed. The Harbingers. "Damn it."

"Yep, it's all the good stuff coming our way."

The Harbingers were the elite special forces of Avalon. You had to be at least a century old to join, and then you underwent a conditioning cycle that a lot of people didn't make it through. Essentially, the candidate was put into a coma for several years so that their minds could be sharpened, their powers improved, and their bodies honed. When they came out, they were considerably more dangerous than when they'd gone in. Not everyone made it through the whole process, and a lot of them came out of their coma too early, or their bodies couldn't handle the stress. But they could only undergo the process once, and if they failed, it was too bad.

"And you're sure they're not here for me?" I asked.

"Not you, no. Robert would have recognized you."

"Who, then?"

"You are not the first person that has been sent here to recuperate. There have been many over the years, but apart from you, only one remains."

"Who?"

Chris let out a long sigh. "I'll explain all tomorrow. It is not for me to say at this time. Please understand. I need to contact people and see how much danger we're in."

"Okay," I said. "Well, I need to get to the Kuro household. Ava's not human. And I told her that once I'd figured out exactly what she was, I would come and talk to her about it."

Chris stared at me for several seconds. "Really? Do you know?"

I nodded. "Yeah. I've been thinking about it all day, and I've a pretty good idea."

"Good luck. I'll speak to you tomorrow."

By the time I drove up to the massive house where the Kuros lived at the far end of town, it was getting dark. The Kuro house sat on a large plot of land, with trees all around it, shielding it from the nearest neighbors' view. It had five bedrooms as well as a turret on the left-hand side above a double-size garage. A balcony ran around the front of the house, and dozens of ornate stone sculptures adorned the large lawn next to the gravel driveway. This was where the wealthy came to live. Daniel and Donna had told me that they had not been born to wealth, but Hades took care of those who worked for him, and because of their involvement, they were able to live comfortable lives as well as know they were doing good in the world.

I got out of the Mercedes as the front door opened and Donna walked out. "Nate, Ava said you were coming over. Did she invite you to dinner tomorrow?" She stopped.

There was a bag of clean clothes in the car, so I'd put on a fresh pair of jeans and a dark-blue jumper before I'd arrived. I didn't really want anyone to see the blood splatter on the clothes I'd been wearing all day.

"She did, yes," I said as Donna hugged me. "But I'm here for something else."

Ava stood in the still-open doorway to the house. "You can tell them," she said.

"I need to talk to you, Daniel, and Ava," I said.

"You sound like it's something bad."

I shook my head. "Not bad, just important."

Donna told me that Jess was putting Simon to bed and that I should go through the house to the conservatory at the rear. I headed through the maze of corridors to the kitchen. The kitchen itself was large enough to have its own dining area as well as an archway that led to a small room with a set of stairs that went up into the tower. There was a door that remained bolted at all times, as only the basement was beyond, and it contained a safe room amid the paraphernalia that Donna and Daniel had accrued.

I removed my jacket, laid it over a nearby wooden chair, and took a seat as Ava, Daniel, and Donna entered.

"So what's going on?" Donna asked.

I explained that Ava had been to my home that morning and that she'd asked me to test her for abilities. Both remained quiet as I told them about the runes, about the glowing. About Ava not being human.

"Is there any point asking if you're wrong?" Daniel asked.

"No," I told him.

"Oh, Ava," Donna said, taking her granddaughter's hand in her own. "Why didn't you talk to us?"

"Because I was scared," Ava said. "I know you both say that it doesn't matter who or what you are, but people at school, and on the news, they're always talking about those who aren't human as if they're monsters. I didn't want to be a monster." Tears rolled down Ava's face.

"You're not a monster," I told her. "No one is born a monster. We decide the kind of person we're going to be. Now, sometimes there are forces at work that want to make us mean, cruel, and unkind. That make it seem like it's okay to be unpleasant to others, to bully and hurt people weaker than ourselves. But it's up to us whether or not we allow those forces to win. Everyone is responsible for their own actions, no matter who or what they are."

"How can you be sure?"

"A long time ago, I was married to a woman by the name of Mary Jane Garrett. Most called her Mary, but I knew she preferred Jane, so I usually called her that. She was murdered by bad people. Bad people I spent a long time tracking down and punishing. I allowed my rage and hate to consume me. I allowed myself to become everything I swore I'd never be. That was my choice. And despite my friends helping me see that I was heading down a dark path, it was my choice to come back from the brink of darkness and become something else. So I know a little something about being responsible for your own actions."

"I'm sorry for your wife," Ava said.

"Thank you. It was a long time ago, when I was much younger."

"Did you ever remarry?" she asked.

I shook my head. "There is a woman I love very much. Her name is Selene, and I hope that one day we'll be reunited." I smiled sadly. When I thought of Selene, my heart ached for her, but continuing down that path brought only sadness and hurt. "But we're not here to discuss me."

Daniel placed a hand on my shoulder and squeezed gently.

"What am I?" Ava asked, taking a deep breath.

"You were born human," I told her. "But when you were young, you almost died after contracting meningitis. Your recovery was seen as a miracle. It wasn't. A spirit bonded with you, healed you, kept you alive. That spirit was a shinigami."

"What's a shinigami?" Daniel asked.

"It's a spirit that senses death around them and tries to bring peace to people who die. But they occasionally bond with children. No one is really sure why, but while they're bonded, the child has no knowledge of the spirit's presence. From that moment on, the child will be stronger, faster; it won't get sick, and it will heal quickly. But in return, it will see death. It will dream of death that happens around it. The child can't stop it; it can't do anything but accept the shinigami. In accepting them, the host can gain some measure of control over them."

"How?" Ava asked.

"I've only ever met two others of your kind in my life, and only one of those was ever interested in discussing his bonding. He said that he asked to speak to the spirit while asleep, and from there they came to an agreement. It's probably the best place to start. Spirits, and anything that bonds with a person, are usually open to discussions. At least at first."

"Just talk to it?" Ava asked.

"Why not?" Donna asked. "Sounds like a good start. We can find more information on them and go from there."

"I have a few old books on spirits," Daniel said. "We can look into shinigami and see how best to help Ava."

The look of relief on Ava's face was easy to spot. "Thank you," she mouthed to me as her grandparents hugged her.

"Thank you for telling us this," Daniel said, leaving Ava's side to embrace me. "I can never repay you for what you've done."

"You've repaid me a hundred times over," I told him.

After several offers of food for the journey home, all of which I had to turn down because otherwise I wouldn't have left the house until the early hours of the morning, Daniel walked me to the front door.

"Do you really think she'll be okay?" he asked me as we both stepped outside. The snow had started up again, although it was light compared to the usual fall.

"Yes," I told him. "Shinigami are not evil; they offer no harm to their host. They are a mystery, but they are a kind one, despite the dreams. She'll need her family, though. I won't pretend it'll be easy for her to learn how to control the visions, but she'll get there."

"How about you?"

"I'm fine," I told him. "I'm still human, which sucks, but I'll be okay."

"Just stay out of trouble."

"Funny, Chris said the exact same thing," I said.

"Because we both know who you used to be," Daniel said.

I climbed into my pickup and started the engine. Feeling the warm air rush out of the vents, I drove away, ready to completely ignore the warning of both Daniel and Chris.

Chapter Seven

Nate Garrett

Parking the pickup outside of the mortuary, I wondered if I was doing the right thing. But I needed to see the body of the dead Nazi to figure out what had killed him, and I doubted that the police were going to let me just have a look at his report.

There were no cars parked outside the mortuary and no lights on inside. Brooke had once told me that aside from two guards, no one worked there at night, a fact that she'd been exceptionally annoyed about at the time, as she'd been waiting for some drug tests to be completed.

My phone rang, and the screen said *Brooke*. "Hi," I said after answering it.

"Get out of your truck," Brooke said.

"What?" I asked, trying to maintain some semblance of innocence.

"I can *see* you in your truck."

"Where are you?" I asked, looking around.

The main entrance to the mortuary opened, and Brooke Tobin stepped out into the night and leaned up against the wall of the building. She wore jeans and a jacket, but I could see her holstered weapon sitting against her hip. "You would suck as a ninja," she called out.

The mortuary was far enough away from anything residential to ensure that no one was going to hear her, but even so, I looked around at the woods on the opposite side of the road.

"We're here alone," she said as I reached her. "I wanted to check on something."

"The dead Nazi?" I asked.

"You're here to check, too, I assume?"

"Well, I was accused of killing him, so I figured I'd at least have a look."

"I heard about what happened. I'm sorry. You seen Antonio?"

I shook my head. "He was my first stop tomorrow morning. I heard he's being kept in for the day, and I know full well that he would hate me to see him laid up in bed."

"I'm certain he is not being a good patient," Brooke agreed. "I'll tell you what. I let you in here to look at this dead Nazi, and you tell me everything you currently know about what's happening."

"I'm not sure I know an awful lot more than you do," I said, unsure if that was actually true or not.

The smile on Brooke's face vanished. "Let's go see our corpse. Just one thing you should know."

I paused halfway through the door. "What?"

"Doug works night shift here this week. I'd hoped he was on days."

"Ah, crap," I said and continued on into the mortuary.

The mortuary in Clockwork, Oregon, looked pretty much like every single mortuary I'd ever been in. The reception area was full of calming paintings on the wall and comfortable seating. Several vases of flowers were dotted around the room, the different colors giving some brightness to what, I assumed, was otherwise a difficult place to work.

"The body is this way," Brooke said, taking the lead. "Lower basement."

Once at the lowest floor, we followed another white corridor to a room with several sinks. I washed my hands, and Brooke passed me a pair of surgical gloves. Once we were both ready, we entered the main morgue. There were twelve silver hatches in the walls of the big room. A large wooden desk sat in the corner. It was spotless except for a computer, a printer, and several notebooks.

"Which one is he in?" I asked.

Brooke walked over to one of the lower hatches on the wall in front of me and pulled open a drawer. She unzipped the black body bag, revealing the dead Nazi. Or what was left of him, anyway.

"Holy shit," Doug said from behind me as he walked through the door.

"What the hell, Doug?" Brooke asked.

"I just wanted to see it," Doug said, in the same voice that a young child might use after being caught doing something they shouldn't have.

"It's a corpse," I told him. "It's not exactly the kind of thing you normally want to see."

"Yeah, but look at it," Doug said, as Brooke mouthed an apology to me and tried to usher Doug out of the room.

"The file is on that desk," Brooke said as I was left alone.

I found the file and took it over with me to the body of Jackson Miller. A swastika was tattooed on his sternum. It was about the size of the palm of my hand, and directly under it in red were the words *Blood and Soil.* There were several more unpleasant tattoos representing his beliefs across his body, and not one of them made me feel bad about being happy he was dead.

"Fuck you, Jackson Miller," I said. "I hope it fucking hurt."

I guessed it probably had, considering something had torn part of his face off and ripped his arm off at the shoulder. The autopsy report suggested that after a large part of his face had been removed, he'd bled out once the arm had been torn free. He hadn't died where he'd been found, which meant nothing particularly good, except that whoever had done it wasn't someone who went around in public ripping people's arms off.

The gouges on his face were deep, to the bone in most cases, and his lips, his nose, and one eye were all missing. One cheek had been torn free, too—the doctor had surmised that it had most likely been bitten off. And indeed, there were large teeth marks on the flesh of the body. The doctor had made a private note on a subsequent page suggesting that if the death had been committed anywhere in the woods, he'd have expected a bear to be involved. He'd also noted that bears were not known to kill in the woods and carry their prey to an alley to dump them. He had a fair point.

"So you see anything interesting?" Brooke asked as she reentered the room.

"The official cause of death is murder," I said. "The doctor has put his personal notes on a separate sheet. He thinks that Jackson went into shock and bled out."

"Any ideas what killed him? The prevailing theory is that it was a werebear, werewolf, werelion, or basically any of the were family of creatures."

I shrugged. "I guess it's possible, but the file says that they found hair in the wound that doesn't correspond to either human or any known animal. Honestly, I have no idea what did this. The list of things that could have is massive, and I can't think that any of them would be good to have running around Clockwork."

"You think it was a message?" Brooke asked.

"Maybe," I said. "Honestly, I think it was an accident, and they dumped the body."

"You think that *this*," Brooke said, motioning toward the body, "was an accident?"

"The body dumping was a panicked thing," I said. "If they'd have thought about it, they'd have buried his body in the woods and been done with it. Let nature take its course. No, this sounds like he died, and people were worried they'd be blamed, but they're also idiots, so they just dumped the body. Otherwise, why bother? What message does this send, and to who?"

"*We'll rip your arms and face off if you cross us?*" Brooke suggested.

"Okay, but who's the threat aimed at? The alley rats? I read in the notes here about where they found him. It was inside a dumpster, in an alley that's one of the first stops on trash pickup. Someone thought they could get rid of him with the use of the landfill. Can't go there themselves, too many cameras, too many witnesses. Can't bury him in the woods, just in case some hiker finds him, and then it leads back to them. Like I said, they panicked and figured this was their best bet."

"I thought you said if they were smart they'd have buried him in the woods?" Brooke said.

"Yeah, well, they would have. Deep down. But I imagine they didn't have time. Which leads back to the idea of them panicking."

"You think his Nazi friends were in on this?"

I nodded. "Without a shadow of a doubt. The biggest question is, What killed him? There have been no other deaths in this town that match this one. People would be talking if a spate of bodies turned up missing limbs. So what do those Nazis have that could accidentally kill one of them? This is just hypothetical, but it also makes sense to me. Not a were, though, not unless it's caged up."

"Could a caged were do this?" Brooke asked.

I looked at the body and nodded. "He gets too close, it attacks him, kills him, and they dump the body."

"But why would they have a caged were?"

"The KOA are working with them," I said. "Maybe they brought one."

"The mayor had a visit from some Avalon personnel. She told us to allow them every freedom to do their job."

"Did you meet them yourself?"

Brooke shook her head. "I did some looking into the KOA, and it looks like they hunt down the enemies of Avalon. I couldn't really find more than that, but the KOA could use a were for that, right?"

"Yeah," I said. "Yeah, they could."

The door to the morgue opened, and Doug walked in again. "You're going to have to leave," he said, fear in his voice.

"Why?" Brooke asked.

"The sheriff is about to arrive," Doug said. "I doubt very much Nate is meant to be here."

"Except my car is out front," I said. "I think he'll have figured it out."

Doug's face paled. "But you *shouldn't* be here. He'll be here any minute."

"I know. Just tell him I stopped off to try and talk you into letting me see the body and that I'm using the bathroom," I suggested. "I'll take the stairs up to the top floor, and he'll be none the wiser."

Doug looked visibly relieved at the idea.

"I'll come up with you," Brooke said.

Doug ran off without another word.

"He really is hard work," Brooke said as we reached the staircase and started the four floors of steps to the reception floor.

"He told me that you're gay," I said.

She stopped and turned back to me. "Seriously?"

I nodded. "I know you told me a while ago, and I know you've been telling people you feel comfortable with, but you should probably know that he wanted me to be aware just in case I decided to hit on you and was rejected."

"He's such a dick," Brooke said with a sigh. "In a roundabout way, it was actually what I wanted to talk to you about the other day. I told my father. He was very happy for me."

"I'm glad," I told her as we reached the top of the stairs.

Brooke went first out of the stairwell, beckoning me to join her in the corridor beyond as the sounds of the sheriff's voice drifted through the hall.

"What the hell do you think you're doing here?" the sheriff asked me as I entered the reception area.

"Peeing," I told him. "Also, washing my hands after. Because that's just nasty otherwise."

The sheriff's eyes narrowed. "You came here to pee."

"Well, no," I said. "I came here to figure out why you'd think I'm a murderer. I thought that if I could get a look at the body, I might be able to work out what actually did do it. But Doug wouldn't let me through, and I needed to pee. Then Brooke arrived."

"And what are *you* doing here?" the sheriff asked his deputy.

"Nate is my friend," Brooke said a little defensively. "We both know that he didn't kill that man. I came to look over the notes from the autopsy."

"And what did you see?" the sheriff asked, his anger deflating somewhat.

"Nothing. I got here about five minutes ago while Nate was trying to get Doug to let him down to see the body. I convinced Nate it was a bad idea and then went with him to the bathroom to make sure he didn't do anything stupid."

"I do have a habit of doing stupid things," I said.

The sheriff stared at me for several heartbeats. The man wasn't an idiot, and I was pretty sure he knew that I'd been down and seen the body, but considering everyone was telling him the opposite, including his own deputy, I also knew he wasn't going to push it.

"Go home, Nate," the sheriff said.

"I'll drive him," Brooke said.

"What about my car?" I asked.

"You can get a cab back here tomorrow and pick it up," the sheriff said, in a tone that suggested this conversation was at an end.

"Looks like I'm taking you home," Brooke said.

"Sheriff King," I said. "Pleasure as always."

"Nate," Sheriff King said as I reached the door. "Don't get involved in this. We know it wasn't you, but you are *not* an officer of the law. No one seems to know exactly what it is you do for a living, but I'm sure you're not a cop."

"I'm independently wealthy," I said. "And you're right—I'm not a cop. Never have been, and it's unlikely I ever will be. On the other hand, I'm not mad keen on the place I live being infested by Nazis."

"Just behave," the sheriff said. I left the mortuary and followed Brooke, who stood next to my car. She'd been to her own car and retrieved a black backpack.

"I thought we were going in yours," I said.

"Yours is much better off road than mine," she said. "I'll direct you. It's about an hour's drive."

The drive was done in relative silence, which was probably for the best when we turned off a main road and started driving up a dirt track through dense forest, as I needed to concentrate. After a few miles the dirt road turned onto another main road, and I could see the lights of a town in the distance.

"Make a left up here," Brooke said.

A few minutes later we were on another dirt road, driving up a steep incline until we reached a large open area near a cliff. Brooke and I got out of the Mercedes and walked across the clearing to a wooden bench that overlooked the cliff itself.

Approximately half a mile away, and several hundred feet below where Brooke and I stood, was a large field housing what appeared to be a hangar along with several dozen buildings. There was a multitude of cars of all shapes and sizes parked on the field, and the sounds of their occupants' party could easily reach my ears.

"What's that?" I asked Brooke, who, after wiping away the snow on the bench, had taken a seat.

Brooke removed a set of binoculars from her backpack and passed them to me. "Take a look."

I leaned up against a large tree and looked through the binoculars at the scenes of revelry in the distance. It didn't take long to find the signs that those enjoying the party were part of the same group that Jackson, Bryce, and his friends were members of.

"A Nazi party . . . ," I said, looking back at Brooke.

"Yep. This is where they all hang out."

"How do you *know* this?" I asked.

"Because I'm a cop, and it's my job to know where the trouble is. Also, I followed one of them here a few weeks ago. I used to live not far from this place growing up; my grandfather used to bring me up here as a kid."

"I assume the Nazi backdrop wasn't here at the time."

"No, it used to just be some old warehouse that belonged to a packing company or something."

"Why did you bring me here?"

"Because I wanted to tell you the truth about why I didn't arrest Bryce, and I hoped that in turn you'd tell me the truth about who you are."

"What truth would that be?" I asked, looking back through the binoculars.

"I've known you for two years. I'd like to think we're friends. We've been out drinking with Antonio, Jess, and others. We've spoken long into the night about life and dreams, but it turns out I don't know a damn thing about you. You're some rich British guy who moved here to get away from the hustle and bustle of everyday life."

"I never said I was anything of the sort."

"You don't have a job that I know of," Brooke said. "But I've never seen you concerned about money."

"I'm not concerned about money," I said. "I'm also not what you said."

"You're also not a cop—I know that much—and I saw you fight at the game. That's training. Real training, not someone who goes to the gym a few times a week because they want to be the next MMA star. You could have killed that man, but you chose not to."

I looked down at the partygoers and caught sight of a young woman who looked like a blonde version of Brooke. She was standing beside Bryce, and I watched as she leaned over and kissed him on the lips. I looked back over to Brooke. "Why is there a woman down there who looks just like you?"

Brooke sighed. "She's the reason we're here. That's my twin sister."

Chapter Eight

NATE GARRETT

"This isn't a rescue mission, is it?" I asked. "Because that would be stupid."

"No, I just wanted you to understand why I let Bryce go."

"He's dating your sister." It wasn't a question.

"Yes. Her name is Addison. She's about as unpleasant a person as can be, and she's dating a Nazi, which I guess makes her one too. When I came out to her a few months ago, she called me some very unpleasant names, and I knew that no matter what happened next, we were done. I tried to get her out of trouble; I even arrested Bryce, but then he got out and sent me pictures of her beating on some woman. That's what he meant by what he'd do. He'd make sure I had evidence to arrest my sister. Evidence I can't pretend I didn't get."

"And if you do pretend and it comes out, then you get charged with obstruction of justice or some other crime. Either way you lose your job."

Brooke nodded. "Addison and I were never close, even as kids," she started. "Our parents divorced when we were eight; I went to live with our dad, and she with our mom. I didn't really get on with my mom—we were too different—and thankfully my parents were grown up enough to see that there was no benefit to making one of us kids miserable just to keep us together. Eventually, my mom got remarried to a rich doctor, and then I basically only saw her at holidays and Christmas. Always with Addison. Who was a bully and cruel. She hated me, and even though I wanted her to like me, to be my sister, she just kept on hating. I never really figured out why."

"But she still plays on that part of you who wants a relationship?" I asked.

Brooke nodded. "Yeah, I still get the occasional call from her asking to meet up. That she just wants to get to know me better. That she's sorry about what happened in the past. It happens every few years, and the last one was a few months ago. Our granddad died six months ago, and she was basically sniffing around for anything she might have been left."

I looked back through the binoculars to the party.

"I don't know what to do," Brooke told me. "I got those pictures; I've seen my sister commit a crime, and if I go to my boss, I'd be all but admitting that I kept it quiet because I didn't want to arrest her."

"And now?"

"And now? Part of me thinks, *Fuck them both; get them arrested.*"

"Where's your mum in all this?"

"Ah, she died when we were twenty-one. Overdosed on pain meds. Husband is in jail for supplying them. My dad lives in Norway with his new wife. She's a lovely lady, but he wants nothing to do with Addison. He tried to talk sense into her, and she got Bryce to threaten him and his wife, so he said she's free to stay a Nazi as far as he's concerned."

"Families are never easy," I said. "From what I've seen, anyway."

"What about your family?" Brooke asked.

"I don't know who my dad is, and I've never met my mum," I said. "I know who she is, but not where."

"You're an orphan?"

I nodded. "Yep. Raised by a man I thought of as my father."

"A good man, I hope?"

I shook my head. "He might have been once, but not anymore. Now, he's bitter and resentful. He's become everything I always thought he hated. It's not entirely his fault; he had someone whispering in his ear for a long time. He tried to protect me, push me away, and by the time I realized what he was doing, it was too late. He's lost to me now. And I think that's probably for the best."

"I'm so sorry," Brooke said.

I shrugged. "You get used to it. I came here, to Clockwork, to heal. I was in an accident, and the man I was working for brought me here to keep me away from my old job. He knew that I would only try to force my way back into a life that would kill me when I wasn't ready. So here I am."

"What did you used to do?"

I'd been wondering how I was going to explain this without actually telling her the truth. I was about to say something when a noise like gunshots sounded out from the party. I raised the binoculars and looked down at several Nazis who were shooting into the air as a Clockwork Sheriff's Department vehicle drove into the area.

"Well, this is about to get bad," I said.

Brooke walked over and looked through the binoculars. "No," she whispered.

I took the binoculars back and watched the sheriff get out of the car, only to be greeted by Robert Saunders. The two men spoke for several seconds before the sheriff shook his hand, climbed back into the car, and drove off.

"Your Sheriff King is working with these people," I said.

"No, he hates these Nazis," Brooke said. "Damn it. I thought he was one of the good guys."

I continued to watch the party as several of those present climbed into three trucks. The men all appeared to carry guns of various kinds. I swept across the area and spotted two people I really didn't want to see.

Both men were people I'd met before, one a long time ago and the other only a few years ago. Both men had tried to kill me in the past. "Fuck," I whispered.

"What's wrong?" Brooke asked.

I passed her the binoculars. "You see the two men with Robert Saunders?"

"Yep. One looks like a bald Viking, and the other one has long hair and a beard and looks like someone I would not want to pick a fight with."

"The Viking is Baldr; the other one is called Orestes."

Brooke lowered the binoculars. "*The* Baldr? The god?"

"Yes, that's him. Orestes is the son of Agamemnon."

"Can they hear us?"

"From half a mile away?" I asked. "They're not human, but they're not capable of hearing over vast distances."

"I don't think you told me the whole truth earlier," Brooke said, returning to her viewing.

"It'll have to do for now."

"Those three pickups are leaving. Lots of people inside, including Orestes. They look ready for war."

Only one place popped into my head. "The Kuros," I whispered.

"Why would they go after the Kuros?" Brooke asked.

"Robert says that Simon is his son. He seems like the kind of person who would use force if he needed to."

"Yes, he does," Brooke agreed. "Let's go see them, just in case."

"You can't call for help," I told her as we got back into the Mercedes. "If they are after the Kuros, we can't let them know we're aware of it."

"Any chance you have a cache of weapons in your truck?"

"Not exactly," I told her as I drove at speeds much faster than those I'd kept to when driving to the clearing.

More than once, I was grateful for four-wheel drive, and Brooke gripped the sides of her seat like she was in a theme park ride, but she never complained or asked me to slow down. I had no idea how quickly the Nazis would get to the Kuro house, but I doubted they were going to drive fast enough to draw any unwanted attention to themselves, which meant I hopefully had time.

"We don't actually know that this is where they're going," Brooke said. "We could be wrong."

"We could be," I said. "But I'd really rather be safe than sorry about this."

We arrived at the Kuro house not long after, and I stopped the Mercedes on the driveway, got out, and ran to the door. I banged on it to wake up everyone inside just as Brooke's phone rang.

She answered with a confused expression, putting it on speaker for me to hear. "Sheriff?" she asked. "It's two a.m."

"Don't talk; just listen," Sheriff King said quickly. "Bad people are heading to the Kuro house. You need to get there before me and get them out."

"We're already here," I said. "We saw you shaking hands with Nazis."

The sheriff paused. "I'll explain later, but right now, you need to get the Kuros to safety."

Daniel opened the door as the phone call ended. "Nate?" he asked, confused. "It's two in the morning."

"Yep, and bad people are headed this way," I said.

"Bad people? What bad people?" Daniel asked as the sounds of powerful engines drifted through the night.

I looked behind me as three pickup trucks parked at the edge of the driveway, having apparently been driven much faster than I'd expected.

"Looks like the sheriff was on the level," Brooke said, drawing her pistol. "We need to get inside."

"Get in," Daniel said, his face etched with worry.

Brooke shoved me forward as one of the Nazis raised a rifle in our direction and took a shot. Brooke grunted as the bullet hit her in the back. We grabbed hold of her and dragged her inside, slamming the door shut behind us.

"Shit," Brooke said, pained.

Daniel examined her. "The vest stopped it," he said. "But you've probably broken a rib or two."

"Everyone to the back of the house," I said, looking out the window to see one of the Nazis yelling at the man who'd taken the shot. "Do you have a gun?" I asked.

"A shotgun, upstairs," Donna told me. "It's in our room in a safe. The combination is zero one four eight five. Shells are in there too."

I took the stairs two at a time, finding Jessica on the landing at the top. Simon stood beside her, fear and confusion on his face. They both wore pajamas and looked as though they'd just woken up. "You both need to go downstairs to your grandparents," I told her. "I think your ex has finally decided to do something about you standing in his way. Where's Ava?"

"Her room is at the rear," Jessica said, picking up her son and starting down the stairs.

I ran down the hallway and found Ava's room after opening every door. She was sitting up in bed, rubbing her eyes. "What's going on?" she asked.

"Bad things, Ava," I told her. "We need to get downstairs."

She stood and stared at me. "I tried what you said. To talk to the shinigami. But I don't remember much else."

"We'll talk later," I told her.

"You were in my vision this time," she said, making me pause at the door. "There were all these dead people in this house. And you were there, but I could see you. Everyone else was a blur, but you were standing above them all. And you were . . . like death. You had an ax in one hand and a sword in the other. You were . . . I can't describe it. How were you not a blur?"

"I don't know," I lied. "We'll talk about it later, okay?"

Ava was soon moving down the stairs as I ran into Donna and Daniel's bedroom and opened the safe, removed the Mossberg shotgun, and put in the seven shells that it took. I carried the loaded shotgun and shells downstairs as someone banged on the door.

"We just came for the boy and his mom," the voice said. "No one has to die here today. We just want to take them to Robert."

I jumped the banister and landed in the hallway as someone tried to force their way into the house through the locked front door. After sprinting through the house to the kitchen, I found everyone huddled on the floor in the darkness.

I passed the shotgun to Jess. "You know how to shoot, yes?"

Jess nodded, determination and fear mingling on her face.

"Good. Daniel, get everyone downstairs to the safe room. Anyone wants to get you, they're going to have their work cut out for them."

"We tried the phones," Donna said, clearly frightened but determined not to show it. "Our cells don't work, and the landline is dead."

"Mine stopped working too," Brooke said, sounding pained.

"I figured as much," I said. "I think Avalon are jamming the signals, but we'll figure that out later. Right now, we need to know their numbers and thin them out a little."

A flashlight swept over the back garden.

"Shit, they're surrounding the house," Jess said, panicking.

"All of you down there," I told them as Brooke's phone rang.

"What the hell?" she asked, answering it and leaving it on speaker like before. "Yes? Who is this?"

I recognized the voice as soon as he spoke.

"This is Orestes," he said. "We have your sheriff. He came to help you, betraying our trust, and now he's going to die unless you all come out the front door with your hands up."

Daniel placed a hand over his mouth and shook his head sadly.

"How do we know you're telling the truth?" Brooke asked.

There was the sound of someone being hit. "Brooke, don't come out. Stay—" Sheriff King's voice was cut off.

"You have sixty seconds," Orestes said before hanging up.

"All of you, downstairs, now," I told them.

"But they'll kill him," Ava said.

"They plan on killing all of you if you go out there," I told her.

Simon began to cry, clinging to his mum.

I crouched down to Simon's level. "Hey, buddy, can you be a big strong boy for a little while?" I asked him.

Simon shook his head, burying his head in his mum's legs.

"Listen, Simon," I said. "I'm going to go stop the bad guys, but you need to be strong for your mum, okay?"

He glanced up at me. "Like Captain America?"

Sure, just without the shield or powers. The latter of which I could really use right about now. "Just like him," I said. "And Cap, he always wins eventually, right?"

Simon nodded.

I watched the family go through the door that led to the basement, until it was just Brooke and me sitting on the kitchen floor.

"Let's go see what Orestes has to say," I said, getting to my feet and walking through the house.

"You should have taken the shotgun," Brooke told me.

"If they get through us, Jess will need it. Besides, those guys out there seem to have enough guns; I'll just borrow one of theirs."

"I'm not sure that's how a gunfight works," Brooke said as we reached the front door.

"Do you have a plan?" I asked, crouching down low just in case someone decided to take a shot at the door.

"Yes, a plan would be helpful," Jess said as she joined us. "Don't argue; I have a shotgun."

I moved the curtain aside and looked out at the front lawn. I counted eight men, all but two with handguns, with those final two opting for shotguns, but I was certain there would be more. Orestes was standing behind Sheriff King, who was kneeling on the driveway.

"I want both of you to go upstairs and keep anyone from getting in," I whispered to Jess and Brooke.

"And where are you going to be?" Brooke asked.

"Down here, keeping this entry covered," I said.

We looked back out as Orestes shouted to get our attention. "So much for loyalty. I guess you don't care," he said, reaching around the sheriff's neck with a blade of ice formed around his hand. He slit Sheriff King's throat and pushed him onto the driveway to die.

"What the *hell* was that?" Jess whimpered.

I guided her out of the way of the window. "Orestes is a sorcerer. A *really* old one, but thankfully, he's not a very powerful one."

"Damn them," Brooke said through gritted teeth.

"I'm sorry, but if we'd opened this door, we'd all be dead," I said. "Stay alive long enough to avenge him."

Brooke and Jess headed upstairs, and I got ready for all hell to break loose. Part of me was aching to get my fists bloody and release the rage I'd felt since encountering these Nazi scum.

The front door burst open, and footsteps came down the wooden hallway toward me. Opening a drawer, I grabbed a serrated silver steak knife. It was one of half a dozen, so I took a few of them, stowing some under my belt, before moving over to the entrance of the kitchen and pressing myself up against the wall, hoping the shadows around me would keep me concealed from whoever was about to cross my path.

The pistol came through the doorway first. The man holding it paused on the other side of the door before taking a step in, and I moved, pushing the man's arm away and holding it there while I drove one of the knives up under his chin and into his skull. The gun fired twice, shattering the window behind me, but he was dead a moment later. I let his body drop to the ground, picked up the gun, and checked for more ammo, but I found none. I sighed and stepped over him out into the hallway beyond. I checked the ammo in the gun, which turned out to be a Heckler & Koch P30L, a weapon I'd used before. Ten rounds left, and no extra magazines on him. I took a deep breath. Time to show Orestes and his people why they'd picked the wrong family to mess with.

Chapter Nine

NATE GARRETT

I moved to the end of the hallway just as the sound of breaking glass reached my ears, followed by the grunts of someone climbing into the house. Looking quickly through the slightly ajar door to the room beyond, I saw two men, both clad in black and wearing balaclavas, standing in the middle of the living room. They both carried pistols and were moving slowly through the room toward the archway that would take them out of my line of sight.

When they were in line with me, I pushed the door open and put two bullets in the head of the farthest Nazi before putting two more into the face of the closer man as he turned toward me. Both were clean kills, and I removed three magazines from them before moving toward the broken window.

The lights were still off inside the living room, and my night vision wasn't as good as it used to be, but even so, I could see the man creeping along the side of the house toward the conservatory. Raising my pistol, I fired twice. The first round hit him in the chest and the second in his head as he crumpled to the ground.

I ejected the magazine and replaced it with a fresh one. It wasn't empty, but I didn't want to run out at the wrong moment. The sound of the shotgun blasting above me made me pause. I hoped Jess and Brooke were okay. While I was certain they could handle themselves, I also knew the kind of man Orestes was, and he wouldn't hesitate to kill them both if the opportunity arose.

Suddenly gunfire exploded through the large bay window at the front of the house. I threw myself to the floor, rolling behind a large wooden sideboard just as the door beside it opened and an armed man stepped through.

He wasn't expecting me to be on the floor, and by the time he'd moved his shotgun toward me, I'd grabbed the barrel and kicked out his knee, hearing it pop from the force of the blow. He fell toward me, trying to grab me around the throat. I stabbed the serrated silver knife into his chest and kicked him away, shooting him in the head as I got to my feet.

Turning back toward the man climbing through the window, I shot him. He fell back out of the window, and I darted through the door beside me, changing the magazine as I went.

Two more shotgun blasts above me, followed by several pistol shots, took the concentration of the only occupant in the room I'd just entered. It was only for a split second, but he still died with a bullet to the forehead before he could raise his own weapon.

Holding him upright, I pushed him out the door, using him as a shield as two more attackers opened fire. As the bullets hit him, I let the dead man drop and shot the first attacker, but the second dived through into the library, the bullet slamming into the wall where his head had been.

I crept toward the open door, but just as I got there, the front door burst open, and I threw myself into the library to avoid the shotgun blast from the new attacker. I hit the floor hard, knocking my gun from my grip as pain coursed up my arm, and rolled to my feet. Two more blasts tore into a nearby bookcase, knocking several of the tomes to the floor. I couldn't spot the gun I'd lost, so I picked up the heaviest-looking book and waited in the darkness for the two seconds it took for the shotgun-carrying man to step into the doorway. I threw the book at him, and it hit his hand, knocking the gun aside, as I launched myself up toward him.

The attacker went to hit me with the butt of the shotgun, but I grabbed the stock with one hand and used my free hand to smash the side of his head into the wooden shelves beside him. The shotgun went off again, destroying the remains of the shelves and showering the room with pieces of paper. I grabbed a handgun from his hip holster and smashed his head once against the bookshelves as a second attacker came into view in the hallway.

I threw myself to the floor, shooting my stolen weapon three times through the damaged wooden door. The bullets passed through it with ease, and the sound of someone in pain on the other side told me I'd hit something.

I got to my feet as the attacker I'd hit with the book charged into me, slamming me against the shelves to my side and forcing his gun from my hand. He tried to aim, but I pushed his arm aside, stepped around him, and stamped on the back of his calf muscle. I continued around him and drove my knee into his stomach as he dropped. He released the gun, which fell harmlessly to the floor.

He pushed me away, but I used the momentum to spin around and land a kick to the side of his head, snapping it around with incredible force and putting him on the ground.

I picked up the gun and aimed it at him. "How many more are there?" I asked.

"Fuck you," he spat.

I shot him twice in the head and put another bullet in the skull of the attacker who was still whimpering on the other side of the door. In the hallway there was a man emerging from under the darkness of the staircase, his gun rising up toward me. I shot him twice in the chest, but the vest must have stopped the bullets, as he continued to struggle, grabbing hold of my gun hand and trying to force the gun aside. A second man walked through the front door as I headbutted the struggling man, who released my hand, letting me use my gun on the newcomer. I twisted to the side of the attacker while he was dazed, bending his arm until it broke, letting me shoot him in the head with his own gun.

More shots upstairs took my attention, and after reloading my gun, I took the steps two at a time, only to find four dead bodies in the hallway above.

"Another couple of cars turned up," Brooke said as she walked toward me. She was bleeding down her arm but had swapped the gun to her other hand.

"You okay?" I asked.

"Shoulder took a round when it hit the window and changed direction. It's just a flesh wound."

"And Jess?" I asked.

"I'm good," Jess called out shakily. "Got three trying to climb up to the window."

"How many did you get?" Brooke asked. "We heard a lot of shooting."

"Twelve or thirteen; I stopped counting," I told her to looks of shock from Brooke and Jess.

Before either of them could say anything, a scream from the front lawn took everyone's attention, and we rushed to the window that overlooked the front of the house. Orestes stood with a gun against the head of a middle-aged man I didn't recognize.

"That's Fred," Jess said. "He's our neighbor."

"Come on out, everyone," Orestes shouted. "Or this kindly man gets to bleed out all over your driveway."

"I have to," Jess said.

"We do, yes," I said. "When it's time—you'll know when—get Fred."

"What are you going to do?" Brooke asked when we got to the bottom of the stairs.

"Piss off a sorcerer," I said with a smile. "Jess, I need you to go out first. I want Orestes to focus on you until I come out."

Jess nodded and stepped outside.

"That's right, Jessica," Orestes said. "Now we're getting somewhere. Where's your boy?"

"Safe," Jess said.

"We're going to need him," Orestes said, tightening his grip on the back of the neck of a clearly terrified Fred.

"You okay, Fred?" Jess asked as she continued to move around Orestes.

"Came to see what was going on," Fred said. "Kind of wish I'd stayed in bed."

"You'll be fine," I said, stepping out of the house, my gun at my hip.

Orestes turned to look at me, the expression on his face changing as he recognized me.

"You're dead," Orestes whispered in horror.

"You first," I said and shot him in the face.

Fred practically threw himself toward Jess as I walked over to a still-moving Orestes and emptied the gun into his chest.

"Is he dead?" Jess asked.

I shook my head and removed two of the silver serrated knives from under my belt.

"Did you forget normal bullets can't kill me?" Orestes asked, his voice raspy.

"How long will it be before you heal?" I asked, kneeling beside him. "An hour, two?"

"When they find out that you're alive," Orestes said, "when Hera and Arthur realize that you're here . . . they're going to take pleasure in turning this entire town and everyone in it to molten slag."

"Probably," I said. "So better make sure they don't." I drove one of the silver knives into his chest.

Orestes screamed in pain, dropping back to the ground and writhing around.

"They're not exactly made for killing sorcerers," I said, turning the other knife over. "But in a pinch, they'll do. Bet it hurts."

"I do not fear death," Orestes hissed at me.

I dropped down over Orestes's chest. "Do you fear pain?" I grabbed the handle of the knife and twisted, causing the centuries-old sorcerer to scream. "The bullets and now the silver means you're too weak to actually use your magic. And you were never that powerful in the first place. Any chance you'll answer my questions?"

"Arthur is going to rip off your head and fuck your skull."

"Now, that's an image I could have done without," I said with a sigh. "You manipulated Mordred all those years ago to try and kill me, didn't you?"

Orestes nodded. "You knew?"

"I do now. I assume Mordred didn't know."

"Not for thousands of years. Once he was reborn, he tried to kill me, though. Didn't do a very good job."

"I'll do better." I drove the second silver knife into his eye, killing him instantly.

Brooke's mouth hung open in shock, and Jess's eyes were wide. "What the hell?" Brooke asked.

"He's a sorcerer," I said. "Or was. Fred, you need to go home, and it would probably be best not to talk about this to anyone."

"Yeah, that's not going to be a problem," Fred said, walking away.

"You think he'll keep it to himself?" Jess asked.

"He's in shock," I said, removing a mobile phone from Orestes's pocket and calling Chris.

"Who is this?" Chris asked.

"It's me. We have a problem," I told him and gave him the address and a rough description of what had happened.

Jess went to check on Simon, and I told Brooke to make sure that no one left the house while I waited for Chris to arrive, which he did twenty minutes later, followed by a white Ford Transit van.

Chris stopped his Chevy pickup near me, got out, and looked down at the bodies of Orestes and Sheriff King. "Fucking hell," Chris said. "He was a good guy."

"Sheriff King?" I asked. "He tried to warn us about them coming, but we saw him shaking hands with Robert Saunders."

"Yeah, he was trying to figure out what the KOA wanted, and unfortunately, that meant having to play friends. There was a cop of his that he was trying to get put undercover too. The deputy who you nearly went for at the station? His name is Devlin Harper."

I was genuinely surprised. "He plays his part well."

"Yeah, he does. We're going to have to get him out of danger now. And by 'we,' I do not mean you."

"The Kuros and Brooke are all inside still. Their neighbor Fred got involved. He's alive, but he's pretty shook up and probably needs talking to."

Two men and a woman got out of the Ford Transit. They all wore military gear and carried MP5s.

"Cleanup crew?" I asked.

Chris nodded. "Something like that. They're here to make sure that the cleanup crew doesn't go crazy."

The woman walked to the rear of the Transit and opened the doors, and two large white men got out. They were both bald, with metal masks fixed across their mouths. Metal bands inscribed with ancient dwarven runes sat on both men's wrists. Sorcerers' bands to prevent people from using their abilities. Anyone trying to rip one off without the key got incinerated in seconds. I hated the things.

"What the hell are they?" I asked as one of the two men looked at Sheriff King's body with what could only be described as hunger.

"Wendigos," Chris said grimly. "They'll eat every corpse in this house by sunrise. Trust me when I tell you you do not want to be here for that. I'll go see Fred and leave my associates to deal with the wendigos."

I'd heard about wendigos being used to clean up particularly incriminating crime scenes over the years. Hence the masks—better safe than dead.

"There's a young boy and teenage girl in the house," I said. "Neither of them needs to see all this."

"Take them to yours," Chris said. "It's safe for now. No one knows you're alive, because the only person who did is now dead. I get the feeling you'll have some explaining to do."

"I can't lie about this," I said.

"I agree, so don't," Chris told me as the occupants of the house came out. Jess carried Simon, his face buried in her shoulder, as they walked over to the nearby double garage and went inside.

"Where do we go now?" Donna asked.

"You're all coming to mine," I said.

"You'll be safe there," Chris told them. "How are all of you?"

"I took one in the shoulder to go along with the one in the ribs," Brooke said. "They hurt."

"I have some medical supplies at home," I said. "We'll get you patched up."

"And explain exactly *who* you are," she said, clearly trying not to look at the dead body of Orestes.

"Yeah, that too."

"Take care," Chris told me as we got into the car. "At some point Orestes's death is going to lead people to you. They weren't here for you, but they will be now."

"Feel like telling me exactly *who* they are here for?"

"Later," Chris said. "We'll talk later."

Back home, after ensuring everyone was settled and the security sensors were all functioning, I had a long, hot shower and changed into some clean clothes. After taking a glass and bottle of whiskey outside to the conservatory, I sat on one of the wicker sofas and switched on the heater. I poured a small measure of whiskey and knocked it back, allowing the warmth to fill me.

It took an hour for Ava to arrive to join me. "Jess will be along shortly," she said, sitting next to me.

And true to her word, Jess was soon along. She put a blanket over Ava and sat in the wicker chair next to the sofa.

"Anyone else?" I asked.

"My grandmother is asleep with Simon," Jess said. "And I think she already knew you weren't who you said. My grandfather has finished patching up Brooke and went to wash up."

"We'll wait for Brooke, then," I said.

Brooke arrived shortly after, while Jess and Ava chatted about Ava's attempts to talk with the shinigami. Brooke had a blanket wrapped around her and an empty glass in hand. She took the bottle of whiskey from the table next to me and poured herself a huge measure.

"This everyone, I assume?" I asked.

"Think so," Brooke said. "Time for the truth." She sat on the second sofa on the other side of the conservatory.

"Okay," I began. "Well, first of all, my real name is Nathaniel Garrett, and this is going to be a long story."

Chapter Ten

LAYLA CASSIDY

Realm of Helheim

A few hours had gone by before Tarron eventually returned to the library. He looked excited, which wasn't exactly something anyone had gotten used to over the short time they'd known him.

"We can *do* this," he said, laying out the elven markings that Layla had given him.

Kase nudged Harry in the shoulder, and he woke with a start. "Sure, what's up?" he asked, looking around.

Hyperion had also rejoined the team, with a sheepish-looking grin.

"What's the plan?" Layla asked Tarron.

"I need to create a new elven realm gate from this realm to there," he said, rubbing his chin. "Unfortunately, this isn't as easy as it has been before."

"Why?" Harry asked.

"Well, I still need blood to make it work," Tarron said.

"There are a multitude of dead bodies all over this realm," Kase said. "They're still being buried, so I don't think that part will be an issue. Gross and awful, but not difficult."

"Okay, well, we need somewhere bigger. Much bigger than anywhere inside the city. And somewhere that Hel won't mind possibly destroying."

"Possibly destroying?" Zamek repeated.

Tarron nodded. "These markings that Seshat gave Layla are locks. They're essentially designed to make sure that no one goes in and out without suitable levels of power, or they know the exact key. This doesn't have the exact key. This has the destination runes, which means I can get us to Jotunheim because there's an elven realm gate already created on the other side, but it's locked."

"And you know that how?" Hyperion asked.

"There has always been a realm gate there," Tarron said, removing a book from the pile beside him and opening it. "But more specifically, this here says that there's a realm gate there. It also says that it was locked, although not by whom."

"And all of this means?" Harry asked.

"Well, I don't know the key," Tarron said, closing the book. "So our choices are . . . one: go through the realm gate without bypassing or using the rune that corresponds to the lock in Jotunheim, and we all die horribly. Or two: we use enough power to break the lock on their end."

"Define *enough power*," Layla said.

"Well, we'll need somewhere with"—he looked down at the writing on his paper—"approximately sixty-two thousand five hundred square feet of space. Also, when we go, we'll be destroying everything in that space."

"Oh," Kase replied with a slow, methodical nod, as if she was thinking about it. "That would be bad."

"I believe Hel would say so, yes," Tarron said.

"Right, you find a place; we'll talk to Hel," Hyperion said.

"We'll help Tarron," Kase said.

"Yes, I'm fascinated about this whole thing," Harry said. "I know that's not the most important part, but my brain likes what it likes."

Hyperion and Layla left the others to it and made their way into the city of Niflhel. The bustle of the people who lived in the city was a stark contrast to when Layla had first arrived. The civilian population had lived under the mountain at the rear of the city while the city itself had been a giant military installation. Layla found it surprising that so many thousands of people had moved back into the city and started their lives again in such a short space of time.

She looked up at the orange-and-red sky, something that had only a few weeks ago seemed alien to her. Now it barely got a second glance.

"You look concerned," Hyperion said as they walked along the cobbled streets to the hall where Hel and her advisers worked.

"Sometimes I remember I'm only twenty-three," Layla said. "And some of you are thousands of years old, and I'm in charge. And that's . . . weird to me."

Hyperion stopped. "Do you know why we follow your orders?"

Layla sighed. She'd had this conversation with people before. "Because I have three spirits and a drenik in my head, and so I have centuries of their experiences to draw on."

"Maybe partly, but we follow you because you're *good* at what you do. You care about your people, and you want to keep them safe." Hyperion rested a hand on her shoulder. "The fact that people trust you to do those things means more to them, and me, than your age. I've seen you in action. I've seen you fight for and defend the people you care about. Do not second-guess yourself because of youth. When I was your age, I was under the command of Alexander the Great, waging war with ten thousand soldiers at my back."

"You want me to go forth and conquer?" Layla asked with a slight smile.

"I'd rather you didn't," Hyperion said. "I think we probably have enough people who want to rule over everything."

They reached the hall, which looked a lot like many other buildings in the city. Made of a mixture of light and dark wood, most were two or three stories in height. It gave the landscape a hodgepodge look, but that was something that Layla found endearing.

The city itself had hundred-foot-high walls surrounding it, although they hadn't been enough to stop Avalon's attack, and large parts of the walls were now being demolished to expand the city out into the lands beyond. The other cities of Helheim had been destroyed over the centuries through fighting with Avalon. Niflhel was the final stronghold and thus was the place where people now felt safe. Layla was pretty sure that the realm of Helheim would soon be resettled, but the memory of what had happened in Niflhel would ensure it remained a potent symbol of defiance against a larger enemy.

The interior of the hall was decorated with a multitude of colored wooden panels and stained glass windows that depicted various mythological stories about the Norse gods, most of which, Layla had discovered in her time there, were complete bollocks. She'd really hoped there had been an actual rainbow bridge. The reality of it just being a bridge to a dwarven realm gate was less exciting, she had to admit.

Hel was alone in the main room of the hall, sitting in front of a large table with pieces of parchment and paper strewed across it like really large pieces of dull confetti.

"I am trying to take a few days off," she said. "I only came back to speak to a few people about the rebuild. Please don't tell me anything has blown up."

"Not yet," Hyperion said, taking a seat beside her as Layla hugged Hel before taking a seat on the other side.

Hel ran a hand through her rainbow-colored shoulder-length hair and sighed. Although she didn't look too much older than Layla, she was thousands of years old. She was also one of the most powerful people Layla could say that she'd ever met. Hel and Mordred had, from what Layla could gather, recently become a couple, which had made Layla happy.

"We need to use the prison," Hyperion said.

"You want to go to Nastrond?" Hel asked. "And do what?"

"Probably destroy it," Layla said. "I'm not entirely sure how this whole thing is going to work. Something will get destroyed."

"Yeah, I'm going to need more than that."

Hyperion and Layla explained Tarron's plan.

"That would be quite the feat," Hel said slowly when they'd finished. "Will it work?"

"Yes," Layla said instantly. "If Tarron says it will, it will. Besides, it means we get a very large elven realm gate on your doorstep. And no more prison, which, let's face it, was horrific."

"It wasn't one of our finest ideas ever."

The prison had been home to people who had been corrupted by magic. Mindless creatures who longed for nothing but destruction and mayhem. They were all dead now, but no one had been to the prison since the battle had finished.

"Do what you want with it," Hel said.

"I'm thinking that what Tarron has in mind is going to make a lot of noise," Hyperion said. "And possibly bring down part of the mountain that the prison is built on."

"So be it," Hel said, standing with a sigh. "Try very hard to not destroy my entire realm. And if you see Mimir, tell him he's a prick and needs to stay down that fucking well."

"Not a fan?" Layla asked.

Hel shook her head. "Do you know why he had his head cut off?"

"I can't remember the story," Layla replied. "Didn't Odin do it?"

"Yes, he did," Hel said. "Because Mimir asked him to. He wanted to know what would happen to him if he lost his head. What happened was we all got a few centuries of peace and quiet. He's an och, like Nabu, except Mimir has all the personality of someone you want to repeatedly punch. If he's alive, he'll probably know something, but you might end up killing him just to shut him up."

"This bodes well," Layla said with a thumbs-up.

"Actually, if you can find the little weasel, send him to Asgard. Now that the Norse realms are unlocked again, they'll need the help. And Odin could probably use someone to have as cannon fodder."

"Enjoy your time off," Layla said.

"I'll be very surprised if something massive doesn't happen in the next few days. Apparently, that's the length of time my life can go before a part of it explodes. Do you need anyone else?"

"Hyperion, Harry, Kase, Tarron, Tego, and me will go," Layla said. "I think the six of us should be enough."

"Excellent," Hel said with a smile and left the room.

"So we get to blow up part of her realm," Layla said. "I wish Remy was here. He'd appreciate that."

Hyperion sighed. "The foxman is . . . a difficult person to talk to. Everything is a joke. It's like talking to oil: always moving, always slippery."

"He has issues," Layla said. "But he's a good guy. I guess those of us with fucked-up parentage get one another."

"That's pretty much all mythology is, I think," Hyperion said. "A group of superpowered individuals with parent issues."

"Well, that's quite the summing-up," Layla said as they exited the building.

"Cronus made every mistake a father could make with his children, adopted or otherwise. Unlike the writings that humans are taught, it was

Cronus who chained Prometheus to a rock for giving magic to humans and essentially creating witches. And I stood aside and watched, because Cronus was my friend and king, and I didn't exactly do a good job with my own children. Selene is off . . . doing whatever she's doing, Helios is dead because he was a psychopath and wanted to help Arthur murder his enemies, and Eos . . . I don't even know where Eos is anymore. And it's not just me; it's every single member of the Titans and Olympians. We all suck at parenting."

"Wow," Layla said. "That is a lot of baggage to carry around."

Hyperion sighed. "Yes. Yes, it is. I'm just pleased to see Hel happy. I hope that once all of this is done, more of us will be able to live the lives we want."

They eventually found Tarron and the others on the city walls, pointing off into the distance of the plains and wildly gesticulating.

Hyperion and Layla filled them all in on the plan. "I assume it was okay to say that you and Harry will be joining us?" Layla asked Kase.

"I figured it gave us something to do," she said. "Besides, I already told my mum and dad I was, and they gave their blessings."

Taking some horses from the nearby guard post, the group rode over the river Gjöll.

The ride was done in silence. Everyone there had experienced the final battle. Everyone there had shed blood or had theirs shed in the name of keeping the people of this realm safe. It had been a hard-fought win, and there wasn't a single person in Niflhel who didn't know someone who had lost their life in the fight against the blood elves and Avalon. Layla had heard that there was going to be a memorial to those who'd died, but Hel wanted to wait until the rebuilding was finished.

The prison of Nastrond was one of the creepiest places Layla could remember ever having gone to. Sometimes you just went to a place, and it felt . . . wrong somehow. Maybe it was the fact that she knew how many people had died within those walls or the horrific crimes committed by those who had been locked away there. Crimes that had happened because people like Arthur had decided they wanted powerful weapons in the shape of human beings. It was hard to feel angry at the weapon when the person who created it had done so for their own amusement and need for power.

Layla climbed down off her horse and patted it, and the animal immediately turned and ran back to the city.

"They going to be okay?" Kase asked as she walked through the gates, turning from wolf to human midstep. Weres and animals didn't mix well, and there was no way a horse would let her ride it, even in human form, so she'd run beside them.

"They'll be fine," Hyperion said. "The guards will pick them up. Animals don't like this prison. Birds don't even fly over this place."

Harry passed Kase a bag of clothes, and she started to get dressed. "Give me a second," she said. Werewolves weren't really bothered by nakedness. Layla had never met one who was even slightly embarrassed about being naked in front of a large number of people.

The rest of the group made their way into the prison, and Layla immediately noticed the large amount of blood that was dried upon the walls and floor. The prisoners had been let out to aid in the fight against Avalon, and Mordred had been forced to kill at least one of them when he'd returned here during the battle to kill Layla's mom.

"You okay?" Harry asked Layla as they walked through the prison.

Layla nodded. Her real mom had died years ago in a car crash, but her body had been possessed by a drenik, who had kept her alive, given her incredible power, and essentially turned her into a complete murder machine. Even though she hadn't really been Layla's mom, she'd worn her mom's face, which had made it especially difficult for Layla to end her life. Kase had done it in the end. It was something Layla was grateful for.

"If you need a moment," Hyperion said.

Layla shook her head. "I'm good. She wasn't my mom."

She walked away from the group, close to the cave that used to be home to the dragon Nidhogg. "Has anyone searched this place?"

"Don't go further," Kase said. "I can smell *drakes*."

"No," Tarron said. "Apparently there's a fine line between grave robbing and archaeology."

"Someone's been watching those Indiana Jones films I lent him," Harry said with a smile.

"He is the *villain*," Tarron said. "I don't understand how no one else is trying to arrest him for stealing priceless artifacts. That boulder should have squashed him, and the Nazis would have never found the Ark."

Kase rolled her eyes. "Any chance we could get on with this?"

Tarron nodded and set about his work. It took an hour for him to put all the runes where they needed to be, and Zamek had joined them to help ensure that the power they contained wasn't fluctuating. Because, in his words, they'd all go boom if they were.

Eventually, Tarron and Zamek were done and returned to the team, both looking tired and muddy, but both also sporting wide smiles.

"This is going to change the way we use realm gates," Zamek said, excited.

"It's amazing," Tarron said.

"If we don't go boom," Kase said.

"It'll be fine," Tarron and Zamek said in unison.

"And now we need blood," Tarron said.

"We not using the dead?" Layla asked and immediately wished she hadn't said that out loud.

"We're going to have to use something else," Tarron said. "The decay will be too great to use the corpses."

"I assume you have an alternative method?" Layla asked.

"Drakes," Tarron said.

Kase immediately took a step away from the cave mouth. "No. No. Not happening."

"They're not exactly my choice either," Tarron said. "But they do need to be destroyed. Nidhogg kept them in check; with him gone, eventually their food source will be gone, too, and then we're going to have a problem."

"But that's future Kase's problem," she said. "Today Kase hates the bastards."

Layla reached out with her power, feeling the metal that was inside the cave, inside the very rock that surrounded it. There were hundreds of tiny pieces of metal inside the cave itself, most only the size of buckles or pins. A few swords, axes, and shields. More than a few coins. She stepped into the cave and listened to the sounds of creatures slithering around in the darkness.

"How many of these things are in there?" Layla asked.

"No one knows," Hyperion said. "Hundreds, maybe."

"How many need to die for this?" Zamek asked.

"A few," Tarron said. "Or they don't need to die; I just need them to bleed. So either a few die, or lots bleed."

"Elven realm gates are messed up," Harry said. "Just saying."

"No one would argue with you, my friend," Tarron told him.

Tego growled. She didn't like this idea any more than Layla did.

Layla touched the metal with her power and shifted it all slightly before quickly moving out of the mouth of the cave. Dozens of large and small drakes slithered out across the markings that Tarron and Zamek had drawn on the cobbled ground.

Layla reached back into the cave, turning more of the tiny pieces of metal into razor-sharp blades, and flung them out, low to the ground, through the throng of slithering drakes. Blood flowed freely from the myriad of cuts that were created, and while most drakes survived with few injuries, a few were killed.

Tarron placed his hands on the ground and concentrated. "Zamek, if you're not coming with us, you'd better leave," he said.

Zamek looked down at the drakes that were moving into the prison. "I don't really want to go through there to get out, so looks like I'm coming with you guys. I'll get a realm gate back home when I find one."

There was a flash of light, and the ground shuddered as the markings lit up a deep-purple color, creating the elven realm gate. A second flash of light, and the team vanished from Helheim.

Chapter Eleven

NATE GARRETT

"To really explain who I am, I need to explain more about Avalon," I said. "If you already know this, I'm happy to move on, but . . ."

"Pretend we know nothing," Brooke said. "That way you can't leave anything out."

"I'm sixteen hundred thirty years old, give or take. The identity of my father is unknown to me, and my mother was a Valkyrie by the name of Brynhildr. I worked for Avalon, a sort of nonhuman United Nations, for several centuries, before it became apparent that they had less-than-altruistic goals in mind for everyone."

"Anything else?" Ava asked.

"We all thought that Arthur was the Second Coming of something or other, that he was going to lead us all into an enlightened age. In fact, he's a monster. A man who lives for nothing but gaining power and using it to subjugate those he deems beneath him."

"The terrorism thing from a few years ago?" Brooke asked.

"All bullshit," I said, remembering the massive number of casualties that Arthur and his allies had inflicted just so that he could ride in on his metaphorical white horse and proclaim himself the savior of mankind. "Avalon had people in all walks of human life for centuries, making sure that you mostly behaved yourself and that you didn't make our presence too widely known. Arthur changed all of that by murdering vast numbers of his enemies and humans and blaming it on Hellequin."

"I remember—they said that Hellequin was dead," Jess said. "That we were now safe because Arthur and his people would hunt down Hellequin's allies."

"Yep," I said. "I was Hellequin. They took my name and blamed me for the murders of millions of people. And then I died."

"Okay, that feels like you missed a step," Ava said.

"I have curse marks on my body. They were put there by my parents to ensure that my magic came to me as I grew in age and power, but Hera—yes, that Hera—screwed around with the ritual, and I spent over a thousand years with those marks and no way to remove them. Well, they started to vanish, but the only way to unlock them all was to die. So I did. And then I returned without any powers at all. Hence me here, right now. Completely human."

"So what are you?" Jess asked.

"I'm a sorcerer," I told her.

"Like that Orestes guy?" Brooke asked.

I nodded. "Sorcerers can use different types of magic. They all use elemental, so earth, fire, air, and water, and most can use two of those, in my case fire and air. I can also mix them to create lightning. There's another set of magic called omega magic, which is mind, matter, light, and shadow. I can use shadow and matter. The third type is blood magic, which all sorcerers can use, and it's all about healing, increasing power, and using blood curses. It's addictive and vicious stuff, and using it too much will turn you into someone who is capable of utter evil just to get their fix. There's a fourth kind, but very few can use it."

"What is it?" Ava asked.

"Pure magic," I said. "It's a destructive force like nothing you've ever seen. I got blasted with some once, and it's not something I'd like to go through again."

"So is you being a sorcerer why I can see you in my dreams as the whole you?" Ava asked.

I shook my head. "My father was a sorcerer, which is pretty much all I know about him, but my mother was a necromancer. A Valkyrie, like I said. So I get both my father's sorcery and my mother's necromancy. That's why you can see me. At least I think it is."

"You can summon the dead?" Brooke asked.

I shook my head. "I can absorb the spirits of the dead to gain power and take their memories. But I can only do it from those who died in battle. And I can't do much of anything at the moment."

"So everyone thinks you're dead?" Jess asked.

I nodded. "My friends all agreed to have blood curse marks attached to them, making them believe I died. When they see me again, those marks should vanish, but until they do, everyone believes I'm dead. I was meant to get my powers back a year ago, but, well, as you can see, I'm still here."

"And your friends are fighting Avalon?" Jess asked.

I nodded. "I hope so. Chris won't give me too much information because he knows that I'll try to get to them and help. And seeing how Hades put me here to keep me alive, that would probably not be a good idea."

"Wait, Hades?" Ava asked. "Like, *the* Hades?"

"When I say the name of someone from mythology, it is a hundred percent certain that yes, it is the person. Most of the people from mythology aren't the same as the stories would have you believe. Hades, in particular, is a kind, intelligent man who loves his wife and children very much. Persephone, far from being forced to marry him, eloped with him. The stories in myths are written by people who have a grudge against the party in the story or by the person in the story trying to make themselves look good. Hades and Persephone were never big on either thing."

"Okay, I have questions," Ava said. "Lots of them. All gods and goddesses are real?"

I nodded. "Don't they teach you about Avalon at school?"

"Yeah, but we get the approved version, apparently," Ava said. "It's all about how great Arthur is and how he helped Avalon save us from those who want to destroy us. We have Avalonian lessons at school for an hour a week. And it's just propaganda. We're kids, not idiots."

"Fair enough," I said.

"So where's Zeus?" Ava asked.

"Dead," I said. "Hera, Ares, and a few others killed him a few centuries ago."

"And the Norse pantheon?"

"They locked themselves away a long time ago. There was a civil war, and Odin apparently wanted no part of it spilling outside of their realms, so he made sure it couldn't. It sounds like it was Avalon's first attempt to take control of the other realms."

"What about Ares?" Brooke asked. "We never hear about him."

"He's dead," I said.

"What happened?" Jess asked.

"I cut his head off," I said.

When no one had said anything for several seconds, I continued. "To be fair, he was trying to kill me at the time, and he'd spent several months torturing me to try and break my mind so that Arthur could have me join his side as his right-hand mass murderer."

"Just how powerful were you?" Jess asked.

"I did okay," I said, downplaying anything close to my full power. No one needed to know exactly what I was capable of, or what I'd hopefully be capable of once my magic returned. "I was powerful enough that people feared me for good reason, but mostly I was just tenacious. I got my ass kicked and just kept getting back up. I think that shakes people."

"What happens when you get your powers back?" Ava asked.

"I have no idea," I said. "Like people keep telling me, it's not a science."

"So you used to be some kind of assassin?" Ava asked.

I shrugged. "Depends on your point of view. I didn't just go around killing people for money or anything like that, but yes, I did kill people."

"So you going all John Wick tonight, that's normal?" Ava asked, a slight air of excitement to her tone.

"This isn't a game," Jess snapped.

"I know," Ava snapped back. "But we both know that Avalon and their rhetoric is bullshit, Jess. We both know that they're only after power for themselves. Granddad told us not to trust them."

"Yes, but Nate still killed a dozen people tonight," Jess said.

"I did," I said without emotion. "If I hadn't, we'd all be dead right now, and your son would be in the hands of Robert Saunders and his Avalon and Nazi friends."

"And you don't mind?" Brooke asked.

I shrugged. "It's them or us. No, I don't mind. I learned a long time ago that sometimes removing people from this planet is doing the rest of the world a favor. I rarely think twice about it."

"That's scary," Brooke said.

"I guess so," I said.

"So what happens now?" Jess asked. "My son is in danger here."

"Is he Robert's?" I asked. "I know you said he wasn't, but I need to know a hundred percent one way or the other."

"No," Jess said. "It's physically impossible for him to be the father."

"So what's his game?" I asked. "This is really just about getting back at you for leaving him?"

Jess nodded.

"He's using the backing of the KOA and Avalon just to piss you off," I said with a slight shake of my head. "That's some deep-seated hate."

"During the trial he had his lawyer give me a letter," Jess said. "It just said that when he saw me again, he would make sure that I didn't forget him. I thought we'd be safe here, especially after so long. I'm not on any mailing lists, I don't have a credit card, and my driver's license is in my nan's maiden name. There's no link to me here."

"Except your grandparents," I said.

"Robert never met them; he never had any indication that they lived here."

"He must have done some digging," I said. "Maybe now that he's working for the KOA, he had to wait until they were back this way before he could really start screwing around with people's lives."

Everyone was silent for several seconds, but the stillness was broken eventually by Ava. "So you're really over a thousand years old?" she asked.

I nodded. "Well over."

"You were in World War Two?"

I nodded again. "Some of it. I was in Germany after the Nazis took control. It wasn't a fun time."

"And the American Revolution?" Ava continued.

"After it happened, yes," I said. "I've met a few leaders of a few countries over the centuries, and I've been in a few places when huge events took place."

"Jack the Ripper?" Ava asked.

"Stop it," Jess said.

"He's dead," I said.

"Did you kill him?" Ava asked, ignoring the glare from Jess.

"I did. There were three of them, but the one in charge was called Enfield. They killed people to collect souls for Merlin. That was the reason I ended up leaving Merlin's employ. It wasn't until after that I discovered that he was doing it because Arthur had addled his brain into doing his bidding."

"So Merlin isn't really a bad guy?" Ava asked.

"Once, I'd have said no. But not now. There's no coming back from the things he's done. The lives he's destroyed all to keep Arthur in power. Whatever was left of the man I'd known growing up is dead. Now, he's just a monster in the service of a bigger monster."

Jess and Brooke both went to bed soon after, and Ava stayed up to keep me company, asking me questions about my life and various historical figures before she fell asleep on the sofa. I put a blanket on her and left her to sleep as I continued to look out the window at the dark. Tomorrow, I was going to have to get everyone to safety. Hopefully with Chris's help. Robert wasn't going to stop with one botched mission, and with Orestes dead, someone in Avalon was going to start to wonder how a sorcerer had been killed by a small, normal human family. Eventually, my identity would be discovered, and if I was still in Clockwork when that happened, it was going to be turned into a war zone.

It took me another hour to go to sleep, and my dreams were of fire and lightning. Of death. Of everything I used to be and hopefully would soon be again.

Chapter Twelve

NATE GARRETT

The sun was out when I woke up, although it had made little difference to the overall temperature. Ava was still asleep on the sofa, so I went into the kitchen to make a large pot of coffee and have something to eat. I'd only had four hours of sleep, but it would have to do.

Daniel was the first person to enter the kitchen once the coffee was done. He took a cup and sat in the chair opposite me at the table.

"So my family finally knows the truth," Daniel said.

I nodded. "I never wanted this to happen, Daniel," I told him. "I stayed quiet and hidden for two years."

"I know," he said solemnly. "The longer you were here, the more likely it was that you would be discovered. There's nothing to be done to change that now."

"Donna knew, didn't she?"

"Not everything, but most, yes. When you were married, did you keep secrets from your wife?"

I shook my head. "Not that I can remember. It was centuries ago, though."

"I learned long ago that Donna is too smart to hide things from. Even things that would put her in danger. Besides, she's much better at keeping secrets than I ever was."

"Jess's ex involved you out of spite and anger," I said. "At least that's what it sounds like."

"To me too," Daniel said. "I knew that sooner or later he might turn up. He was a possessive, violent man who would not allow Jessica to talk to her family. He tried to distance her from everyone she knew, and when he was deployed, she realized there was more to life than the house she lived in. She met someone else, and she finally escaped Robert's grasp. Unfortunately, Robert discovered her affair and attacked the young man, but that got him put in jail and gave Jessica time to vanish."

"And the young soldier Robert attacked?"

"Chris helped with that. He kept an eye on him and made sure he was nice and safe. Paid off to keep quiet by Robert's family, and last I heard, he now lives in Toronto with his wife and children."

"Is Simon his? The other soldier's, I mean?"

Daniel nodded.

"Does he know?" I asked.

Daniel nodded again. "Once he was out of the hospital, Jess went to see him. Neither wanted a relationship, and the father was . . . concerned about Robert reappearing. They agreed that it would be best for Simon if he wasn't involved."

"Any chance that Robert tracked him down and got Jess's location that way?"

Daniel shook his head. "The father knew that we lived here, but that's as far as it went." Daniel stared at me for several seconds. "You think that's how Robert knew to look here? He came here looking for Donna and me and wound up finding Jess and Simon?"

I shrugged. "It's as good a theory as I have. He's using Avalon resources to get revenge for being dumped. It doesn't look like Avalon are all that bothered about it, but there's no way the KOA and Harbingers came all this way to piss off Robert's ex-partner and take a son who can't possibly be his."

"He wants to hurt Jess."

"He does. I guess he figures taking her son does that pretty well. Honestly, I don't know. People like Robert have a warped sense of relationships. He sees Jess as property who was taken from him. I assume her son coming back to him is as good a recompense as any other."

"If she'd stayed, he would have killed her," Donna said as she entered the kitchen.

I nodded. "I have no doubt."

"Are you going to kill him?" she asked me as she made herself a cup of the green tea I kept in the cupboard.

"Yes," I said. "Or at least I need to figure out a way to remove him as a problem so that the KOA and Avalon don't decide to get their own measure of revenge on this town."

The front doorbell went; it was Chris along with three combat-armor-clad men armed with shotguns and two women dressed identically but carrying MP5s. Their three large black BMW SUVs glinted from the curb.

"You come for a war?" I asked.

"We're getting everyone out of town and over to Portland," Chris said. "It's less than a two-hour drive from here, but I'm not taking chances."

"Come on in," I said. "You sound more concerned than you did last night."

"Last night was nothing compared to what I've just been told," Chris said, stepping into the house but not removing his jacket.

"Okay, who are those people with guns, and what happened last night?"

"They're part of the rebellion against Avalon," he said. "There's a large number of factions on the West Coast of America and Canada.

After what happened in Red Rock and Thunder Bay, they scattered and formed new cells. One of them has taken up residence in Portland."

A year or so ago, Red Rock and Thunder Bay had been attacked by Avalon, which was hell bent on routing out anyone opposed to them. A lot of people had died during the fighting. Chris had told me that Hades and Persephone, both of whom controlled the territory there, had gotten out in one piece, but it had been a close thing.

"Let's get everyone together, and I'll let them know the plan," Chris said.

It took a few minutes to get the whole group assembled in the dining room, with Simon being given full access to my games console in the living room so he didn't have to hear whatever awful things Chris had discovered. Ava was asked to stay with him, which she clearly didn't want to do but did anyway.

"Okay, what happened?" Brooke asked.

"You know Devlin Harper, yes?" Chris asked.

"I work with him." She paused. "I mean, I used to. I'm not really sure what to do now that the sheriff is dead."

"Well, the sheriff's office was torched last night," Chris said. "You probably didn't hear the emergency services heading toward it, but there's nothing left. Two deputies were inside; both were killed. I don't know their names. I'm sorry."

Brooke closed her eyes and nodded.

"Was it done before or after the attack on the Kuros' house?" I asked.

"After," Chris said. "Why?"

"Could have been a revenge thing," I said. "The sheriff turned out to be playing them; he was trying to put a cop inside their organization. Maybe they figured it was time to make sure everyone knew that the police in town weren't in charge."

"Well, speaking of the deputy inside the organization, it gets worse," Chris said. "The Portland Police Bureau found Devlin in a nearby alley.

He'd been tortured and then killed. His body was all torn up, but his head was nailed to a wall. His badge was inside his mouth."

"Oh fuck," Jess said, putting her hand over her mouth.

Chris shook his head. "I only just got off the phone with the Portland Police Department. I have some friends there. There are some human allies of Avalon who have been doing the rounds on the news networks to peddle their bullshit about how the crimes in Clockwork are linked to the previous protests where violence occurred. They're saying that it's a conspiracy against Avalon and that the Portland protest is just an excuse for more death and mayhem."

"Great, so Avalon are trying to make these protesters into some kinds of monsters," I said. "Well, it certainly sounds like an Avalon ploy."

"They're expecting over a hundred thousand people," Chris said. "If the KOA or ITF or some other bag-of-dicks organization decides to make these people look like murderers, then something bad is going to happen."

I sighed. "And Avalon will point to it and say, *See, look what these people are doing—they're murdering innocent police officers.* Yep, that's probably not going to end well."

"So how do we stop it?" Brooke asked.

"Firstly, we get you all to Portland," Chris said. "We can protect you there, and yes, I know that means missing parts of your lives here, but frankly your lives here are now unsustainable. I told Hades that I would keep an eye on Daniel and his family, and that's what I aim to do."

"We'll come," Donna said. "But will Robert Saunders find us?"

"Find you? No," Chris said. "I think Baldr is looking for someone else I'm keeping safe. I think he's here to find them and using Avalon resources to do it, under the cover of whatever bullshit reason he dreamed up. The protests, presumably."

"Who?" I asked.

"It would be best that I show you in Portland," Chris said. "I can see this turning into a million questions otherwise."

"I'm going to the hospital first," I said. "They've already shown they'll go after friends to get me to comply, and I doubt they'll leave Antonio alone just because he's hurt."

"You'll have to take your pickup," Chris said, writing down an address on a piece of paper and passing it to me. "Memorize it and then destroy it."

I did as he asked.

"I'm sending someone with you," Chris said.

I shook my head. "These people are after Jess more than me. I'll be fine."

"It wasn't a suggestion," he said, pointing to the large man who stood beside my truck.

"Fine," I said, accepting the help. "But it feels like we're missing something."

"What?" Chris asked.

"I'm not sure. I get that Robert wants revenge, but there's something else. The dead Nazi, Jackson . . . he was killed by an animal, but I've seen no more evidence of whatever it was that killed him. And the sheriff mentioned that there have been more reports of violent crimes. Robert and the KOA arrive at places and cause discord, so what if he's here to do just that, but finding Jess made him more interested in revenge as a side mission?"

"You're trying to find the reason inside the mind of a psychopath," Chris said. "All we need to know right now is that Robert isn't going to stop at last night, and Baldr is almost certainly here for something a lot more personal than a protest."

As people loaded into cars, telling me they'd see me later, Brooke stopped at the front door. "Am I still a deputy? I mean, officially, I am, but I'm not sure that's where my loyalty lies anymore. The sheriff is dead, deputies are dead, and I don't even have my badge on me."

"The best thing you can do now is go with everyone else and help keep them safe."

"I got shot," Brooke said. "Remember? I don't think I'll be doing a lot of fighting."

"You don't need to fight to help, Brooke. But they still need you. And besides, if you stay here, I'm pretty sure you won't be far down their list of victims. Especially considering Bryce and your sister aren't exactly your biggest fans."

"This all got really bad really fast," she said with a resigned sigh.

"That's pretty much how it usually goes, yes," I agreed.

"Take care of yourself," she said. "Bring Antonio in one piece too."

"I plan on doing just that," I said, and she walked off to get into one of the cars.

"If you're not at Portland two hours after we arrive," Chris said as he walked down my hallway toward where I was standing at the front door, "I'll come looking for you. Please don't make me come looking for you."

"I'll try my best," I said. "Four hours to get to the hospital, grab Antonio, and get to Portland sounds doable."

"Do you need any weapons?" he asked.

I shook my head. "I have that covered."

He placed his hand on my shoulder. "Be careful. We could really use your magic right about now, but until it arrives, don't put yourself in any dangerous situations."

"I'm hoping they won't even think about me or Antonio. For a few hours, anyway. Not until they figure out that Orestes is gone and a large number of their people didn't come home last night. I assume the wendigos had their fill."

"It was not a pleasant thing to be around," Chris said. "They're exceptionally handy, and they require very little, but they are the creepiest things I've ever had to work with. The bodies will never be found, although the bullet holes and general damage to the house are going to take longer to fix. Except for the sheriff. We deposited his body in the woods close to where he lived and called it in. I don't want any family or friends to wonder where he is. After all that, I had a chat with the neighbor and told him if he kept his mouth shut, I'd pay for the extension on his house. Shockingly, money really does make some people happier to do what you want them to."

Once everyone had gone, I ran upstairs and removed a painting from my bedroom wall, opened the safe inside, and took out a Heckler & Koch HK45, two extra magazines, and a holster. Placing it all on my bed, I also removed a belt containing half a dozen silver throwing knives, which I put on, pulling a jumper on to cover it all. The last thing I removed from the safe was a few thousand dollars in twenty- and fifty-dollar bills. After strapping on the gun in its holster and tossing the money and ammo in a black rucksack, I closed the safe back up and replaced the painting.

"You ready to go?" the guard asked me as I left my house.

"Sure," I said. "What's your name?"

"Ben," he said, offering me his hand, which I shook.

It was still early in the morning when we drove through the deserted streets of town. Most people were not out and about yet, which hopefully meant that I could retrieve Antonio and get out of Clockwork before anyone had the bright idea to go check on him.

The hospital was at the edge of the town and was large enough to cover Clockwork and the two closest towns to it.

Chris had given me the floor and room number where Antonio was, which meant using the stairs to run up to the fourth floor. I considered using the lift but wanted to check that there was no one waiting in the stairwell, and after emerging onto the fourth floor, I was happy that no one was going to be an issue. At least not yet.

Antonio was in the second to last room before the emergency exit stairs, which I was sure was in no way, shape, or form a foreboding premonition of future events. Ben joined me on the journey through the hospital before stopping at the end of the corridor and telling me to hurry.

I knocked twice on Antonio's door, then opened it to find Antonio lying on a bed with a female nurse beside him checking his blood pressure.

"Hey," Antonio said with a grin. "Gail here is just making sure I'm okay. Am I okay, Gail?"

"Your blood pressure is a little high, and the doctor was worried about your concussion, but you'll be able to go home today."

"Am I okay to take Antonio home?" I asked.

"I'll need a doctor to okay it, unless he wants to discharge himself, which, by the way, I do not recommend."

"How long before a doctor can see me?" Antonio asked.

Gail looked at her watch. "An hour or so. Depends on how busy he is."

"Thanks," Antonio said as Gail left the room.

"We're leaving now," I told him once we were alone.

"I'm sorry, what?" Antonio asked.

I gave a brief rundown of the previous evening's events.

"If people want to try and kill me, they'll get more than they bargained for," Antonio said, a little anger creeping into his voice. "I won't be blindsided for a third time."

"No, you'll be shot instead," I snapped. "Trust me, now is not the time for tough-guy bravado. Now is the time to leave this town before exceptionally bad people come and kill you. And when I say 'kill you,' I obviously mean 'torture you first to try and get information on where Jess or anyone else might have gone.' They know you're friends, and seeing how they've all left, that means you're their quickest way to get hold of them. I imagine my house is going to be ransacked in the not too distant future too."

"I am loath to run away from racist pieces of crap like this," Antonio said.

128

"And I'm loath to bury another one of my friends," I replied. "Now get some bloody trousers on so we can leave."

Antonio got dressed, and I opened the door to look out into the corridor beyond and didn't see Ben anywhere.

"Damn it," I said as Bryce and two of his friends left a room at the far end of the corridor, closing the door behind them and beginning to walk toward us. "Shit," I snapped. "I think we have a problem."

"You bring a gun?" he asked.

I removed the H&K from the holster under my jacket and made sure it was loaded. "I'd rather not use this in a hospital—far too many innocent people to get into a gunfight." I put the gun back in its holster and removed a silver throwing knife.

"You're going to use a knife?" Antonio asked.

"Your point?" I asked him, standing behind the door and ensuring that the blinds in the window and in the glass panel on the door that looked out into the corridor beyond were closed.

"Do I get to have some measure of revenge now?" Antonio asked.

"You get to fight, if that's what you mean," I said.

Antonio had the sense to look concerned when the door opened and a bald man stepped inside. I pushed the door closed on the arm of whoever was behind him and reopened it to kick Bryce in the chest, sending him back into the large man behind him as Antonio tackled the man in his room to the ground.

Bryce scrambled to get back to his feet, so I kicked him in the nose and stepped over him, ducking a punch from his friend and driving the four-inch blade of the throwing knife into his thigh. I twisted the knife before removing it as he cried out in pain and dropped to the floor.

"Your friend's femoral artery is cut," I said to Bryce, who was back on his feet, looking angry. "He's in the right place, but you delay, and he'll die. I personally don't care either way, though."

"You'll die first," Bryce said, removing a six-inch dagger from a sheath on his belt and waving it at me. "Your guard didn't expect one of us to already be here. That was what killed him. Well, the silver knife to the heart killed him, but you get my point."

In a knife fight, you get cut. There was no way to avoid it. If someone came at you with a knife, you ran away. You didn't try to disarm him or be clever; you just ran. Unfortunately, running wasn't an option, so I reached for the nearest thing to use as a shield, which turned out to be a fire extinguisher.

Bryce darted forward with the knife, and I brought the fire extinguisher down onto his wrist as I stepped out of the way. The sound of his wrist breaking was quickly followed by him dropping the knife. I smashed the extinguisher into his wrist once more, just to make sure it was broken, and he fell to his knees in pain. Pushing him to the ground, I locked his arm in place behind him and knelt on his back. I bent down and pressed the tip of the blade against his throat.

"The world will be better off with you not in it," I said.

"Please, don't," Gail shouted from behind me. "I know that he's a bad person, but you can't murder him in this hospital."

"They killed Ben," I said. "He was only here to help me."

"Don't add to their horror," Gail said. "*Please.*"

Antonio left the room, putting on a coat as he closed the door. His knuckles were bloody, and I wondered just how much pent-up aggression and frustration he'd managed to work out.

I turned to the sounds of more voices at the far end of the corridor and saw several of Bryce's Nazi friends burst through the door. I sighed and broke Bryce's arm at the elbow before dislocating his shoulder and leaving him a whimpering wreck on the ground. "Tell Robert and his friends I'm coming," I whispered.

I pulled Bryce to his feet and used him as a shield as Antonio, Gail, and I backed toward the door behind us, which needed a password to open.

The Nazis swore and called us unpleasant names, but they were easy enough to ignore, as none of them wanted to risk getting Bryce killed. Gail opened the door and allowed Antonio through first, with me following. I smashed Bryce's forehead into the wall and shoved him back toward his group of friends as I darted through the door, closing it behind me.

We used the emergency stairwell to go down one flight before using the lift to get out at the ground floor.

"I'm sorry this was brought to your hospital," I told Gail. "Please don't go back up there without police help. Those men are dangerous."

"So are you, apparently," she said. "Thank you for not killing him."

Antonio and I ran out of the hospital as sirens rang out, and we reached the pickup as the first police cars appeared outside the hospital entrance.

"Why didn't you kill him?" Antonio asked as we both got in the vehicle.

"Because Gail asked me not to," I said honestly. "And then Bryce's friends showed up, and having a live shield is better than a dead one."

"You think there will be a next time?" Antonio asked as we passed a state police car on the road toward Portland.

"Yes, and when there is, there won't be any innocents around to stop me from ending them."

Chapter Thirteen

Nate Garrett

We arrived in Portland a few hours later without incident.

The address that Chris had given me took me to a warehouse on the outskirts of town that was right next to what appeared to be a large five-story office building. I parked outside, where dozens more cars sat, and looked at the mass of gray concrete and glass.

"Ummm, not that I wish to mock," Antonio said, "but that looks like the kind of place that sells insurance rather than any kind of safe house."

Getting out of the car, we walked toward the steps and ramp that led up to the front doors. The words ELEMENTAL INCORPORATED were etched onto the glass.

"It *is* an insurance company," Antonio said from beside me.

The doors to the building slid open, and Chris walked out. "Welcome to Portland," he said. "Where's Ben?"

"I'm sorry," I said.

Chris sighed, saddened at the loss of one of his people. "Damn it," he whispered. "He was a good man."

We were all silent for several seconds before Chris motioned for us to follow him into the building.

"What is this place?" I asked him as we all went inside.

"This is an insurance business with approximately four million members in the United States, Canada, and Mexico alone," he told me with a forced smile.

At reception, there were security guards standing next to a set of turnstiles that needed a pass to get through, and three receptionists—two men and a woman—sat behind the large desk. There were several people who appeared to be having meetings at one of the half dozen small tables in the reception area, each one next to a couch and chair.

"We do insurance differently here," Chris said as if reading off a brochure.

"Do you do it on drugs?" I asked, looking around. "Because this is *really* weird."

Chris nodded to the two guards—a man and woman who both wore dark suits and looked like they were auditioning to be members of the Secret Service—before swiping a key card against one of the turnstiles and leading Antonio and me through.

"Seriously, what the hell?" I asked as we entered a nearby lift and Chris selected the button for the top floor.

"Elemental Incorporated was set up a year ago. We have sixteen branches in the United States, twelve in Canada, four in Mexico, and a number in Europe, Asia, and Africa. In total we have seventy-four branches around the world."

"Is this Hades's idea?" I asked.

Chris shook his head. "No, Hades and his rebellion have been off the grid for a long time now. Last I heard, they were in Greenland, which was raided by Avalon troops."

"Is everyone okay?" I asked, shocked and concerned.

"Information suggests that yes, most of them are. Selene was not there, before you ask. No, I don't know where she is."

"So none of you are human?" Antonio asked, clearly fazed by the idea that this was all happening.

The lift opened, and we all stepped out onto the fifth floor.

"Not even a little bit," Chris said. "Although I guess technically Nate is currently human."

I forced a smile.

"So what do you *really* do here?" Antonio asked Chris as I looked around the floor.

Apart from the hallway that we stood in and the paintings on the walls, which appeared to depict various battles and landscapes throughout history, there were only doors leading into unseen rooms.

Chris took us down one part of the hallway and around the corner, where the floor opened up, showing a huge amount of open space with televisions mounted on the walls in front of chairs and tables.

"We do some work here," Chris said. "But mostly we use this floor as a staging area or as somewhere to bring people new to the organization."

"Who runs this?" I asked. "You?"

Chris shook his head as we walked across the open space and through a set of double doors at the end. This area had a desk large enough to fit the four people who worked behind it, all of whom waved at Chris as he walked by. Two armed guards, both carrying spears and bucklers, stood in front of a set of mahogany double doors. One of them bowed his head slightly while the other pushed open the doors, revealing a large office with floor-to-ceiling windows on both sides. Two desks sat at the far end of the room, and the occupants of the chairs behind them got to their feet and came to greet us.

"Don't freak out," I whispered to Antonio.

"Why?" he asked, before catching sight of the two women and realizing who one of them was. He put his hands over his eyes and turned away.

"Oh, for crying out loud," Medusa said, the snakes that were entwined with her dark hair barely moving around her shoulders. She wore a white T-shirt and black jeans with dark-green trainers. Her skin was olive colored, and her short fingernails were painted black. One of the snakes moved over her shoulder languidly, showing absolutely no interest in anyone in the room. "I'm *not* going to turn you to stone."

"She really isn't," the woman beside her said. I'd never met her before. She had dark skin and waist-length black hair that was braided with small silk bows of various colors. She wore a pale-yellow dress that stopped just above her knees and a thin golden necklace with a gold-and-diamond pendant of a falcon on the end.

"Medusa," I said with a smile. "It's been a long time."

"Nathaniel Garrett," she said, returning the smile. "It has been *too* long." She walked over and hugged me, the snakes on her head moving away from my face.

"This is Isis," Medusa said, introducing me to the second woman.

"An Egyptian goddess?" Antonio asked, only now peeking through his fingers as I shook her hand.

"I am sorry for your loss," I said.

Isis smiled warmly. "Thank you. It was many centuries ago."

"I know, but it feels like something I need to say."

"What happened?" Antonio whispered.

"My husband, Osiris, was murdered by his brother Set," Isis said. "It was a ploy by people working with Hera to ensure that the strongest of us who opposed them were no longer an issue. When Avalon came to fruition, many of the Egyptian deities fled, died, or joined them. My son, Horus, fled. I have not seen him in nearly two thousand years." She touched the pendant on the necklace. "I hope to one day see him again."

"I'm sorry," Antonio said. "That's awful."

"Thank you," Isis said. "Our mutual friend brought you here to see us."

"Chris hasn't exactly explained why," I said.

"How come your snakes can't turn me to stone?" Antonio asked, before assuming the expression of a man who had just said something aloud that he'd only meant to think.

"Mythology is bullshit," Medusa said. "There are two types of stories. Either one deity had their followers create a story to tell the world about how awesome they were, or the enemy of a deity had their followers tell a story about how evil their opponents were. In my case, there was a story about Athena turning me into a Gorgon. I was *born* a Gorgon, and the story was concocted by Hera and Perseus. Perseus hated the Olympians. His father, Zeus, was about as good at being a father as he was at keeping his dick to himself, and Perseus was a judgmental little shit who believed every evil thing he was fed about them. Hera sent him after me to kill me and take my head." She tapped her neck. "Guess how well it went."

"But the rest of the story?" Antonio asked. "What happened?"

"Well, seeing how Perseus was unable to kill me and barely left with his life, he took the head off the body of a soldier I'd taken. From what I hear, he then killed some snakes and sewed their corpses into the head. He took it to a king of somewhere or other, and when he got laughed at, he butchered him and told everyone that the head turned people to stone if they're not nice to him. My head does that. The decomposing head of a soldier does not. Still, he got rich and famous off it, and I decided to lie low and not do anything that would make Hera come after me again."

"But your snakes can turn people to stone?" Antonio asked.

"No, they're snakes," Medusa said. "*I* turn people to stone. My snakes are just a physical part of me, like fingers or something else that would bite you with venom designed to dissolve flesh and kill in seconds." She smiled at Antonio, whose eyes went wide.

"Relax," I said. "She's not someone who would turn you to stone just for being there, no matter how much the stories suggest otherwise."

"The Kuros arrived this morning," Isis said. "They were taken to the warehouse. We have belowground floors there that double as accommodation."

"How did you manage to spring up under Avalon's nose?" I asked.

"Money," Medusa and Isis said in unison and then laughed.

"We've always had organizations like this," Isis said. "But over time it was necessary to change and adapt into something that is out in the open but still leaves us able to operate."

"This is a place for people to hide from Avalon, yes?" I asked.

"Hide and fight back," Medusa said. "Originally we fought against the oppression from people like Hera and her allies. But now that Avalon's true colors have been revealed, we've had to increase our scope somewhat."

"So what happens now?" I asked.

"Now, you stay here and hide," Isis said. "You are human; you cannot hope to defeat Baldr and his allies."

"As a human, I defeated Orestes," I told her.

"You really think Baldr will fall as easily?" Medusa asked softly. "You are a warrior of great strength, Nate, but you are human. Until your power returns, you will not be able to defeat someone with Baldr's power. Nor his Harbinger allies."

"Do we know who those allies are?" I asked.

"Two teams," Isis said. "One led by Adrestia and one by Apep."

I groaned.

"Is that bad?" Antonio asked. "Sorry, my ancient mythology is a little rusty."

"Adrestia is Ares's daughter," Chris said. "Nate killed both her father and her brother."

"You killed Ares?" Antonio asked, astonished.

"A long time ago," I said. "But Adrestia's not exactly someone who forgives and forgets. She's also a negative empath, so she feeds off people's pain, misery, and the like. It makes her stronger. Deimos had a similar power, and he was just a joy to be around."

"And Apep?" he asked.

"Never met him," I said. "He's snake-kin, which basically means he can turn into a really big snake. It's said that snake-kin are descended from the children of Tiamat, the Mesopotamian dragon."

"Who you also killed," Chris said.

"Yes, apparently I get around a lot and leave dead bad guys in my wake."

"Both Tiamat and two of her children," Chris continued.

I sighed. "Okay, I get it—both Apep and Adrestia will want me dead."

"And Baldr," Chris said. "He *really* hates you. Always has done, ever since you were little."

That made me pause. "You knew me as a child?"

Chris quickly shook his head. "Just heard stories from Hades."

"It's helpful knowledge," Antonio said, sounding a little like he'd been overwhelmed with information.

"I'll take Antonio to his lodgings," Isis said.

"Okay, there's one thing I don't understand," I said. "Actually, there's a lot I don't understand, but let's start with why Baldr is in this part of the world. I said to Chris earlier that something felt off about Baldr being here. If he's here to make yet another protest into a blood-bath, then why the stopover in Clockwork? And surely this is all way below his pay grade. Apep and Adrestia could just as easily have done all of this with Robert's help. Who, I might add, is another person whose actual reason for being here I'm not entirely sure of. No one needs to sow dissent in Clockwork. Is this just all about the protests?"

"Not exactly," Medusa said. "I think they would like to find who are helping the humans and protesters, but I'm pretty sure that's not why Baldr is here."

I looked between Chris and Medusa. "Anyone want to say why?"

"Best if we show you," Chris said.

Medusa and Chris led me out of the office and down the corridor, stopping at the last door before it opened up into the large area on the floor. Chris opened the door and motioned for me to step inside.

There was a woman in a bed. Runes had been carved into the wooden posts and headboard, the bare wooden floor, and even the walls and ceiling. They blinked yellow, white, and orange as the power they contained ebbed out of them.

The woman was unconscious, but there were no tubes giving her nutrients or machines checking her heartbeat. Just a woman with long silver hair sleeping in a bed. She looked peaceful.

"Who is that?" I asked.

"Frigg," Medusa said. "Baldr's mother."

"How long . . . how . . . why?" I asked, unable to articulate the shock I felt.

"About four hundred years ago, she was the target of assassins," Chris said. "They obviously didn't kill her, but the weapons they used were coated with a venom the likes of which we've never seen before. There is no antidote, as the venom destroys it. You can't study it, as it's always changing. All we've been able to do is keep her alive by the use of these runes."

"Baldr was behind her attack?"

Medusa nodded. "Yes."

"And now he's back and wants to finish the job?" I asked.

Chris nodded. "Yes. He's been looking for Frigg for centuries, always wanting to end her. He's made his intentions well known, and over time he's figured out that she's here."

"How?" I asked.

"We had a leak," Medusa said. "A . . . well, excuse the pun, but a snake by the name of Apep. He worked with us for a while, but in another office. Eventually, he became trusted enough to learn Frigg's whereabouts. At the time it was Vancouver. Apep then killed six people. Six people I considered friends."

"I'm sorry. How long ago?" I asked.

"Four years. Baldr has been busy in another realm, apparently, and only recently came back to this one. It's one of the reasons we set up this front. We couldn't just stay where we were, but we can't move her far either. Realm gates are out of the question without some pretty serious dwarven runes to help her stay alive during the trip, and I don't see many dwarves around here. Oregon was the furthest we could go, and they've been searching the state for a few months now. A week ago, two human allies of ours were killed. They didn't have Frigg's exact location, but they knew she was in Portland."

"Baldr?"

Chris nodded. "He carved his name into their chests."

"Yeah, he always was a dick," I said. "Out of curiosity, why does he hate Frigg so much? I assume the whole only being able to die with mistletoe is a made-up story."

"He's always been jealous of those he thought were given more attention than he was," Chris said. "Thor, for one."

"Loki, for another," Medusa said.

"Yes, Loki too," Chris said sadly. "Baldr thinks he deserves to be held up as a shining beacon of brilliance. For people to bow down to him and kiss his feet. Like you said, he always was a dick."

"But what did Frigg do to deserve this?" I asked.

"Apart from have more children after Baldr?" Chris asked and sighed. "I guess you might as well know the truth."

"That would be helpful," I said.

"Baldr had a vision as a child that his mother and father would be the death of him. It's hard to say if it was a genuine vision or if someone was manipulating him into only seeing what they wanted him to see."

"One of Arthur's people?" I asked.

"Probably Gawain," Medusa said. "They were friends, and they're both evil bastards, so it's not hard to believe that they helped create one another."

"Baldr helped start the civil war that forced Odin to shut the realm gates to the Norse realms. He murdered countless people, people who trusted him. He gave the fire giants aid to attack the frost giants and began the civil war to help bring about Ragnarok."

"The end of the gods?" I asked. "Isn't his death meant to start it? Loki tricks Hodhr into starting it; he gets imprisoned; Loki escapes and starts Ragnarok. I remember something about it when I was a kid, but I never paid much attention, considering it sounded batshit crazy. Even by the standards of nonhuman craziness."

"Mythology is bullshit, remember?" Medusa said. "Except in the case of Ragnarok—it's a real prophecy."

"Only a handful of people actually heard the original as it was being recited by the soothsayers of the court. Thor, Loki, Frigg, Freya, Odin, Baldr, and a few others," Chris said. "I think the soothsayers had been paid off by our enemies to help sow fear and to show Baldr that Ragnarok was real."

"Sounds like it worked," I said. "So why the change from that one to the one in the books?"

"Odin wasn't sure if the original prophecy was totally fake or if part of it was real," Chris said. "Unfortunately, some people started spreading rumors about it all, and Odin decided that the best thing to do was to head it off at the pass.

"Odin had it changed to say that Baldr's death starts it all simply because he knew that no one in their right mind was going to try to murder the son of Odin. Besides, Baldr heals too quickly; you'd have to be incredibly powerful to kill him, and Odin didn't foresee his own son's betrayal and attempt to murder the true catalyst for Ragnarok."

"So Baldr wants to start Ragnarok?" I asked.

Chris nodded. "He thinks that aligning himself with Arthur will bring about the end of days, after which he and those who stand by his side will be victorious and shall live as gods."

I knew where this was going. "Oh crap."

"Yep," Chris said. "It's not Baldr's death that's meant to start Ragnarok. It's Frigg's."

Chapter Fourteen

NATE GARRETT

It had been a very long day. I looked at Frigg, who was unconscious in bed, and wondered how her own son could have put her there just so he could gain more power. That was what it was really about. If Ragnarok happened, everyone who was an enemy of Avalon would die, and Baldr would be left to help rule over the pieces that survived.

I rubbed my eyes with my fingers and took a seat on a nearby chair. "So . . . looks like Baldr needs to die."

Chris laughed. "You think people haven't tried?" he asked. "Odin tried. Thor tried, and look where that got him. Baldr heals too quickly. He's too strong."

"I fought him once," I said. "With Mordred's help we managed to fight to an unconvincing draw. However, no one is invincible. Everyone can be killed; we just need to figure out how."

"Nuke?" Medusa asked helpfully. "I fought Baldr several centuries ago, when he was too close to finding Frigg once before. I turned him to stone. He healed before my eyes. The amount of power it would take to destroy him is immense. We're talking maybe Merlin-level power."

"What happens if we kill Baldr and Frigg wakes up?" I asked.

"Frigg had been all but lost in despair about Baldr before he attacked her," Chris told me. "I would hope she'd understand."

"Wait just a second," I said, getting to my feet. "Avalon knows that Frigg is in the city, just not where. So are they here to disrupt the protests and cause a distraction? Because I'm not sure that's right. It feels like we're missing something about *why* Avalon are here specifically. They can't keep disrupting protests indefinitely. The 'they were terrorists, honest, guv' excuse isn't going to wash forever. What's their endgame here?"

"They're going to use it as an excuse," Medusa said. "That's why they want the protests to go ahead. They want to do something horrific, giving them the excuse to come into Portland with force. They're going to tear this city apart looking for Frigg and those helping her."

"That's my thought too," Chris said.

"Okay, but that's not connected to what happened in Clockwork. They're one organization, but it feels like they're here for two totally separate reasons. Robert wants revenge on Jess, but I honestly can't see any way in which a human would be given Avalon forces so he could go get a grudge resolved. Even one working for the KOA. Which leads back to the idea of why the KOA are in Clockwork. They should be in Portland getting ready for the protests. And why are Avalon letting the protests carry on? They could just find out who the ringleaders are and execute them."

"This will be the sixth protest in the USA alone," Medusa said. "Each one marred with violence. Each time, they use the violence as an excuse to raise the level of security in that city. And at each protest the violence has increased, affording Avalon the ability to get more powers and a greater foothold in state and city law and order."

"Six protests all across the country?" I asked, my mind trying to put links together. "Whatever happens in Portland, it will be big, not just because I really do think that Baldr will use it as a distraction but also because Avalon needs it to be big."

"Each one getting worse," Chris said.

"Hera said it already," I said. "On the news the other day, she said *legislation*. Avalon are going to get the human governments to give them more legal freedom to do what they want. They can go to these governments and say, *Hey, look what our enemies are doing—we need more help to protect you all*. It's similar to what they did when they were outed in the first place. Make someone else out to be the bad guy, claim you're only helping, and then get legislation to give you the powers you need to crack down on dissidents."

"They'll turn this entire world into one giant police state," Medusa said.

"And they'll do it with human approval," I said. "Most leaders are already in Avalon's pocket, but they can't just give Arthur and his people free rein—they'd have riots in the streets. More than they do already. But if they got the world's governments to *give* them that power under the guise of protecting people . . ."

"We'd all be more fucked than we already are," Chris finished.

There was a knock on the door, which opened a second later, revealing a young black man with a slightly worried expression on his face.

"You need to see this," he said, pushing the door open.

We followed him downstairs to where Isis, Antonio, the Kuro family, and Brooke were watching a large TV on the wall. There were maybe a hundred others inside the room, which appeared to be used primarily as a mess room for everyone staying here.

I stood at the back near the doors, with Chris and Medusa beside me. Ava saw me walk in and made her way through the crowd, her eyes red with tears.

"What happened?" I asked.

"Duke's has burned down," she said. "The news said that it was an act of terrorism, that it was anti-Avalon forces who were involved."

"Why would anti-Avalon forces burn down Duke's?" I asked. "That makes no sense."

"I don't think those in charge care," Daniel said. "They just peddle their lies and expect to get away with it."

I shared a worried expression with Chris before making my way through the crowd to get closer to the news broadcast. I watched the TV in silence as a female reporter interviewed Baldr, who smiled gently at the screen.

"This *heinous* crime attacked an innocent man's work," Baldr said. "It's fortunate that there was no one inside when the attack was carried out. The owner of Duke's, one Antonio Flores, was in the hospital at the time, having already been targeted once by these cowards."

I glanced over at Antonio to see that he radiated anger, his jaw set and his eyes focused on nothing but the television.

"I could call them," Antonio said. "Tell them the truth. That this was done by Avalon and their Nazi thugs as revenge for our escape."

"We will find the people responsible," Baldr continued, "and bring them to justice."

"And what about the attack on a house inside the city?" the reporter asked.

"We're treating them as linked," Baldr said. "Dr. Kuro and his family are valued members of this community, and their disappearance after the attack on their home is being treated as a kidnapping and murder."

"Murder?" the reporter asked.

Baldr nodded. "Their next-door neighbor was found dead this morning. We believe he disturbed the criminals and paid with his life as he tried to call for help. He was a hero."

"Goddamn it," Daniel snapped. "They didn't need to kill Fred."

I kept watching until the end of the report. Baldr reveled in the spotlight, radiating charm and showing the exact amount of anger and determination that would win him many supporters within the human community. Big, bad Baldr sent by Avalon to help find these criminals.

When the newscast was over, a silence lingered over the room. It ended when Antonio stormed out. I followed him and found him outside on a bench next to a koi pond.

"So this has been a bad few days," I said, taking a seat beside him.

"They didn't need to destroy Duke's. I worked hard on that place. I put everything into it. It was good." Antonio sighed and rubbed his eyes. "I failed my friend. I named it after Duke Wilson. A friend of mine in the Rangers. He was killed in the explosion that took my leg. We'd talked about creating a diner together once we got out."

"You'll rebuild," I said. "You'll rebuild it so grand and large that God will look down and say, *Damn, that's where I want to eat.*"

Antonio laughed. "If my mom heard you say that, she'd smack you around the head."

I smiled. "It'll be okay, man," I told him. "It doesn't look like it now, but it will get better."

"This Baldr always been an ass?" he asked.

"Yep. Only met him once, but he tried to kill me, tried to kill one of my best friends, kidnapped and hurt another of my friends, and basically was a giant dick weasel of epic proportions."

"Dick weasel?" Antonio asked.

I shrugged. "I was thinking about a friend of mine who would think that was really funny."

"He another sorcerer?" he asked.

"No, he's half-man, half-fox. With a real interest in bladed weapons and a need to tell everyone around him to fuck off on a regular basis."

Antonio stared at me for several seconds, presumably trying to decide if I was lying or not. "You have a weird life," he said eventually.

"You have no idea," Medusa said from behind me. "You mind if I talk to Nate for a second?"

Antonio nodded and stood before pausing. "Does that mean that *all* mythological beings are real?"

"Most," I said. "A lot are dead or very different to how you might think of them."

"So the Aztec gods?"

I nodded. "There are some who are alive, yes. Some work within Avalon, and more than a few died defending their homes when the Spanish came."

"My mom, she had an old picture of Mictecacihuatl that she used to put out on the Day of the Dead festivals. She said it had been passed down through the generations of her family. Supposedly given to my great-great-grandmother by Mictecacihuatl herself."

"Mictecacihuatl is real," Medusa said. "Haven't seen her in a long time, but she's an interesting woman."

Antonio shook his head. "This is the weirdest day I've ever had."

"Antonio, why don't you talk to Isis about getting your story out there?" Medusa said. "She has a few contacts with reporters who aren't happy churning out Avalon-sponsored bullshit on a daily basis. I think it might be good to get the real story out there or at least let some people know that Avalon are aligning themselves with a bunch of Nazis. I'm sure that'll go down badly with the vast majority of people."

"Will do," Antonio said and left Medusa and me alone. He muttered to himself about how weird everything was as he walked away, which caused Medusa to smile.

"I think it's going to take some getting used to," Medusa said.

"He'll get there," I said. "I meant to ask you when we were upstairs, but how likely is it that someone here will know my face?"

"Slim to zero," Medusa said. "Most of the people here are humans. It's not like Nate Garrett had a lot of photos of himself all over the place, although I think more than a few will know the name Hellequin."

"Hellequin is gone."

"He was gone before," Medusa said. "Then he came back."

"He's now synonymous with terrorism and the murders of hundreds of thousands of innocent people. Avalon made sure that name was tarnished for good. I think Arthur really believed that if he took everything from me, even my name, it would make me easier to crack."

"Well, then no one here will know you as you. The only nonhumans here are the security and people who work on the top floor. This is a business, after all." Medusa sat beside me. "I have to say, it was odd seeing you alive. I was never a fan of Avalon, and we didn't always see eye to eye, you and me, but I always thought you were honest and gave everyone a fair shake. I was sad to hear of your death."

"I wish I hadn't stayed dead so long," I said.

"I've been told I'm not allowed to tell you how certain people from your old life are doing, because Chris is worried you'd arm yourself and go all vigilante on your enemies, getting yourself killed in the process."

"Apparently, I'm a flight risk."

"Baldr will eventually discover that you're alive," she said. "What happens then?"

"Hopefully by then I'll have my magic back and I can kick the shit out of him," I told her.

"Chris worries about you," she said. "Hades asked him to take care of you, to keep you safe, and you go get yourself in a fight with a bunch of Nazis. Who, I'd like to say, I thought we'd gotten rid of the last time."

"Yeah, they're the chlamydia of hate groups."

Medusa laughed. "That is certainly one way of putting it. I came here to ask you something, though. About Diana."

Diana was a very old friend of mine. She was half-werebear and probably the greatest warrior I'd ever met. At one point she'd been considered a goddess by the Romans, although she rarely brought it up.

"Last I heard, she was good," I said. "But that was two years ago."

Medusa nodded nonchalantly. "Good, good. Did she ever, you know, *mention* me?"

I tried very hard not to smile. "You still have a thing for Diana?"

"A thing?" Medusa shook her head unconvincingly, making one of the snakes hiss.

"Your snakes, they give away your emotions," I said. "How long were you together?"

"A few centuries, and then she wanted to work for Elaine and Avalon, and I . . . didn't. We went our separate ways. That was about four hundred years ago. But every now and again, we'd meet up, and flames would be rekindled. But I haven't seen her in a long time. I . . . miss her."

"And you're too stubborn to just contact her, just like she's too stubborn to contact you?" I asked.

"I am not stubborn," Medusa said. "The word is . . . *independent*."

"Stubborn," I said with a slight laugh. "The word is *stubborn*."

Medusa sighed. "Seeing you today just made me realize I haven't seen Diana in such a long time. And seeing how she now hates Avalon, too, I figured it was no longer a sticking point between us."

I laughed out loud. I couldn't help it.

"I don't think it's very funny," Medusa said.

"Not you," I assured her. "Not like that anyway. I'm sitting here talking about love with someone who is thousands of years old, and Avalon wants to kill us all, and it's just the most normal conversation in the world to have. It doesn't matter what awful shit is happening in the world, what horrible acts are going on—normal things like love and friendships still happen. Love still blooms, even in the darkness."

Medusa stared at me for several seconds before laughing. "Damn it, Nate, did you get all soppy in your time away?"

I smiled. "Fine, you and your cold, dead heart can sit there and pine. But I still think it's sweet that amid all of this"—I waved my arms about in emphasis—"you're still thinking about the one you love."

Medusa glared. "Damn it. I inspire fear in men and women the world over, and here I am missing someone who makes me feel good about myself. I sound like a goddamn teenager. You don't go telling anyone I said that."

"Lips are sealed," I promised.

"You miss Selene, yes?"

I let out a small breath and nodded. "Every damn day."

"I heard you got back together just before you died. I always liked Selene. She didn't take shit from anyone. Ever. I'm sorry you can't contact her."

I patted Medusa on the hand. "Thanks. In the meantime, I need something to do to keep me busy."

"Tomorrow," Medusa said. "We'll find you a job in town, somewhere out of the way, where no one knows you and you can't possibly get into trouble."

"Trouble has a way of finding me. You know that, right?"

Medusa kissed me on the cheek as she got to her feet. "Of course. It's one of the reasons I like you."

"Any chance you can show me where I can sleep?" I asked.

"Top floor; take room F. I know you packed a few things, but there are more clothes in the wardrobe should you need them. We had a wild guess about your sizes, so if you need more, you can always go shopping tomorrow. The rooms also have their own bathrooms, so you don't need to worry about sharing. I would say have a shave, but I think the rugged bearded look suits you."

"That's what I was going for," I said.

"Don't push it," Medusa said with a smile. "Go shower and sleep. Tomorrow will be a whole new day for you to cause trouble."

I thanked her and did as she asked, going up to the top floor, where the Kuro family were entering two separate rooms closer to the lift. Jessica smiled at me as she closed her door, while Donna came over to ask if I was okay.

"I'm good," I said. "You?"

"Tired," she said with a clearly forced smile. "It's been a long day. Days. Weeks. It's all sort of blurred into one. Daniel thinks this is his fault. He's sleeping now, but I think tomorrow the worry will return."

"At least he's sleeping," I said. "That will hopefully help."

"I gave him two shots of vodka in his hot chocolate," Donna said with a devious grin. "I'd have drugged him, but I think that's probably frowned on. He needed to relax a little. Vodka relaxes him."

"How are Jess and Simon?"

"Tired and scared. Jess more than Simon."

"And Ava?"

"Oddly fine," Donna said. "Just taking it all in stride. It's a bit strange, but maybe that thing in her head just keeps her calm about stuff like this."

It was certainly possible. "I guess it's better than her climbing the walls."

After saying good night, I opened the door to the shared living area to find Ava sitting on a red beanbag chair that looked incredibly comfortable. She was reading a book.

"How are things going?" I asked.

She shrugged. "I should probably be more freaked out by all of this. Also, I'm not allowed to use my phone. It sucks."

"Yeah, sorry about that."

"I like my phone."

"I like having people who want to kill me not know where I am," I told her.

Her eyes narrowed. "I want to argue with you about that, but you make a good point."

"What's the book?" I asked.

"It's about Death," she said. "It's funny, and I could use funny. I get the feeling that Death and I are going to be friends."

"At least you've come to terms with it," I said.

"I've been talking to my shinigami for the last few nights, but it's hard work, and I thought it might work better if I was suitably relaxed beforehand. I still see you, you know. Standing above the dead. The location changes, but you're always there. I get the feeling this isn't over."

"I get the same feeling, but for tonight it is. Tonight we rest and sleep, and then tomorrow we try to figure out what to do next. One day at a time, Ava. That's all we can do right now."

Ava nodded. "I'll try."

I yawned. Sometimes I forgot that I was human and needed sleep. "I'll see you tomorrow."

Leaving Ava to her reading, I found my room and discovered that there was a king-size bed inside with several piles of clothes on top of it. The room was a nice size, with a large window at the far side that, with a touch, turned into darkened frosted glass.

A pair of blue shorts and a white T-shirt were quickly selected to wear for bed, and I put everything else away before climbing into the world's most powerful shower and literally blasting the grime of the day away.

I got dried and dressed and climbed onto the bed, ready to relax, but before I knew it, I'd slipped away into sleep.

Chapter Fifteen
Layla Cassidy

Realm of Jotunheim

The giants looked both confused and unhappy to see the group.

They'd arrived in Jotunheim inside a temple with a whole bunch of giants standing before a dais, where another giant—Layla presumed some sort of cleric, considering he was wearing purple-and-golden robes and a big pointy hat—was giving a speech.

Weapons were drawn, and, seeing as they were wielded by giants, they were about the same size as your average human. Layla considered it somewhat intimidating to fight someone whose idea of a weapon was a maul that was as big as you were.

"Wait," Tarron said in perfect Dwarvish.

The giants and dwarves shared a language. They had lived and worked side by side for hundreds if not thousands of years, and over time the giant language had been used less and less. Some still practiced it, but it was more for curiosity or a need to feel connected to ancestors than for day-to-day use.

Everyone stopped what they were doing. From the looks on their faces, Layla figured that they were either surprised to see a shadow elf, surprised to hear someone speak their language, surprised that the group hadn't all wet themselves in mortal terror, or all of the above.

When not using their power, giants were usually about seven to ten feet tall, which was the case with those in the temple. The average giant could grow a lot more than that. A fire giant friend of Layla's, Dralas, had reached fifty feet in height and had done so while fighting Mammon. Dralas had given his life to save many people. And as Tarron's best friend, he was someone Layla knew would be deeply missed for a long time.

"Shadow elf?" the cleric asked.

"High priest," Tarron said.

The high priest looked at the group. "What is going on? That elven realm gate has been disused for thousands of years. We only kept it because removing it would probably destroy the temple."

"We're looking for the elves and dwarves," Layla said in Dwarvish. She'd learned the language when in the dwarven realm of Nidavellir. Everyone on the team knew the language and could speak and understand it with ease. The dwarves had a machine they used to implant their language or other information into people's heads as if they'd always known it. Everyone who had been through the process came away thinking the same thing: that it was a strange experience they didn't want to ever repeat.

"They're right there," the high priest said, indicating Zamek and Tarron, clearly confused as to what was going on.

Zamek waved. Harry forced the dwarf to lower his arm.

"I'm just trying to be nice," Zamek whispered. "They outnumber us a hundred to one, and they have *really* big weapons."

"You're a walking weapon," Harry whispered back. "Don't make any sudden movements."

"I think we should go to my chambers," the high priest said. "We don't appear to be getting anywhere here." He waved at the congregation, who all lowered their weapons or at least didn't look like they were about to use them.

The group followed the high priest through the massive temple hall, which, while certainly made for those who were much larger than human, was almost dwarven in its influences. The white bricks and dark wood were joined together seamlessly. Layla found the whole thing quite stunning, especially with a roof that was in large part made of what appeared to be glass. It let her look up at the bright-blue sky above. The whole thing was beautiful.

The buildings outside the temple were just as impressive. The group stood on top of a large hill overlooking the city below, and to Layla's mind, it really did appear as though it had been made for dwarves. Except on a much larger scale. The city stretched as far as they could see. It was easily the same size as a human city but appeared to have considerably fewer people.

"Did you guys do this?" Layla asked Zamek.

"We learned how to craft from the dwarves," the high priest said as they descended the stairs to the town. "They taught us a lot before they vanished. But yes, they built these buildings. Maybe two thousand years ago now."

"They look new," Layla said.

"We know how to make things last," Zamek said proudly.

The high priest looked back at them. "If you are looking for the rest of your people, I think you'll have had a wasted journey."

Zamek shrugged. "I'm used to it."

"So who were you when the dwarves were around?" he asked. Layla noticed the six guards who followed at a respectful but cautious distance.

Zamek looked uncomfortable with the topic of conversation, but he sighed and answered truthfully, "I was . . . am, I guess, Prince Zamek."

The high priest stopped in his tracks and turned back to Zamek, staring at him intently. "I knew your father," he said. "He was a good dwarf, but arrogant and full of pride. Have you learned from his mistakes?"

"Probably not," Zamek said.

The high priest laughed. "At least you can admit your failings," he said. "It was more than your father and brothers were able to do. Your sisters too. Actually, the whole royal family. Dwarves are a proud people. Royal dwarves are . . ."

"Blinded to anything not happening in front of them," Zamek said. "Yeah, I've met them before."

"Your father would never have allowed you to wear armor like that. He would have wanted it to gleam."

"My father isn't here," Zamek said. "And I'm not a prince anymore. Besides, armor that shines is stupid and just makes you look pretty when you're dead."

The giant slapped a huge hand on Zamek's back. "Too right," he said. "I tried explaining that to him, but I was a young man, and he was not one to be easily moved."

"No, that he wasn't," Zamek said. "What were you doing for the giants at the time?"

"I was a soldier," the high priest said. "Not a very good one either. Or an excellent one. I forget how that works. Either way, I left one order and joined another. This one has less people being stabbed, though."

"How many less?" Harry asked.

The high priest laughed. "I like you."

The expression on Harry's face suggested he wasn't sure if that was good or bad.

"And you have a saber-tooth panther," the high priest said conversationally as the stairs ended and they started walking along the brick roads of the city, getting several strange glances from the giants that lived there, as their buildings towered over the group like an entire town of ten-story skyscrapers.

Several giants, probably no more than children, ran over to the team. Each one was already Layla's height. Their parents barked commands at them to leave the newcomers alone.

Layla stopped outside a building that, while only two stories, was over sixty feet high. The high priest opened the door, and Layla suddenly felt like Alice after drinking a shrinking potion. The group walked through the house, most rooms of which were big enough for an entire human family to live in. The table in what Layla assumed was a dining room was higher than her head. Layla smiled at the thought of needing a stepladder to get onto the chairs. They all left through a door at the rear of the property and stepped out into a garden.

"My people can shrink to about seven or eight feet," the high priest said, "but we feel more comfortable in our homes at taller heights, so it would be impossible for us all to talk in there. But I have a place for when the dwarves used to visit."

At the end of the garden, which was about a quarter of a mile in length, was a building that, while not quite human size, was also not quite giant size.

"This is awesome," Harry whispered.

"Thank you," the high priest said. "Whispering doesn't work here. Our hearing is better than yours."

Kase laughed and gave Harry a playful hug as he sighed with embarrassment. "Apologies," he said. "I wasn't trying to be rude."

"Oh, no need," the high priest said as he removed a bunch of keys from a pocket in his robes and unlocked the door with the smallest one. "Humans are a strange species. There are so many rules and ways to behave. Giants are easier. It is difficult to offend us. Be kind. Be respectful. Crush your enemies. After that, we don't worry too much."

"Crush your enemies?" Zamek asked.

"We're a peaceful society," the high priest said, beckoning everyone into the building. "But we're capable of laying waste to those who cross us if need be."

"Like flame giants?" Layla asked, stepping into the building.

"Ah, yes. A sad story," the high priest said, following after them but leaving the door open so his guards could join them.

The room contained a large table that could have easily seated twenty people, chairs, a tapestry on the wall that appeared to depict some kind of battle, and a set of stairs that led to whatever was above them.

"What's up there?" Tarron asked.

"It's empty," the high priest said. "Back when this building was first used, the dwarves who came here would stay upstairs. It's basically one large room for everyone to sleep. There's a washroom up there, too, although I don't think it's been used in a thousand years, so I can't vouch for its cleanliness." ·

"This room looks clean, though," Kase said as she took a seat at the table.

"It's kept tidy," the high priest said. "We hoped that one day the dwarves would return and sit with us again. My name is Fuvos. I am one of three high priests within the city limits."

"How big is the city?"

"It contains approximately a hundred thousand giants. We like to build up, not out, so most homes will have at least two families in them. Giants are a social species, although the writings of mythology would suggest otherwise."

"Why don't you socialize with Avalon and people outside of this realm?" Tarron asked. "Why lock yourself away?"

"The war with the flame giants, or fire giants, or whatever you want to call them," Fuvos said sadly. "They live shorter lives than us, primarily due to their use of the magic that is inside of them. The more they use the power, the quicker they age. There are very few flame giants who can control their use of the power inside of them.

"They resent the fact that their own power kills them and wanted us to help them find a cure. When we said that was impossible, we fought. Thousands, tens of thousands, died. And then they brought in the sorcerers, elementals, and weres of Avalon, those who were trying to overthrow Odin and destroy Asgard. The population of giants was halved. We managed to push back the flame giants, but it wasn't quick enough. We disengaged all realm gates and shut ourselves off from everyone. Odin asked for our help to destroy those who attacked him, but we'd lost so much already. We couldn't risk burying more of our children in a war we wanted no part of."

No one spoke for several seconds.

"So if you're here to ask for our aid in combat, you will probably find many unreceptive," Fuvos continued.

"We're looking for the shadow elves and dwarves," Layla said. "We were told to come here and speak to Mimir."

Fuvos laughed. "Someone clearly doesn't like you, if they sent you to speak to him. But he would know where they've gone. He lives down a well. Actually, he lives in the catacombs that the well is an entrance to. Finding him will be easy, but getting his help will not be. I cannot give you giants to help. I am sorry, but I would need to take that to the council of elders, and it would be a long, hard discussion."

"Avalon will be back," Layla said softly. "They're still trying to conquer Asgard. And they're going to take everything else, including the Earth realm, if we don't stop them. I know you've lost much. I know your people have suffered because of your involvement in this war, and I cannot tell you that you won't lose more. But if you can help, please do. I've fought the Avalon machine. I've seen what they do. I've seen friends die because of it. I don't want to see more people fall to their cruelty."

"You are asking us to go to war?" Fuvos asked.

Layla noticed the stern faces on the heavily armored guards. "I wasn't going to," she said. "I was going to ask you to point us toward Mimir, and then we'd have been on our way, but yes. I think you could be a great ally."

Fuvos looked around the table, settling on Tego. "You are a strange human," he said to Layla.

"Umbra," Layla said.

Fuvos raised an eyebrow. "Now, that is a surprise. The dwarves and sun elves were trying to design a weapon, a weapon that could bond human and magic. The umbra were that weapon."

"The sun elves were helping Avalon," Layla said. "No one has seen them in a long time, but their taint is on *everything* that has happened over the centuries."

"Do you know where they are?"

Layla shook her head. "Once we find the dwarves and shadow elves, we'll hunt the sun elves."

"They were involved in the civil war between giants, and they helped turn the shadow elves into the blood elves. A fact that I took to Avalon members and was shot down." Fuvos stood. "We have horses here, and if you can build a carriage, you can take a few. Be aware they are three times the size of a human horse."

"Thank you," Layla said.

"A dwarf, an elf, a saber-tooth panther, a human, and a were all follow you," Fuvos said before looking over at Hyperion. "And a Titan. I have heard tales of the Titans. Powerful beings who are controlled by no one. Not even Zeus. It's why he locked you away in Tartarus, so the story goes. Atlas is among your numbers, a giant who could not live with giants. I assume he's alive."

"Last I heard, yes," Hyperion said.

"Why do you follow Layla?" Fuvos asked him.

"Because she's right," Hyperion said. "And the stories are old and not entirely accurate. Also, Zeus is dead."

"I am sorry to hear that," Fuvos said. "I met him once. An odd man. Bristling with power, and a need to use it, but also capable of great compassion and love. I will take your case to the elders. Do not expect a quick reply."

"Thank you," Layla said.

"Avalon will come," Kase said. "Eventually, they will come for you, like they do everything else. They lost at Helheim, but they've beaten countless realms into submission. Whether you help us or not, you need to prepare for that."

"We will," Fuvos said. "It appears that a lot has happened in the time we were hidden here. A lot of it bad. We thought that by hiding away, we'd be free of Avalon's influence, but I think maybe we just delayed the inevitable. Stay; rest. I will have food and drink brought to you. When you're ready, please feel free to come find me at my home. If I'm not there, someone will take a message. A guard will be posted outside this building. I am not against trusting outsiders, but not everyone will agree, and I'd rather not have anyone think they could release any of their anger about past transgressions on you."

Fuvos left the building, and they all breathed a slight sigh of relief.

"You think he'll try to get the giants to help?" Harry asked.

"He appeared to be sincere," Tarron said.

"The giants are not known for treachery," Hyperion said. "They are honest about their intentions. If he wished us harm, he would tell us. If he says he will talk to his people, he will do it. Atlas often spoke of their need to be honest."

"They're incapable of lying?" Harry asked.

"Oh no, they can lie," Zamek said. "They can be deceitful and mean, but to do so would tarnish them. It would take a great act to turn a giant into a liar and scoundrel. It happens, but it's rare."

Zamek asked the guard to show them the materials he could use to build a carriage to carry them, and the group was taken to a nearby yard that was full of dark wood. The horses were kept in a massive field beside it, and Layla realized that Fuvos hadn't been kidding when he'd said they were larger than human horses. They looked *exactly* like huge human horses, except for one thing.

"That's a unicorn," Layla said, pointing to the one closest to her, which was about the size of a minivan.

"Yes," Kase said. "And they don't appear to be afraid of me."

"Not afraid of anything," said the guard, who'd introduced herself to them as Jidor.

"But it's a unicorn," Layla said.

"Horse," Jidor said. "I've never heard of the word you're using."

Layla turned to Kase and Harry, who were both too busy being absolutely enthralled with the animals to care much about the technical term for them.

"Fine, horse," Layla almost whispered, and she saw the ghost of a smile on the face of the guard.

It took Zamek an hour to put together a coach that was large enough for everyone. Tego would have to run alongside it, but she was much faster than they were, so no one thought it was going to be a problem.

"One horse will pull this," Jidor said, inspecting the coach. "It's well made."

"Thank you," Zamek said, sounding proud.

Layla watched as Jidor harnessed the . . . she forced herself to think of them as horses, not unicorns. The act of harnessing the animal was much simpler than she'd imagined it would be.

"It's quite gentle," Layla said, allowing the massive animal to sniff her hand before rubbing it on the nose.

"They are tame," Jidor explained. "Wild horses . . . unicorns . . . are not so pleasant. If you see one, avoid it. They are known to attack without provocation."

"Avoid giant killing machines," Tarron said.

"I don't think that's going to be a problem," Harry said.

"You still coming?" Layla asked Zamek. "Or are you going to use the dwarven gate here?"

"I don't want to reactivate their gate," Zamek said. "It feels wrong to do so. I'm with you until we find one I don't have to piss anyone off to activate."

"I could take you back through the elven gate and then return," Tarron said. "I will admit that they might not be happy about it being used so frequently."

"Let's not do anything to upset the giants," Zamek said.

Jidor climbed onto the top of the carriage and took the reins. "I will drive," she said. "I know the way to Mimir. Most giants do; it's why we're able to avoid him."

Considering Zamek hadn't spent a huge amount of time on the coach, the interior was spacious and quite lavish, with comfortable seating and curtains that could go across the barred windows.

The group rode through the city, stopping when they reached the gates. Fuvos appeared beside the coach. "I came to wish you good luck," he said through the open door. "I was surprised to hear that you were leaving so soon."

"Thank you for your help," Layla told him. "But we need to see Mimir."

"The elders are debating the possibility of joining you. I am not convinced the end result will be favorable to you."

"Thank you for at least trying," Layla said, feeling a little guilty. She hadn't come here to ask for their help in the war, but it had seemed like something she needed to try.

"Jidor and Goretis will accompany you," Fuvos said, pointing to a giant who dwarfed even other giants. He wore metal-and-leather armor, with a dark helm that had a face guard giving him the appearance of a demon. "They're both excellent warriors and will help keep you all safe. When you return, I will hopefully have an answer. Either way, I've also petitioned for the dwarven realm gate to be opened; I would rather the elven gate stay unused for the moment. I told them it was a one-way trip for you."

The team left the city and rode through the countryside for several hours, passing a large stream and a great plain that stretched for as far as Layla could see. At one point they rode past several unicorns, all of which made furious noises and beat at the ground with thunderous hooves as they continued past them.

"I don't like unicorns," Harry said. "Wild ones, anyway."

"Yeah, they weren't friendly," Layla said, glad to have them far behind soon after.

They eventually stopped just as the sun was beginning to set. Getting out of the carriage, they looked around, and Jidor climbed down from her perch. "This is the well," she said, pointing to a large stone well.

"Okay, I thought it was going to be metaphorical," Harry said.

"Gotta admit, I didn't expect a . . . well, a well," Kase said.

"There're stairs inside," Jidor said. "It's too small for me to walk down, something Mimir did on purpose. I will need to carry on to the entrance to the catacombs, which is just by the hill over there."

Layla walked over to the well and climbed up the stone stairs that led to the top. She looked down at the darkness beyond and the wooden spiral staircase.

"Is it safe?" Layla asked.

Jidor nodded, climbing back up onto the carriage. "I'll take the horse to the catacomb entrance."

"I will stay with it too," Goretis said. They were the first words to leave his mouth since they'd left the city.

"Tego, go keep them company," Layla said.

Tego pawed once at the ground and followed Jidor.

The rest of the team slowly descended the stairwell, the lamps on the stone walls bursting alight after only a few feet. It took them some time to reach the bottom, where the well opened up into a huge cavern.

Wooden boards had been placed over slippery rock, with rope handles dotted along the rocks to ensure no one fell. It was slow going, and more than once the sounds of something scuttling in the darkness could be heard, but eventually the wooden panels ended and were replaced with a dry stone floor.

"This has been crafted," Zamek said, placing his hand on the ground. "Dwarves did this."

They followed the catacombs for half an hour, never worrying about being lost because there appeared to be only one direction they could walk in. Eventually the increasingly narrow walls ended in a large metal door. Layla used her power to push the door open, checking for booby traps as she did, and then stepped into another large cavern; this one was clearly lived in. It was decorated with hanging silk and tapestries that adorned every wall. The floor was made of red brick, and in one corner of the cavern sat a pile of gold and jewels that was easily twice Layla's height.

"You could have fucking knocked," a man shouted as he walked toward the group. "I assume you're here about the dwarves and elves. You must be Layla and co." He was just over six feet in height, with long dark hair that was adorned with golden beads. His long beard had jeweled rings attached to it, and his every movement drew a noise from the number of bangles and rings he wore.

"Mimir?" Tarron asked.

"Of course I fucking am, you cretin," he snapped. "Now close the fucking door so we can discuss your future."

"Can I kill him now?" Zamek asked.

Layla watched the walking jewelry ad move back over to a silk couch. "Maybe later."

Chapter Sixteen

LAYLA CASSIDY

Realm of Jotunheim

"Do you live here because Odin forced you to?" Hyperion asked as he took a seat on a sofa that he appeared to almost sink into.

"No," Mimir snapped. "Well, yes. The bastard. And no."

Layla exchanged a confused glance with Kase as Mimir left the group alone and walked away through a nearby dark tunnel. Everyone sat in uncomfortable silence for several seconds.

"Anyone else think he's a dick?" Zamek asked. "Just curious."

"Mimir was always meant to be difficult," Hyperion said. "Apparently, difficult and surly are the same thing."

Mimir returned with Jidor and Tego in tow.

"Don't let that fucking cat get on the sofa," Mimir said as Tego snorted and lay down next to the chair Layla was sitting in.

Jidor looked around for somewhere suitable for her to sit, decided against it, and leaned nonchalantly against the nearest wall. "Goretis is going to stay outside," she said. "He wants to keep an eye on things just in case."

"Good idea," Hyperion said.

"How did you know we were coming?" Layla asked Mimir as he lit a pipe and began puffing away.

"I'm an och," he said patronizingly. "I know shit."

"You know, you could take the attitude down a few notches," Kase said. "We're not your enemies."

"Oh, I'm sorry, am I offending your delicate sensibilities?" Mimir mocked. "Fuck you, weregirl."

Kase blinked in shock before regaining her composure. "Oh, I'm gonna knock you the fuck out."

She took a step forward, but Tarron got between her and Mimir. "Enough," he said. "Mimir, I don't want to have to keep our werewolf friend from reenacting the moment you had your head removed, so please don't be an asshole."

Mimir sighed. "Fine. Not apologizing, though."

This is going to be a long day, Layla thought to herself. "Why are you down here? How did you know we were coming? And before you say anything, know that if your answer is telling me to fuck off, we're going to have a *serious* problem."

Mimir furiously smoked his pipe for a while, the smell of pot wafting around the cavern. "This is the only thing that keeps me mellow," he said after well over a minute of him getting more and more stoned. "Otherwise, I'm just angry all the damn time."

"Why?" Harry asked.

"Because when I touch someone, I know everything about them. *Everything.* All their dark, nasty little secrets. It's why Odin put me down here, and it's why I agreed to be here. I was being driven insane living in Asgard, and in turn, I was driving Odin insane."

"How'd you know we were coming?" Layla asked.

"Oh, well, that part was easy. Apart from being able to see the past of a person, I can also see my own future. Sort of. It's spotty and irritating, but I can pick out people pretty well. I can't tell you what's going to happen to the war, though. Mostly because, apart from you people turning up, I'm not leaving this cave to see anyone else. Ever. I have enough shit in my head without needing to add to it."

"Seshat said you might be able to help us," Hyperion said.

"With the dwarves and shadow elves," Mimir said, sucking on his pipe again. "The dwarves were here. It's where they came after they fled their home realm. But they were betrayed."

"What happened?"

"Arthur was told where they'd gone, and he arranged for the flame giants to finally start that war they'd been so damn keen on. In the end the dwarves were handed over to Surtr and taken to Muspelheim. I assume they're still there. That was a thousand years ago, and I doubt very much that they've had a lot of fun being trapped there, but then we haven't heard much from the flame giants, so maybe the dwarves have been giving the bastards a good go. The shadow elves, last I heard, were trying to stay one step ahead of the sun elves. I heard something about the sun elves being in Midgard, but that was a long time ago. You do all know that Midgard isn't Earth, right?"

Everyone nodded.

"Well, the sun elves *really* want that place for themselves. No idea why. I heard they'd retreated to their own realm, and that was a thousand years ago, and I have no further information about them. Either way, Muspelheim is where you want to go. And therein lies your biggest problem."

"What is it?" Zamek asked.

"One of the giants in Jotunheim isn't who he pretends to be. You see, when the flame giants were pushed back, one of them stayed. One of them ingratiated himself with the giants here and pretended to be something he isn't. You know him as Fuvos. And he knows that I know."

"Fuvos is working with Avalon?" Hyperion asked.

"You've met him?" Mimir asked.

"He's a high priest and someone I thought we could trust," Hyperion said.

"Then you're a fucking idiot," Mimir said before puffing on his pipe again.

"If he's working with Avalon, why didn't he just have us killed when we arrived?" Layla asked.

"Because that would be stupid. He's meant to be a high priest." Mimir sucked on his pipe again. "High priests don't go around telling their guards to murder people just for showing up. They certainly don't have dwarves and shadow elves—traditionally the allies of the giants—executed. He probably took you all aside, somewhere quiet and out of the way, while he tried to figure out what the hell to do next."

"Ah, shit," Harry said. "So what comes next?"

"You ever heard of a summoning circle?" Mimir asked.

Hyperion and Zamek nodded, but everyone else looked confused.

"Fucking youth," Mimir muttered. "They're sometimes called vision circles."

"Yeah, I still got nothing," Kase said.

"Damn it, what is wrong with you people?" Mimir shook his head. "Anyway, they're used to communicate with people, but the special thing about them is that they can be used to talk to someone in another realm."

"That sounds helpful," Tarron said. "Why aren't they used more widely?"

"They're spotty," Hyperion said. "And they don't always work. And you need to have your intended recipient agree to talk to you. And they need to have the right runes. And *you* need to have the right runes. And if anything goes wrong, your circle explodes and fries your brain."

"It was created by the Norse dwarves," Zamek said. "And then promptly kept to ourselves for an exceptionally long time before we shared it with Avalon. You'd have been long frozen, Tarron. It's not exactly the safest way to communicate, but it'll do in a pinch. And it can only be done between two people who share a connection: friendship, love, hatred—something strong."

"So I assume that Fuvos is still connecting with someone in another realm," Harry said.

Mimir nodded. "Was last time I met him. I saw his memories a few decades ago when I had to go to town for something. I've been trying to reach Asgard ever since, to let Odin know, but Odin appears to have blocked all access to the realm. Which, honestly, I don't even know how that's possible, but there you go. I don't know who Fuvos contacts; I can only see *his* actions, and I saw him make the circle and use it to communicate and discuss the betrayal of everything he's meant to hold dear."

"Right, let's get this straight," Jidor said. "You're saying that the high priest Fuvos is a traitor to the realm of Jotunheim?"

"I'm sorry if this is a lot to take in," Layla said.

"It's impossible," Jidor said. "There's no way he's capable of such things. I haven't worked for him long, but I've known him all my life." She turned and left the cave without another word.

"Any chance that if Fuvos is involved, he has a plan for us before we return to Utgard?" Layla asked.

"It's a certainty," Mimir said. "It would be difficult for him to do anything on the road here. The horses tend to be attracted by the smell of blood. His people would be in just as much danger as you."

"I think I can officially say that unicorns suck," Kase said. "Exactly what's Fuvos's play here? Tell the elders that we're Avalon spies and have us thrown in jail?"

Mimir shook his head. "They would want a trial and independent investigation. It would slow you down, but as soon as they saw Hyperion, Zamek, and Tarron working together, they would know that no self-respecting Titan or shadow elf would help Avalon, and the dwarves are the friends of the giants. Fuvos would be made to look foolish for any such claim."

"He'll take us somewhere quiet and do it there," Tarron said.

"The house he took us to," Zamek said. "It's far from anything residential. And I doubt they're expecting a drawn-out battle."

"Can we find out who he's using the summoning circle to talk to?" Layla asked.

"You could ask him," Mimir said, sounding only slightly sarcastic.

Layla was about to argue that it was unlikely that Fuvos would tell them anything when she wondered if Mimir was right. "We could do that," Layla said. "I think with the right persuasion, we could get him to tell us a lot."

"You can't torture a giant to give you anything," Zamek said.

"No torture," Layla said. "But what if we made a deal with him? He tells us what we need, and we don't go to the elders, who I'm pretty sure would be unhappy, yes? Surely the elders would be keen to ensure that there was no repeat of the civil war."

"Why is it that the dwarves, elves, and giants all had civil wars, or at least wars that displaced them, one after the other?" Harry asked.

"Long-term planning," Tarron said. "The dwarves, shadow elves, and giants were allies, who in turn were allied with Asgard. If you want Asgard and you're willing to wait, getting rid of your most troublesome problems first would go a long way."

"The sun elves must have had a hand in this for thousands of years to set this up," Layla said.

"They helped create Arthur," Mimir said. "They helped destroy civilizations; they helped people win wars. You could go back through the history of Avalon, the Olympians . . . hell, even the Seven Devils with Abaddon and Lucifer, and their fingerprints are all over it. They must have an endgame, but I'm fucked if I know what it is."

"To rule everyone?" Harry asked, putting more than a little sarcasm in his voice.

"That's possible," Mimir said, completely ignoring Harry's tone. "And they say humans are idiots."

Harry shook his head slightly.

"Okay, well, sun elves are a problem for later," Tarron said. "Right now, we have the problem of Fuvos waiting for us back in Utgard and whatever he has planned."

Layla got to her feet. "Thank you for your help."

The group started to file out of the cavern, using the entrance that Jidor had used. Harry, Kase, and Layla were the last three to leave.

Mimir sighed as he followed them down the tunnel to the exit. "I don't see a lot of the future, but I did see you coming, and I did see one other thing. Ragnarok."

"The death of the gods?" Layla asked.

Mimir nodded. "There's a prophecy about it. Baldr thinks that he's meant to bring it about. But the prophecy was bullshit. I touched the soothsayer after, and I know what they made up. It's not the story you all read in books; it's different. It's not the end of the world in biblical terms, but it's the end of how everything is right now. Baldr thinks that the prophecy starts with the death of his mother. That's why he's trying to kill her."

"He's trying to kill his mum?" Harry asked.

"Shush," Mimir said. "Right, where was I? Yes, Baldr thinks he needs to kill his mother to start the prophecy, but he's wrong. It's not *mother*, it's *brother*. 'Death will come for the son of Odin.' That's the exact phrase."

"But he killed Thor, so has the prophecy already started?" Harry asked.

"Why are you telling us this?" Kase asked when Mimir didn't say anything for several seconds.

"Because you can't stop it," Mimir said. "'The flame giants will return.' That's part of it. But by *return*, it means *attack*. The second you open that gate to Muspelheim, you're going to start the countdown to them returning to Asgard to lay waste to the realm."

"We could just not do that," Layla said. "And we'd be leaving the dwarves in flame giant hands."

Mimir nodded. "Ragnarok *has* to happen. It's the only way to bring peace. But to achieve it, a lot of bad things will happen first. I'm telling you this because you deserve to know that the road you're on will lead to bad things happening. *Ragnarok* is a made-up word with no real meaning. It's just the end-of-the-world crap that people like to spout and cause panic so they feel big and important. But the change *is* coming. And you're going to help it happen. If you really want peace, then you have to go through the darkness to get there."

"Anything else?" Layla asked.

"Prepare for war," he said.

"We're already at war," Kase said.

Mimir shook his head. "No, this has been a skirmish. The real war is coming. Arthur will throw everything at you and your allies to break you. Don't let him. Don't let him win."

"You can't see if he does or not?" Layla asked.

"There are pivotal moments in time that people like me can't see beyond until they've happened. Ragnarok, or the end, or whatever you want to call it, is one such moment. I can't see how it ends. I just hope I'm around when it does. I wouldn't mention this to too many people. Stories of death and destruction don't tend to go over well with the majority of right-minded people. Tell Mordred next time you see him; he knows about it."

"You've met Mordred?"

"When he was evil and crazy," Mimir said. "I assume he isn't anymore."

Layla shook her head.

"In that case, be *really* glad he's now on your side," Mimir said.

"What about Jidor?" Layla asked, fully aware of how lucky everyone was to have Mordred on their side. "Any chance she's working with Fuvos?"

Mimir shook his head. "I brushed my hand over hers when she came into the catacombs. She's not a part of it."

"You want us to say anything to Odin when, or if, we see him?" Kase asked.

"Yeah, call him a motherfucking bag of giant dicks," Mimir said and walked away.

"I'm going to miss him," Harry said when Mimir was out of earshot.

"Really?" Layla asked.

"Nope," he replied. "Not even a little bit. I think it's probably a good thing Remy wasn't here, or he'd have either killed him or moved in with him."

Layla smiled at the thought of Mimir and Remy in the same space at the same time, and then she shuddered at how horrible that would be after about ten seconds.

They left Mimir to his catacombs and met up with everyone else outside. No one looked particularly thrilled about the information discovered. Jidor marched up and down a short distance from the carriage.

"So what are we meant to do now?" Harry asked.

"Fuvos is a traitor," Jidor said, almost shouting. "I told Goretis, who walked off after telling me he knew."

"What?" Layla asked. "He knew?"

"Apparently, the elders sent him to work for Fuvos to investigate him," Jidor said, waving her arms around in an exaggerated manner. "They *trusted* him to keep an eye on Fuvos, but not me. They just let me work for a man who wants to bring about the end of peace."

"I'm sorry," Kase said softly. "I know this must be hard."

"Do you?" Jidor snapped. "How? How do you know?"

"When I was a kid, I was told about the great and wonderful Arthur," Kase said. "About how when he returns, things will improve. That they'll get better and the world will be united under one leader. That he was a good man. And then I learned the truth. I saw the death and destruction that he brought with him. I saw people, friends, die because of him and those who follow him. I never worked for Arthur, so you're right, I can't possibly know what that's like, but I did have faith in him. I had faith that he would make things better, and everything I was ever told was a lie. So many people had their hearts broken because they'd wanted to believe in something *better*. Fuvos betrayed you. He betrayed everyone."

"Fuvos will be waiting for us," Jidor said. "Goretis said Fuvos knew about Mimir but let him live because he wasn't actually sure that Mimir can be killed or how much Odin is linked to him."

"We could just go back into town, take Fuvos aside, and kill him," Hyperion said.

Everyone stared at Hyperion for a second.

"Let's call that plan B," Layla said.

"Why haven't they sent anyone after us?" Zamek asked. "Anyone else think that's weird? Fuvos knows that Mimir knows his plan. He knows we'll find out. So what does he plan to do about it?"

Everyone immediately looked around the clearing.

"This feels like one of those moments in a horror film where someone walks into a dark house and doesn't switch on the lights," Kase said.

"Where is Goretis?" Harry asked.

"He walked off to the woods," Jidor said.

"Right," Layla said, feeling more than a little concerned about the possibility of an ambush before they returned to the city. "Let's find Goretis, and then we can figure out how to get back to the city without Fuvos and his people waiting for us."

The group moved toward where Goretis had walked off, with Tego emitting a low growl as they reached the edge of the clearing.

"What's wrong?" Layla asked.

"I've learned to trust Tego's nose," Harry said. "If there's something in there she doesn't like, it would be best to stay away from it."

"Goretis is in there," Jidor said.

Layla looked down at the saber-tooth panther. "Can you find Goretis?"

The cat nodded and began to walk into the woods. The rest of the group followed behind. Many of them had already drawn their weapons.

It took five minutes to find Goretis. He was kneeling in front of a large knotted tree that twisted up high above them. Several runes had been drawn on the tree itself, but most were hidden from view by the mass of Goretis's body, which had been nailed to the tree by a large sword through his back.

"A summoning circle," Hyperion said as Layla used her power to remove the sword.

Goretis's body dropped to the grass as the ground beneath their feet began to shake.

"What's that sound?" Harry asked, concerned.

"Prepare for battle," Jidor shouted, unsheathing a huge claymore sword.

Chapter Seventeen

NATE GARRETT

Waking to the sound of banging on my bedroom door, I sat bolt upright. There was no clock telling me what time it was, so I swung my legs out of the bed and opened the door. Donna was standing in the hallway looking as though she were positively crushed by worry.

"What's wrong?" I asked, moving aside and letting her into my room. I walked over to the window and tapped it twice, changing it back to normal clarity and blinking furiously as the sunlight streamed in.

"I'm really sorry for waking you," Donna said. "But Jess and Daniel are missing."

That got rid of any semblance of sleep that remained. "What?"

"Daniel needs medication for his high blood pressure, and we didn't bring it with us, so he was going to go get some from a nearby pharmacy. He left this morning before anyone could stop him. He left me a note telling me he was going to wait for the pharmacy to open and that he wouldn't be cowed into hiding away."

"That fucking idiot," I snapped. "Sorry."

"No, you were right the first time," Donna said. "I sent Jess out to get him, but that was an hour ago. The shops are a ten-minute drive from here." The concern in her voice told me exactly how seriously I needed to take this.

"I'll go check up on them," I said. "Have you told anyone else about this?"

"Medusa," Donna said. "She suggested I come wake you up."

"I'll go find Medusa," I said. "You stay here with Simon and Ava, and I promise you I'll find them."

"Thank you," Donna said, placing a piece of paper on my bed with the address of the shop.

I got dressed in the first things I could find and was still putting on a T-shirt as I ran toward the lift at the end of the floor, where I met Medusa, who was leaving it.

"Just the man I wanted to see," she said, carrying a black rucksack in one hand.

"Daniel and Jess are missing," I said, stepping into the lift. "You can tell me on the way down."

"Jess told me this morning that her grandfather is a stubborn man. I expected them both back by now. You're going after them?" Medusa pushed a button on the panel to take us to one of the three basement levels.

"I'm going to go check," I said. "It'll be quicker for me to jump in a car and go than to wait for your guards to get there."

"Agreed," Medusa said. "If it helps, I sent three guards with Jess. I'm sure whatever is happening, they're fine. There's no way that Avalon knows of Daniel or Jess's location. They're probably just trying to find the right medicine."

"You don't believe that for one second," I said.

"No," Medusa said. "My people haven't returned, and that was an hour ago. They are not usually ones to dawdle."

"Any chance any of them could have turned?" I asked as the doors opened.

Medusa took the question as it was meant, without offense. "No. I trust them all. And yes, I know Apep worked here, but I never once trusted that little shit, so it's not the same."

We walked down a short flight of stairs to a parking garage with dozens of cars inside. A tall, muscular woman stood behind a desk inside a small hut.

"Nate needs something fast," Medusa said.

The woman grabbed a set of keys from under the counter and threw them to me. "Don't scratch it," she said, her booming voice echoing around the garage.

"Wouldn't dream of it," I said, looking down at the set of keys in my hand, which said *Aston Martin*. At any other point in my life, I would have smiled, but the concern for Daniel and Jess overrode the emotion, even when I found the gunmetal-gray Vanquish coupe and got inside.

Medusa passed me the rucksack. "Heckler and Koch," she said. "MP5 and a HK45. Suppressors for both should you need them. Both have five magazines, hollow-point silver bullets, as standard. If you need to put anyone down, do so. Once you figure out where they are, you call me, Isis, or Chris. I assume you don't want to wait around for me to have another team ready?"

"Not even a little bit," I said.

"In that case, I trust you not to get involved in anything before notifying us of a threat. Please don't get yourself killed. They were driving a black BMW model X7 SUV."

I placed the bag in the footwell of the passenger seat. "I'll try."

"Don't break the speed limit either. If you get pulled over in this with those guns, you're going to jail."

"Yeah, I figured that bit out, thanks," I said with a smile. "I'll contact you and let you know what's happening."

I ignited the V12 engine and drove up through the garage until I came to the exit, which was barred by a large metal gate. As I stopped the car by the switch to open the gate and wound down my window, my passenger door opened and Brooke climbed in.

"Ummm, what are you doing?" I asked.

"Coming with you," she said. "Don't argue; we don't have time."

She opened the bag, removed the pistol for herself, and left the MP5 inside. "I haven't had much practice with those," she said by way of explanation. "I'm more comfortable with a pistol or shotgun."

I sat wordlessly as the gate rose up, spending the time putting the address of the shop into the satnav inside the car, before I drove out of the garage at a relatively sedate pace. The ten-minute drive took me less than five, which made me feel like it was slightly pointless to take a car capable of the speeds the Aston Martin was. I pulled up outside the pharmacy and switched off the engine.

Two black BMW X7 SUVs sat in the car park. The pharmacy was bigger than I'd expected, but there were no other cars there, which I had to admit was a bit weird. I got out of the car and stared at the sliding front door of the pharmacy.

"There's a note on it," I said to Brooke.

"I'll check the cars; you go read."

I left the MP5 in the car, mostly because if someone decided to come into the car park and saw me standing there with it in my hands, I might soon after be hearing sirens nearby, and I could do without that.

The lights inside the pharmacy were off, which was kind of strange considering it was nearly nine a.m. The note on the door said that it was closed today due to an outbreak of a dangerous pollutant. It gave no more information than that and had been written by hand in someone's neatest capital-letter handwriting.

Brooke said as she stood beside me, "Cars are clean, both locked, no one inside either. You think they came here, saw the note, and went further but got lost or something?"

I shook my head. "Nope. I think they came here, and shit went south fast." I looked back over to the cars. "It's seventy feet from the furthest car to these doors. I very much doubt the guards would have gone inside with Daniel and Jess, not to begin with. So they sat there and waited, and something happened that made them get out of the car."

"A noise?"

I nodded and peered through the window again. "If there's a dangerous outbreak in there, then there should either be a manager out here waiting for a cleanup crew or an employee out here waiting for their manager." I walked back to the car, retrieved my MP5, and aimed at the supermarket door.

"Whoa," Brooke said. "The second you pull that trigger, anyone around here is going to know what's happening. Even with that suppressor."

"Trust me," I said, pointing to the glowing purple runes on the suppressor. "Runes can take away noise. And about a million other things, but in this instance, it's more the noise thing."

"Well, even with that, you're still not going to smash through the glass here with a bullet," Brooke said. "It's tough glass; it's designed to absorb impacts. It'll splinter the glass but not shatter it. Besides, what if the people who caused trouble here left the door unlocked?"

I lowered the gun, and Brooke pushed the door. It slid open.

"Let's pretend that didn't happen," I said, stepping into the dark pharmacy with the MP5 at the ready.

"You smell anything?" Brooke asked.

"Blood," I said, pointing to the smear on the ground next to the counter. I walked around and found the three bodies of the guards, all of whom had been shot twice in the head and chest and dumped behind the counter.

"Shit," Brooke whispered.

"Where are the staff?" I asked as we stepped around the bodies and pushed open a door to a short corridor beyond. There were three doors in the corridor, two opposite us and one at the far end. "No cars out front, no staff out there." I pushed open the door closest to us.

"My God," Brooke whispered as we both stood looking at the bodies inside what had once been some kind of staff room. They looked like they'd been torn apart. Blood splattered the entire room, and pieces of what appeared to be flesh had been torn and ripped off the victims. Of the four bodies, all of them were covered in blood, three of them were missing their throats, and all of them had gore adorning their fingers. One had two holes in their head, presumably because they hadn't died as quickly as their executioners wanted, or they'd been the last survivor. I was going to make sure to kill everyone responsible for this atrocity.

"They did this to themselves," I whispered. "Holy fuck."

"What?" Brooke asked.

I looked around the room at the runes that had been drawn all over. The same runes that adorned my suppressor. "They ensured no one would hear them," I said. "And do you smell that? There's a weird scent in the air. Something happened in here that drove these people to tear each other apart."

"Why leave the front door unlocked if they go to this trouble?" Brooke asked.

I didn't have a good answer to that question that made me feel better.

"Call Medusa," I said. "Let them know that we have a lot of bodies, including those of their own people, but none of them are Jess and Daniel."

"How did they know where to find them?" Brooke asked, taking out her phone. "No reception."

"It's the runes," I said.

We both left the staff room and used the door at the end of the corridor, stepping out to the rear of the pharmacy, where the loading bay sat. There were black tire marks on the ground next to a large lorry and three more cars, which I would have bet money had once belonged to the staff. While I walked off to see if I could spot anything or anyone, Brooke made her call to Medusa.

She found me a few minutes later standing outside the rear of the pharmacy. "This was done fast and hard," I said. "No way in hell this was those Nazi fuck-knuckles. They weren't going to get the jump on Medusa's people."

"So who was it? Avalon?"

I nodded. "Harbingers."

"I would have thought they'd use their abilities to do this kind of thing."

I shrugged. "They normally would have, but I'm guessing this was an order to keep it low and quiet. You start throwing around magic and elemental powers, and you get a lot of noise very fast. And coming in here as werewolves or something is just going to cause issues if anyone loses control. Harbingers are all about control. And they like to get things done quickly. My guess is they grabbed Daniel and Jess while they were inside here, forced everyone to the rear of the pharmacy, and executed everyone they didn't need."

"You think they've been taken to Clockwork?" Brooke asked. "Medusa told me to tell you to stay here, by the way."

I removed my own phone and called Medusa. "If you're going to Clockwork, I'm going to kick you in the ass," she said upon answering.

"I'm going to Clockwork," I said. "I'm already closer than you are."

"By five minutes."

"Yes, but I think I know where they'll have taken Daniel and Jess, and I'd rather a small group of people checked it out before anyone descends on it. If we can get them out without turning the area into a war zone, that's probably a good idea."

"Nate, it's Isis," she said. "Medusa has you on speaker. We'll contact Chris and have him meet you at the outskirts of Clockwork."

"Deal," I said.

"We still don't know why Clockwork is so damn important to them," Medusa said. "Beyond Robert wanting revenge."

"That's why they've taken them to Clockwork," I said. "Robert wants revenge. If he can't get to Jess through Simon, he'll do it another way."

"Yeah, that sounds like a plan to me," Isis said.

Brooke tapped me on the shoulder, and I turned around to see several armed men wearing black tactical gear advancing toward us. I didn't recognize any of them, but their guns were aimed at Brooke and me, and one of them raised a finger to his lips to ensure I understand their need for me to behave. The guns already ensured that.

"Gotta go," I said. "I'll see you both soon."

One of the men removed the phone from my ear and, after ripping it in half with his bare hands, tossed it aside.

"Well, this is nice," I said as I was pushed to the ground and my hands tied behind my back.

Brooke suffered the same treatment, until we were both left kneeling on the tarmac, our hands bound with cable ties as the five armed men stood guard.

A car pulled up, and a young man stepped out. He had dark skin, and his eyes certainly didn't belong to a human. They had a reptilian sheen to them, and when he looked down at me, a tongue flicked out, separating into a fork and then reforming into one.

"Apep, I assume," I said.

"Nathan Carpenter," he said, crouching down in front of me. "Daniel and Jess said that you'd be coming to find them. Congratulations."

"I am a lucky man," I said. "Why not do this while we were inside the pharmacy?"

"Well, you're lucky enough to stay alive," he told me, not answering the question.

"The others in this shop weren't," I snapped back. "All of this just because Robert is pissy that he got dumped?"

Apep stared at me and laughed. "That's what you think this is about?"

"I did before I got here," I said. "You tested some sort of drug on those people. That's why you didn't take us in the pharmacy—you were worried we might have come into contact with it, and you didn't want to kill either of us. Nice open space, lots of room to watch from afar before deciding how to proceed. What's the drug?"

"You'll see," Apep said. "You have been requested by Robert to be our guest. Apparently, you made quite the impression on him."

"And me?" Brooke asked.

"Oh, you too," Apep said. "If you both behave and do as you're told, maybe you'll both live through this."

I doubted that very much.

"Get up; get into the car. Do not misbehave," Apep said.

Brooke and I both climbed into the gray Jeep Grand Cherokee. Two Harbingers climbed into the rear two seats of the seven-seat vehicle, sitting behind Brooke and me, but not before making sure we knew that they had guns.

Apep climbed into the front passenger seat, and another Harbinger sat between Brooke and me. The fourth Harbinger got into the driver's seat, leaving the last one to drive the Aston Martin to wherever we were going, and I felt a pang of irritation at having one of the Harbingers remove the keys from my pocket and pass them over.

"You break it, you bought it," I told him.

"I'll be real gentle," he said with a grin that obviously meant the exact opposite.

"Off to Clockwork, then," I said.

"This should be a nice surprise for you," Apep said with a lot more happiness in his voice than I liked.

I wondered whether or not calling him a dick was worth being hit. I decided against it, which was considerably harder than I expected. I didn't want to be at anything other than peak condition by the time we arrived wherever it was we were actually going.

I looked down at my hand and willed my magic to return to me. I closed my eyes and tried to feel it, tried to bring it out, but there was nothing. Just a void where it had once been. I opened my eyes again to see that Apep was staring at me.

"Don't be scared, little human," he said with a creepy smile. "If Robert does decide to kill you, I'm sure it won't be quick." He laughed, turning back to face the road.

"What about Baldr?" I asked.

Apep's head snapped around toward me. "Baldr? How do you know about Baldr?"

"Heard someone talk about him," Brooke said. "He was on the news."

The Harbinger beside me hit Brooke in the ribs after Apep nodded at him, and then he did the same to me.

"I asked *you*, Nathan," Apep said. "Not your friend. She needs to remember her place."

"Like she said," I stated. "We saw him on the news."

"Where is Frigg?" Apep asked.

"Who?" I replied.

Apep smiled again. I was getting really sick and tired of seeing that. "Don't worry, Nathan. You'll be singing all of your secrets soon enough. Baldr will definitely want to talk to you before the day is over. And I don't think you'll like the way he asks questions."

An image of my friend Mordred popped into my head. He'd been asked questions by Baldr for years, breaking his mind and spirit along with his body. Baldr knew how to keep you alive, how to make you suffer far beyond what you might think was possible. On top of that, I was pretty sure that the second Baldr saw me, he was going to recognize me, and then all hell was going to break loose.

Come on, magic, I thought to myself. *If there was ever a time for you to burst free and come back into my life, now is a good time.* But still nothing happened. *Erebus, if you're still in there, come say hi. I could really do with the help.* Nothing happened, not that I'd expected it would, and I looked out the window, hoping to figure out exactly how I was going to get out of this mess. I was being driven to meet the man who would torture me to death. Who would kill Brooke without a second thought. Who would get information out of us, because no one stayed silent forever. And once he had that, he was going to kill Frigg and everyone protecting her. And I had no magic to stop it. I sighed. It turned out being human could really suck.

Chapter Eighteen

Nate Garrett

The drive took a few hours, but thankfully, Apep stayed quiet for most of it, and the Harbingers were about as conversational as a brick wall. A long time ago I'd gone through their mental training regime, although at the time I'd had no idea, as it had been forced upon me under some misguided attempt to make me a better warrior. I understood why Harbingers tended to socialize only with other members of the same order—those who understood the kinds of things they'd gone through—but I also knew that it helped them appear scary and mysterious to anyone having to deal with them.

The car stopped, and the door beside me was opened. The Harbinger gave me a shove out onto the tarmac next to a huge hangar that I'd seen through binoculars only a day ago. There were oil drums still burning next to the warehouse, but all other signs of the frivolity that had occurred were gone.

The smell of cooked meat wafted through the air, and my stomach growled in response. The Harbinger forced me to my knees on the snow-covered ground, with Brooke joining me a few moments later.

"This isn't going to end well, is it?" she asked.

"Nope," I said, looking over at the buildings next to the nearby field. There was no way we could make it over there without being killed or captured. For now we were at the mercy of Avalon and their cronies.

Robert Saunders exited through the open door of the hangar and walked over to us. "Hello, Nathan and Brooke," he said, clapping his hands together. "We were only meant to have Daniel and Jessica today, but this is a nice surprise."

"How'd you find them?" I asked. "Just curious."

"We had a trace on the phones of the Kuro family. It seems that Daniel needed to contact his other grandchildren to let them know he was okay. And then we got them. Don't worry; we don't need to go after anyone else. We have all we need right here. Shame about the innocent lives, but if Jessica hadn't been a bitch all those years ago, we wouldn't be here now."

"This is a lot of effort to get revenge for being dumped," I said.

Robert crouched down to my level and grabbed my jaw in one of his hands, forcing me to look at him. "She humiliated me. She fucked another man and then *left* me. People laughed at me behind my back. That kind of behavior can't go unpunished. Took me a long time to find her, though, as she went off grid. And then we were sent here for another reason, and I found them. Call it coincidence, but I like to think of it as fate. I get to come here and deliver the justice I need, and I get to do my job at the same time. Everyone wins. And on top of it all, we found out that Frigg was in Portland, and so Baldr came along for his own little mission. I'd already been looking into Clockwork and knew I needed help doing my job, so I hired some local talent."

"Hence the Nazis," I said. "Although they're not exactly local, are they? I've never seen them before."

"Yes, hence the Nazis," Robert repeated. "They're from all over several states. I brought them together to be something more than the ineffectual small groups who met in dingy bars in the middle of nowhere. A few of them, Bryce, Jackson, and several others, they lived in Clockwork as kids. It wasn't hard to get them to go back and do what I needed. They're idiots, but they *really* hate people who aren't white, and they *really* like money. Surprisingly the second one more than the first. Bryce is looking forward to seeing you." He looked over at Brooke. "And Addison is . . . chomping at the bit to get back in touch with you, Brooke. We're all really looking forward to the reunion."

"Why are your eyes yellow and black?" I asked. "I didn't notice it the last time we met. Does it only happen when you're emotional?"

Robert smiled at me. "That is a surprise I'm almost shaking with excitement about. Why don't you both join me at the facilities around the rear of the hangar? I think you'll like this."

Apep hauled me to my feet as the Harbingers did the same to Brooke.

"Quick question, Apep," I said as Robert strolled off in front. "Why are the KOA using humans? I thought that Avalon was all about only using the best."

"Humans are helpful," he said. "They can go places we can't. Runes can't take power that doesn't exist." He shoved me into the hangar wall hard enough to knock the air out of me. "Sorry, slipped."

"That's okay," I said. "Not everyone is capable of simple things like walking."

Apep's eyes narrowed, and he shoved me inside the hangar, which instead of containing a plane was actually a garage for a dozen cars, most of which appeared to have seen better days.

I was marched through the throng of people working on the vehicles and out through the rear of the hangar, across a hundred meters of tarmac to the field beyond, where someone had constructed a much smaller version of a coliseum.

The structure was horseshoe shaped, with the open end pointing toward the hangar. There was a tall chain-link fence that separated the staggered seating area from the arena floor, which mostly seemed to consist of the frozen field. The whole thing was big enough to seat a few hundred people comfortably, and the arena floor itself was about the same size as two wrestling rings placed side by side. A pickup drove toward the arena, with a man standing in the back holding an AK-47. The pickup had a large cage in the back, although I couldn't see what was inside due to the black tarp that partially covered it.

As we reached the edge of the field, I spotted Jess and Daniel in the front row of spectators, with Robert standing behind them at the top of the seating, looking down on the full arena as if he were a Roman emperor.

"I'd just like to welcome Nathan Carpenter and Brooke Tobin to the festivities," Robert said.

"I'm going to enjoy this," Apep said from behind me before walking away to take his seat.

I looked around the crowd and saw no one I knew, although quite a few of them were obviously Harbingers, as they all sat together around Jess and Daniel.

"It's a shame that Baldr and Adrestia couldn't be here to witness this," Robert continued. "But they've given me their blessing to continue. As some of you know, we like to celebrate our victories with a test of strength among the faithful. I've worked with you fine people for several weeks now, and I've seen how strong and capable you are, and you've seen just how dangerous the Harbingers are, but today we're going to see something else."

The rear door of the pickup with the AK-47-wielding man on the back opened, and Bryce stepped out, shame easy to read on his face.

"Bryce has failed me," Robert said. "He was given a simple job. Retrieve the Mexican. A job that was made even easier because the Mexican in question has to use an artificial leg. Not only did Bryce get outplayed by our guest Nathan here, but Nathan broke his wrist and elbow and dislocated his shoulder. Bryce was beaten like the bitch he is."

There were some calls of support for this, and Bryce's shame vanished as he looked over at me with rage-filled eyes.

I winked at him, which shockingly didn't help matters at all.

"You see, Bryce has told me that his girlfriend, Addison, was responsible for him being late to the hospital. He blamed his loved one for his own mistake. But hey, we all have loved ones who are about as smart as a piece of wet bread, so that's forgivable."

Nasty laughter sounded throughout the arena, and I had a very bad feeling about what was going to happen next. I risked a glance at Brooke, whose expression said she had the same concern.

"Bryce has been given a choice," Robert continued. "In the tradition of the Harbingers, he can atone for his mistake by running the gauntlet. He will fight five of his peers chosen by us, one at a time, and if he gets through all five or is physically capable of continuing, his crime will be forgiven."

There was a big cheer for that. The sound was larger than I'd have assumed a few hundred people could have made.

"Bryce, will you run the gauntlet?" Robert demanded.

"I broke my arm," Bryce whined. "I can't fight."

"You can," Robert shouted. "You can, and you must. If you want forgiveness, you *will* fight."

"I broke my arm," Bryce said again. "He broke my damn arm."

I waved and got a punch in the gut for my trouble from one of the Harbingers closest to me, causing me to drop to my knees as I sucked in air.

"If that's the case," Robert said, "as sad as it is, then your girlfriend, who you have said was responsible for your ineptitude, will have to run it for you."

Addison was hauled out of the pickup and marched next to Bryce. She was shaking with fear, and her eyes widened with surprise when she saw Brooke.

"Addison," Robert said. "Do you agree to run the gauntlet?"

"I don't know," she said softly. "I don't understand."

"You don't understand?" Robert mocked, causing more laughter. "Well, you're going to get the shit kicked out of you by five people I select, as punishment for making Bryce miss his opportunity to grab the Mexican. Now, I know that in hindsight we didn't need him anyway, so because of that, I'll just make it one person you have to beat."

"Who?" Addison asked.

Brooke was marched forward and shoved into the center of the arena. "Your sister," Robert said, causing a mixture of laughter and bays for blood.

Addison's look of fear changed to a smirk, and she charged forward, wrestling Brooke to the ground and smashing her elbow into Brooke's face. Brooke tried to stop her sister without hurting her, but when that was clearly never going to happen, she blocked a punch, moved around Addison, and applied a choke hold, causing her to pass out. Even with a wounded shoulder, Brooke was clearly the better fighter, although the occasional wince on her face showed that she was still in pain.

"Ding, ding," Robert shouted. "That's enough."

Brooke released the hold, shoving her sister away and wiping the blood from her nose.

"This is madness," I shouted. "You're fucking insane."

Robert climbed down from his seat and made his way toward me, his expression radiating anger. "Insane?" he asked as he reached me. "This is how the Harbingers settle matters."

"They're sisters," I said. "Not Harbingers."

"Well, one is a lesbian cop, and the other hates everything the first is and stands for. I think it's time for their family squabbles to come to an end."

"By killing one another?" I asked. "You're not right up there."

He headbutted me before I could react, kicked me in the ribs several times, and dragged me into the arena, shouting at people to move out of the way.

"Let's see how good you are," Robert said.

"What the hell are you?" I asked, my vision spinning from the force of the blow.

He hit me in the ribs as I tried to get to my feet and smashed a forearm into the side of my head, knocking me to the ground.

"Not much fight, is there?" he whispered into my ear. "You thought I was human, but when I take my medicine I'm so much more."

He picked me up by the collar of my T-shirt and threw me across the arena into the nearest wall. I dropped to the ground and tried to get back to my feet, but he sprinted across the arena and kicked me in the ribs. I felt them break. My body hurt, and dark spots flashed in my vision.

"I want you to see this," he said, propping me up in a seated position. He walked over to Brooke and hit her in the stomach, forcing her to her knees. "This is *your* fault."

I watched in horror as Robert removed a syringe from his pocket and grabbed hold of Addison, injecting it into her arm. He walked away as Addison screamed in pain and fury, then launched a horrific attack on Brooke, who tried to defend herself, but she was no match for the stronger and faster Addison, who punched and kicked her sister until Brooke stopped moving. Addison roared as she repeatedly stamped on Brooke's head, until Addison was shot with a tranquilizer dart and dragged away.

"Bryce, all is forgiven," Robert shouted.

I ignored the pain in my body to get back to my feet, keeping my eyes on Robert the whole time.

"You got something to say?" Robert asked as he walked toward me.

"I'm going to *kill* you," I told him, unable to do anything but stare at the body of my friend. A cold hatred began to spread through me.

Robert hit me in the stomach. The power of the blow lifted me from my feet and dumped me on the ground. "Baldr wants to talk to you," he said. "I assure you, you'll wish I'd killed you."

"You didn't need to kill her," I said.

"I'm going to eradicate every single person from the place that kept Jessica from me," Robert told me. "She was mine. She will regret ever trying to run away."

He motioned to some of his thugs, and I was dragged away.

I drifted in and out of consciousness for I had no idea how long, but I had the vague awareness of something near me. Something big and dangerous.

Opening my eyes, I felt the pain run through my body. I went through the checklist of what was and wasn't hurt, and apart from a few busted ribs, which didn't feel great, and a lot of bruising, I appeared to be in one piece.

I rolled onto my back and looked up at the room. The only window had been covered over, letting in only a small amount of sunlight and making it hard to see. But the room was about twice the size of a normal cell, with a huge cage next to me that took up nearly all the available space.

Getting from a supine to a seated position was an exercise in pain and discomfort, but I eventually managed it, only to notice that there was something very much alive inside the cage.

"Oh shit," I said, immediately knowing what had killed Jackson and what Robert had injected Addison with when she'd killed Brooke.

The creature inside the cage growled low, a warning that it wasn't to be messed about with.

"I'm not here to hurt you," I told the creature, who was still shrouded in darkness.

The creature walked toward me, and I got to see the grendel for the first time. Grendels were a species of omnivore that lived in the northernmost reaches of Norway and Finland and, for the most part, pretty much kept to themselves. Because they walked on two legs and looked like a cross between a troll and a gorilla, people assumed they were either cave trolls or some kind of cursed men.

Unlike cave trolls, who would very much like to kill everything they came across just for fun, grendels only killed for food, and they rarely killed humans unless provoked. They mostly ate deer and rabbits, and ever since that damn poem, their numbers had declined exponentially.

Beowulf had been an asshole who'd murdered a bunch of innocent creatures because a king had decided that they scared him when one had broken into his dining hall and killed some people as it tried to escape. Grendels were animals, but they were smart, and Beowulf had known this. He'd murdered the grendels for nothing more than gold and glory and then had a poem written about him to make him out to be some sort of dragon-slaying hero.

"I'm not here to hurt you," I repeated to the grendel, who sat down in front of the bars beside me. "I'm going to guess that the Nazi you killed was less than friendly, and one day he got too close."

The grendel stared at me.

"The bad man hit you?" I asked.

It nodded.

"You tore his arm off?" I asked.

It nodded again.

"Good."

It bared its teeth in something resembling a smile.

There was no way to tell in the darkness if the grendel was male or female, and I wasn't sure if it would understand the question. It wrapped its thick fingers around the bars, its short but sharp nails more than capable of removing a man's face.

"I'm sorry about what happened to you," I said. "They take your blood?" I mimicked the act of an injection.

The grendel nodded and turned its huge face to one side, showing me the mark where the dart had hit.

"They knock you out and draw your blood," I said. "That's why Robert's eyes were yellow and black. He takes the blood to make him stronger. It's why Addison went nuts. She's never had it before, and I'd heard that the first time would turn you into a berserker."

Thoughts of the bodies in the pharmacy drifted to the forefront of my mind. "They used the blood on those people," I said to myself. "Did they inject them? Did they do it some other way?"

The grendel continued to stare at me.

I tapped myself on the chest. "Nate," I said.

The grendel mimicked my action and made a noise like a cross between a howl and a monkey call.

"I don't think I can make that noise," I said. "Sorry. Can I give you a name?"

The grendel stared at me for several seconds before shaking his head.

"Fair enough. I guess these assholes call you enough horrible things. How old are you?"

The grendel tapped twenty-four times on the bars. An adult.

I was about to ask more when the door opened and the grendel almost threw itself into the dark farthest corner.

"You heal quick," Robert said. "It's only been a few hours."

"Not quick enough, apparently," I said.

"On your feet."

I sat and counted to five in my head.

"On your feet, or I move you," Robert said.

I counted to three and pushed myself upright just as Robert took a step toward me.

"Out the door, turn right, downstairs, first left door, sit down," Robert ordered.

I did as I was told. Leaving the room, I discovered that it was just a bedroom inside a house. I followed Robert's directions, although the stairs didn't feel great, and I had to stop once when I thought my ribs were on fire, but I eventually made it to the bottom.

Robert followed behind me in silence as I walked past his Harbingers and entered the room. I didn't know what the room used to be, but it had been repurposed as a torture room. There were several unpleasant-looking hooks hung from the ceiling, and a metal chair with secure fastenings on the arms was bolted to the metal-covered floor. A drain sat in the floor at the end of the room, and Robert forced me to sit in the chair. Although I hated doing so without a fight, I'd learned long ago that you needed to save your energy in situations like this.

"Stay here," Robert said. "Baldr is going to want to get a lot of information out of you. I look forward to seeing what he does."

He left the room, and I heard the sound of the locks closing behind him.

I counted to sixty five times over before the door opened. "Nathan Carpenter," Baldr said without looking at me. "I have some questions . . ." He paused as he turned toward me, and a smile crept over his face. "Oh, this is *glorious*."

Chapter Nineteen

NATE GARRETT

I expected Baldr to launch an all-out attack on my person, but instead, he placed a chair calmly in front of me and then stared at me for a solid five minutes.

"Are you planning on killing me with uncomfortable silences?" I finally asked.

"I thought of all the *awful* things I was going to do to you after you ruined my fun in the dwarven realm," Baldr said. "And then I found out who your father was, and frankly, now I hate you even more."

That got my attention.

"Yep, I know who dearest Daddy is," Baldr said with a slight chuckle, noticing my interest. "We all thought you were dead; everyone did. But instead, you're in the ass end of nowhere, and you're human."

"I like to keep people on their toes," I said.

The door burst open, and a young woman ran in, screaming in Latin about how she was going to rip my head off. Baldr intercepted her, but not before she managed to kick me in the chest hard enough to send me over the chair and onto the floor with a painful thud.

"Adrestia, nice to see you again," I said through clenched teeth.

"Fuck you," she shouted in English. "You murdered my father and brother."

"Your father and brother were psychotic assholes, the former of whom tried to tear my brain apart, and the latter . . ." I shrugged. "Deimos was just someone the world is better off not having around anymore."

Adrestia tried to launch herself at me again, but Baldr kept hold of her. "We will give him to Arthur and Hera," he said. "They will let you watch as he is torn to pieces. They will probably let you have a go yourself, but for now, he remains in one piece. Am I clear?"

Adrestia stared at me with a burning hatred behind her eyes. "Agreed," she said, radiating anger. "But if he becomes a problem, I'll put him down hard."

"Heaven forbid," I said, climbing back into the chair and wincing.

"You'll get your chance," Baldr said, shoving Adrestia out of the room and closing the partially broken door behind her.

"She's just as nice as I remember," I said.

"She would make you suffer given the chance," Baldr said, picking up the chair he'd been sitting on before Adrestia had knocked it out of the way to get to me. He put it back in front of me. "She's not *officially* a part of Avalon. It means she can be disavowed if she gets caught doing anything awful, like killing large numbers of humans."

"What are you going to do, then?" I asked. "We just going to talk about things until I want to stab myself in the ears?"

"You will not be harmed while I'm here," he said. "You will be kept safe until all of my plans are done, and then you'll be taken into Portland to witness the deaths of everyone you care about."

"Why do you have a grendel?" I asked, completely ignoring his posturing.

"What?"

"The grendel," I said slowly and slightly more loudly than necessary, as if I thought he was especially stupid. "Why do you have one?"

"You don't know?" Baldr asked.

"If I knew, I wouldn't have asked, dumb ass," I said.

He punched me in the stomach, and I tried exceptionally hard not to show it hurt as much as it did, but I still had to gasp for several seconds.

"Grendels are rare," Baldr began. "And there's an entire . . . pack, I guess, of them in the forest around Mount Hood. Eight in total, we think—enough to ensure that we have a steady supply of blood for generations to come."

"You're weaponizing their blood," I said.

Baldr smiled. "Very good, Nate. Yes, we are. You see, when injected into a human, grendel blood gives you an increase in strength, speed, durability—basically everything you could want in a human soldier. The first time is . . . rough, I'll admit, but over time we can make an army of humans who are actually better than human. But we messed around with the blood and created a way to give it to a lot of humans in a short period of time."

"Airborne," I said. "That's what the smell was in the pharmacy."

"Yes, that's exactly it," Baldr said with enthusiasm. "I've seen the film of those humans tearing each other apart in seconds; it's very entertaining. We came to find more grendels, and we found Jess for Robert. And obviously, my mother is in Portland. You're going to tell me exactly where."

"Am I bollocks," I said.

Baldr slapped me across the face, knocking me out of the chair. "For someone in the predicament that you're in, you're just a little too smug, I think."

I rubbed my jaw. "I've been tortured by the very best the world has to offer," I said, remaining on the floor. "Then I killed them. Guess where this is heading."

Baldr laughed. "You're *human*," he said. "What are you going to do, make my fists ache when I beat you to death? And you couldn't even do that because I heal so quickly."

"Avalon arranged the protests, didn't they?" I asked. "It feels like something you'd do to get your enemies in one place."

"Not all of them," Baldr said. "In fact, most of them we just hijacked and told everyone that they were violent toward our forces."

"That can't possibly go on forever," I told him.

"Oh, it won't. Portland will be the last protest."

"You're going to use it to get more powers at a government level, yes?"

Baldr laughed. "You worked for Merlin for a long time; you know how he thinks."

"Get the enemy to do the work," I said. "Get the government to welcome you with open arms and allow you to take control. Yeah, I've been there before."

"You going to tell me it won't work?"

I shook my head. "We both know it'll work. You do something in Portland so big that the world sits up again. You're going to use the grendel-blood thing to drive people crazy, aren't you?"

"Partly," he said with a smile. "The rest is just a big surprise."

He got up, opened the door, and left me alone until he returned a short time later with Robert in tow.

"Hi, Rob," I said. "Baldr thinks you're a dick."

Robert looked at Baldr, who nodded, so the former walked across the room and planted a kick to my ribs.

"You see, Nate, I can't be seen attacking you," Baldr said. "The punch earlier was one of anger, and I can't allow that to happen again. I might lose control and *really* hurt you, and then Hera would know, and Arthur would certainly not be happy. But if you were roughed up by guards, well, that's out of my control. Also, Adrestia and I would be able to kill you with one punch, and that would be far too quick. It's better this way."

Robert slammed on my already-broken ribs, causing me to cry out.

"You're saying I shouldn't have asked about the grendels?" I asked as I took another kick, this time to the back.

"Robert, do not kill him," Baldr said.

The beating didn't last long, and it mostly consisted of Robert methodically kicking me in the ribs and back. Occasionally, he stamped on my arms or legs, but he never did anything that would result in serious long-term injury.

"Today, this town will burn," Robert said, crouched beside me. "Metaphorically, anyway. We've got plans for a large test run of the grendel blood."

"You haven't used it before?" I asked, unable to keep the surprise out of my voice.

"Not at large public gatherings," Baldr said. "We're going to film it so that Arthur can sign off on our plan to give it to humans. Right now, we're just in the planning stages. Clockwork has happily agreed to be our first guinea pig."

"And if it works, then the protests?" I asked.

"Got to keep checking those variables," Baldr said. "We've had a lot of people using it in isolation, but it's time to go big or go home."

"And obviously, you want to kill your mummy," I said. "I assume because you were so shit at it the first time."

Baldr punched me in the jaw, knocking me to the ground. "You know *nothing*," Baldr almost screamed.

"You know, you suck at not hitting me," I snapped.

He went to kick me, but Robert surprisingly stopped him, presumably so Baldr didn't actually kill me.

"You want to start Ragnarok, and you think that your mum's death will accomplish that," I said. "But you're delusional, because Ragnarok isn't going to happen. There are no end-of-the-world myths that are anything more than tall tales."

"You think so?" Baldr asked. "Thor said the same thing. He tried to convince me that I was wrong, but I'm not. Ragnarok will cleanse this world. It started with him."

"Let me guess," I said. "One of Hera's people told you about it, or maybe it was someone close to Arthur."

He punched me in the face again. I spat blood onto the floor.

"Sir," Robert said.

"I know," Baldr snapped. He got down on his knees and pushed my head against the ground until I cried out. "I want you to see what we're going to do to this town. I think you've earned that much." He looked up at Robert. "Get him ready to ship out."

Baldr released me and stormed out of the room.

"Baldr's little lapdog?" I asked.

"Do you think that calling me names is going to help you?" Robert asked me.

I shook my head. "No, I think you want to kill me, and it's burning you up inside that you can't. So I can say anything I like, you vile little twatwaffle."

The anger on Robert's face was easy to see. "You want to play games?"

"Sure," I said. "How much grendel blood do you need to inject into yourself before you can get an erection?"

Robert dragged me upright and punched me in the stomach. "You think you're funny?"

I nodded. "Come on, Robert, all that pent-up sexual tension because no one wants to touch you? Maybe that's why you're such a massive bellend."

The punches came thick and fast, knocking me to the ground, where Robert started stamping on my ribs until I nearly passed out from the pain. Abruptly, he stopped.

"Can't finish, eh? Maybe you need some more grendel blood?" I said through broken lips. "Come on, Robert. Just kill me already."

Robert flinched. I'd said too much. "That's it, isn't it? You die, and you don't go to Arthur and Hera. You die here, and you'll avoid them tearing your mind apart and forcing you to do horrific things once they're done." Robert laughed. "That's funny. Because I almost fell for it, and if I give you over as a corpse, I won't be far behind."

He dragged me out of the room, and I passed out again. When I woke up, I rolled over as pain laced every part of me. I couldn't open one eye, and it hurt to breathe.

I reached out and found the metal cage beside me. On the opposite side, the grendel sat watching me.

I tried to say something, but I was pretty sure my jaw was broken, and it came out as a gurgled mess.

The door opened, and Robert came in with two of the Harbingers that I'd seen with Apep. One of them knelt beside me as the other smashed a baton against the cage, causing the grendel to run to the other side.

"You need to live," Robert said. "My friend here is going to help."

I looked over at the Harbinger kneeling beside me. He raised his hands, and I saw the blood that covered them, but before I could say anything, he placed them on me. My body convulsed from the pain as the blood magic coursed through my body. Blood magic was primarily used to hurt and cause pain in others and to heal the sorcerer using it. Some blood magic users could manipulate their power to heal others, but the pain that came with it was exactly the same as if they were using it to kill.

I screamed. There was no way not to. The raw and complete agony that exploded inside of me felt like something was trying to claw its way out. And then, as quickly as he'd started, he stopped. I remained there on the ground, covered in sweat and trying to remember my own name.

"Heal up," Robert said. "See you in a few hours for the festivities."

Everyone left, and it didn't take long for my body to respond to the power placed inside it. My ribs knitted themselves back together, and my eye healed. All of it was done slowly, with the maximum amount of pain, and eventually my body could take no more. I passed out.

I woke to the sounds of gunfire outside the room. My body was mostly healed, although it hurt like I'd been hit by a truck. The door was flung open, and a man stepped inside.

"Chris?" I asked. "Oh *shit*, am I glad to see you."

"We need to go," Chris said. "I wasn't exactly able to get a lot of people together to get you out, but most of this place's inhabitants are in Clockwork now."

"Jess and Daniel?" I asked.

"I watched them get loaded onto a Jeep and driven away," he said. "That's when I knew I had to come get you. How's it going?"

"Been lovely," I said. "I'd give it four stars because the breakfasts suck, and the staff nearly beat me to death before using blood magic to fix me."

"Oh shit," Chris said. "Can you stand?"

I nodded and got to my feet with a little help. "We need to get the grendel out," I said.

"And do what with it?"

"They're torturing it," I said. "There's a whole pack of them in the forest, and they plan to find them and use the blood to make this toxin that makes people crazed the first time they use it. They're going to use it to create some sort of fucked-up supersoldier, but first they're going to use it to cause a whole lot of death and mayhem in Portland."

Chris grabbed the lock, twisted it, and ripped it free, then opened the cage for the grendel. "You're free to go," he told it.

The creature left the cage tentatively.

"Good luck, roomie," I said. "I hope these assholes don't find the rest of your people. Go hide. Stay there; stay safe."

It stood before me, grunted, and then ran out the door.

I followed Chris out of the room, stepping over several bodies of those who had tried to stop him, including a few Harbingers. Chris was more formidable than he'd led me to believe. Eventually, we made it outside and ran across the tarmac to Chris's pickup. I sprinted around the truck and opened the door, just as I got shot.

I opened my mouth to say something but found I couldn't breathe properly to get the words out. Chris reached over, dragged me into the truck, and floored it, getting us out of danger as I half lay, half knelt in the footwell and passenger seat. I felt blood pour down my back and spat up blood as I tried to tell Chris what had happened.

"You've been shot," Chris said, looking worried. "We need to get you somewhere to look at it."

I nodded in agreement, hoping I didn't look as terrified and pained as I felt. As a sorcerer, only silver bullets could kill me. And even then, it had to be a heart or head shot. As a human . . . well, being shot meant I'd never felt quite so fragile. Still, dying in the footwell of Chris's car while dusk settled around me was better than at the hands of Arthur and Hera.

Eventually the car stopped, and Chris manhandled me out of it, took me into a warm house, and placed me facedown on a table or sofa. Frankly, he could have put me in a giant vat of pudding, and I wouldn't have been able to tell the difference at that point, but I was hoping he'd picked something nice.

I looked over and blinked at Erebus, who was sitting in a nearby chair and staring at me.

"Hey," I said to the living embodiment of the magic inside me. "It's been a while, Erebus."

"You're dying," he said.

I nodded slowly. "Yes, turns out this sucks."

Erebus smiled. It was weird seeing someone with my face smile at me differently than how I smiled. "You need to know the truth of who you are," he said softly. "That's the last link. I said nothing because you were meant to regain your powers on your own, and because you were human, I was too deeply buried in your psyche, but as you die, your human consciousness and sorcerer subconscious are more fluid."

"Meaning what?"

"Chris will not save your life. You will die. Your friends will die. Avalon will win. Those are simple facts. The bullet inside you is not silver, but it has shattered ribs, punctured your lung, and created an internal bleed that cannot be controlled outside of a hospital. And you'll be dead before you get there."

"How do I stop it?"

"You need to remember who you are."

"I can't," I snapped. "I don't know who I am—that's why I'm in this goddamn position at the moment. No one knows who my father is. No one. No, that's a lie; Baldr does, and he *really* didn't seem to be interested in telling me."

"He told you that he hated you more for it."

My subconscious mind turned to look back at Chris, who was trying everything he could to keep me alive.

"Do you know who he really is?" Erebus asked.

"Chris?" I shook my head.

"Ask him. And you know, Nathaniel Garrett is only part of your whole name. Ask him to tell you your missing name."

"Why can't you just tell me?" I asked Erebus.

"We both know why. I can't tell you information you don't already know. And this information is blocked from you. I will push your mind back to your consciousness, but you will not have long to ask."

I nodded and cried out as I was dumped back into wakefulness. Chris knelt beside me. "I'm sorry," he said, taking my hand in his. "I'm so sorry."

"Who are . . . you?" I asked, before realizing that was the wrong question.

"Loki," he said. "That's my real name. I was told to keep you safe from harm, and I failed you. I'm sorry. I didn't know you were alive for so long, and then I was forbidden from ever interacting with you, so when Hades contacted me about helping you, about keeping you safe, I jumped at it. I wanted to get to know you."

"What is . . . my name," I asked.

Chris stared at me for a second before nodding. "You deserve to know the truth. Your mother and father wanted you to have a part of his name, but giving you it would have painted a target on you."

Thunder rumbled above, and the sound of rain drummed against the building, creating an echo all around me.

I looked at my hand and saw lightning jump between my fingers.

Loki stared at my hand and smiled. "Your full name is Nathaniel Garrett Woden."

I recognized that word. It was Old English. A variation on . . .

"Your father was—" Loki continued.

"Odin," I said, my voice low and guttural, as pure, untamed power flooded my body.

Chapter Twenty

LAYLA CASSIDY

Realm of Jotunheim

The team ran back to the clearing as Kase changed into her werewolf beast form, her body growing several inches in height, increasing in muscle mass, and becoming covered in dark fur. The first unicorn charged through the trees at high speed, its head down, horn ready to gore whoever it hit first. Zamek's ax caught it in the neck, causing the creature to fall to the ground short of its attack, and the dirt was quickly drenched in its blood.

Five more wild unicorns ran toward them, with two giants herding them. One of the unicorns turned back to attack one of the twenty-foot giants and received a kick for its trouble, which sent the creature airborne. It crashed into a tree in front of the team.

"Jidor, can you get our ride away from here?" Kase asked.

"You will need help with the giants," she said, climbing up onto the carriage and taking the unicorn's reins as Kase practically threw Harry into the carriage.

"Then hurry," Hyperion said.

The carriage was twenty feet away when all five unicorns burst into the clearing, kicking up huge amounts of dust and dirt.

The team split off, forcing the unicorns to separate from the herd they'd formed and attack individually. Hyperion had turned into his dragon-kin form and hovered over the clearing, his massive wings occasionally beating to keep him airborne as ice exploded from his mouth. It hit the closest giant in the chest and sent him sprawling to the dirt with enough force that the ground beneath Layla's feet shook.

Tego leaped up at one unicorn that got too close to Layla for her comfort. The massive saber-tooth panther's jaws clamped on the unicorn's neck with an awful sound of bones being crushed beneath her powerful bite.

Layla pulled metal out of the earth and wrapped it in tendrils around the legs of the unicorn closest to her, pulling them tight and tripping the animal. It tried to gore her with its horn as it fell, but Layla was too far away, and she wrapped more tendrils around its body to keep it in place.

Tarron had used his two black swords to remove the head of the unicorn that had attacked him, and a second was no match for Kase, who picked it up and threw it into a nearby tree. More tendrils of metal tore out of the ground, dragging the remaining unicorn down before it needed to be killed to stop it from hurting anyone. Layla wasn't keen on the idea of killing animals for acting out their nature, but if it was between that and a friend getting slaughtered, it was an easy choice to make.

The giant got back to his feet just as the second giant pushed apart two trees and stepped into the clearing. He punched Hyperion in the chest, and despite the fact that the Titan was in his dragon-kin form, he flew back through the trees at the other side of the clearing with incredible force. The first giant kicked Kase across the clearing as his body began to turn bright orange.

"Move," Tarron screamed, diving for cover behind a large boulder as fire erupted from the mouth of the giant. The fire wasn't magical fire, which looked normal; this was thick and had the appearance of lava.

Jidor, now over twenty feet in height, charged through the clearing and caught the flame giant under the jaw with an uppercut that took her opponent off his feet and dumped him on the ground.

He blocked a second punch and threw Jidor over him. Layla was reaching out to gather more metal from the earth when Hyperion returned, and a blast of ice hit the flame giant in the eye. He screamed in pain, flailing at his face in an attempt to pull out the six-foot blade of ice.

While he was distracted, Jidor punched him in the jaw, sending him crashing toward the clearing. The flame giant shrank in size as he hit the ground, the blade of ice puncturing the back of his skull. Tarron drove one of his blades into his head, killing him.

The second giant had been dealing with Tego, who had torn out a large part of the giant's leg, causing him to drop to one knee. The saber-tooth panther ran rings around him, never getting close enough to be injured. Tarron ran toward the giant, and Hyperion poured a blast of ice onto the ground beneath the giant's legs, which Tarron used to slide past the giant, slicing through the tendons in his ankle and causing him to hit the ground with an almighty crash.

Layla used the metal in the giant's weapons and armor to make a noose that she wrapped around his throat, ensuring it was tight enough to hurt but not cut off the air.

"Who are you?" Layla asked.

"He works for Fuvos," Jidor said. "How can you do this?"

"Flame giants were almost exterminated," the giant said. "It's time you knew how that felt."

"You started a war and lost," Hyperion said. "I'm not sure you get to blame anyone else for how that ended."

"What do we do with these unicorns?" Kase asked, pointing at those Layla had kept tied to the ground.

"Whatever we do, it should be quick," Layla said. While the three unicorns had calmed and had stopped trying to get free, keeping them still while also wrapping the iron mixture around the giant's throat was taking a lot of power.

"Can we just let them go free?" Harry asked as he reentered the clearing.

"They will attack again," Jidor said. "There's too much blood here. They might seem calm at the moment, but they are not."

The flame giant laughed. "You care about those stupid animals?"

"Animals *you* used as a weapon," Kase said. "They don't deserve to die for you being an asshole."

The giant struggled, and Jidor punched him in the face hard enough to knock him out.

"He a flame giant too?" Layla asked.

Jidor shrugged. "No way of knowing until he activates his power. Apparently, we've had enemies in our midst for centuries and didn't know. Living and working alongside us, coming to our homes, being friends. It makes me feel sick."

"I'm sorry," Tarron said before turning to the unicorns. "Can they be moved to another area before being released?"

"That might work," Jidor said. "But whoever released them would need to leave in a hurry."

"I have an idea," Hyperion said. "I'll go with Layla and her panther to deal with the unicorns. The rest of you, try to get something out of the giant. Kase, can I borrow you for a moment?"

"I think it's safe to say that Fuvos knows we're onto him," Harry said.

"Good," Kase said. "I hope he's worried."

Hyperion and Kase used their ice power to create a sled before the three unicorns were dragged aboard, their metal tethers allowing Layla,

Kase, and Hyperion to move them with relative ease despite their bulk and weight. Layla thought that the unicorns watched Tego with a mixture of anger and fear.

"You see it, too, don't you," Kase said. "They look at me the same way. They fear Tego because they haven't seen one of her kind before, but they're angry about it because . . . actually, they just seem to be angry at everything. I always thought of unicorns as peaceful, beautiful creatures."

"They're still beautiful," Layla said. "Just in a bloodthirsty, crazed way."

Kase stared at her friend for a heartbeat. "That's either really sweet or really scary."

"I haven't decided either," Layla said, matching her friend's smile with one of her own.

When the unicorns were on the sled, Hyperion wrapped them in tendrils of ice, allowing Layla to remove her power, much to her relief.

"You know, these would be easier to just kill," Jidor said.

"I know," Layla said. "That's why we're not killing them."

Moving the unicorns didn't take long, as Hyperion and Kase were able to push the ice sled away from the clearing and toward a nearby field, where everyone stopped.

"This should be fine," Hyperion said, taking off and hovering a dozen feet above the ground. "You two head back to the clearing, and I'll release the unicorns."

Layla and Kase stopped at the nearby dirt path and watched as the ice melted and the three unicorns made their displeasure known to Hyperion, who was far too high for them to be a threat. The creatures turned and ran off toward the distant plains.

"I feel good for doing that," Layla said. "There are enough times when we need to kill things that actually saving something makes a change of pace."

"I get the feeling that the killing isn't done," Kase said.

The pair entered the clearing to find Fuvos's giant ally in the exact same position as when they'd left.

"He told you anything?" Kase asked.

"He keeps telling us how we're all going to burn in the fires of flame giant justice," Tarron said with a roll of his eyes.

"I got help," Harry said, emerging from the catacombs with Mimir in tow.

"Is that helping?" Kase whispered.

"Fuck off," Mimir said. "I can hear you."

Kase shrugged.

"So where is the big prick?" Mimir asked.

"It's the giant," Jidor said, pointing to him.

"Yeah, I was being facetious," Mimir told her. He stopped, removed a pipe from his pocket, and lit it before taking a long drag. "Some days I really need this stuff. Dealing with other people makes it a worse day than usual."

"Can you get answers out of him?" Layla asked.

Mimir sighed but made no comment. Instead, he stood by the giant and slapped him around the face hard enough that it echoed all around the clearing.

"Damn," Harry said. "That was harsh."

The giant growled, low and threatening.

"You're a nasty little fucker, ain't you?" Mimir said, shaking his head slightly. "This one likes killing horses . . . sorry, unicorns. He's not a nice giant. And you'd be better off killing him and dismembering the body as a warning to others."

"No one is being dismembered," Layla said. "Not at the moment, anyway."

Mimir tapped the side of his nose. "Saving it for later? I get it."

"I'm not . . ." Layla stopped and took a deep breath. "What did the flame giant have in his memories?"

"Mostly awful stuff that he's done to unicorns. Some really nasty things he did to a few people who figured out who Fuvos really was. He was looking forward to what he had planned for all of you. He wanted those unicorns to rip you apart. Lots of other unpleasant things. He has issues with his parents. He has issues with women. He has issues with a lot of stuff. I'm pretty sure Fuvos kept him in check from going full mass-murdering fuckwit, but only just."

"Okay, he's a bad guy," Kase said. "But does he know what Fuvos has planned?"

Mimir shook his head. "Nope. No one does, apparently. Fuvos keeps that information to himself, because he doesn't trust anyone. He killed your giant friend, by the way. Sneaked up on him and stabbed him through the back like a coward and then ran off to help the other giant round up those unicorns." Mimir stopped and looked back at the giant. "Interesting. Fuvos is having to move his plan up. He wasn't quite ready for it to be completed, and you people arriving really fucked up his timing."

"But we don't know what that plan is," Harry said.

"Nope," Mimir said, taking a long drag of his pipe and blowing rings with the smoke. "My guess is you need to get back to Utgard pretty damn quick." He looked over at Zamek. "There were dwarves involved."

"You sure?" Zamek asked.

Mimir took a long breath. "I'm going to be diplomatic, because that ax looks exceptionally sharp. So, yes. Yes, I'm sure."

Zamek walked over to the giant and rested the edge of his battle-ax against his throat. "What dwarves?"

"Not even Hades himself could drag it out of me," the giant said.

"He doesn't know," Mimir told everyone. "He's trying to act all tough, but actually he's scared."

"Of dying?" Zamek asked.

"Of Fuvos discovering that he's failed," Mimir said. "Fuvos does not deal with failure well. Not really feeling a lot of sympathy for him, to be honest."

"The shadow elves were here," the giant said. "They were good playthings for so long, but eventually, like all things, they broke."

Tarron moved like lightning, darting toward the giant, but Layla created a wall of metal between them.

"He's goading you," she said when Tarron punched the wall. "He wants to die."

"Let him," Mimir said. "He's no longer useful to you. I'm going back to smoke some more." He walked off without another word.

Layla removed the wall. "Go nuts."

She walked over to the carriage as Tarron drove one of his swords into the giant's eye. The giant screamed in pain. Flame cascaded from the wound, forcing everyone to get back as the fire fell over the grass. Layla reached out and turned the metal she'd used as a noose earlier into a spear that pierced the flesh under the giant's chin and exited at the back of his skull.

"You okay?" she asked Tarron.

The shadow elf nodded. "I didn't expect that."

"He was preparing to attack," Jidor said. "He will not be the only flame giant we face today."

"No," Layla said. "And I'm willing to bet he won't be the only one we kill."

Everyone climbed back into the carriage, and they set off at a fast pace. No one said anything on the journey back to Utgard, and Layla was thankful for the silence. She wasn't entirely sure how she was going to deal with Fuvos. She was certain that Fuvos would prefer being killed to being taken for questioning, but there was so much they didn't know and so much he could tell them. Through force if necessary.

"You need to see this," Harry said, pointing out the window of the opposite side of the carriage.

Layla looked out and was horrified to see black smoke billowing up from the city of Utgard. She wondered just how much Fuvos was willing to do to the place he'd called home for so long and what would make him betray everyone who called him a friend. Layla banged on the carriage roof.

"I see it," Jidor said from above.

I hope we get there in time to help, Layla thought.

Chapter Twenty-One

LAYLA CASSIDY

Realm of Jotunheim

Part of the city of Utgard was on fire.

The carriage raced into the city, bumping over cobblestone roads. Everyone was thrown into a tangle on the floor as it came to a halt. Before anyone could ask Jidor to maybe be slightly more careful about her passengers, she'd already leaped from her seat and was racing toward Fuvos's home.

Thick black smoke billowed from the roof, and several dozen giants were throwing water on it in a futile effort to help quench the flames. The house was only a few hundred feet away.

Layla climbed out of the carriage and tried to figure out how best to help. "Hyperion, as much ice as you can manage, please."

He changed forms without a word and took to the skies. A massive sheet of ice formed over the house, and a moment later the heat from the fire was already melting it, throwing up clouds of steam.

The constant rain from the ice would help, but it wouldn't stop the flames.

"Kase, Tarron, anything you can do to get this fire out," Layla said.

"And me?" Harry asked.

"See if you and Zamek can come up with a way to divert any water supplies to the effort. With your brains and his alchemy, there should be something you could do."

Layla got the feeling that it was no accident that it was Fuvos's home aflame, and whoever had started the fire clearly didn't care about those houses next to his being caught in the inferno.

Layla considered using her power to smother the flames, but she didn't want to leave red-hot metal all around the place. Instead, she manipulated the underground steel water pipes, bursting them up out of the ground and spraying water. Zamek and Harry found a large water tower on top of a building only a few away from Fuvos's. With a few dwarven runes placed around it, the water shot out like a cannon, drenching everything that had caught fire around the building. When the fire was out, Layla put the pipes down under the ground—although someone else was going to have to come along and remove the foot of water that remained inside the property—and put the torn earth and stone back in place.

The smell of burning was all that remained of the blaze. As the giants thanked everyone for their help, Jidor arrived with two extravagantly dressed giants, one male and one female, whom she introduced as Tisor and Wedver, elders. Their robes were a mixture of yellows, purples, and reds, and they wore silver laurel wreaths. Both elders asked if they could all go somewhere to talk.

"How about Fuvos's cabin?" Hyperion asked. "We were going there anyway."

The two elders exchanged a glance as the rest of the team and Layla walked around the remains of Fuvos's property.

"We know what happened to Goretis," Tisor said. "He was in contact with us when one of Fuvos's guards killed him. He will be missed."

"Fuvos's people killed him," Jidor said with more than a hint of anger. "Because you knew that Fuvos was a traitor and didn't stop him."

Layla noticed that the last sentence she spoke was definitely not a question. "Let's try not to piss off the people we're here to help," she whispered to Jidor.

"We knew he was working against us," Wedver said. "We just didn't know exactly *what* he was doing—or who was working with him. You included."

The two elders had been joined by a half dozen giant soldiers, all of whom stayed a respectful distance behind.

"You worked with Fuvos?" Layla asked while Jidor walked off, clearly unhappy about how everything had gone down.

"He is a high priest," Wedver said. "*Worked with* is probably an inaccurate term. We are separate branches of the governing system of this realm. We deal with the law of the land, and the high priest deals with spiritual well-being. He is one of six."

"Are you planning to investigate the others?" Zamek asked, his voice tense.

"Do we need to?" Tisor asked.

"You have a high priest working with Avalon and the flame giants to undermine your realm and threaten the people who live here," Zamek almost snapped. "I would be checking everyone he had any contact with."

"Are you suggesting that more of our high priests are involved?" Wedver asked, his voice matching the anger in Zamek's. "We have spent many months looking into Fuvos. And I assure you, we have checked anyone else who had any contact with him. Whatever his betrayal, he was not working with other members of the priesthood."

"Why didn't he burn that one?" Tarron asked, pointing to the dwarven meeting hall.

"How do you know that Fuvos burned down his own home?" Wedver asked.

"We don't," Tarron said. "But he's a flame giant. And his house is now on fire. So I'm going to take a not-huge leap of faith on that one."

Layla shrugged, thinking about Tarron's question. "Maybe he needs something in the hall?" It was a wild guess, but it wasn't like she had a lot of other ideas as to what was going on in Fuvos's head.

Tarron and Zamek spent a few minutes checking to ensure that there weren't runes or booby traps in the building. When they gave the all clear, Kase kicked the door in, turning the mass of wood into thousands of splinters in the process.

Once inside, they searched the downstairs thoroughly but found it in the same state as they'd left it earlier. Layla hadn't expected to find anything, as she doubted that Fuvos would have let them stay there if it had been important to him or whatever he had planned, but it was worth checking, all the same.

Tarron stayed downstairs with Harry, Hyperion, Tego, and the other giant elder while their guards remained outside on their orders. Layla and the rest went upstairs, which they found exactly as Fuvos had described, with a large room, a bathroom that had seen better days, and a locked door that Zamek opened by writing a dwarven rune on the wood and activating it, causing the door to disintegrate.

"Nice trick," Jidor said to Zamek.

Inside was a small room with large amounts of dwarven runes written all over the walls, floor, and ceiling.

"What does it say?" Tisor asked.

"It doesn't make any sense," Zamek said, staring at the runes. "It's using the ancient dwarven runes, which, as far as I was aware, exceptionally few people know."

"So what do they do?" Layla asked.

"Normally, they're capable of massive amounts of power, but these ones do nothing," Zamek said. "It's gibberish." He pointed. "These are runes for realm gates, but these are runes for power fluctuations and transfer. And these ones on the floor, they're just complete nonsense. It's something to do with merging energy forms. I honestly don't understand it."

"Take some time to keep looking," Layla said. "Hopefully something will jump out."

"Find Fuvos," he said. "Maybe he can explain what this all means."

"Jidor, can Wedver keep Zamek company?" Layla asked. "Just in case he manages to blow up the roof or something."

"One time," Zamek said. "That happened *one* time."

Layla smiled. "I'll go see what everyone else is doing."

"Not going to blow anything up," Zamek muttered as he was left to his investigation.

"This has all been quite traumatic," Tisor said as they descended the stairs back to the rest of the group. "A high priest working with Avalon behind our back, trying to kill our guests, doing who knows what in concert with the flame giants. Mimir should have told us this."

"Mimir doesn't strike me as the kind of person who likes to talk to people about what he's seen," Layla said. "Also, I get the feeling he didn't think he'd be believed."

"Fuvos was highly regarded, so . . . maybe not. The vast majority of people had no idea that he was even being investigated, and frankly, Mimir lives down there for a reason."

"Yeah, he's a real peach of a personality," Layla said with a smile. "Did Fuvos come to the elders to ask about your help with this war?"

"He did come to us," Tisor said as they reached the bottom of the stairs. "He said we should not aid you any further than necessary. He said we should be afraid about what your being here would do, what it would bring to our door."

"It's already at your door," Layla said.

"Hiding in plain sight," Tisor said. "Whoever was helping him will be found and dealt with."

"At least two members of his guard were helping him," Layla said. "They drove the unicorns at us. Both were flame giants, and both were apparently capable of hiding their power for a long time."

"If flame giants don't access it, you can't tell the difference," Tisor said. "I assume they aren't alive to question."

"You assume correctly," Layla said.

The rest of the team had left the floor and gone through the rear of the building, leaving the door open so Layla could see them searching the grounds.

Tego padded back into the building and purred as Layla stroked her behind the ear. "I assume you haven't found anything," she said.

"Something is wrong here," Tarron said, walking back into the building. "Kase said she can smell Fuvos; he walked up toward the mountain at the north. She doesn't want to go too far ahead without the rest of us, but I have a feeling that something is wrong *here*. The property feels off. Like it's hiding something."

"Any chance he has something under the floor?" Layla asked.

"It's possible," Tarron said. "But we haven't found—"

"Everyone out of the house, now," Zamek shouted as he bounded down the oversize stairs with the elder and Jidor following behind.

No one needed to be told twice, and they sprinted out the door to the rear of the property just as the upper floor exploded. Layla used the metal in her arm to create a large shield that kept Tarron, Tego, and her safe from the thousands of bullet-size pieces of wood and metal that were shot over the back of the garden. Tisor had grown in size and run with Jidor—who held Zamek in her arms—and Wedver, getting far enough away from the explosion.

"That was interesting," Tarron said as the upper floor of the building continued to smoke, and they jogged over to where the others were. "No fire, just an explosion."

"It was power," Zamek said before he thanked Jidor for the assistance. The giant blushed a little and nodded her head.

"What do you mean, power?" Harry asked.

"Those runes were gibberish," Zamek said. "But some of them were there to focus power. They'd been there a long time but only activated a few hours ago. Power built until it reached a limit and exploded. Fuvos didn't write the runes in the way a dwarf would; he linked ones on one wall with ones on another surface."

"He made a bomb out of dwarven runes?" Harry asked.

Zamek nodded. "Yeah, but that's not all he did. There were runes in there that had been altered. It's why they didn't mean anything. He was trying to shift a massive amount of power from one realm to another. He used the room to practice getting the runes and power shift right."

"What does that mean in simple terms?" Layla asked.

"He was trying to create a realm gate that would move one part of a realm to this realm. And I think he managed it."

Layla couldn't help but mimic the look of confusion that crossed everyone else's face. "What?" several of them asked at the same time.

"While you need a gate to move between realms," Zamek began, "you can, in theory, create something that would let you link two realms in the same space. It would be incredibly dangerous to do, but it's possible. I think that's what Fuvos is attempting. I think that's what burned down the house. I went through that building when putting the fire out, and there was lava in it. You see a lot of lava around here?"

"That mountain range up there is a dead volcano," Wedver said. "But there's still lava underground; we use it to heat the city."

"This wasn't bursting up through the earth," Zamek said. "It was like a layer of lava on the stairs and hallway. Someone could have created it through magic, but Kase didn't smell any magic, right?"

Kase shook her head. "And I would have, even over the burning."

"Fuvos is trying to bring something from one realm to here?" Tisor asked. "That sounds . . . very bad."

"Could it be a person?" Layla asked.

"Sure, it could be anything," Zamek said. "It essentially finds a space in another realm and opens a breach between the two realms to merge. The only problem is that since you're essentially removing it from one realm and placing it in another, it can't go back; it can't be . . . unmerged, I guess. Anyway, it can be a person, but you'd have to bring everything around that person with them. You need to extend the breach for a number of meters, and everything in that breach would be taken to the new realm."

"How big can this breach be?" Jidor asked.

"There's no real limit," Zamek said. "But the amount of power it would take to create a large breach grows exponentially as it increases in size."

"Could an inactive volcano be used?" Layla asked. "One that still has lots of lava underground?"

"That's a huge amount of power," Zamek said. "You could use that to bring *a lot* to another realm."

"Like a whole realm?" Hyperion asked.

"You think he's trying to merge a different realm with this one?" Harry asked.

"Mimir said that the flame giants will return," Hyperion said. "Maybe he meant to this realm. If Fuvos is trying to merge the flame giant realm and this one, then what happens?"

"Depends where the merge takes place," Zamek said. "Muspelheim is considerably smaller than Jotunheim. You could fit Muspelheim in here hundreds of times over. Theoretically it's possible, but there would need to be more to it than just causing a breach. That room in Fuvos's property also had a summoning circle in it. That's part of the runes that were changed. No idea who he was talking to, but Muspelheim is as likely a location for whoever it was as anywhere else."

"Whatever he's doing, we need to stop him," Layla said.

"I'll bring the carriage," Jidor said, walking off toward where she'd left it.

"You staying or coming?" Layla asked the two elders.

"I will go to the other elders," Wedver said. "I will talk to them about the possibility of aiding you in your war. It seems that Fuvos had plans to bring it to our doorstep well before you arrived."

"We'll start walking," Layla said. "Jidor will soon catch us up."

They'd barely made it half a mile when Jidor rode up, and they all piled into the carriage, Tisor sitting up top with Jidor.

"You really think he can merge two realms?" Harry asked Zamek.

The dwarf shrugged. "I've come to believe that nothing is impossible. I didn't think we'd ever win back my home realm, yet we did. I didn't believe we'd beat Abaddon, yet we cast her into a realm with—as far as I can tell from my fairly exhaustive research—no way of getting out. Merging two realms would be difficult, dangerous, and most of all incredibly foolish, but it's certainly possible. It's all about the runes and the power used to do it."

No one had much to say after that, and Layla watched Tego out the window as she looked up at her while keeping pace with the unicorn-driven carriage. People had told Layla that Tego was a wild animal and would turn on her if given a chance, but Layla knew she never would. She had shown herself to be loyal time and time again. Layla trusted her with her life, and Tego trusted Layla with hers. Also, she could crush metal with her jaws, and that was a talent that Layla had to admit had come in useful on more than one occasion.

The carriage stopped just as the scenery changed from open plains to cracked earth and the smell of sulfur.

"I thought you said the volcano was dead," Harry said.

"It doesn't smell dead," Kase agreed. "It smells alive and really unpleasant."

The ground beneath the carriage moved, and the earth cracked open. A small stream of lava began to pour out.

"This is bad," Zamek said, climbing down from the carriage.

"He's reactivated the volcano," Layla said. "How?"

"It has been dead for thousands of years," Tisor said. "The dwarves put runes around the mountain to ensure it wouldn't erupt."

"They stopped working, then," Hyperion said.

"No," Zamek said. "No, they didn't."

Layla followed his pointing finger to the blazing rune that sat on one of the ridges of stone around the volcano. The rune was fifty feet high and thirty feet across and burned bright red.

"It's an ancient dwarven rune for power," Zamek said. "That's new. And that wasn't done by Fuvos. No giant has the power to pour into a rune that big. He drew it, no doubt about it, but he didn't power it."

"Who did, then?" Layla asked.

"Dwarves," Zamek said. "There are dwarves here." He unhooked the battle-ax from his back. "And I aim to find out whose side they're on."

"And if they're not on our side?" Hyperion asked.

"Then they will be dealt with accordingly," Zamek said grimly.

Chapter Twenty-Two

Nate Garrett

"Took you long enough," Erebus said from beside me as I ran through the forest of Mount Hood. My bullet wound had healed, along with other injuries I'd sustained.

I'd run from the house Chris had brought me to, which it turned out was the house where I'd been living for the last two years. Lightning struck the building and trees around me dozens of times, and my body moved on pure instinct: *Get to higher ground, away from people. Protect the people. Protect your friends.* Somewhere inside me there was another voice: *Make everyone who hurt them suffer. Turn them to ash.* That would come soon enough.

I couldn't respond to Erebus, as my mind was concentrating on running and climbing as high as I could go. I moved quicker than any human could, not just because my air magic cut through any vegetation in my path but because I was capable of speed and agility that they simply couldn't match.

Eventually I came to a clearing and looked behind me, seeing the flaming footprints on the ground where I'd stepped. The vestiges of light were vanishing from the sky, and I crashed to my knees and screamed as the power inside me began to increase. The glyphs of orange and white, of gray and purple, ignited over my arms and hands, looking as though my skin were cracking apart.

I tried to control the magic but failed and collapsed to the ground. Any vegetation around me burst into flame, and once-healthy trees turned to kindling as power flooded out of my body.

I blinked, and the world vanished around me, replaced with rolling hills and a beautiful stream. There was a table with two chairs, and Erebus sat on one, drinking from a cup of tea. An ornate china teapot sat on the table, along with a second cup.

"Ummm . . . what the hell?" I asked.

"We don't have long," Erebus said. "Your near-death experience and the memory of your father appear to have unlocked your power. Congratulations. Do you remember what happened when you discovered who your mother was?"

I sat at the table and poured a cup of tea. "She'd left a message in my head. It was a strange experience."

"Well, your father has done the same."

"What's happening to my body right now?"

"The power inside your body is building. I know it looks like it's flooding out over the landscape, but honestly, that's just the excess. Once your magic fully releases, it will be quite spectacular," Erebus said. "My power here is waning. I will vanish soon and not return."

"I promised you I'd find the real Erebus. He . . . you allowed yourself to lose a part of your soul and have it merge with my nightmare. And I intend to keep that promise."

"I know. And I told you I was proud of you. That is still the case." He got to his feet and held out his arms for an embrace, which I was happy to return.

"It has been a pleasure and a privilege to watch you grow over the centuries into the good man you are today," Erebus said.

I blinked tears out of my eyes. "Thank you for everything you did. I don't think I would have made it this far without you."

"You will do great things. You can help stop Arthur and his people."

"Portland first," I said. "I can't let those people die to further Avalon's aims."

Erebus smiled. "Like I said, a good man. Goodbye, Nathaniel Garrett Woden. I love you."

"I love you too, Erebus," I said, and he vanished from sight, leaving me alone and my heart aching. I'd first thought that Erebus was an enemy, someone not to be trusted, but over the years I'd discovered the truth about him and his desire to see me thrive and grow as a sorcerer. He'd been invaluable on more than one occasion, and his disappearance from my life was going to take time to get used to. I walked over to the stream and splashed water onto my face. It wasn't real except in my mind, but the coolness made me feel a little better.

"My son," a voice said from behind me a few seconds later.

I turned to see Odin. Though I had no knowledge of ever meeting him, my memories told me it was him. A few more seconds passed as the truth settled in my head. I was wrong about having never met Odin. I'd met him when I was only three or four. I hadn't known I could remember back that far. I remembered his smile and his sadness when I'd left.

Over the centuries, I'd heard stories about Odin, but the knowledge now, that he was my father, made it different. His hair was short and white, and he had a long beard of matching color. Several beads had been threaded through the beard, and a nasty scar went from his cheek up over his eye, which I noticed he had two of.

He wore Viking leather-and-silver armor, and his arms were big enough that he looked like he was walking around with tree trunks strapped to his shoulders. He was imposing, and I would not have wanted to be on the opposite side of the battlefield to him.

"I thought you had one eye," I said.

"Maybe. I don't know," he said. "I can only answer questions up until the day you were born and Erebus's spirit was placed inside of you.

I do not know how long it has taken for you to remove the blood curse marks that would be on you, and I do not know how your life is, but I hope you are happy. I hope you are a good man. I hope you will not hate me for not being a part of your life. It was the only thing I could do to keep you safe, to send you and your mother away.

"I'm sure you heard I hate your mother. I do not. I did not love her, but I did care for her a great deal. Frigg had agreed to your birth, which, let me tell you, was quite the goddamn conversation. Then, before you were born, I began to hear talk of people who were planning on waging war against me. So I am sending you away . . . sent you away. Damn it, this whole talking-to-you-in-the-future thing is weird."

Odin ran his hand through his hair and sighed.

"Your mother is one of the finest warriors I've ever met, and I am sure you will take after her. I'm also sure you will have heard horrible stories about me and the things I've done. I assure you that some are probably true. I was not always a good man, although I am trying to change that. You were born to be a weapon. There were to be seven of you, although I fear a few will not survive. You were an insurance that Avalon and its various factions wouldn't fight among themselves. There's a boy born in Avalon; his name is Mordred. He's the son of Merlin, and I'd like to think that despite your power, the two of you will be friends. Maybe if the seven of you do all make it, do all grow up to be friends, then that friendship will ensure that none of the factions use you for war. I know that this is a great burden, and I am sorry to place it on the shoulders of someone so young."

"So young," I said, mostly to myself. "Hera fucked up the ritual. It was a bit longer than you expected."

Odin's image did nothing for a second, as if the information I'd given it was outside the remit of what it could discuss.

"I held you the day you were born," Odin said. "I hope you never needed to go to war. I hope that you never needed to fight and kill and that you were able to be happy, but if that's not the case, I really hope you destroyed everyone who stood between you and happiness."

Odin smiled. "Right, that's the information done. One last thing. If I'm still alive, I'm in Asgard. Come find me. There's a realm gate in Munster, near the southern coast, that will only open for the blood of my kin. A little dwarven gift for your birth. I have no idea if it's still called Munster, but I'm sure you'll figure it out." A raven landed on Odin's shoulder, and he sighed. "I have to go. I probably haven't answered anything because I have no idea what the bloody hell I'm meant to say, but I really hope you decide to come find me. I want to see how you turned out, and I want to show you off to the world. The last time I saw you, you were four. You were this bundle of questions and inquisitive nature, you were stubborn and smart, and I was very proud to see that you were kind to others. There isn't enough kindness in the world, especially from those who wield power. Maybe one day that will change. In the meantime, I look forward to seeing you, Nathaniel Garrett Woden. My son."

Odin vanished, and I found myself on my knees in the clearing once again, screaming as pressure inside my chest and head continued to build. The trees surrounding me were aflame, and lightning continued to strike the ground around me. My vision turned purple, and I looked up to the sky and roared in defiance as the pressure vanished in an instant.

My magic exploded out of me, instantly incinerating everything in the clearing and carrying on into the dark forest, destroying everything in its path. Dirt and rock were thrown up as the magic created a crater beneath where I knelt and a shield of air that prevented it all falling back onto me as it returned to the earth. Magic continued to surge, turning the forest into an inferno. I fell onto all fours, vomiting flame onto the ground, cooking the dirt, before lightning struck my back over and over, rolling me over and forcing me supine. Shadows moved over my hands, and I felt the touch of the wraith that lived in my shadow realm. It was cold but oddly reassuring.

I had no way of knowing how long I remained lying in the dirt, but I didn't pass out; I remained conscious for every single second of the expulsion of my power. When it finally seemed to be over, I got to my feet, looking up at the maelstrom of fire and air that towered all around me. I remembered being told that for only a few hours, I would have full access to the power that existed inside of me.

At that precise moment, the power that I'd expelled rushed back toward me like a nuclear sonic boom. The force threw me onto the ground again, where I remained until the ringing in my ears stopped and I could breathe normally.

I looked up at the sky and saw a helicopter high above me. How long had I been here? The forest was no longer ablaze, although whether that was from the recalling of my power or from the fact that everything was now ash, I didn't know. The crater was large enough to hold a sizable house, and I climbed out of it slowly until I reached the crater's edge and stood upright for the first time in what felt like hours.

I felt no different than I did prior to my "death" two years ago when facing my enemies, but I knew I was. I felt the power seething inside me. How I could wield it, the things I could do. I walked back through the forest, then jogged, and finally broke into a flat-out sprint. After five hundred meters the forest was no longer burned beyond all recognition. It was a near-perfect line of ash to green.

The helicopter wasn't in the sky when I reached my house and found Loki outside, which hopefully meant I wasn't about to be plastered all over the evening news.

I stopped beside Loki, offering him my hand. "Thank you for all you did for me."

He shook it. "My pleasure."

"You chose your name based on the actors who play Thor and Odin in the films."

Loki nodded and smiled. "I figured 'Tom' was too on the nose. I saw the films over the years, and I liked that while I was the villain, I was entertaining. So now you know. Baldr is your half brother."

"Baldr is my half brother," I repeated. "And he knew."

Loki nodded. "I guess so, yes."

"I'm going to *kill* him," I said. "No games, no playing. He will die by my hand. I don't care if he's family; he's a psychopath who murdered countless thousands of people over the years."

"Judging from what I just saw, you might actually have the power to back that up. You have about eighteen hours, by the way. Minus the time you spent up on the mountain. After that, your power reduces to more manageable levels while you relearn how to use it. It'll take a few years before you're back up to this level again."

"How long was I up there?" I asked, looking up at the night sky.

"It's just after three a.m., so about six hours," Loki said. "Never seen anything like it. Not once. That's the kind of power that will make people take notice. Your parents certainly did a good job."

Six hours, I said to myself, completely shocked. "I assume you're not *my* half brother?"

Loki smiled and shook his head. "Not related to Odin by blood. I was given by my parents to Odin and Frigg to look after. It was a sort of pact between the frost giants and Norse gods. That's my understanding of it. Giants are weird."

"So what are you?"

"A little bit of everything," he said. "My father was a giant. My mother was half-conjurer, half–earth elemental. So I sort of got a bit of all three. And they reacted strangely to one another, so I can shapeshift my face and body. I'm an anomaly, according to Thor." Loki's smile was tinged with sadness.

"Baldr really did kill him, then?" I asked.

Loki nodded. "I couldn't stop him. I tried. Thor threw everything at Baldr, trying to get him to stop, trying to get him to listen to reason, but it didn't work, and Thor was eventually overpowered and killed. Baldr used a poisoned blade like the one he used on Frigg. Thor disarmed him, but not before Baldr caught him with the blade. After that it was just a matter of time."

"I'm sorry," I said.

"You'd have liked Thor. He was a spoiled brat on occasion, but he was loyal and friendly, and there was no one else I'd have wanted watching my back in a fight."

I placed my hand on Loki's shoulder. "Let's go kill Baldr and give Thor, and all of the others whose lives Baldr has ruined, some justice."

"You should know that while you were gone, the Harbingers took over Clockwork. They burned a few of the buildings down and marched pretty much the entire population to either the high school or town hall. There's a truck outside of the school; it looks like it's used for transporting petrol or oil or something."

"Get to Portland. Warn everyone there that Baldr has a plan about the protest. He's going to use that grendel blood to cause the human protesters to attack everything around them. There's something else, too, but I'm not sure what yet." My mind went back to when Addison had been injected with the blood, just before she'd gone wild and killed Brooke. I told Loki.

"You think that the truck has this airborne version of the blood in it?"

I nodded. "I'd put money on it. They were going to do a test run here before using it on the protesters. They want to make something happen that's so bad that the human governments will happily give them more free rein. That the people of this country will support them having more powers. It's all about taking what is given, little by little, until you're in a police state that they'll claim is for your own safety."

"You going to be okay by yourself?"

I smiled and raised my hand, and lightning leaped between my fingers. "Once this town is free of Avalon and Nazi control, I'll head to Portland, and we'll stop Baldr."

"I know you have your magic back, but I figured you'd want these." He threw me a bag full of leather combat armor adorned with runes. I quickly changed into them and used the hose at the front of the house to wash my face and hair, removing a vast amount of dirt.

"Good shout," I said when I'd finished getting dressed. "I must have looked like some sort of monster walking down the hill."

"It wasn't your finest hour," Loki agreed. "The leather armor is inscribed with the usual runes for Hades's people. They'll stop some serious magical power, but a silver bullet is still going to go through. Do not forget that. You're not immortal, Nate. Or impervious."

I put my jacket on over the armor. I looked bulky, but Loki was right; the armor might well save my life.

"You need any weapons?" Loki asked.

I shook my head and set off at a run through the forest toward the town of Clockwork. The high school was at the far end and the town hall in the center, and seeing as how I didn't want anyone to start firing at the people who were being kept there, I had to be silent until I got to the school. I reached the outskirts of the town and knelt in the forest, watching for patrols. The town hall was only a few minutes from me, but I didn't want to get surprised by anyone in the town. I looked down the main street to the far end where the town and forest met. There were at least two vehicles down there. Time to go to work.

Chapter Twenty-Three

NATE GARRETT

I ran along the rear of the properties, using my air magic to give me an extra boost of speed, white glyphs covering my arms and hands, until I stopped outside the shop where I'd seen the pickups. Casting my air magic out, I picked up the conversations of the three men inside the shop. They were going through the jewelry of the now dead, picking the best pieces to steal. They'd done it a few times in the last hour. They were quite proud about it.

I easily scaled the ten-foot-tall wooden fence, vaulted over the barbed wire that sat atop it, and dropped without a sound to the concrete yard beyond. I'd really missed my magic.

Sprinting the twenty feet across the yard, I stopped next to the open door that led into the property. There was a dead dog on the floor, a retriever. They'd shot it twice in the head. If I wasn't going to kill them before, I damn well was now.

The room I entered was a large kitchen-diner. It looked like it hadn't been redecorated since the 1970s and must have been the living area to the shop at the front. A man stood in front of an open fridge. The remains of food packets had been discarded on the linoleum floor as he'd tucked into the owner's food. I snaked tendrils of air magic around him, silently wrapping them up his body, unseen, until they were near his head, when I snapped them shut, wrapping more around his mouth so that he couldn't yell out.

With a slight movement of my hand, the man was turned toward me.

"My name is Nathan Garrett," I told him. "Your Nazi friends kidnapped me, killed a friend of mine, and have generally been a giant pain in the ass for the last few days. How many are there with you in this building? Use your fingers to show me."

The man raised three fingers.

"Thank you," I said and used the tendrils of air magic to crush his skull like a grape. I walked away as the dead man's body fell to the kitchen floor, opening the door to a short hallway with stairs at one end and two doors opposite me.

I pushed open the first door, which led to the shop area. It was a hardware store. It felt remiss that I couldn't remember the owner's name, but I knew that he and his wife were quite elderly and had lived in Clockwork all their lives. It wasn't a massive store, but it was well stocked, and I'd been inside on several occasions to pick up a few things.

I walked between the rows of tools to the front door, the glass of which was all over the floor. The door itself had been hit with one of the pickups, destroying the door, window, and register area. Change covered the floor amid the mess that had been made. I created a blade of fire in my hand and drove it through the grille of the pickup, using a large amount of power to increase the heat as I pulled it up through the engine bay. Water covered the floor a moment later, and the front of the truck burst into flames, which I smothered with air magic. No one was using that truck again. No one was escaping.

I saw the bodies of the owners in a side office, the door of which was ajar. Both were definitely dead. Shot several times in the chest.

I stormed through the hallway, throwing out air magic to bounce around the house like sonar in an attempt to figure out where the other attackers were. *Upstairs, third bedroom on the right.*

I walked up the stairs without bothering to mask the noise—let them know I was coming. The bedroom door was ajar, but the lights inside were off, so I kicked it open, spooking the first Nazi. He took a blade of flame to the throat while I threw a dagger of air at the second one, pinning his arm to the wall.

I widened the blade of fire, decapitating the man closest to me, and looked around the room, which had been trashed.

The Nazi was yelling about his hand while frantically trying to remove a blade that I had complete control of. It was fruitless, but there was no use in telling him that.

"Why kill them?" I asked.

"They looked down their noses at us," he said.

I turned the dagger of air, causing him to yell in pain.

"You are not worthy of anything but *contempt*," I said. "People *should* look down their noses at you. You're fucking idiots. You're bottom-feeding thugs who think that they can wrap themselves up in hate and blame everyone else for their own shortcomings. You're pathetic. You're losers who got picked by Avalon because you're expendable and you know how to shoot people."

"You'll die here," the man said.

I flicked on the bedroom light and looked back at the thug. "You first."

A skeletal hand flew out of the shadows that had been created with the light's activation. It grabbed the waistband of the man's jeans, and I removed the dagger as he was pulled into the shadows. His screams and pleas stopped the second he was gone.

By the time I'd made it to the bottom of the stairs, I felt the familiar surge of power flood my body. The wraith that lived in the shadow realm I had access to killed anyone I sent down there and fed that energy back to me. I wasn't sure if it was a hard death, but I couldn't imagine it was a fun one.

I left the building through the front of the shop, using air magic to push the pickup out of the way and fire magic to cut through the tires of the second pickup.

As I walked through the deserted town, passing several buildings that had been set alight, I found a number of townspeople hiding. I told them to either leave town or go to my cabin. Twenty-six people were all huddled in a church not far from the town hall. I had to talk one down from shooting me with the shotgun he held, but eventually they saw sense, and I watched them go on their way.

The church in question had been a target of mine simply because it had an old bell tower that, while no longer functional, gave excellent views of the town hall and surrounding areas. Many of the streetlights around the town hall had been broken, and the only light came from the three oil drums that had been used to start fires. There were several dead on the steps of the town hall, and I closed my eyes, using my shadow magic to give me night vision. When I opened my eyes again, everything was in shades of black and white, but I could see just as well as I had during the day.

There were four bodies on the steps of the town hall, all police—both local and state—and two more had been killed at the door. The blood splatter on the white brick of the building suggested they'd been lined up against it and executed.

I swept my gaze across the small park that sat in front of the town hall. There were four guards, all Nazis, based on the insignia they wore as bands around their arms. They carried AK-47s and patrolled like they were professionals, although I doubted very much that any of them had ever been in any kind of real combat situation.

At the top of the two dozen steps to the town hall were two large columns. During the day, they were white and looked a little bit like cut-price Roman architecture. Right now, one of them had the body of the mayor's aide impaled on it. The other had the body of her deputy. I didn't even know the name of either man. I felt bad about that—that I'd been here two years and never bothered to learn their names. The mayor I'd met twice, both times because Loki had dragged me along to a party that she'd been throwing; he'd been there as a benefactor. Her name was Kathleen Stone. She'd been nice enough, and I got the feeling she genuinely cared for this town. I wondered if she was okay inside or if something worse had befallen her.

I heard a cry somewhere in the darkness and closed my eyes, changing my night vision to thermal with the use of fire magic. Tommy had once asked me if it was like the Predator, and he'd had to show me the film for me to actually understand what he was talking about, but I'd had to agree that yeah, it kind of was like that.

Apart from the four thugs I'd seen earlier, my thermal vision picked up three more on one side of the town hall and another on the first floor balcony. I ignored them for a moment and looked across the square to figure out where the cry had come from. There were dying heat signatures for dozens of people, all leading away from the town hall, and I hoped that those people had gotten to safety. Or if they were the bad guys, I hoped they'd gotten attacked by a rabid badger.

I scanned the surrounding area and picked out three heat signatures about two hundred feet to the east of me. On the field where Antonio and I had first met Bryce and his merry band of assholes.

I removed the thermal vision and vaulted over the tower, using my air magic to slow my descent to the ground. I didn't land soundlessly, but it wasn't enough to attract any of the guards, and I was soon moving away from the church, taking the alley between two rows of houses, and crossing the road beyond to move into a second alley that brought me to the rear of Antonio's burned-out diner.

There was a second cry and the sound of two shots, all of which came from the park. I ran toward the noise as a third shot rang out, wrapping myself in a shield of air just in case someone decided to take a potshot at me.

I ran onto the field, and the lights around the area showed what had transpired. Doug was slumped on the ground about halfway up the field, leaning against a lamppost. He had his hands over his chest, and blood soaked through his shirt. Addison Tobin was lying on the ground beside him. Although I couldn't tell what had happened to them, I was pretty sure they were dead.

Bryce was standing nearby, looking at them both. He turned the gun toward me and fired, but I extended my shield and dived to the side, and the bullet hit the outside of the shield and harmlessly dropped to the ground. I moved faster than Bryce was prepared for and struck him in the arm with a whip of air magic, slicing through his wrist and forearm, forcing him to drop the gun to the ground as he cried out in pain.

I lost the shield and walked calmly toward Bryce.

"Bitch was going to leave me," he said. "Told me she couldn't deal with what she'd done to her sister. She went to Doug, and they were going to go to the police with proof," he continued. "Fucker deserved to get two in the chest for that. You don't play games with another man's woman."

"What is it with you assholes and your desire to think of women as objects to own?" I asked. "I'd ask you if you could actually hear the stupidity leaving your mouth, but I think we both know you don't care." I heard a rustling noise behind Bryce. I turned on my thermal vision and spotted several masses of heat creeping up toward the whimpering thug.

Bryce got to his feet and pointed a finger at me. "This is your fault," he said. "If you'd stayed out of it, we'd all be sitting pretty, getting paid, and going on to spread our word, but no, you had to turn out to be some kind of fucking assassin."

"I told you to leave," I said. "I told you to not hurt anyone. I told you several times. And you ignored me. And now you're all going to die, and I'm going to go on with my life and forget any of you ever existed. No one will mourn you; no one will care. You'll be a blip on the radar of history. An anomaly. And even that is more than you deserve."

"Kill me, then," Bryce said. "Go on. Do it."

"No," I told him. "Because while you deserve to die, you do not deserve a quick death, and I don't have time to make it linger. That, however, does."

I pointed behind Bryce, who turned just as the grendel from the compound pounced, taking Bryce by the throat and throwing him to the ground. The grendel straddled Bryce's back and looked over at me as several more grendels moved toward Bryce.

"Take your time," I said. "No one will come to help him. I'll make sure."

The grendel leaned down to Bryce's ear and growled, low and menacing.

"Please kill me," Bryce begged.

"The grendels will," I said. "I think some might call this karma, but I'm pretty sure you're too stupid to know what that means. Enjoy being digested."

I ran back toward the diner as Bryce's fear-filled screams were turned into a gurgle of pain. I knew from past experiences that grendels liked to remove the tongues of their prey to ensure they didn't scream and bring in rival predators. Bryce was about to have a horrific night.

When I reached the outskirts of the square where the town hall was, I reapplied my night vision and moved through the darkness, keeping away from the light of the oil drums. I reached the left-hand side of the town hall and quickly scaled the building. I moved slowly over the roof until I was directly above the thug on the balcony. Sitting down, I concentrated, starting to remove the air from around him. I started off slow until I heard him cough, and then there was a slight hissing noise, followed by a sharp intake of breath as he used an inhaler, but I continued to thin the air, creating an invisible bubble of nothing around him. He took a step forward, and I removed the air from around his head as quickly as possible, and before he could do anything else, he fell unconscious and dropped to the balcony floor.

I climbed over the roof and dropped beside the unconscious Nazi. I looked through the glass door to the room beyond, but it was shrouded in darkness. A small noise escaped the lips of the Nazi, so I dragged him into the town hall and broke his neck before dropping him out of sight.

A quick ping of air magic under the door told me that there was no one in the immediate vicinity, so I pushed the door open and stepped out into the well-lit hallway. A set of stairs led down, and there was a second hallway between where I stood and a door forty feet in front of me. I looked over the stairs and heard muffled talking below, but I didn't have time to hang around and check. I used my air magic to spread under the doors and find hostages or hostage takers, but there was no trace of anyone alive. As I walked past the rooms, those with glass doors showed that there were several dead inside, all shot at their desks, and more than one room was completely trashed.

Moving back to the top of the staircase, I looked over the banister at the fifty-foot drop to the polished floor beneath me, but I saw nothing there, so I headed to the first floor. Thirty feet from the bottom of the staircase, I heard the sounds of an AK-47 beneath me. That made my decision pretty fast.

I vaulted over the banister and landed on the floor below, readying a blade of fire, but the entire foyer of the town hall was empty. I ran across the floor to the first door, opened it, and found a Nazi inside with his rifle pointed at a group of hostages. A bolt of lightning through his chest ended him as a threat, and I removed the gun from his grip.

"Mayor," I said as I recognized Kathleen Stone sitting on the floor among the hostages. She'd been shielding her staff members from the threat posed as I'd entered the room, and from the looks of the bruises on her face, she'd pissed off more than one of the bastards responsible for what had happened.

"You're one of them," she said. "A member of Avalon?"

"Not last time I checked," I told her. "I need you all to stay here, keep your heads down, and stay out of my way. Do you know how many hostages are left?"

"A few dozen were taken to the main hall," Kathleen said.

"And how many assholes with guns?"

"Four or five in here," she said. "More outside."

"The ones outside can wait," I said. "The ones inside are my first priority."

"There's a leader," she told me. "Robert is his name. He's not like the others; he's here for revenge. He thinks this whole town kept someone from him."

"We've met," I said.

"You need to be careful of him," she warned me. "He keeps using these drugs, and they're making him delusional. He took me into the main hall and demanded answers. When I couldn't give them, he killed two people. I have no idea where he is now, though. I've never seen anything like it."

"Just stay here until I come give the all clear," I said. "I can't have hostages running around while I'm trying to remove the threat of these Nazis."

"Thank you," the mayor said. "The school is in danger too."

I nodded. "I know. They're my next stop after here." I left the room and moved to the next door, where a second set of hostages was being watched by another Nazi. He died just as quickly as his friend in the room adjacent. Once everyone was safe, I used my magic in the same way as I had on the floor above, checking for threats and people who needed help. When nothing came up, I turned my full attention to the main hall.

I'd been in the hall a few times since moving to Clockwork. I knew that it was big enough to seat four hundred people with relative comfort. There were two doors at the far end of the hallway, and one of them led down into the basement, where chairs and tables were kept, and the other door led to an office used by members of the mayor's staff. There was a spiral staircase inside the office that led to an identical one upstairs. Loki had given me a tour of the place, which at the time had felt mind-numbingly dull but now made me thank him.

Stopping outside the door to the main hall, I paused. I had no idea how many people were in the hall, nor how many of those would be a threat. I looked around and saw shadows cascade across the brightly lit foyer. I moved one of the shadows toward me and sank into it, ending up in my shadow realm.

Every sorcerer who had access to shadow magic had a shadow realm, a place where they could move between the shadows. Time was strange inside the realm, and somewhere in the darkness my wraith patrolled. It was no threat to me, though, so I didn't give it a thought as I looked around.

There were dozens of pockets of light dotted all around the realm, each one linked to a shadow that was above me. With a slight use of power, I knew which shadow would take me into the hall. I moved the shadows in my realm until I was under the one I wanted. Taking a deep breath, I moved up through the shadow and appeared inside the hall.

There were twenty-four people huddled in a corner, hostages for the Nazis to use as needed. They were away from the windows that sat along one wall, but the lights in the hall hadn't been killed, giving me access to a whole bunch of shadows that belonged to the five Nazis in the room. Five Nazis who were justifiably surprised to see me.

The shadows exploded out from beneath their feet, wrapping around guns and legs, dragging each of them down until they were no longer in the room. It took a lot of power to use so many shadows at once, but it was quicker and safer than throwing bolts of lightning about.

"Where's Robert?" I asked the crowd of people.

No one knew.

"Stay here," I said. The five men who had been dragged into my shadows died at that moment, giving me more power. The wraith couldn't feed indefinitely; it could usually only manage a dozen or so people before I couldn't take any more down into my shadow realm. The more powerful the people, the less it could feed on.

The sounds of gunfire echoed outside the building. I ran through the main hall and sprinted through the foyer to the front door, which opened just before I got there.

Loki stepped inside, wearing black leather armor and carrying an MP5. There were several men and women behind him at the front of the town hall who were busy executing any remaining enemy forces.

"I thought I said go to Portland," I said.

"Yeah, but we figured you'd need help," Loki said. "My people arrived a short time ago, and we have more on the way. We stopped off at where you were being held, but it's empty, sorry."

I'd hoped that Jess and Daniel would still be there. "Robert Saunders is unaccounted for," I said. "I imagine wherever he is, Jess and Daniel are. The high school is overrun with who knows what, but there are a lot of people scared in the town hall."

"I'll leave some people here to get the hostages to safety. They'll search the hall for anyone else, including Robert, before joining us at the school. You want to get going?"

I nodded.

"I assume you're enjoying having your magic," he said as we climbed into an SUV.

"Yeah, it's been nice," I said. "You think we can get everyone out of the school without people getting hurt in the process?"

Loki floored the accelerator. "We damn well better," he said. "I plan on showing the bastards who work with Avalon that they picked the wrong town."

Chapter Twenty-Four

Nate Garrett

We moved onto the school grounds on foot. There were no lights on at the front of the school, and we decided to do a circuit of the grounds before heading inside, so it didn't take us long to find where the hostages were being kept.

"They're at the back of the school," Loki said from beside me as he returned from his patrol. "There's the gymnasium back there, and all the hostages are inside. About two thousand of them. Mostly families and teachers. From what I saw, there were no Harbingers inside, though. Which means they're all patrolling the football field."

"There was some sort of PTA meeting here tonight," I said. "I think Jessica mentioned it a few weeks ago. All the parents, teachers, and kids in one place."

"Yeah, lots of nice hostages for the taking until they use that grendel blood to make them all kill each other. And to make things worse, the Harbingers are patrolling a huge open area, where they'll see us coming. That's not my idea of a good approach."

I used fire magic to scorch a rune on the ground and activated it, masking our scents from any of the Harbingers that were able to smell us. It wouldn't last long, and it wasn't the most powerful of runes, but it would do while we tried to figure out the best way forward.

"When you were looking around the school, any chance you counted the number of guards?" I said.

"Nine hostiles," Loki replied. "How do we get nine hostiles away from a huge amount of hostages? And do it without anyone activating that truck full of shit?"

I looked over at the truck. It was large enough to contain a lot of the airborne blood mixture, although it didn't look like they'd attached it to the school by a hose or anything like that. "I haven't figured that bit out yet. How are they going to get that crap into the school?"

I continued watching the Harbingers as they patrolled the perimeter of the football field. They moved differently to how the Nazis had patrolled the town hall. The Harbingers were more confident; they moved with an assurance that they were more than capable of taking care of whatever problems might arise. It wasn't quite cockiness, but it was pretty damn close.

"I need you to create a diversion," I said. "A big one."

"Why?" Loki asked.

"I'm going to go through the school, checking for hostiles along the way, and then I'll leave through the gymnasium to the fields behind the school. That means that hopefully I'll be hitting the Harbingers from the back after defusing any of the grendel blood. Should make it easier to ensure that none of the hostages get killed, used as leverage, or turned into a threat."

"Okay," Loki said, as if thinking things through. "I'll try to get some of the Harbingers to come around this way before I run off to the woods over there and cause some problems. By the time I get there, you should be ready to come bursting out of the school."

"Don't get killed," I told him.

"You too," Loki said. "I mean again."

I flipped Loki off, which made him chuckle.

Getting into the school was easy; I used air magic to cut through one of the large windows close to the reception area and had just climbed through it as several car alarms behind me were set off. Unfortunately, I'd never been in the school before, and it took me a short while to get my bearings.

I finally found some signs attached to the walls that led me in the right direction, and a few minutes later, I was crouched down behind a wall, out of sight of the gymnasium double doors. I looked around the corner at the man who stood there. He wore black tactical armor with runes inscribed on it but appeared to carry no weapon that I could see.

"I can *smell* you," he said, taking several steps toward me and turning into his werewolf beast form midstep. All were creatures had three forms: human, animal, and beast form, which was basically an amalgamation of the human and animal but much bigger than either.

I stepped around the corner with a loud sigh. I waved at the werewolf. He had dark fur and stood about seven feet tall. His armor was designed to move with his changing, and a low growl showed a muzzle that was all sharp teeth and power. He smelled like blood.

"You've killed recently," I said.

"Some people in town wouldn't do as they were told," the werewolf said in a raspy voice. "Bit like you."

"Yeah, I think I might be a tad more difficult to kill."

The werewolf laughed and lunged toward me. I moved aside, bringing a blade of flame up under the werewolf's outstretched hands and removing one of them at the wrist. I stepped to the side of the giant beast as it howled in pain, and I drove the blade of fire into the side of the werewolf's skull, just above the temple.

I was slightly disappointed. There was no way this werewolf was a powerful version of his kind. No werewolf with actual power would have been subdued so easily. Either Harbingers were slacking, which boded well for their removal, or this one was just too cocky and sure of himself. Either way, I removed his head with a swipe of the fire blade. Weres could only be killed through the use of silver or removal of their heads. They could grow back a lot of body parts, but a head was beyond even the most powerful of them.

I opened the gym doors and was overwhelmed by the noise of crying, begging, and more than one person praying to whatever god they believed in. Large numbers of them turned to me, and several recognized me. I explained they all needed to stay inside the school until someone came to collect them. The school principal—a large man with a bald head and a beard that would have made Vikings proud—asked me what was going on, and I told him that he needed to keep the people calm. He responded by showing me several metal canisters painted red that had been placed along the walls. They had valves on them that were currently closed. I breathed a sigh of relief.

"Don't let anyone touch these," I said to the principal.

The windows inside the gymnasium all had their blinds closed, presumably so that no one inside could check on the Harbingers watching them, and while I didn't want to alert any of them to my presence, I did want to know how many were a problem directly outside the door. I switched off the lights at the edge of the hall and moved one of the blinds, risking a quick glance outside at the field, just as a large explosion rocked the building and a fireball tore into the sky from the edge of the football field.

What the bloody hell did you do, Loki? I wondered. But as suspected, the second the Harbingers outside saw the blinds move, one of them opened the door and took a step inside.

"Who switched off the damn lights?" he demanded.

I walked toward him as his torch moved over people in the dark half of the gymnasium, terrifying them in the process. He carried an MP5 and a second pistol against his hip, turning the former toward me when I was only a few steps away.

He held the torch up toward my face as a blast of air struck him in the legs, knocking them out from under him and sending him to the hardwood floor. He rolled with the blow, coming back up to fire at me, but I hit him with another blast, sending him out the doors he'd entered through. Once again, he hit the ground and rolled to get back to his feet, but I'd moved more quickly than he'd expected and had my soul weapons ready.

Apart from being a sorcerer, I'd also inherited my mum's necromancy, although, like her, I could only use it to power my abilities when I'd taken the spirit of someone who had died in battle. But one thing all necromancers had access to was their soul weapons. Weapons formed through the power the necromancer processed. Each weapon was unique to the individual wielding it. I drove the jian sword through the Harbinger's chest, the weapon decimating the runes on his armor.

The soldier's mouth dropped open in shock. Soul weapons didn't physically harm a person, but they did a pretty good job of ripping through a person's spirit. And that would kill you just as quickly.

The jian emitted a slight blue glow, and I twisted it before it vanished from view. I'd spent a large part of my life in China and been given a jian as a gift by the people I'd lived with. It had meant a lot to me, and I assumed that was why it was one of my soul weapons. The original sword had probably been destroyed, but it was nice to know that there was still a reminder of the time I'd spent there.

The Harbinger dropped to the ground, and I drove my other soul weapon, a battle-ax, into his head, leaving no mark but killing him all the same.

Most of the other Harbingers had run toward the fire in the distance, leaving only me, the dead Harbinger at my feet, and a second attacker, who ran toward me, throwing balls of fire as she moved. Each ball of flame was deflected by a blast of my air magic, until she was within arm's reach. Then she wrapped the fire around her fists and threw a punch. I darted to the side and pitched a bolt of lightning at her exposed head, forcing her to fling herself aside to get out of the way. The ground beneath my feet erupted, and I propelled myself back as a second Harbinger ran toward the pair of us, tearing up large chunks of earth to throw at me.

I moved back, putting distance between them and me.

"You will stay away from my sister," the newcomer said, a young-looking man with a stern expression and slim build.

"You're killing innocent people," I said. "You leave, and we won't have a problem."

"You are a traitorous cur," the man said.

"Did you just call me a cur?" I asked, slightly disbelieving what I'd heard. "An actual cur? Is that an in word the youth of Avalon are using?"

The woman threw a ball of flame at me that hit my shield of air and harmlessly vanished.

"You can't beat me," I said. "You can't win. The only reason I haven't turned you both to ash is because I don't want innocent people to die."

"Once you're dead, we're going to watch as the grendel blood makes everyone tear apart their loved ones," the woman said. "You can't stop it."

Thunder rumbled above us, and I shook my head. "This is going to go badly for you," I told her.

"You were Nathaniel Garrett," the man said. "You betrayed Arthur. You mocked his friendship. He will rule this world, and he will kill all who oppose him."

I launched a bolt of lightning to the side of the man, forcing him to move closer to his sister, as another rumble sounded above. I darted forward, creating a sphere of air in my hand and spinning it faster and faster as I moved toward the pair. They put themselves in a defensive stance, remaining side by side; then a shield of earth and fire surrounded them.

I plunged the incredibly power-filled sphere into the shield and detonated the magic inside. The effect all but obliterated the shield, the ground the pair stood on, and thirty feet of field all around them. The pair of Harbingers bounced along the ground and came to a rest after fifty feet, their bodies smoldering. I ran toward them, removed a silver dagger from a sheath on the hip of the girl, who was on all fours trying to relearn how to breathe, and plunged it into the man's eye as he moved toward me. My soul weapon battle-ax to the woman's head ended her struggle.

I considered using my necromancy to absorb her spirit and hopefully learn Baldr's entire plan in the process, but I'd seen the spirits of Avalon members booby-trapped before, causing anyone accessing them incredible pain. Reaching out with my necromancy, I just tested the spirit, hoping to find any traps, but stopped as a loud hissing noise came from the nearby woodland.

Trees rustled and creaked as something moved between them, and the head of a giant snake moved out from the tree line. It was four feet tall from the bottom of its head to the top and looked like a massive python. It opened its enormous mouth and hissed at me. Each fang was two feet in length. If I got bitten, I was not going to be feeling very good for a very long time.

Eventually the whole snake left the trees, and I estimated that it was about forty feet long.

"Hey, Apep," I said as thunder continued to rumble. "You're a bit more impressive as a snake than in human form. Probably about the same level of personality, though, yes?"

"Traitor," Apep hissed. "Had I known who you were, I'd have killed you in Portland."

"Yeah, well, now you know who I am, so feel free to give that a try."

Apep continued toward me.

"You know what's irritating?" I asked. "I like snakes. I think they're actually kind of cool. Not you, though; you're just a massive bellend. Actually, your head looks a bit like a penis."

The snake hissed at me again.

I started walking toward Apep. "I want you to know," I said, "this is *personal*."

The snake reared back, ready to strike once I was in reach. I smiled and wondered if Apep really had any idea who I was and what I could do or if, in his extreme arrogance, he just assumed he could beat me. I'd been holding back since my magic had returned; the need to be quiet or to keep innocent people safe had dictated what I could do. But the only thing behind Apep was woodland, and we were in the middle of a huge field.

The snake sprang toward me, his mouth agape, and I activated my air magic, wrapping it around me as Apep bit down. I moved the shield in front of me, effectively jamming it between the snake's jaws, and as lightning streaked down from the heavens, I raised my hand to the sky. The lightning hit my hand and passed through my body, and merging with an incredible amount of power, it exited through my other hand toward Apep's open throat. I removed my air magic as the lightning hit, traveled down the snake's throat, and exploded inside him. Apep died as his entire body vaporized, leaving nothing but a dark stain on the grass.

A cry for help came from near the football field where I'd watched Ava play only a few days earlier. I ran toward it, using fire magic to cut through the chain-link fence, and saw Daniel on the ground. Daniel held his ribs but smiled as he saw me round the corner, motioning over to the far edge of the field, where Robert dragged an uncooperative Jess along by her arm. Jess's knee connected with Robert's stomach, and she punched him in the jaw, but he backhanded her and sent her to the ground.

"I would stop," I said, using air magic to ensure that my words reached him.

"Fuck you," he shouted back, stepping around Jess, who ran over to help her injured father. "Do you know who I am?"

"An utter wanker," I said, approaching him. "Like, I've met some wankers in my life, but my word, you are a *peak* wanker."

He walked toward me, rolling his shoulders and cracking his knuckles. "I have the power of a grendel in my veins," he said. "I'm going to fuck you up."

"Good luck with that," I told him.

He started running, and I activated my matter magic, bracing for the impact as his fist connected with my jaw with a punch I didn't even try to defend against. It snapped my head aside, and I theatrically dropped to one knee.

"Grendel strength, bitch," he said confidently as he stood above me.

The shadows around Robert moved, and the wraith emerged. Its shadowy robes billowed out around a terrified Robert as its bony hands reached out for him. Robert took a step away from the wraith and bumped into me as I got back to my feet.

The wraith roared in rage, grabbed Robert, and dragged him down into the shadow realm to be consumed. "Sorcery, bitch," I said, before Robert vanished from sight.

I ran over to Jess and Daniel and checked on the latter as Loki entered the field, covered in blood.

"Have fun?" I asked, helping Daniel to his feet. He had a few broken ribs, and at his age, that was a cause for concern, but it didn't look like anything that was going to be a huge problem.

"Yes, I got to teach the Harbingers why they shouldn't piss off someone who is a whole lot stronger than them," Loki said. "Where's Apep?"

"Apep is a smear over the field," I said. "He didn't realize that sorcery isn't something to take lightly."

"My people are done cleaning up at the town hall," Loki said.

"Is Robert dead?" Jess asked.

I felt the rush of power and knew that the wraith was done with feeding on people for the time being. "Yep," I said. "And I doubt it was a fun one."

"It has been a trying day," Daniel said as we reached the school parking area. Two SUVs pulled up in front of the school. Loki's people got out, and he went over to talk to them.

"Sorry I took so long," I said.

"Baldr is still out there," Daniel said. "He will not care that Robert is dead. He is here for his mother. He spoke about her at length while we were prisoners."

"I don't think he likes her," Jess said. "At all."

I was about to comment when the sounds of a helicopter above grabbed my attention. "Loki, they friends of yours?"

Loki looked up. "No, but they are friends. Well, I hope they're friends, anyway. Just so you know, I've got my people removing that grendel shit from the school. The truck was empty, so I guess it had all been put in those canisters. There was more of it at the town hall. I'm not entirely sure *what* we're going to do to destroy it, but it will be destroyed."

The helicopter landed on the football field, and I ran over to meet it as the door opened and a three-foot foxman bounded out. He ran over to me and jumped up to hug me around the neck.

"Damn it, Remy," I said as the foxman's bristly maw made my neck tickle.

"You're alive, you fucker," Remy said, dropping to the ground. He wore a pair of swords strapped to his back and specially designed leather armor with runes inscribed to keep him safe from magic.

Tommy Carpenter was next. He hugged me tight, lifting me off the ground with ease. "Damn it," he said as I hugged him back. "Damn it, you're alive."

"Now I know how Han Solo felt when Chewie found him in *Return of the Jedi*," I said.

Tommy let me go and grinned from ear to ear before making a Chewbacca-like noise. "I know I agreed to have my memories wiped," he said, suddenly serious. "But damn it all the same."

Diana was next. Like Remy and Tommy, she hugged me, not saying a word until she was done. "I've missed you," she said softly.

"You too," I told her.

"Someone missed you more," she said, moving aside as Mordred got out of the helicopter. He waved at me.

"Not Mordred," she said with a slight sigh. "Seriously, Mordred, move."

Mordred, who had gone completely bald and grown quite the beard since I'd last seen him, gave the thumbs-up and stepped out of the way as Selene exited the helicopter. Selene was just over five four and, in my humble opinion, the most beautiful woman I'd ever seen. The top half of her hair was black, while the bottom, which cascaded over her shoulders, was silver. She walked over to me without a word and kissed me on the lips. We stayed that way for several seconds before we pulled apart. Her green eyes were glistening with tears, and I was sure mine were doing the same.

"I can't tell you how much I missed you," she said softly as everyone else left the field and a second helicopter landed close by.

"I'm sorry you had to go through that," I said.

"I agreed to have my memory wiped," she said. "But I didn't realize that losing you would still hurt after so long. That I just wouldn't stop needing you. When I remembered everything, my heart hurt so much. I love you, Nathan Garrett."

"I love you too," I told her.

I felt a tap on my shoulder and looked up to see Hades and Persephone. "While we are glad for your reunion, we need to decide what to do next."

"Now we're going to protect Frigg and the people of Portland from Avalon's wrath," I said. "And I'm going to tear Baldr's head off."

"Anything else?" Persephone asked with a smile.

I paused. "Oh yeah, I guess you should all know. My father is Odin. So technically, Baldr is my half brother."

Chapter Twenty-Five

Nate Garrett

"You know something?" Tommy said to me as we flew in the helicopter toward Portland. "If someone asks you if you're a god, now you can actually say yes."

"I thought you were always meant to anyway?" Diana asked from opposite me.

"Fair point," Tommy said.

I shook my head slightly and squeezed Selene's hand. We hadn't been able to spend much time together since Clockwork, but I'd promised her that we would once we landed. It was just before four thirty a.m., so we had a long time before the protest was due to start. I was sure we'd have enough time to talk things through.

Loki had joined us in the helicopter, leaving his people to help the inhabitants of Clockwork and dispose of the grendel blood. The helicopters were Black Hawks that had been modified to be slightly larger and carry considerably more fuel than the standard model. They were owned by Hades and his organization, and I was glad to see that no matter what had happened in the two years I was away, the people who worked for him were still around.

"So, Mordred," I said, activating the mic on the headset I wore. "How's things been with you?"

"I'm good," he said with a warm smile. "I'm seeing someone, so I'm in a good place."

"Who's the lucky . . ." I paused. I wasn't entirely sure of Mordred's sexual preference. When we'd been younger, he'd been more interested in the person than whatever their sex or gender might have been. And then he'd spent over a thousand years trying to murder everyone who came into contact with him, and since his return to whatever passed for normality in our world, we hadn't really discussed his dating life.

"You don't know how to finish that sentence, do you?" Mordred asked, grinning.

"Sorry, I just . . . no," I admitted.

"Her name is Hel," Mordred said.

"Like Loki's daughter, Hel?" I asked.

Mordred nodded. "I'm in love, Nate. It's a weird feeling."

"Hey, Mordred," I said with a sly smile. "Meet Loki." I pointed to Loki, who winked at Mordred, and Mordred's face pretty much collapsed. Being sixteen hundred years old means very little when you meet the father of the person you love for the first time.

Loki offered Mordred his hand. "Pleasure to meet you," he said.

"Sure," Mordred said, looking my way. "Thanks for the introduction, Nate."

I shrugged and started to laugh. "That was literally the most fun thing I've done in a year."

"I'm beginning to regret coming to save you," Mordred said.

Remy started to laugh out loud. "Oh damn, I've missed stuff like this," he said.

"Me too," I said, noticing that Loki and Mordred were now in conversation.

"He really is in love," Diana said. "It's sickening."

I laughed. "I'm glad. What's Hel like? I've never met her."

"She doesn't take any of his shit," Diana said.

"So she's perfect for him, then," I replied.

"Pretty much, yeah," she said, smiling.

"Oh, I should mention," I told her. "I saw Medusa. She asked after you."

I'd known Diana for centuries, and I'd always been able to tell when something had gotten to her, to make her either sad or happy. She tried to hide surprise behind stoic nods, but I could usually tell. And right at that moment, I could tell she wanted to ask how Medusa was.

"She's good," I told her. "Misses you. Sounds like it's been a while since you last spoke."

Diana nodded. "Yeah." Her voice was tight.

"I'm sorry," I said. "I didn't mean to upset you."

"It's okay," Diana said, reaching over and patting me on the hand. "I haven't seen her in ages. We were close for a long time, and then we went different ways. She was always anti-Avalon. Always. Hated that they allowed people like Hera and her ilk in. Gave people power who didn't deserve it or abused it. Well, it turns out she was right about them all along, but it caused friction. We parted on angry terms."

"If I've learned one thing from these past two years," I said, "it's that you can't let things go by. When you see her, talk to her. Don't leave things unsaid. You'll just regret it."

"Thank you for your sage advice," Diana said with a smirk.

"When did you get all philosophical?" Remy asked. "You sound like you should be on a radio show giving out advice about love."

"And what about you, Remy?" I asked. "What have you been up to?"

"I can change into human now," he said. "Also, I can teleport. It's a bit weird, and it looks like I can only do it for this life, but there we go."

"Wait, what?" I asked.

Remy nodded. "That's right—I evolved. Well, actually, it's more like I just got taught how to use the powers I didn't actually bother to find out about, but I prefer the word *evolved*."

"So you could do this all along?" I asked.

"Yeah," Remy said sheepishly. "Turns out I had a few hidden talents I didn't know about. When those witches turned me into . . . this bundle of sexual magnetism"—he motioned to himself—"they used a spell that basically meant with each life I'd have a different power. Don't know what any of them are until I die, though, so, you know, yay for me."

"That's good," I said, not really sure what else to say.

"Honestly, it's a bit weird," Remy said. "The human thing too. I'm basically immortal as a human, but I'm also . . . human. So I can't do fuck all except look like everyone else. Turns out I prefer being a foxman. I like my bushy tail and my senses and the fact that I look nonthreatening and then stab people. Also, and I don't know if you know this, but being a human is not much fun. Even one who is seemingly impervious to harm."

"Just spent two years being human," I said. "It sucked."

Remy gave me the thumbs-up. "But now you're back and ready to incinerate people."

"Not specifically," I said. "So did I miss anything else while I was away?"

The following hour was a barrage of information as everyone told me everything that had happened since I'd become human. The world had changed, old friends had fallen in battle, and new ones had joined the cause. By the time we'd reached Portland, I was pretty much ready to drink whiskey and try to absorb all the information I'd been bombarded with. Unfortunately, as we landed on a helipad on the roof of Elemental Incorporated, I got the feeling that taking some time to myself wasn't going to happen in the near future.

We were met by Medusa, Isis, and a host of armed guards, including Antonio, who had been given an HK416 and a set of combat armor. When everyone was gathered, we were led to a large meeting room.

"How are things?" Antonio asked me as we walked side by side.

I told him about what had happened in Clockwork.

He stopped walking. "Shit," he said, his voice low and emotional. "Brooke didn't deserve that. The town didn't deserve that!"

"No," I said. "They didn't. So you're working for these guys now?"

"I made a deal," Antonio said. "I help them out during the protests, and they all come order food from a newly refurbished Duke's. Also, it's nice to be doing what I was trained to do. I didn't realize I missed it."

Antonio walked off to do his job, leaving me sitting beside Selene and Tommy as Daniel came over to talk to me. He appeared to be quite sprightly considering his recent injuries. Jess had already gone to see her son, and I doubted there was any part of the conversation that was about to be had that she wanted to take part in.

"Your friend Mordred is quite the healer," Daniel said.

"Yeah, he's got a talent for it," I said. Mordred's light magic allowed him to heal in minutes wounds that would take much longer to heal with normal medicine. Unfortunately, it took a lot out of him to do it, and it worked best on humans, as someone else's magical power sometimes interfered with it. Sometimes I thought that Mordred tried to do too much to make up for all the centuries *he'd* been the bad guy.

"Thank you for what you did in Clockwork," Daniel said, grinning and shaking my hand with vigor. "For finding us, for stopping Robert."

"No thanks needed," I said, retrieving my hand from Daniel's over-enthusiastic shake. He looked like he'd been given some pain meds for whatever had happened to him during his stay with Robert and his Nazi friends. "I was never going to let you guys stay in Robert's hands. And he couldn't be allowed to live. He would have just come back. People like him always do. They don't think they're doing anything wrong. Bit like Baldr and Arthur, to be honest."

Daniel beamed. "Good to hear. No one deserves to be in the company of people like Baldr and Robert."

"Couldn't agree more," I said. I hoped that the grendels near Clockwork would be safe and manage to live their lives free from any more contact with Avalon's cronies. "You staying or going to see Donna and your family?"

"I'm going," Daniel said, waving over at Hades, who smiled and nodded in his direction. Daniel slapped me on the shoulder and grinned at me. "Don't get dead, Nate."

"I don't plan on it," I promised.

Daniel left the room, and I took a moment to look around at Hades, Persephone, Medusa, and Mordred, who were all deep in conversation at the far end of the room.

Isis sat down next to Selene and Tommy. "Nate Garrett has returned," she said with a smile. She kissed Selene on the cheek before doing the same to Tommy. "It's good to see you both again."

"What's the long, pointed conversation about?" Tommy asked. "And what are you over here to ask for?"

Isis clutched her hands to her chest in mock indignation. "Why, whatever do you mean?" she said in her best southern-belle accent.

"Isis, it's been a long day," Selene said. "So you'll excuse my bluntness when I say *get on with it.*"

"A few hours ago, we received intel from Hades's people, who discovered that a few of Avalon's spies have been moving into the city over the last few days," Isis said. "These are humans with the ITF, and they've been working within organizations around the world who are arranging protests against Avalon. Several of the same people have been seen at multiple protests, which turn into riots or worse. And three of them are in this city."

"Nice to see Big Brother coming in handy once in a while," Tommy said. "How did you track them?"

"Turns out Hades has people inside the ITF, which no one knew about," Isis said, sounding slightly irritated.

"That's the problem when you get a whole bunch of different organizations fighting against one cause, but none of the smaller groups share info," I said. "We need to come together on this. All of us under one banner."

"Agreed," Isis said. "But that's a problem for tomorrow. Right now, we have about six hours until these protests are due to start. And then, according to the intel that Nate has supplied, all hell is going to break loose."

"Okay," I said, doing the math in my head. "I have about nine hours before my power levels subside to a whole lot less than I currently have access to. Baldr is going to be in hiding until the protests start so as to ensure he's not stopped or delayed. He's using the protests as a way to cover his own need to find his mother, so keep an eye on him. If he finds out where she is—and at the moment I'm not convinced he really knows her location—he will come here in the confusion. Unfortunately, that means I'm going to have two or three hours to find and stop Baldr. That's not long."

"Thankfully, we have a plan," Isis said.

"It involves me, doesn't it?" I asked.

Isis nodded. "Yep. That's sort of why Mordred and Medusa are currently in a very heated whisper over in the corner. You see, Baldr knows who your father is, and he hates your father . . . his father . . . you know what I mean. We're going to put the word out that you know where Frigg is."

"I do know that," I said. "You showed her to me."

"Yes, but he doesn't know that, does he?" Isis asked.

"No," I agreed.

"You want to use Nate as bait?" Tommy asked.

"Yes," Isis said. "Mordred is against the idea because, well, he thinks Baldr will almost certainly try to kill you again. In a populated area."

"But I need to be seen at the protest so he knows it's not a trap," I said. "So the trick is getting Baldr away from a populated area once he knows I'm there."

"We want to put you at the head of the protest," Isis said. "Mordred isn't against you being bait—"

"I'm against you being at the head of the protest," Mordred shouted from across the room. He walked over to me. "You won't just be painting a target on your head for Baldr to hit; you'll be painting a target for Arthur, Hera, Merlin, Gawain, and anyone else who wants you dead. There will be news cameras there, Nate."

"Everyone will know I'm alive," I said.

"And in seven hours your powers are going to drop to levels low enough that you can't beat them. You're going to be vulnerable for the next, I don't know, maybe five years until they increase back to your full potential. And there's nothing we can do to keep you safe for five years. It's great that you're back, Nate, but if you go on camera to tell the world you're back, Avalon is going to try and crush us like bugs."

"They've already been trying to crush us," Selene said. "We literally went to war to stop them."

"Okay, fair point," Mordred said. "They'll try to crush Nate. Arthur *hates* you. Hera *hates* you even more. You don't think they're going to go all scorched earth on this planet and any other realm to find you?"

"What was Hades's idea?" I asked.

"We could hide you away once your powers lessened," he said.

"No," I said.

"But—" he started.

"No," I interrupted. "I will not have people fighting and dying to keep me hidden. It's one thing that everyone believes I'm dead, but it's quite another to try and stop people from actively hunting me."

"There's another option," Persephone said, running a hand through her long dark hair. "It is not a great option. In fact, it's probably untested, highly dangerous, and could do who knows what worth of damage to your body and mind."

"Awesome selling approach," Remy said, putting his thumbs up. "Don't know about you, Nate, but I'd like to have a go after you're done."

I had a pretty good idea what Persephone was suggesting, as it was also what I'd been considering. "Harbinger trials," I said.

Persephone nodded.

"Have you all lost your minds?" Tommy asked. "Nate went through them once before; he can't go through them again."

"Actually, he might be able to," Diana said. She'd been lying down on a beanbag chair with her eyes closed. She looked over at me and winked.

"How?" Mordred asked.

"Because I died," I said.

Diana nodded. "It's just a theory, because everything in our lives is just a theory until someone stupid enough tries it, but yes, he died. Therefore he might be able to go through it again."

"That's my hypothesis too," Persephone said. "We have some evidence that Arthur has gone through the process since his return, and that's why he hasn't been seen in two years. It's not concrete because those who tend to him are loyal to the last, but it's pretty likely."

"Arthur didn't die," Tommy said.

"But he was comatose," Mordred said. "Do we know if he went through the process before?"

Medusa nodded. "I know for a fact that he did, because Merlin told me. This was back before Merlin was Arthur's own personal fanboy, but he definitely went through it."

"And Nate was conceived using a similar ritual," Selene said. "Mordred, you never wanted to try the process?"

Mordred shook his head. "I went through it once. Just after I nearly killed Arthur and put him in a coma. Spent about a century there to try and hide away from everyone who wanted to find me. After I died and recovered my mind, I decided that going through it again might unlock things in my head I'd rather stayed locked. Like memories . . . and desires to murder everyone who took pleasure in breaking me."

"Don't you want to kill them all anyway?" Remy asked.

"Yes," Mordred admitted. "But I also want to keep people safe. I'm not singularly focused."

"Okay, so it's *possible*," I said. "And we're going to try it. I don't want any more arguing about what *I* will and won't be doing. I've been out of action for too long, and frankly I'd rather get Baldr to come to me. Which I really don't think is going to be a problem." I turned to Medusa. "Can you guys really let Baldr and his people know that I'm aware of Frigg's location?"

"Already being set in motion," Medusa said. "We couldn't wait for everyone to agree."

"Good thing I'm okay with it, then," I said. I didn't blame Medusa for moving ahead with the plan. I'd rather be the target than thousands of innocent people.

"So this grendel-blood thing they've got planned," Diana said. "Any idea how they're going to disperse it?"

"Out in the open, I'm not sure," I said. "Maybe canisters again, but I think they want something with a higher chance of success when the wind could blow it all the wrong way."

"We're just going to have to keep an eye out and hope that we can grab people who show the first signs of impending psychosis," Selene said. "I assume that Medusa and Isis will be deploying their entire security personnel."

Medusa and Isis shared a glance. "We have a few hundred people in and around Portland who can help," Isis said. "We'd have had more, but we couldn't get that many people here in time."

"And we'll have to leave a contingency here to protect the humans and Frigg," Medusa said. "We're not exactly a military organization."

"It'll be fine," I said, getting to my feet. "Right now, we have a few hours before we're ready to go. Eat, sleep, go shoot video game things, watch a film—I don't care. Just be ready to go when that protest starts. I want all of you up front with me. Anyone not in this room should be deployed throughout the protest, but if Baldr sees me, he'll come for me, and anyone around me will be in danger."

"That means us," Remy said. "You want us to be in danger?"

"Aren't you glad you came and found me?" I asked with a smile.

"No," Remy said. "I'm beginning to wish I'd had a prior engagement or gone with Layla and company. I bet they're having a lot more fun than we're about to have."

Chapter Twenty-Six

LAYLA CASSIDY

Realm of Jotunheim

It took Zamek some time to use his alchemy power to tunnel through the rock where the rune had been drawn, destroying the rune in the process and, Layla hoped, putting an end to whatever awful thing Fuvos had planned.

Tego and Kase took point inside the mountain, and Zamek practically had to be restrained to keep him from rushing off.

The heat inside the mountain was nowhere near what Layla had expected, considering that, at best guess, Fuvos had restarted a dormant volcano. And after a few minutes of walking, the team ended up in a large tunnel inside the mountain range.

"What is this?" Layla asked. "I can feel traces of metal all around us."

"I don't know," Jidor said, looking over at the elder, who looked to be as confused as anyone else.

"This was dwarves," Zamek said.

The tunnel was thirty feet high and large enough to put two trains in side by side. The rock was red inside the tunnel, and someone had placed rune-powered lanterns every ten feet or so.

"Why would anyone need this?" Hyperion asked.

"Let's follow it and find out," Tarron said, setting off down the tunnel.

"I'm not sure that wandering blindly down tunnels where enemy giants are is necessarily the best idea," Harry said, being the voice of reason.

"He has a point," Layla said. "We don't even know the route."

Tego sniffed the ground and pawed at the stone.

"You want us to go this way?" Layla asked.

Tego snorted.

"I smell fresh air this way," Kase said, taking a long sniff. "That way, I don't smell anything."

The team decided to follow Tarron, who was already making good progress up the tunnel. After ten minutes of walking, the fresh air became more prominent, and a strong breeze rushed through the tunnel. Two minutes later, they were outside, standing atop the rock where they'd originally seen the rune.

Layla took a step closer to the edge and looked down at the ground where they'd been standing not too long ago. It was on fire.

"Whatever is happening, destroying that rune didn't stop it," Zamek said. "There must be more of them. Probably dozens spread out around the mountain and volcano. How far back is the volcano from here?"

"For you, a day or so walk," Jidor said. "It's in the middle of the mountains, but there's no straight way to it. The old paths were destroyed by—"

"Fuvos," Tisor said. "He had them brought down so as to ensure that no one was hurt in the constant rockfalls that were happening. That was a few centuries ago. He put together an archaeological team of giants to keep an eye on the volcano and ensure that it maintained a healthy level of power output."

"Apparently, it did a bit more than that," Zamek said.

"I think we need to keep going," Kase said, pointing over to the mouth of another tunnel at the top of a slope from where they stood.

The tunnel was smaller than the one they'd walked along before, but it was set up in a similar way, with rune-based lighting and loose rock and dirt on the ground. About a hundred feet inside it, everyone stopped.

"What the hell is that?" Harry asked, pointing to a shimmering mass on the tunnel wall.

"I don't know," Zamek said, looking closely at the black and gray swirls that moved around the four-by-five-foot piece of wall.

"Let's keep moving," Layla said. "Who knows what Fuvos has done in the time it's just taken us to get here."

The end of the tunnel opened into a huge chamber with a wooden bridge suspended above a fall of several hundred feet onto some very unpleasant-looking rocks. The bridge was wide enough for a giant to walk comfortably along it, but no one looked particularly eager to be the first person to test it out.

Layla took a step onto the first wooden panel and held on to the rope on one side as she moved onto the second panel. "It's four hundred feet long," Layla said. "Don't run it; just move at a nice easy pace."

"You get a few more along, and we'll join you," Hyperion said.

Tego was next to join her on the bridge, the panther looking suspiciously at the wooden panels with every step. She stayed directly in the center of the bridge, pausing to see how Layla was doing, and snorted at her.

"I'm going," Layla told her.

It took a few minutes for everyone to get to the other side of the bridge, and relief was etched on all their faces.

"I'd rather not come back this way," Kase said. "I know I'd survive the fall, but I don't really want to test the theory."

"I can *fly*, and I hated every second of it," Hyperion said with a shiver.

The tunnel from there led back outside, although on the adjacent side of the mountain to where they'd been. Snow had settled on a set of steps that led farther up into the mountains.

"What's up there?" Layla asked.

"An old temple," Jidor said.

"It's where the high priests go on pilgrimage," Tisor explained. "It's a holy site."

"Not today, it isn't," Zamek said, starting up the stone steps as the wind whipped around them.

"This is most irregular," Tisor said.

"Yes, but if Fuvos is hiding in this place, hoping you won't come here because of its religious sentiment to you, he's making a mockery of your beliefs. He's already done that just by lying to you all for so long."

Tisor nodded, but Layla could tell she wasn't thrilled about the idea of climbing up the steps herself.

"If you want to stay here, you can," Layla said.

"No," Tisor replied with a shake of her head. "I need to face him. To know why."

Layla ran to catch up with the others, while Tisor followed behind at her own pace. Layla knew she couldn't blame her for not wanting to be somewhere she wasn't meant to go, but whatever Fuvos's plan was—and if he was planning on merging two realms, it could be disastrous—he needed to be found before more died.

The steps and temple at the top had been carved out of the mountains themselves, using a ridge joining two peaks that towered over the group as a means of moving from one to the other in relative safety. They were hundreds of feet above the ground at this point, and Layla could easily see the city they'd left not that long ago.

They were halfway there when the earth began to shake. At first it was a small tremor, nothing to be concerned about, just something to make everyone hurry a little. But it escalated, becoming more violent in moments. Rocks high above them tumbled down the mountains, narrowly missing the path they were on.

Hyperion and Kase joined forces to create a massive sheet of ice that sat ten feet above their heads. Rocks continued to fall, occasionally striking the ice and causing chunks of it to fall over the side of the path, but none of the stones hit anyone.

The group was flat-out sprinting by the time they'd reached the temple, and three giants rushed out to meet them, swinging huge clubs. Hyperion froze one club in place, allowing Kase to run up it and dive onto the giant's face. The second quickly found himself preoccupied with an exceptionally pissed-off Zamek while Tego ran toward the giant at full pelt, and the third charged straight at Layla, punching Jidor in the face as he ran past.

Layla changed her metal arm into a razor-sharp whip, mixing in the silver from the dagger in the sheath she wore, which made her arm feel as though it were too close to an open oven. Layla ignored the discomfort, swinging the whip toward the legs of the giant just as Jidor punched him back, knocking him off balance. The whip wrapped around his leg, causing him to scream in pain as it cut into his flesh. Layla moved the pieces of the metal around his leg, faster and faster, like a chainsaw, then pulled back on the whip, and the giant's lower leg was torn free. He stumbled back, and a well-placed kick from Jidor sent him over the side of the path, crying out as he fell.

The other two giants were already dead as Layla recreated the arm, removing all traces of silver from it to create the dagger too. She gritted her teeth at the last bit. Taking the silver into her arm had been considerably easier than removing it.

"You okay?" Tarron asked Layla, wiping his bloodstained sword on a cloth that turned out to be a piece of the giant's tunic.

Layla nodded. "You?"

"Kase got thrown into a wall, which I think did more to anger her than hurt, but by the time she'd torn out the giant's throat, I'd stabbed it through the heart. As far as teams go, we appear to be working much better together."

Harry walked up the steps to the white stone columns that sat at the entrance of the temple.

"Harry, move back," Tarron said.

Harry didn't need to be told twice and stepped back down the stairs.

"You see that, Zamek?" Tarron asked.

"I did," Zamek said.

"You feel like filling in the rest of the crowd?" Layla asked.

"Runes," Zamek said. "They flashed when Harry moved toward them."

Harry moved away at a quicker pace. "You think they're a bomb?" he asked, the words tumbling out of his mouth all at once.

"No," Zamek said. "If they were, we'd all be dead, as would the giants when they left." He ascended the stairs and knelt beside one of the columns, where a purple rune flickered.

"It safe?" Kase shouted.

"Yes," Zamek said. "It's essentially a doorbell."

"So Fuvos knows we're here?" Jidor asked.

"I get the feeling he's known for a while," Layla said, walking up the stairs, past Zamek, and into the temple.

The temple itself got taller the farther in you went. The walls were decorated with murals that were partially covered in gold, and there was a large area in the center of the temple that was sunken into the white brick floor and filled with water. A cool breeze came through the open wooden windows that sat at the top of each wall, and the incense that burned made Layla think of Christmas cooking. Behind a large stone table at the far end was a set of double doors that were five times larger than Layla was. Runes adorned the doors, and Zamek ran over to read them. He stopped next to the stone table and looked under it.

"Shit," he whispered, his voice echoing around the temple.

"What's wrong?" Layla asked as she joined him and everyone else entered the building.

"These are dwarven," he said. "They say *Help us*. There's no power in them, just two words. Written in haste, by the looks of it."

"We'll find them," Layla promised.

Tarron and Hyperion stood before the large doors. "So we need to get this open," Tarron said. "Is it booby trapped?"

"No," Zamek said after glancing over at the door. "It says *Welcome, guests*."

"Well, that's not at all creepy," Kase said as Hyperion pushed open the doors with a creak, allowing a rush of air into the temple.

"Where does that go?" Layla asked Tisor.

"No idea," she said. "There's not meant to be anywhere else up here to go. The path to the volcano is on the ground floor around to the side of the mountain range. Up here is just the temple."

"They remodeled, then," Harry said.

The team all left the temple and found more stairs, these ones created out of the very mountain, leaving a thin layer of rock to protect them from the elements. They followed them up for several minutes until the steps opened out to a large space containing a second temple.

"That's gigantic," Jidor said.

"It looks like an old Roman palace," Hyperion said.

"Someone clearly has a high opinion of himself," Kase said.

"Dwarves made this," Zamek said, his voice tense as they went closer to the palace. "I can tell. There are runes inside the stone. They blaze with power."

"What do they do?" Layla asked, looking up at the dozen stone columns of white and red and the deep-red stone that made up the exterior walls of the palace. The hundred-foot-high walls of the building hid the group from the view of anyone below.

"Provide warmth, protection from the elements, that kind of thing," Zamek said.

"Should we go say hello, then?" Tarron asked.

"You go," Layla said. "I'm going to climb up and see if I can figure out how to get in from up there. I want to check for traps or anything we can use to our advantage."

"I'll come with you," Zamek said. "These walls look easy enough to climb for a dwarf."

The pair started to climb the nearby wall away from the palace, watching as their friends walked inside to face whatever Fuvos had planned. The climb itself was simple enough, Layla's metal arm allowing her to scale the stone with ease behind Zamek, who created holds with every touch of his hands to the surface.

They'd scaled a hundred feet at almost a complete vertical when they reached a spot where they had to swing toward the roof of the palace. Zamek had wanted to stay away from the palace walls in case any runes in them disliked being manipulated by his alchemy, but that meant having to make it over the thirty-foot gap between where they held on and where the roof of the palace started.

"I'm going to go up onto the ceiling of the cavern," Zamek said. "This will be tricky, even with your arm to help you. Hope you've been doing arm day at the gym."

"Just get on with it," Layla said through gritted teeth.

Zamek went first, using his alchemy power with every touch to change the wall into hand- and footholds exactly where he needed them. The sound of battle erupted from below, making Layla want to hurry, but she knew that doing so would mean greatly increasing the possibility of falling. So she remained behind Zamek and took to the roof of the mountain cavern, edging her way across until they were directly over the palace roof. Layla anchored her metal arm into the stone, manipulated it into a lengthy metal rope, and slowly lowered herself to the red-tiled roof before remaking the arm.

There was a gap in the roof that let Zamek and Layla look over the edge down on the battle that their friends were waging against . . . blood elves.

"I thought they were all dead," Zamek said.

"They soon will be," Layla told him, attaching her arm to the wood and stone that sat around the opening and beginning to lower herself inside the temple. It looked like their allies were winning. Fuvos stood behind a dais, commanding his troops to "kill the intruders," and fourteen dwarves huddled in the corner. They were dirty, wore only rags, and were malnourished in appearance, and the sight of them increased the anger inside Layla, who released the anchor she'd created and fell thirty feet before using the arm as a whip to catch one of four huge pillars at the end of the temple and swinging down toward Fuvos. The giant didn't look up until the last second, and Layla barreled into him feetfirst, causing him to stagger back.

The roof of the temple tore apart, creating steps for Zamek to run down, screaming words in Dwarvish that Layla was pretty sure would have made Remy blush. He dived onto Fuvos as he got back to his feet, driving his ax into the giant's chest.

Fuvos grew in size and swatted Zamek aside, sending him flying across the temple into a batch of blood elves, who quickly discovered that an angry dwarf was no one they wanted to be close to.

Layla got back to her feet and breathed out slowly, taking in the large number of runes that had been painted on the walls forty feet above her head. One of them was larger than Layla and pulsated power.

"When you arrived, I didn't know why you were here," Fuvos said. "And there was no way to kill you all and keep my secrets hidden. But sending you to Mimir and sending those guards to remove you all was meant to end you as a problem."

"And when I kill you, that problem will stop," Layla told him. "You have dwarven *slaves*."

"Of course," he said. "After the dwarven civil war, many came here. I gave them over to the flame giants but kept a few for myself. They built me great things."

The floor beneath Layla's feet began to shimmer much like the rock wall had done earlier, and she threw herself back in case it exploded, which caused Fuvos to laugh.

"Part of the realm of Muspelheim will soon be transported to this realm. Just a small piece, enough to fill this temple. When it works, we will then move on to bringing the whole realm here. My flame giant brethren will lay waste to Jotunheim and bring about the coming of Ragnarok and end Odin's reign. Avalon will reward us, and the flame giants will take their rightful place at Arthur's side."

"You're delusional," Tisor said, running into Fuvos and punching the high priest in the face with a fist that was the same size as Layla.

Tisor had grown to forty feet by the time she kicked Fuvos in the chest, sending him flying up against the far wall. "Get the dwarves," she shouted.

Layla didn't need to be told twice. She ran over to the dwarves, all of whom appeared to be transfixed by Zamek as he cut through several blood elves.

"Prince Zamek?" one of the dwarves asked.

"Long story," Layla said. "Right now, let's get you all out of here."

Layla avoided the swipe of a blade by a blood elf, turning her arm into a blade and absorbing the silver dagger before spinning around and catching the elf across the midriff, opening his belly. Layla plunged the tip of her blade into his skull as she walked past with the dwarves and flicked the blood free before parrying the strike of a second blood elf, who was knocked to the ground and had his head torn off by Tego before Layla could kill him.

"So, blood elves," Kase said as the giant cat finished with its prey. "They suck."

"Always have," Layla told her. "Get the dwarves out of here. I'm going to check on Tisor."

Layla turned back to watch the high priest and elder fight at the far end of the temple, each blow sending one of them into a wall or column, tearing off chunks of stone in the process. The temple wasn't made for two giants of over forty feet in height going at it like they were in a boxing ring.

Jidor joined the fray, but Fuvos held his own against the pair. The walls had started to shimmer as the last of the blood elves were killed. One of the dwarves broke away and sprinted across the floor, avoiding Zamek and picking up a blood elf sword to throw at Fuvos like a spear. Fuvos shrank, allowing it to sail over his head and into Tisor's throat.

The high priest grew in height an instant later, catching a surprised Jidor in the jaw with an uppercut before punching Tisor in her wounded throat.

"Get those giants to shrink," Layla shouted to the others. "Not Fuvos. Hyperion, no flying. Everyone stay on the ground."

"You have a plan?" Zamek asked.

"You remember what you told me about breaking runes? What happens when these ones break?"

"I don't know."

Layla smiled and turned her arm into a long spear as Hyperion, Kase, Tarron, and Zamek brought the fight to Fuvos, who remained large as he tried to fight them off. Jidor was semiconscious on the floor of the temple, and Tisor had slumped to a seated position as blood poured from the wound in her throat. She began to shrink in size, making the wound even larger as Layla threw the spear of silver, titanium, and steel at the large pulsating rune. As it hit, she tore the metal apart, razor-sharp spikes ripping through the stone.

At first, Layla thought that she'd been wrong, that eliminating the rune had done nothing. But there was a flash from the wall, and then everything twenty feet above her head vanished in a rush of noise and power. One minute the temple had a roof, and the next there was nothing, including the top fifteen or so feet of Fuvos. The remains of the giant fell wetly to the ground next to Tisor, who Harry rushed over to check on. He shook his head as Jidor sat next to her. The giant guard wept at the death of her elder.

"I'm sorry," Layla said.

"She will be buried with honor," Jidor said, picking Tisor up and carrying the dead elder over her shoulder.

"Let's get back to the city," Hyperion said as there was a deep rumble from somewhere above them. "I think we need to leave. Now."

The first pieces of rock falling from the top of the cavern hit just as they emerged from the temple, and soon after they were sprinting through collapsing tunnels, with Tego and Jidor helping to carry several of the dwarves.

Zamek and those dwarves who could help managed to keep everything together so that everyone could leave the mountain, but as soon as they were all out, there was a landslide, and one entire part of the mountain fell away as the volcano erupted.

Chapter Twenty-Seven

LAYLA CASSIDY

Realm of Jotunheim

"We couldn't leave the mountain," one of the dwarves told the team, lifting his tattered tunic to show the black blood curse mark on his stomach. It was fading. "We kept the volcano inactive. You destroying the palace set us free."

"That might have been information to tell us *before* we started running away," Tarron said.

"What were we going to do?" Zamek asked. "We couldn't have left them there."

"Of course not," Tarron said, his tone softening. "But it would have been nice to know."

They were a few miles away from the volcano, not quite halfway between it and the city of Utgard. Jidor and Harry had gone ahead to tell everyone what was going on—and to take Tisor's body to the other elders—leaving everyone else to try to figure out a way to stop the slowly moving lava that had started to flow out of the cracks in the mountain.

"How long before it reaches the town?" Layla asked.

"At that speed, about six months," Zamek said. "I know lava is slow, but this stuff is moving at a snail's pace."

"There must still be runes inside that release the volcano's full power," a female dwarf said. "Fuvos wanted to use the power of the volcano to bring forth the entire realm of Muspelheim if moving the temple worked."

"Well, on the plus side, it worked for him," Tarron said. "A big piece of him got to go to Muspelheim."

"What is happening?" Kase asked, pointing up to the mountain as large chunks of it shimmered slightly before vanishing.

"What the hell?" Layla asked.

"You disrupted the rune," one of the dwarves said.

"I didn't expect it to make parts of the mountain disappear," Layla almost shouted.

"How do we fix it?" Kase asked.

Several of the dwarves shared a glance before looking back at everyone else and shrugging.

"There will be another rune in Muspelheim," Zamek said. "You can't have energy flowing one way like this. There needs to be a link. You broke the link at this end, but not at Muspelheim."

"So we have to get to Muspelheim and break the link?" Kase asked.

"I'm not sure we can," Tarron said. "I think Muspelheim is coming here."

He pointed at the mountain, where more of it was disappearing, but it was being replaced with black rock that rained down from the sky.

"Okay, so I made it worse," Layla said.

"Define *worse*," Zamek said. "There were more runes around the volcano, yes?" he asked the dwarves.

"Yes, hundreds," one of them told him.

"You broke the rune where the breach was going to take place, Layla," Zamek said. "But in doing so, I think you just stopped the movement of the temple and triggered Fuvos's plan of bringing the realm of Muspelheim to Jotunheim."

"The *entire* realm is coming here?"

Zamek nodded. "Muspelheim is a realm, but it's really just a collection of mountains and volcanos with lakes of lava between them. Everyone who lives there lives in the mountains because it's the safest place. The mountains in front of us are only a small part of the range, which stretches far enough north that if you looked at it from above, it would be like a scar on the land."

Harry returned with Jidor, Wedver, and several other giants, who all wore similar robes and similar expressions of concern.

"Tisor's death will lay heavy on many hearts," Wedver said.

"I'm sorry for your loss," Layla told him. "But right now, we don't really have time to grieve. We have to move out of the way of an erupting volcano as Muspelheim arrives on your doorstep."

The ground shook, and a few hundred meters away, a fountain of flame shot out from it.

"That was both cool and horrific," Harry said.

Everyone started to move back toward the city. "Can we stop it?" Layla asked the elders.

"It was foretold that the flame giants would come back," Wedver said. "Fuvos and the other high priests warned of it."

"Right," Tarron said. "I'm not big on prophecies, especially when it's provided by someone trying to make it happen, so let's just ignore that. How do we get to Muspelheim so we can remove the rune and stop this?"

"We would have to access the dwarven realm gate," Wedver said. "It has not been used in centuries. I'm not even sure it is usable."

"Time to find out," Zamek said. "Lead the way, because either we get to Muspelheim and stop this, or you're going to have some new neighbors."

The streets of the town were packed with giants, most of whom were watching the unfolding disaster with fear. Huge plumes of smoke had started to rise out of the volcano, darkening the sky and giving a general apocalyptic vibe. It wasn't exactly how Layla had imagined she'd be spending her day, but then she'd thought that most days since becoming an umbra.

The dwarven realm gate was deep underground, beneath one of the council buildings that sat in the center of the town. Layla lost count of the number of guards who had to be waved away as the group walked through the ornate wooden building, descending the huge number of stairs to a temple underground.

"There sure are a lot of temples in giant culture," Harry said.

"They're good for storing lots of different things you don't want the average citizen to bugger around with," Zamek said. "Also, they look pretty."

Tego rubbed her head against Layla's hand and purred slightly. She didn't like being this far underground, understandable considering the beginning of her life had been deep underground in the care of blood elves.

"This is masterful," Zamek said, walking over to the dwarven realm gate, which was three times larger than any Layla had seen before.

"How can we get it working?" one of the dwarves asked. "There are runes missing. And this destination isn't set to Muspelheim—it's Earth."

Zamek nodded, but Layla wasn't entirely sure he was listening. "The gate is badly damaged, but it'll take me about an hour with the other dwarves' help. Tarron, you think you can get anyone who needs to evacuate out of here and back to Helheim?"

Tarron nodded. "You think we'll need to?"

Zamek shrugged slightly. "Well, if this doesn't work or we can't destroy the rune in Muspelheim, then everyone in this town is well and truly fucked."

Harry accompanied Tarron and the contingent of giant elders back upstairs. Layla hoped the evacuation wouldn't be necessary, but it was worth activating the elven realm gate they'd come through, just in case.

"Anything we can do?" Layla asked.

"No," Zamek said, already using his alchemy to shift the stone and wood of the realm gates. Layla knew he wasn't being rude; he was just concentrating on what needed to be done.

"How is he doing this?" one of the dwarves asked.

"He figured out how to change the destination of any dwarven gate," Layla said. "Ancient dwarven runes, or something like that. It's not a permanent change, but it's enough. Also, we found out that all of the dwarven realm gates are linked to the great tree Yggdrasil. Apparently, the wood that intertwines with the stone is from the tree; it's what gives it the power."

As if on cue, the dwarven gate began to hum and glow a light-blue color before stopping.

"All okay?" Layla asked.

"Yes," Zamek said. "I think I know how to get this to work."

"You know the Muspelheim address?" Kase asked him.

"It's there," Zamek said, pointing to a list of runes that sat on the wall behind the realm gate.

Layla walked over with Wedver and Kase, looking at the wall full of dwarven runes. "Are all of these addresses?" Hyperion asked.

"Yep," Zamek said, almost absentmindedly. "Although most are incomplete, like they were rushed for time. The one for Muspelheim, Earth, Helheim, and a few others are there, though."

No one asked any more questions for some time as Zamek directed the other dwarves to move and change parts of the realm gate as he needed. Occasionally they made mistakes, but Zamek was never angry or upset and remained quietly patient in explaining what was required, even when it was apparent that they were slightly awestruck by the fact that at one point he'd been a member of their royal family.

When it was done, the realm gate glowed bright yellow. "Muspelheim awaits," he said. He turned to the fourteen dwarves. "You cannot come with us. You are tired, hurt, and need treatment and rest."

"But my lord—" one of them began.

"I *am not* your lord," Zamek said strongly. "I am a dwarf like any other. But I am more experienced in these matters, and I haven't been used as a slave for centuries. You will go through to Helheim, you will join the other dwarves there, and you will help our people flourish once again. I will find those responsible for what has happened, and I will see that justice is done."

The dwarves bowed their heads, but one of them—a female with a scar on the side of her head—walked over to Zamek and shook his hand. "Thank you," she said. "For all of us."

"Go; be safe," Zamek said.

"The elven realm gate is operating on its own," Harry said as he ran back into the temple.

"How long will it operate like that?" Layla asked.

"A few hours," he said. "Hel and a dozen guards are currently at the site we blew up. She said something about how she was meant to be on holiday, and Tarron explained what was happening. Giants are already fleeing through. We won't be able to get the whole city evacuated in a few hours, but it gives you time. Tarron has to stay here, though; that's the burden of being the only shadow elf."

"You're staying too," Kase told him firmly. "You know about dwarven runes; you know how to get them to work, even if you can't operate them yourself." She walked over to Harry and kissed him on the lips. "And I want you *safe*."

"There's a volcano here," Harry said. "It exploded."

"The entire realm of Muspelheim is lava," Zamek said.

"He makes a good point," Harry said, kissing Kase. "Get back here soon."

Zamek activated the realm gate, and the remainder of the team, half a dozen giant guards, and Jidor, who had been relatively quiet since returning to the city, moved through the gate into Muspelheim.

"You okay?" Layla asked Jidor when they were on the other side. They were in a temple that looked identical to the one they'd just left, although it was noticeably warmer, and there was no roof. The red-and-orange sky was clear for all to see.

"A high priest betrayed us all and is now dead. Surtr wishes to invade my home with his flame giants, and the volcano is erupting, threatening to destroy everything I love anyway. It's a lot to take in."

"We'll save the day," Kase said. "It's what we do."

Layla left the temple and looked across the realm of Muspelheim. The group was standing on top of a mountain that was hundreds of feet above the ground. When they looked down toward the expanse of lava below, the air had a heat shimmer, and occasionally huge geysers of flame would shoot up in the distance.

"No wonder the people here want to move," Layla said.

"The dwarves told me that the rune is to the north," Zamek said. "It's closer to us than the similar rune was in Jotunheim. It's a spatial thing, and honestly I've had it explained to me, and I still don't get it."

"Like Doctor Who's TARDIS?" Kase asked.

"I don't know what that is," Hyperion said.

Kase's eyes lit up, and for the next twenty minutes, Hyperion was regaled with tales of the mysterious Doctor Who, Daleks, and anything else she could think of. Hyperion, for his part, appeared to find the whole thing fascinating, but then he'd been stuck in a realm with no TV, radio, or forms of entertainment other than plays for the better part of five thousand years, and TV appeared to be the one thing that he was constantly both bemused and intrigued by.

Layla actually found it to be a fairly pleasant walk up the gentle slope to a second temple, almost identical to the one they'd just left. It was at the front of what appeared to be a village built on top of the mountain, where the air was cooler as it was partially above the clouds. It began to rain as they got closer, turning the loose dirt on the path to mud pretty quickly, and by the time they'd actually reached the temple walls, Layla was grateful they didn't have to continue the climb, for fear of sliding off the edge of the cliff.

"I don't smell anyone," Kase said after changing into her werewolf beast form. "I've been around flame giants before. They smell."

Hyperion, who had already transformed into his dragon-kin form, froze the wall, and Kase punched it. Tego was the first into the temple, followed quickly by the rest of the group.

"Ummm," Layla said. "I'm not an expert on bad-guy tactics, but shouldn't there be someone here?"

The rune pulsated on the far wall, and then a rumble outside caught Layla's attention and she turned back to watch a large chunk of a nearby mountain vanish, only to be replaced with white rock from Jotunheim.

Zamek threw his ax into the rune, and the pulsating stopped.

"Did we do it?" Jidor asked.

Layla shrugged and moved to the front of the temple, looking out through the large open doors to the village beyond. The top half of Fuvos lay at the bottom of the temple steps, blood smeared up to where she stood.

"That's really unpleasant," Hyperion said from beside her.

"Where is everyone?" Layla asked no one in particular before taking the steps to the village beyond.

There were a few dozen buildings, all looking much like the ones in Utgard, although these were made with red-and-black stone.

Tego ran through the open doors of several houses but returned with a slight shake of her head to signify there was no one there.

"Okay, this is *weird*," Kase said.

"I was expecting battle," Jidor said. "I was practically aching for battle." She kicked the remains of the high priest.

"Feel better?" Zamek asked.

"No," Jidor admitted.

Kase sniffed the air. "Wait, I have something. Big building to the south of here."

Everyone ran along the dirt road to the building in question, which sat at one end of a large clearing where the ground was covered in dwarven runes.

Zamek drove his ax into a rune, and each one in turn flicked out of existence.

"Well, I smell that," Layla said, putting the crook of her arm over her mouth and nose to try to ward off the stench.

"Sweet lord," Kase said, spitting onto the floor in disgust. "Dead people."

Layla walked to the large building, the feeling of worry building up inside her. She pulled open one of the large golden double doors and promptly wished she hadn't.

There were piles and piles of bodies inside the building. Some giants, but mostly dwarves.

"What the hell happened here?" Zamek asked, taking a step into the building before dropping to his knees.

The dwarves appeared to be wearing a similar style of clothing to those they'd found working for Fuvos, although with the amount of blood that was inside the building, it was hard to make out anything with much fine detail.

Layla moved back into the courtyard and looked up at a huge black stone monolith that had dwarven runes written upon it. On the side facing away from the building of death, the runes had been traced over in blood. It was still wet. The stone shimmered, and she immediately changed her arm into a whip, caught it around the nearest wooden post, and pulled herself away from the stone, which continued to ripple.

"Hello," a voice said from inside the monolith.

"Ummm, who are you?" Layla asked as everyone else rushed over to join her.

"Surtr," the voice said as the shimmering grew until the entire space around the monolith changed, showing a giant wearing red-and-gold armor and carrying a massive sword. The giant's skin slowly pulsed red and orange.

"You did *this*," Zamek said, throwing a knife at Surtr. The blade hit the portal and harmlessly bounced off.

"You can't come through, I'm afraid," Surtr said calmly. "I saw what you did to Fuvos. You cancelled the rune in Jotunheim and broke the ritual. Fuvos was really counting on us going there and killing you all, but unfortunately for him, turns out I had other ideas."

"You're not in Jotunheim?" Kase asked as Layla studied the rolling hills behind him, the forests and waterfall in the distance.

"You murdered all of those dwarves and giants," Hyperion said.

"Needed the blood," Surtr said in the same tone as if he were talking about needing to buy milk from the shop. "Had to practice on some first, though, just to make sure we got it right."

"Needed the blood?" Layla asked. "You murdered hundreds of innocent people because you *needed* the blood?"

"Slaves," Surtr corrected. "Not people. Slaves."

"I'm going to find you and end you," Zamek said.

"Good. Come find me, Prince Zamek. I've killed many of your bloodline over the centuries; I always hated you royal bastards for thinking you were better than everyone else."

"You feel like telling us where you are?" Jidor asked. "I'd be happy to come find you as quickly as possible."

"Yeah, I'm pretty good with that plan," Kase said.

Surtr laughed. "Jotunheim was *never* the target. I don't much care what happens to the giants, but we needed the power of that volcano's runes to cause a breach between realms. And we found some interesting people to help us." He stepped aside and revealed two rows of twelve shadow elves, kneeling with chains around their necks and their hands manacled. They all kept looking at the stone floor.

"You son of a bitch," Kase said.

"I have no idea who my mother was," Surtr said with a chuckle.

"Why bother telling us all of this?" Layla asked. "Gloating seems especially stupid."

"Because I want you to spread the news of the return of the flame giants," Surtr said. "I want the realms to know that we will lay waste to our enemies. That we will decimate everything before us. That Ragnarok begins *now*. See you soon, little prince." The vision ended.

"We need to get back to Jotunheim," Kase said.

"I saw the landscape behind him; I know where he is," Hyperion said. "We need to hurry."

"Where is he?" Layla asked.

"Asgard," Hyperion told everyone.

Chapter Twenty-Eight

Nate Garrett

After we were all done talking, I went to get a bite to eat, grab a bottle of water, and go to my room with Selene. I had missed her more than I'd ever thought possible, and while we started to talk about everything that had happened in the years we'd been apart, we ended up doing very little talking. Which—I'm not going to lie—I was perfectly okay with.

We took a shower after, and as we were getting dressed, there was a tap at the door, and Diana opened it before either Selene or I was able to say anything. "Five minutes," she said.

"We'll be ready," Selene said.

"Glad to hear it," Diana said and closed the door behind her, leaving us alone again.

"So when this is done, you're really going to go back through the Harbinger trials?" Selene asked casually as she pulled a set of leather armor on.

"Yes," I said. "I have no idea how long I'll be under for, though. The shortest amount of time possible to let me learn the most from my magic."

"It'll be dangerous," she said.

"I know," I told her, lacing up my boots.

"You were gone for two years, Nate," Selene said softly. "That's a long time. I lost myself in battle. I fought every single day. I fought and killed and hurt the enemy, because I just wanted to feel that rage at having lost you. If I'd thought for one second that I'd have to endure that, I never would have agreed to let you go and pretend to be dead. I'd have gone with you, or . . . I don't know. I just . . . it hurt."

"It wasn't meant to," I said, walking around the bed and taking her hands in mine. "The ritual was meant to spare anyone that hurt. I'm sorry it didn't. I'm sorry you went through all of that. I will make that up to you every single day for the rest of my exceptionally long life." I kissed her on the lips. "I'm going to do this Harbinger thing, but I'll be back once it's done."

"Can you kill Baldr?" she asked me. "Honestly. No bravado or bullshit. Can you kill him? Because he sure as hell can kill you if you're not careful."

I nodded. "Yes. Yes, I can kill him."

She wrapped her arms around my waist, brought me toward her, and kissed me on the lips. "I know. I just wanted to hear you say it. Promise me you won't do anything stupid."

I raised an eyebrow in question.

"Fine, more stupid than normal."

"I promise," I told her.

"And that when we're done here, we can take a few days to . . . catch up, before you plunge into a damn simulation of life so you can learn how to use your magic."

I raised my right hand. "I'm sure we can manage something."

"That's not how you swear on your right hand," Selene pointed out.

"You want me to swear on a Bible?"

"You're an atheist."

"Okay, you want me to swear on an issue of *The Amazing Spider-Man*? I'm a hundred percent certain that Tommy has some."

Selene laughed, and the sound went through me, warming my heart.

"I missed that sound."

"You missed a whole bunch of stuff," she said with a sly smile.

"That is also true," I said. "I might need to relearn how to do a few things."

The sly smile intensified. "Oh, I think we can get you up to speed as soon as possible."

"I didn't think it was possible, but I hate Avalon even more for making me leave you here."

"Here next to the bed, or here up against you?"

"Both of those things," I said and kissed her. "Be safe today."

"You too."

She hugged me tightly, and I longed for the day when neither of us had to go to war. Eventually, we left the room and made our way to the exit of the building, where we found the rest of the group. Diana, Mordred, Hades, Persephone, Remy, and Tommy had been joined by Medusa and several members of her security operation, while the majority of them, including Antonio, were staying behind to defend against any threat that might arrive.

"Right, then," I said. "Is this it?"

"We have a few dozen others who will be joining us," Hades said. "But they're already heading toward the protest march to integrate with the crowd, along with a few hundred of Medusa's people. You will be at the head alone with only a few nonhumans at your side. The rest of us will join the protest and blend in. The second Baldr sees me or Persephone there, he might think twice about attacking openly."

"Thank you for that," I said to Medusa.

"I like this town," she told me. "I'd rather it wasn't turned into a bloodbath. Besides, it's been such a long time since I've actually gone and pissed off Avalon; I figured it was something I needed to do."

The entire group climbed into identical black SUVs and set off toward the protest route. None of us carried guns. In fact, while I had a few silver daggers on my belt and Remy had his swords, no one else had much in the way of weapons at all. We didn't need to add to the craziness of what was about to happen with the sound of gunshots. And seeing as how Remy was wearing a coat that was big enough to pretty much cover his entire body, no one was going to see his weapons.

"We had a chance to make Remy up to look like that big bird in Robin Hood when Robin goes to the tournament, and we didn't take it," Diana said. "I'm thinking that's a missed opportunity."

"What are you talking about?" Remy asked.

"Oh, she's comparing you to a Disney character," Mordred said. "I never considered it before, but it's pretty apt."

"So he's like our very own Disney Princess?" Tommy asked.

"A Disney Princess that is more than happy to fuck you up," Remy said from under his hood, which made everyone laugh, easing the tension that had grown inside the car. "However, you're right: I'm going to be a bit noticeable in this march, which is why I'm going to be moving through the buildings and alleyways around it to check for any nasty surprises."

"Today we're going to let the world know that Nate is alive," Tommy said. "We're going to have to get all of our fragmented groups together to fight Avalon. Even with Nate's help, we can't keep going like we have been."

"We'll get the help we need," I said, certain of that fact.

The SUVs pulled up in a car park just behind where the main protest route was going to be marching down. It was just after half past twelve, and the sounds of the people gathering and coming toward us meant that the protest had already begun. No one in the car thought that Avalon would try anything this far out—they'd want to wait until the mass of protesters got to the news cameras that had been set up a mile away.

"We have an issue," Hades said, coming over to us.

"Of course we do," Remy said. "Can't possibly have a mission without something going wrong."

"It would be weird to have clear sailing," Tommy agreed.

"Unnatural, even," Diana said.

"You done?" Hades asked.

Everyone nodded.

"Just before the place this march reaches the large amount of news cameras that are going to be there, the ITF have set up shop. They've brought in a lot of armed personnel."

"How many is 'a lot'?" I asked.

"Forty or fifty from best guess at the moment. They've also placed sharpshooters on rooftops around that area."

"It's almost as if they're looking forward to trouble," Diana said, not bothering to hide her disdain.

"So what's the plan?" I asked.

"Honestly?" Hades asked. "I think we should go ahead as is. If we take them out, we're dangerously close to looking like we're instigating violence in the eyes of any of those TV crews, and frankly I'm not sure we can stop them without innocent people getting hurt."

"So we stick to the plan," I said. "Remy, do me a favor."

Remy threw back his hood. "Sure, what can I do for the mighty son of Odin and Brynhildr?"

"I'm beginning to reconsider having missed you," I said. "You were going to look through the alleyways and the like, but instead, go keep an eye on those snipers. If you think they're going to be a problem, remove the issue. Quietly."

"You say that word like I'm normally incapable of being quiet," Remy said. "Stealth would be my middle name, if I had one, but I don't, so it's not Stealth."

Everyone stared at Remy.

"Yeah, I sort of lost my train of thought there. I'm going."

"He can't do all of that alone," Mordred said.

Hades removed a phone from his pocket and made a call, walking off while he spoke. He returned when he was done. "I've had some of my people help out."

"I'll go with him anyway," Mordred said. "If I see Baldr, there's a chance I might lose my temper."

He walked away, and I caught up with him. "You okay?" I asked.

Mordred nodded. "He enjoyed hurting me. And I had my chance to kill him and couldn't do it."

"Neither of us could kill him," I said. "Even with our magics together, he jumped out of a tower to avoid us."

"I know," Mordred said. "I just . . . I really would like to break him in half. And then send each part to a different country. I don't even know what that means. I just *really* hate him." Mordred started to hum the theme tune to *The Legend of Zelda* under his breath.

"You do that less now," I said.

"I do it when I'm stressed or nervous," he said. "It calms me down. Hey, do you think Baldr has played that *God of War* game I sent you?"

"I really doubt it," I said, recalling the game in question.

Mordred smiled. "In that case, that whole opening scene should be new to him."

I laughed. "Yeah, I'll let you know how that goes."

"Be safe, Nate," he said, grasping my forearm.

"You too, Mordred," I told him. "Don't let Remy blow anything up."

"I'm only one person, Nate," he said before walking off.

"You think he'll be okay?" Diana asked from beside me.

"Remy or Mordred?"

"Both. Either. No, let's go with both."

"Yeah. I think I pity anyone who gets in Mordred's way today. He has some issues he'd like to work out."

"I think by the end of the day, we'll all have gotten out a few frustrations if Avalon's plan comes to fruition. Or we'll be dead. You know, it's one of those."

"You've spent way too much time with Mordred and Remy," I told her.

"You are not the first person to tell me that," Diana said with a grin.

The next twenty minutes were all about preparing for whatever was going to happen next. We waited on the sidewalk as the massive crowd of people came around the corner of the street a few blocks away.

"Holy shit," Tommy said from beside me. "That's a lot of people."

He wasn't wrong. The crowd just kept on coming. A veritable swarm of people that looked as though it were unending. The police had set up barricades along the route, ensuring that cars didn't come anywhere near it and that people couldn't run down the alleyways that sat between several of the large multistory buildings around us. The Willamette River wasn't far from where we stood, and from the planned route of the protest, it looked like the march would keep the river close by the entire time. I hadn't decided if that was a good or bad thing, but it certainly couldn't be worse than whatever Baldr had planned.

"We still don't know how this grendel blood is going to be delivered, yes?" Tommy asked.

"Nope," I said.

"I love it when we all come together to fight something we have no idea how to fight and no idea what they're actually going to do."

"Uncertainty. It's the spice of life," I said.

"You just made that up," Tommy said.

I nodded. "A hundred percent, yes. So how's your daughter?"

"Kase has a boyfriend. Name of Harry. Nice guy."

"You threaten to kill him?"

"No," Tommy said as the din of the crowd grew ever closer. "It's her life. I can be there to help when she needs it, but I can't be helicopter parenting her every move. She's in her twenties now. She's a grown woman. All I can do is hope that Olivia and I have given her all of the tools she'll need to make the right decisions."

"Ah, Tommy, you're all grown up."

Tommy grinned. "See, without you around I had to. You're a bad influence on me."

The crowd stopped beside us and started chanting about how Avalon was evil and killed innocent people. It wasn't what you'd call a catchy chant, although some of the placards that a lot of the people carried were either funny, poignant, or obscene enough to make Remy blush. ARTHUR CAN FUCK HIS OWN SWORD was a particular favorite of mine.

"Avalon equals murder!" a young black woman shouted through a megaphone from the front of the march, followed by cheers of agreement from everyone around her.

We all joined the crowd. Tommy and I managed to get to the front of the protest, while the rest of the group was either right behind us or a few rows back. The protest continued on through the city, moving at a relatively sedate pace and passing several people on the sidewalk who clapped along enthusiastically. Occasionally, there were people shouting abuse, but they were drowned out and soon moved on, presumably to find a computer and get onto whatever internet site they frequented.

We turned a corner of a block, and I spotted the ITF in the distance. They were wearing riot gear, and while there weren't a lot of them, they were carrying guns. You didn't need a lot of people to do a lot of damage if they were all carrying assault rifles.

The protesters stopped fifty feet away from the ITF and began chanting at the Avalon forces, who stood their ground for several seconds until one of them stepped forward and raised a bullhorn to his lips. He remained like that for some time as the chanting grew louder.

Eventually, he spoke. "Go home," he commanded. "Go home to your loved ones. Go home to your lives before we are forced to intervene in this situation."

"We have the right to march," the black woman from earlier shouted.

"We have information that states that you will cause violence," the bullhorn-using soldier said. "You will be treated in the same way as those in other cities when they used violence to carry out their aims. It will not be tolerated. We are authorized to open fire."

At the side of the street were dozens of journalists with cameras, handheld and video, documenting the exchange.

"Go home," the man said again. "We don't need violence here today. No one wants that."

"We are allowed to protest," a middle-aged man shouted back. "You won't stop us."

The crowd broke out in a "You won't stop us" chant, and I felt the air growing thick with tension.

"This is going south," Tommy whispered to me.

"You smell Remy or Mordred?" I asked him.

He raised his head to the sky and took in a good long sniff. The buildings on either side of us were over four stories high, and if Avalon wanted to take shots at the crowd, that was a good place to do it from, but I wasn't convinced that they would do that if they'd planned to sow drug-induced acts of violence throughout the protesters.

"I got Remy," Tommy said. "Top of the building there. I know it's him; he smells . . . distinctive. But there's something else too." He turned around to face the thousands of people behind him just as a scream sounded out, followed quickly by people running to the sides of the street to avoid whatever had happened.

I pushed my way through the crowd, but the second I reached the edge, someone ran at me, snarling and waving a large butcher's knife. Persephone grabbed him by the throat, lifted him into the air, and slammed him down onto the ground, knocking the wind out of him. Earth moved over his body, keeping him in place and ensuring he wasn't a threat.

Two more attackers were subdued by Diana and Persephone and a fourth by Hades, who flicked a young woman on the head, disrupting her spirit and knocking her out. I'd seen it done before, but it was never any less impressive.

"Him," I shouted, pointing to a man in dark clothes walking along the side of the crowd. Tommy ran after him, grabbed him, and removed his hood to reveal a completely nondescript white man with a swastika tattooed on the back of his neck.

Tommy dragged him over to the side of the road as the ITF barked orders to disperse and aimed their weapons at the protesters.

"They expected more fighting," I said. "They look confused that no one has attacked them yet."

"We've got this," Tommy said, putting his foot on the back of the Nazi's head and pushing it against the tarmac. "Go stop a massacre before it starts."

I ran to the front of the crowd, my hands out, hopefully showing no signs of aggression as the crowd behind me continued to chant, although now there was an undertone of fear in the sound.

"My name," I said, using my air magic to take my words to anyone within a few hundred feet of me, "is Nathan Garrett." Several people in the ITF either recognized the name or were concerned about a sorcerer standing in front of them. "These people have done nothing wrong, and those cameras there will show that."

A few of the ITF officers looked over at the journalists as if seeing them and the dozens of innocent bystanders for the first time.

"If you do this, people will die," I said. "No one needs to die here today."

"I disagree," a female voice said from inside the crowd of ITF agents.

The human agents moved aside, showing Adrestia and a dozen Harbingers, all of whom carried similar weaponry to the ITF agents.

"These people are scum," Adrestia shouted, snatching the bullhorn from the ITF guy. "Did you hear me, protesters? You are nothing but *scum*. You are not worthy of standing before us. You are not worthy to breathe our air."

"You always were a blowhard," Selene said from beside me as Diana and Tommy joined us.

"I think that maybe your friends aren't as dangerous as ours are," I said, pointing over to Persephone, Hades, and the others, who had made it to the front of the march. "You can't possibly think that your plan will work if all of these people see you kill innocents."

"These people," Adrestia said, waving at those standing on the streets watching, "will say what I want them to say. Any journalists here work for us. The story will be whatever we decide the story is."

"No," I said. "The story will be how you got all of your people killed."

"Open fire," Adrestia shouted.

The bullets left the assault rifles of the ITF agents closest to her, and I placed a dense shield of air across the entire street between us and them. The bullets hit the air, and several pinged off harmlessly, but some were silver, forcing me to increase the power of my magic to the shield to stop them from going through.

When they were finished, there was complete silence from the crowd behind me. Several people patted me on the back, their smiles and nods wordless thank-yous. I nodded but didn't turn around. Instead, I poured more power into the shield as the Harbingers opened fire again. Their silver bullets tore into the barrier, forcing me to keep flooding more and more power into it as the screams of those behind me became all-encompassing.

If I let the shield falter, not only were the innocent protesters going to die, but my friends would too. Tommy and Diana were werecreatures and would both be killed with silver. The rest of us would fare little better. By the time the firing stopped, I was on my knees, the power flowing out of me forcing the tarmac to crack.

I stared at Adrestia, who smiled. "You can't keep that up all day," she shouted.

"Wasn't going to," I whispered back and released the magic directly in front of me.

The ITF, the Harbingers, and Adrestia were hit by enough air magic to pick them all up and throw them fifty feet away. The power also moved parked cars, tore tree branches free, and swept up anything else that wasn't nailed down. Windows exploded, raining the glass down on our enemies.

I got back to my feet, and Selene was beside me. "You okay?"

I nodded. "Lot of power."

"No shit," Tommy said.

"Anything we can do to help?" Diana asked.

I glanced over at Adrestia as she and the rest of her people struggled to get back to their feet.

I pointed toward our enemies. "Smash," I said.

"With pleasure," Diana replied with a wry smile.

Chapter Twenty-Nine

Nate Garrett

Diana had transformed into her werebear beast form well before she'd reached the mass of bodies that I'd hurled up the road. Mordred jumped off the roof of a building, using his air magic to glide to the ground, with Remy sitting on his shoulders. The fox jumped off onto the head of an ITF agent, who screamed in terror.

I turned to the crowd as the rest of my allies went to subdue the ITF and Avalon. I found several hundred people all staring at me intently, while thousands more stood behind them. So many people from all walks of life, from all age groups, all just wanting to take a stand and say they wouldn't let Avalon walk all over them.

I heard the shouts and cries of battle behind me and turned to see Mordred use a spear of ice to stab through a Harbinger's chest, before Selene—now in full dragon-kin form, hovering over the melee—beat her massive wings, opened her mouth, and sprayed ice over any of her enemies who were too slow to move aside. Her scaled skin was a brilliant silver, her fingers elongated to form talons. I knew from experience that her eyes would be a reptilian orange. She tore a car apart to get to the ITF agent who had hidden inside. Dragon-kin were feared for a reason.

I heard whispers from the crowd of protesters—"Who is he?" "Is he going to kill us?"—and wondered if these people would ever trust those of us who weren't human. A lot of the people were running away, and I couldn't say I blamed them for that. But more stayed than left. Either because they wanted to show defiance to those who had tried to put them in their place or because they were curious about what would happen next.

"We are not a threat," I said, with a little air magic to ensure that everyone heard me. "Avalon is your enemy. Avalon is not here to keep you safe. They're not here to ensure that you're happy and free from being targeted by their enemies. They want you cowed, they want you obedient, and they want you subdued. They *need* it. There are millions of nonhumans the world over. Tens, maybe even hundreds of millions. There are billions of humans. And Avalon needs you to behave so that they can do whatever they want."

"Who are you?" the young black woman from earlier shouted.

"My name is Nathaniel Garrett," I said. "I once thought that Arthur and those who stood with him were my allies. I once thought that he was a good man with only the best intentions. I was wrong. He's a murderer, an evil tyrant who will lay waste to those who dare question him. Avalon controls the governments of this world. They have control in all aspects of those who lead you, who say they protect you, who create wars for you to die in. I am here to say, 'No more.' Avalon will not have free rein to do as they please. Arthur and his minions will not be allowed to walk over those who stand up and say, 'No more.'"

I pointed to the Nazi, who had been placed partially inside the brick wall of a building. Two more, a man and a woman, were now beside him. "Those people were given the task of spraying people in the crowd with a drug that induced psychosis. They did this because they wanted the ITF to have an excuse to kill you. They wanted Avalon to have a reason to say that you people here today are the enemy of Avalon. That you are vile, corrupt murderers. They killed police officers and were ready to blame you all for it. You've all seen the news. You've all heard the whispers of how protests in other cities have turned violent. These people . . ." I pointed back to the Harbingers and ITF, who were busy getting their asses kicked by my friends. "These people have done this time and time again. Gotten good people killed because they don't want anyone to speak out. All of this was in an effort for them to go to your government, to the people in charge, and say, *We need more power to stop this.* They were going to turn your country and any other country to agree to their terms into police states. More people missing who disagreed with them, more murders, more crime, all for Avalon to tighten its grip on power over this entire planet."

"So you're here to save us?" a young white man asked.

I shook my head. "You can save yourselves. I can only do so much. I can't protect everyone all the time. But I can help you bring Avalon down around Arthur's knees. I can ensure that he and his people are met with justice. I know that you all want to be here to protest against Avalon, but I need you to go home. I need innocent people as far away from what is coming as possible, because I'm here."

"We're not going anywhere," the young woman from earlier shouted.

I sighed and looked up behind me, noticing that while my allies had managed to subdue the Harbingers and ITF, there had been a lot of damage done to the nearby buildings. Diana had thrown a car at one Harbinger and was busy picking it up to smash back down on them.

"Where's Adrestia?" I asked.

Selene turned to me, having heard my magic-carried words, and shrugged. I walked over to the fighting, took hold of a Harbinger by the throat, wrapping tendrils of shadow around him, and dragged him down a nearby alleyway while he squirmed.

"What are you?" I asked him.

"Fire elemental," he said.

"Where is Adrestia?" I asked.

He turned away from me.

"Look," I said, using my shadow magic to push him up against the wall. "We both know that this is nowhere near all of you here. So where is Adrestia, and where are the rest of your people?"

He opened his mouth, and I wrapped shadow around it.

"Before you tell me to fuck off, know this: I will kill you and either drag the information from your corpse or send you into my shadow realm to see what happens when a wraith gets hungry. Which one?"

"He knows where Frigg is," the Harbinger said.

"How?" I asked. "How is that possible? Were we betrayed?"

When the Harbinger didn't answer, I constricted the tendrils of shadow around his throat. "Do not test me," I snapped. "I am not in the mood and don't have time to play games."

"One of Frigg's attendants," the Harbinger managed to say.

I released the tension around his throat. "They betrayed us?"

"Adrestia," he said. "She can do things to people. Get in their heads, make them see things. Make them tell her things. No one wants to work with her."

I removed the shadows, and the Harbinger fell to the ground. I looked down toward the mouth of the alley and saw Diana there, still in her werebear beast form. She towered over me and the Harbinger.

"She's going to take you into custody," I said. "You're going to answer whatever questions you're asked, and you'll live to see the next few hours. If you think I'm bad, she'll tear you in half."

"We're new," the Harbinger said. "All of us were conscripted to the Harbingers. The tough ones, the ones who have been doing this for centuries, they don't leave Avalon anymore. Or they go on missions of extreme importance."

"And this wasn't that important?" I asked.

"Baldr selected us for this project," the man said, rubbing his neck, which was still pink from where I'd throttled him.

"You all chose to fight for Avalon," Diana said, her voice echoing all around us.

"Or die," the man snapped. "Not much choice, is there."

"So your excuse is 'because I was ordered to'?" Diana asked.

"I would very much not piss her off," I told him and left him to Diana's care. While he was an elemental and a Harbinger, he wasn't anywhere near as powerful as the Harbingers I'd met in the past. I thought of something and turned back. "How long is your training?" I asked. "How long do they put you under for the trials?"

"What trials?" he asked. "None of us were put under for anything."

"Were there any more of you that went with Baldr to get Frigg?"

"There were a dozen others," he said. "They were Adrestia's personal guard. They didn't socialize with the rest of us. We were all lumped in with the humans in the ITF and told to open fire on the protesters the second they started to attack. I . . . I couldn't do it in Texas at the massacre that happened there. I couldn't fire. I just stood there, and then I was told to come here."

"Remy," I shouted and waited for him to join me. "The snipers on the roof—how trained were they?"

"They were the real thing," he said. "A rifle with silver bullets that would have turned anyone into putty the second they hit. These Harbingers don't deserve to use the name. They're sloppy, ill prepared for actual combat."

"They were sent here to die," I said. "They disobeyed orders before and refused to kill people. Baldr knows where Frigg is and has gone after her, but something is planned here. Something where Avalon doesn't care about collateral damage. Those rifles had silver bullets in them; they were not there for the human protesters."

"They were going to kill the Harbingers," Mordred said as he joined Remy beside me. "It's what I would have done. You know, before I stopped being evil. Sent your useless idiots out there to do a job, and then, because you need some sort of spark to ignite the horrific shit you have planned—in their case, get more power—you kill your own people."

I stared at Mordred for several seconds. "That is actually what I thought they'd do too. Which means we're both probably messed up."

Mordred held out a fist, which I bumped. "Solidarity in being really fucked up," he said with a smile, before it faded. "But then you'll have a bunch of ITF shooting civilians, so I assume the reporters would all need to die too. At least the ones who aren't working for Avalon. And there will be people with phones who are filming. Can't have that getting out. And that's hard to do."

We shared an expression. "There's a bomb," we said in unison.

"Mordred, you need to find it and get rid of it. I need to go stop Baldr from killing Frigg and anyone else in his way."

"Need a lift?" Selene asked as she hovered over my head. She winked.

"We'll join you once we're done," Mordred said and began relaying information to the rest of the group while Selene picked me up, and we set off at speed toward Elemental Incorporated.

"You really think there's a bomb?" she asked as we flew over the rooftops.

"Something big enough to ensure that no one got out of there alive," I said. "They have the Nazis drug people, it starts a fight, but they'd want a backup, and shooting your own people is certainly not outside of Avalon's remit for horrific plans. Those Harbingers were sent there as collateral damage. So my guess is yes, there's a bomb there. Something that Avalon can blame on the protesters, sacrifice those who have disappointed them, and say that the Harbingers have been targeted by the protesters. Those Harbingers down there never even underwent the trials; they were picked up to use as collateral damage. Avalon would have needed some of their own people to die so that the legislation has more traction. Using the people who failed you once is the smartest move they have. I wonder if Adrestia opening fire was part of the plan or if that was just her hatred of me."

"You do have that effect on people," Selene said. "Not everyone, thankfully. So you think this bomb was meant to kill a whole bunch of people while the grendel blood set the stage for Avalon to fight back?"

"Pretty much. The bomb was just the icing on the 'really evil plan' cake."

"They'll find it," she said.

"I know," I told her as the Elemental Incorporated building came into view, and I spotted three Harbingers standing outside the building.

"You think there's fighting going on in there?" Selene asked.

Part of the building exploded, raining brick and glass all over the car park. "Probably," I said. "Drop me off on the roof, and then go get help."

"I need to help you," Selene said as we touched down on the roof of the building.

The door was thrown open, and the appearing Harbinger was shocked to find both Selene and me there. His shock was amplified when he got hit by a blast of ice from Selene's mouth, quickly followed by a bolt of lightning from my hand, which tore through his skull, leaving nothing but a hole where his face used to be.

"You think he'll heal from that?" Selene asked me.

I walked over to his body, picked up his assault rifle, and checked the ammo. Silver bullets. I put two into what remained of his head.

"No," I said, turning back to Selene.

An armored personnel carrier pulled into the car park, with a soldier on the massive cannon that sat behind the driver, and opened fire on us. Selene dropped to the ground, avoiding the bullets as they tore through the concrete around us like it was paper.

We both ran across the roof, the sound of a helicopter coming our way hurrying our steps. Just as we made it inside the building, the Apache AH-64 opened fire on the roof.

"I guess we have a change of plan," Selene said as we huddled in the stairwell and tried to figure out what we were meant to do next.

I dialed Hades on my phone. "We have a situation here," I shouted over the noise of the helicopter.

"We found a bomb," he said. "It's a very big bomb. It's in a building nearby, and it's large enough to level a city block."

"We have an Apache helicopter and an APC trying to blow this building apart. Also, lots of Harbingers, from the looks of things. Isis's people aren't going to be able to hold out against this onslaught for long."

"Do you have a plan?" he asked.

"Anyone you can spare who are crazy enough to fight an Apache," I said.

"You want Mordred." It wasn't a question.

"If he's not too busy."

"I'm sure he'll be happy to help," Hades said and ended the call.

"So what's the plan?" Selene asked as we cautiously made our way down the stairwell to the floor below. "Before Mordred shows up and blows up half the building, I mean?"

We stopped outside a door with a security panel that required an eight-digit code. "Frigg is in this room," I said. "I'm going to get the code from Medusa, so if you can go down to the bottom floor and basically kill everyone trying to kill you, that'd be really helpful."

"Did I detect a note of sarcasm in your voice?" Selene asked.

I kissed her on the lips. "Please go. I'll be fine."

Her eyes narrowed for a second, but her expression softened, and she took my hand in hers. "I am afraid to lose you again."

I hadn't lost anyone. Not really. I'd known I was alive and that my friends were, too, despite the fact that they were all fighting a war. The idea of losing Selene made me feel ill, and I couldn't imagine how hard it had been for her to believe I was dead. The fact that the spell hadn't worked properly and she'd been allowed to continue to grieve for me made me want to hold her and not let go.

"I don't think there's anything I can do to make up to you what you went through," I said. "But I will try every day to be the man you deserve. I'm *not* going to be killed by a piece of shit like Baldr. I'll be fine. And as soon as we've secured this building, you're more than welcome to come find me and help me kick his ass."

Selene smiled and kissed me on the lips. "The second I'm done, I'm coming to find you."

"Please do," I said.

Selene ran off down the stairs, taking them two at a time, and I called Medusa, who gave me the code for the door. She sounded like she was somewhere windy, but before I could say anything, she said, "Mordred stole a motorbike, and I'm on the back of it. We'll be with you shortly."

I put in the code and pushed open the door. The building shook as the Apache launched missiles at the car park. These were Avalon vehicles and Avalon personnel waging open war in a human city. Either the rules of engagement had well and truly changed in the last half hour, or Baldr had lost his mind.

I moved across the floor, a sword of lightning on my arm that occasionally crackled with power. When I was thirty feet away, the door to Frigg's room opened, and Antonio stepped outside, his assault rifle aimed at me.

"Antonio," I said calmly.

"Oh, Nate," Antonio said, lowering his weapon. "Am I glad to see you. It all went to shit. Baldr turned up; people attacked the building. There's an Apache helicopter outside."

"Considering the last few days, that sounds like a logical step forward," I said. "Also, I have someone coming to deal with that."

"Couldn't you just do it?"

I shook my head. "If I did it, I wouldn't be able to make sure that Baldr doesn't get to Frigg. Besides, these windows are rune scribed and pretty much impervious to bullets or missiles."

"He's got a real thing for killing his own mom, hasn't he? You think it'll bring about the end of the world?"

I shook my head. "Prophecies of doom and destruction are pretty much always utter bullshit. Baldr was fed this so that he'd be more willing to join Avalon's side and help them rule all. He wants the end of the world because . . . well, I assume because he's just that full of bile and hate at his own people."

"Daniel is in with Frigg. He's a doctor, so they asked him to keep an eye on her while hell arrived. There's a guard with him too."

I looked over at the window and saw the rune drawn in blood. A guard walked over to it and turned back to me. "Adrestia says hello," he said and slammed his hand against the glass, which exploded.

Hovering, the Apache opened fire through the destroyed window, turning the guard to pulp and forcing me to protect Antonio and myself with a shield of dense air. It only lasted a few seconds, but when it stopped, Baldr was stepping over the remains of the guard, unclipping a rope from his belt.

I spun toward him as he blasted me in the chest with a bolt of light. I managed to stop it from doing any serious damage, but I couldn't prevent being blinded by it. Several bullets were fired by Antonio, but a cry soon after signaled the end of his part in this fight.

Daniel came out of Frigg's room firing a gun at Baldr, who laughed as the bullets struck home. Baldr kicked me in the ribs, sending me flying up against the wall.

I blinked, gasping, only to see Daniel being forced to kneel in front of Baldr while the Norse god held a blade of light to the back of his neck. Antonio was unconscious on the floor, a bloody wound in his side.

"Baldr," I said softly, getting back to my feet.

Baldr looked over at me. "I brought a friend," he said. "I want you to know that the guard helped me find my mother. Took us a long time to get one of you who actually had information we needed. Adrestia is pretty good at her job, although she wasn't meant to open fire on you at the protest. She'll have to be punished for that. Good thing all of the others are being killed anyway."

"I know," I said. "One of your fake Harbingers told me all I needed. We found the bomb too."

"Just the one?" He removed a detonator from his pocket and pressed the button, followed a few moments later by tremors and the sound of a large explosion somewhere in the city. "I wonder how many of your friends died in that explosion."

I felt power flood my body as rage became my only focus.

"I assume you're going to want to fight now," Baldr said. "Guess I should make the first move." He plunged the blade of light through Daniel's neck, killing him instantly.

"I guess—" Baldr went on, but he was interrupted by a sphere of magical energy that I drove into his side and detonated. But Baldr had wrapped himself in a dense shield of light, forcing my power up and over him, obliterating every wall between where we stood and the far end of the floor.

Baldr drove a blade of light into my stomach, twisted it as I cried out in pain, and detonated the magical light inside of me. I was thrown through the wall behind me and landed in the reception area of Medusa and Isis's office.

Blood poured from the wound in my stomach as I scrambled to get back to my feet.

"I'll deal with my *mother* in a second," Baldr said, stepping over the ruined wall closest to me and kicking me in the chest with every bit of matter magic at his disposal. The blow sent me through the window at the side of the building. I tumbled through the air and smashed into the concrete next to the small park that sat at the rear of the building.

I'd managed to encase myself in a shield of air, which saved me from serious injury.

Baldr stepped out of the window and landed beside me, the force of the magic he used as he fell enough to throw me back a dozen feet.

"You can't protect your friends," Baldr said. "You can't protect yourself. And when you're dead, I'll drag your corpse over to your lovely lady, Selene, and show her that you can't protect her either. Looks like you're going to die for real this time."

My body was burned, cut, and broken. I placed a hand against the entry wound that Baldr had created and activated my blood magic. I mixed it with enough power to ensure that the wounds I'd received healed in moments, and Baldr clapped.

"Glad you're feeling better," he said, cracking his knuckles on his palms. "I wanted a bit of a challenge."

A bolt of lightning flew from the sky above, straight onto Baldr's head, destroying everything in a ten-foot circle surrounding him. I got back to my feet and rolled my shoulders, ready for the fight ahead. Lightning crackled all around me as Baldr got to his feet without a scratch on him.

"You're going to have to do better than that if you want to kill me," Baldr said with a sneer.

I smiled. "Happy to oblige."

Chapter Thirty

Nate Garrett

A bolt of light narrowly missed my head as I closed the distance between Baldr and me, trying to cut through him with a sword of fire. He forced me to put distance between the two of us and bounced from foot to foot in a show of enjoying himself.

"You know, you could just make it easy on yourself," he said. "Just take a knee and let me end it."

I threw a blade of air at him, and when he moved, I wrapped his legs and lower torso in shadows, forcing him to stay put. But a blast of blinding light caused the shadows to vanish. Painful feedback ran up my arms in response. I needed to get him away from the fighting that raged on all sides around the building. The sounds of gunfire and the Apache were still easy to hear, and I couldn't use my power to its full extent until I was sure it wasn't going to kill innocent people in the line of fire.

Baldr's light and matter magic combined to allow him to heal almost instantly, whereas I needed to rely on my blood magic to boost my healing. And blood magic was addictive and dangerous. I could use it to boost the power of my magic, but it wasn't something I wanted to do again unless I was out of options.

"Do you want to know what makes me hate you more?" Baldr asked. "You get to use pure magic. It seems like it's a hidden benefit of the way you were created. I don't. I was born normally to two parents who had me because they loved one another, not because they wanted to create a weapon. So I'm punished for not being a freak of nature. Not sure how that's fair."

I remained silent and felt the magic inside me swell. Pure magic was only destructive, and once used it would deplete my ability to use it again for some time. I had about an hour before my magic reduced in power, which meant I probably had only one shot with pure magic. And that was if it would even work at all.

Darting forward, I created a blade of flame and brought it up toward Baldr's chest. A mass of earth broke free from the ground, forming a shield in front of him, and I sank into the shadows and came up behind him with my soul weapon jian ready to go, but he moved through the shield of earth, putting it between us.

"Come on, Nate," he said. "Are you holding back because innocent people are nearby?"

I used a sphere of air to destroy the shield, throwing a whip of fire at Baldr a second later; it cut through his stomach and gave me an opening. I created two blades of lightning and drove one into his chest, then dragged it down and out of his stomach, while the second punched into his side. I pulled it up and out of his back, just by his shoulder.

Blood cascaded out of the wounds, and I moved around to Baldr's back, stabbing him over and over, until I punched one final blade through the back of his skull, detonated the magic that the blade contained, and turned the inside of his head into soup.

I pushed him forward, and he fell to the ground, lifeless. I let out a small sigh, wondering whether he was actually dead. I wasn't sure what else I could do to a person after liquefying their brain and opening their body up like they were being carved up to send to a butcher.

Stepping forward to finish the job, I suddenly felt a euphoric happiness wash over me. It was as if all of my dreams had come true at once and nothing else mattered.

Adrestia exited through a nearby door and walked over to me. "I *really* want to kill you," she said. "Instead, I'm going to let Baldr do it, and I'll watch. And you're not going to fight back, are you?"

I shook my head, although inside I was screaming at myself to kill her. "Empath," I managed between gritted teeth, and I pushed her away.

The surprise on her face was enough to break the trance for a moment, but then she regained her concentration, and I was right back to being happy and content.

"I don't know how you did that," she said. "But it won't happen again."

A blast of ice smashed through the door that Adrestia had walked through a moment earlier, crashing into her and waking me up from my dream of contentment. Selene burst through and charged into Adrestia, taking her off her feet and throwing her through a nearby window.

I shook the weirdness from my head as Selene winked at me and took off after Adrestia. Selene wouldn't be able to let up on her assault, or she might well end up in the same position I'd been in only moments earlier.

"You know," Baldr said as he looked up at me. "That really *fucking* hurt."

I dived toward him, but he caught me with a jet of flame that forced me to wrap myself in dense air and shadow to ensure I wasn't incinerated. A column of earth shot out of the ground and slammed into my chest, throwing me back against the nearest tree with a crack.

I was on all fours when Baldr slammed a magically powered boot into my ribs, shattering them and puncturing my lung in the process.

"I'll admit," Baldr said as he towered above me and brought his boot down onto my jaw, "you hurt me more than I've been hurt in a long time."

He picked me up and smashed my back against the tree, over and over again, until my vision darkened and pure survival instinct took over. I threw lightning at everything in a ten-foot radius of where we stood and followed up with a wind strong enough to tear trees from their roots.

Baldr released me and was driven back into the now-burning building, allowing me to slump to my knees and use blood magic to heal my pain-laced body.

My broken jaw and ribs were healed in mere moments, my lung not long after, but the toll it took on my magic was high. I couldn't keep getting hurt and expect to be able to heal myself as quickly as I'd need to. I was running out of time.

Baldr stepped out of the fire. His face was scarred from the heat, but a few seconds later it was back to normal.

"You've got to be kidding me," I said, getting back to my feet. "Why won't you just *die*?"

"You know, your friends are fighting for their lives against the Harbingers I brought with me," he said. "These walls have runes on them to stop magical attacks, but it turns out that if you damage enough of them, the building can catch fire. I might bring the whole place down when I'm done. Just pave over this whole area."

I breathed out and got into a fighting stance to wait for Baldr's next onslaught.

"Do you know why I hate you?" he asked conversationally as he walked the length of the path in the garden, putting himself at the opposite end of the small area of grass from the burning wall. He leaned up against the wall there, and I looked up at the three walls that stood around the garden. Instead of a wall behind me, there was a large empty car park, presumably where those who worked here parked.

"I don't care," I said.

"We're *brothers*," he said. "That's not a very nice way to treat your own family."

"You're a psychotic prick," I said. "I know what happened to our other brother, so I don't really feel like being nice."

The ground beneath my feet broke apart, and lava began to pour out, forcing me to jump up onto the railings that separated me and the car park. I flung myself aside as the ground where I'd been standing exploded in a shower of magma, and I used a shield of air to stop any of it from hitting me.

I threw a torrent of air at Baldr, who activated his matter magic and ran into the storm, forcing me to add more and more magic just to keep him at bay. But he didn't stop moving forward until I added lightning to the maelstrom of power that I'd unleashed, which obliterated part of the wall he'd been standing in front of. The runes over the concrete structure flickered once before their color faded.

"Impressive," Baldr said, clapping his hands. "A lot of power. I expected nothing less from the little freak. I killed Thor because he got in my way. I didn't want to—I wanted him to understand my hate, my need to correct all of the mistakes that the pantheons made over the centuries. How I *should* be king. He should have understood that I deserve to be king. But he didn't. He called me deluded and mocked me. So I killed him. You, though . . . you I'm going to kill because you're a mistake. You should never have been born, never have been thought about. You are the problem with our kind. A weapon designed to stop a war that might never happen. Instead, you're going to die, and I'm going to bring about a real change when I kill our father and ascend to the throne of Asgard. Ragnarok will see me blessed as the ruler of the Norse realms."

I blinked. "Do you ever actually hear the words that are coming out of your mouth? Do you ever stop and think, *Shit, I sound like a fucking lunatic?* Just asking."

"I've played with you enough," Baldr said and threw a spear of light at me that I easily avoided.

"We could do this all night," I said.

"I know," Baldr said and clicked his fingers.

I turned and wrapped myself in air just as the spear of light that he'd thrown, which had jammed into the wall, exploded out toward me. The magic that hit me was fairly low in power, but it was enough to force me back, right into the path of a second and third spear, the latter of which broke through my shield and slammed into my chest, knocking me off my feet and throwing me to the ground.

"Come on, Nate," Baldr said, punching me in the jaw as I got to my feet. "Why aren't you doing all you can to kill me? No one is innocent. No one."

I drove a sphere of magic into his knee and detonated it, causing him to be thrown back across the garden and into the damaged wall opposite. The runes no longer flickered as part of the structure fell down to fill the hole that Baldr had made.

I ran toward the hole in the wall, pouring magic into my fist as I moved, but when I was halfway there, the Apache helicopter appeared and opened fire at me. A shield of air saved me from being riddled with bullets, and the second the Apache stopped, I used all of the power I'd built up, merged the fire and air magic with my lightning, and threw it at the helicopter. It caught the machine just below the rotor, ripping it apart and causing the Apache to fall toward the car park. With a deafening explosion, it drove into the concrete and exploded. One of the pieces of the rotor was flung toward me, and I moved to avoid it but was caught in a tackle by Baldr, who drove me into the ground.

Baldr rained punches down on me, and I moved, grabbing his leg and twisting it until the knee snapped. I kicked out at the other leg and punched him in the groin with a fist wrapped in lightning, then kicked out at his face as I saw his knee had already healed. He punched me in the jaw with so much power that it drove my head into the ground. When I turned to move, he hit me again and again, each time the power of the blow causing loose dirt around me to shower over my body with the shock wave. Even the shield I'd managed to create to stop him from doing any more damage was broken after the fourth punch, leaving me dazed and hurt on the ground.

"Why won't you just die?" he asked me, throwing my own question back at me before spitting in my face.

He raised his fists high above his head, and the glyphs over his arms glowed brilliantly as he brought them down onto my chest, just as I gathered my own magic and poured it out of my body to meet the blow. The resulting shock wave threw Baldr away, but there was no respite, as he was back a second later, dragging me out of the hole that had been created with the blast and over the inferno that spilled out of the building nearby. He smashed my face into the wall before driving a knee into the side of my skull and punching me in the stomach when I didn't immediately fall to the ground.

"I want to see the monster inside of you," he whispered. "I know it's there. I know that darkness is there. I heard all about the things you did after your wife died. I saw what you did to Kay. I saw what you did to everyone who crossed you. So where's the monster now? Come on—stop playing games and show me what you can *really* do."

I took a deep breath and exhaled slowly. I'd been fighting angry. I'd been wanting to hurt Baldr, wanting to make sure that he knew he'd been beaten. But I realized I couldn't fight him that way. I couldn't hold back and expect to win. I sent out a mass of air, trying to find out how many people were inside the building behind me, but I found no heartbeats.

He punched me in the face again. "Fight me!" he screamed. "Is this it? Is this the weapon my father put so much time and effort into creating? Pathetic!"

He punched me in the face again.

I caught the third punch in my hand and looked up at Baldr, increasing the pressure of the air magic until I heard bones break and tendons snap. Baldr's eyes widened as the pain hit him, and I kept hold of his hand as I got back to my feet and black, smokelike swirls spilled out of my eyes, the power inside me growing.

Baldr tried to pull his hand free. He went to punch me, but my shadow magic leaped up to block the blow. I pulled my free hand back, and a black orb appeared, spinning rapidly until it was a blur. I drove it into Baldr's chest and detonated the magic.

The wall behind Baldr was partially vaporized as he was thrown backward, through the side of the building behind me, and down the slope outside. I walked through the rubble and noticed that he had come to settle near the main road. Cars braked as he scrambled over the metal barrier and sprinted across the road to the park beyond, next to the river.

I ran down the slope, vaulted the barrier, and used my air magic. "Everyone in a car, get away from here. Now."

Most people appeared to take the hint, and after a bolt of lightning slammed into the road beside me, the rest followed suit.

Baldr leaned up against a tree, his chest a mass of red. "Why won't it heal?" he shouted, more to himself than anyone else.

"I didn't want to use my pure magic," I told him. "I wanted to stop you without it. Pure magic is only destructive, and I didn't want to kill people who were in the wrong place. But there was no one there."

"Why am I not healing?" he screamed at me.

"Because I was designed to be a weapon," I told him.

He tried to stab me with a blade of light, but he was slow and awkward, and I easily deflected it with one of shadow before stepping to his side, grabbing his arm, and snapping it at the elbow. I headbutted Baldr and punched him in the stomach, and then I unleashed a blade of lightning that cut up through his body.

A second later the wound and broken arm healed.

"What did you do to me?" he screamed, throwing a punch that I blocked. I hit him in the chest with another blast of pure magic.

He bounced fifty feet along the ground as the tree he'd been standing in front of was turned to ash from the power of pure magic.

"Damn it, now I have to plant a tree," I said, stepping over the remains of the trunk.

"What is this?" Baldr screamed.

"This," I said, "is pure magic. You think you know what it is, but you don't *really*, do you?"

The wound on his chest was healing again, but it was bleeding and sore and healed much more slowly than any other wound he'd received.

"When my magic rushed back into my head and my nightmare finally vanished, I had a lot of stuff up here," I said, tapping the side of my head. "Lots of info about exactly *what* I am. Like you said, I'm a weapon. But I'm a weapon designed for one purpose. To kill people like you. I was designed to be a god killer. The wounds caused by pure magic will take a lot more strength to heal than you possess."

Baldr's eyes opened wide, and for the first time I saw fear in them. "Please don't," he said.

"You could have done *so* much to help this world," I told him.

He tried to stab me with a blade of fire, but it was weak and feeble, and a bolt of lightning through his shoulder ended that attempt for the moment, although his body started to heal the wound almost instantly.

"I'm healing," he said with a bloody grin.

"Yep, but only where the pure magic didn't hit," I said, feeling the magic build up inside me once more.

"I'm your *brother*," he said. "Doesn't that mean anything to you?"

I shook my head. "Did it matter to you when you killed Thor? You're *not* my brother. You just happen to share some of the same genes as me. You're nothing. A waste of power and talent."

Baldr pushed me away, but my shadow magic tripped him, causing him to land on the ground and cry out in pain. "Whatever you do to me, I'll heal," he shouted.

Pure magic continued to spin in my hand, growing faster and faster the larger it got. When it was the size of a basketball, I ran up to a kneeling Baldr and plunged it into his chest before detonating the magic.

The park for thirty feet on either side of us vanished. Trees were torn apart, and the ground behind and to the side of Baldr was ripped up and thrown into the river as the magical inferno engulfed him. The metal railing that separated the park from the river became molten, and the water boiled where the magic hit it, until it stopped a hundred feet out from where I stood.

When the magic ceased and all reserves had left my body, the ground looked as though a bomb had gone off. There was nothing but dirt.

I stood over what remained of Baldr and kicked the ashes. "Heal from that, you utter bastard."

Chapter Thirty-One

Nate Garrett

Loki was the first one to find me as I walked back up the slope to the ruins of the building. He looked dirty and had dried blood on his face and clothes but was otherwise unharmed. "You okay?" he asked.

"I just found out I had a brother who not only murdered my other brother but who I then had to kill," I said. "It's been a bit of a strange couple days. Even by my standards."

"You had no choice about killing him," Loki said. "He was psychotic."

"And evil, I know." I patted him on the shoulder. "How is everyone else?"

"The fighting is done. The Harbingers that Baldr had were the real deal and put up quite a fight. The Apache helicopter is toast, which I assume is your doing."

"Guilty," I said with a slight smile.

"So it's just gathering the injured and helping those who can be saved."

"What about the explosion I heard?"

"Everyone is fine," Loki said. "Some of the Harbingers, the fake ones, well, they had these blood curse markings on them that caused them to explode when activated."

"Yeah, I've had some up-close meetings with people and those runes," I said, remembering all of the people two years ago who had been killed by sorcerers turning themselves into bombs.

"No serious injuries to those of us who were there." He paused. "You know, except for the people who blew themselves up. They were definitely dead."

With Loki beside me, we made our way through the partially destroyed building and out to the car park at the front, where the APC had been mostly melted on one side. Remy sat on top of it, wearing a military helmet. I didn't want to know where he'd gotten it.

"You look happy," I said.

He tapped his knuckles on the APC. "I'd ask to keep it if it wasn't for the fact that it looks like melted cheese on one side," Remy said, jumping down from the top and landing by my feet. "Baldr dead?"

I nodded.

"I'm sorry you had to kill your brother," he said, suddenly serious. "That's a shitty thing to have to do."

"Thanks," I said. "But he was not a good person, so I don't exactly feel bad about it. Where's everyone else?"

"Inside," Remy said. "There was a lot of mopping up to do once these guys were dealt with. I heard the Apache blow up. Sorry I didn't see it. Was it impressive?"

"Yeah, a bit," I admitted. "Not something I want to do again anytime soon, though."

"You heard about the sorcerers who blew themselves up? Again."

"Loki told me."

"Can you have a word with your people and tell them to stop doing that?"

"We don't have a newsletter, Remy," I said.

"You need to get on that shit, then," he said. "You don't see us fox-men going around blowing ourselves up."

"You're the only one," I pointed out.

Remy paused. "Not the point."

"Is he really always like this?" Loki asked.

"Yes," Remy said cheerfully. "Apparently you get used to me."

"You don't," I corrected and received a playful punch to the ribs from Remy as we reentered the building and moved toward where the fighting had been the fiercest.

Mordred and Diana were tending to the wounded, and Hades was in the corner, talking to Persephone and Medusa.

"Can I help?" I asked Mordred.

"No, you can rest," he told me. "Your power is about to drop like a stone, if it hasn't already, and when that happened to me, I passed out."

"So don't pick up anything heavy," Diana said.

"I'll keep that in mind," I promised.

"Selene is upstairs with Frigg," Diana said. "I know you were going to ask."

"How many did Medusa and Isis lose?" I asked.

"A few dozen, and Isis got hit pretty badly," Diana said. "One of the Harbingers was a werelion and tore her up before she could be stopped. Isis will heal, but it was just after another Harbinger stabbed her with a silver blade, so it'll take time."

"She's discussing moving the whole operation to work with Hades and his people. I think that would benefit everyone concerned," Tommy said, dropping a large barrel of water next to Mordred.

"Where are you all based now?" I asked.

"Well, we were in Greenland for a while," Tommy said. "And then that got destroyed by Avalon."

"The whole country?" I asked.

"No, just one bit," Diana told me.

"It sucked," Remy said.

"So we moved to Shadow Falls," Tommy continued. "We took precautions to increase security, and it seems to be working okay so far. And Helheim."

"Go find Selene," Diana said.

"I'll go talk to Hades," Loki said. "I think we're going to need all the help we can get, though. And at some point, you're going to have to consider visiting your dad."

"Do you know where my mum is?" I asked.

"Last I heard, she was with the other Valkyries," Loki said. "And they don't like visitors."

"Or anyone. At all," Mordred added.

"What Mordred said," Loki agreed. "We'll have to find a realm gate to get you there and hopefully not get you killed the second you step foot in Valhalla."

"A problem for tomorrow," I said and left everyone to their work, taking the stairs two at a time to the top floor, where I found Selene playing cards with Antonio.

"Glad you're okay," I said.

"He means you," Antonio said to Selene, who laughed.

"He bloody well better," she told him.

"I'll leave you alone," Antonio said, getting to his feet and wincing from the pain in his side before offering me his hand. "Duke's can wait. I'm coming with you guys. Human or not, I can shoot, and frankly Clockwork isn't for me anymore."

"Welcome aboard," I said.

"Before you get all loved up, Daniel's family is in the office at the far end. They know what happened to him."

"I'll be back in a minute," I said.

I walked through the floor, noticing the missing windows and several rooms that no longer had all their walls, until I reached the office and entered after knocking.

Jessica sat on a sofa near the far wall with a sleeping Simon beside her. Ava was sitting at a meeting table with her head in her hands, and Donna was beside her, one arm around her granddaughter.

Apart from Simon, they all looked up when I walked in.

"I'm so sorry," I said, my voice cracking.

Donna was the first to her feet, rushing over to me and enveloping me in a tight hug. "It's not your fault," she whispered in my ear. "None of this is your fault. Or Hades, or Loki, or anyone but Baldr and Avalon. They started this. They murdered him. I'm sorry you had to witness it."

Tears stung my eyes. "He was a good man, a good father, a good husband and grandfather."

"I'm coming with you," Ava said.

"Ava, not now," Jess snapped.

"Yes," Ava snapped back. "I didn't see my granddad's death. I saw you and piles of bodies, but that was it. I need to learn how to control this. Just talking to the shinigami isn't going to get the job done. I need to learn how to control it."

"It won't be safe with us," I said.

"It's not safe anywhere," she countered.

"She has my blessing," Donna said. "Hades has told us we all have a place with his people. I will be taking him up on the offer too. I don't know what I can do—I'm not a warrior, and I don't have powers—but I'll do what I can."

"I don't know what we're going to do," Jess said. "It's just . . . so much to take in."

"I know," I said.

"Hades has arranged transport for us to Shadow Falls," Donna said. "We'll be gone in an hour or so."

"Will we see you there?" Ava asked.

I nodded. "Yes, I can think of nowhere better to rest and get ready for what happens next."

"What happens next?" Ava asked.

"We finally go to war with Avalon," I said. "You should know that. You should know that what happens next will be hard, and more will die. But if we don't do this, Arthur and his people will eradicate everyone who disagrees with him in his quest to rule all of the realms. I don't plan on allowing that to happen."

I stayed and talked with them all for a few minutes before telling them I'd see them later and going back to find Selene alone.

"You coming to Shadow Falls?" she asked.

I nodded. "Sounds like the best way forward."

Selene got up and took my hands in hers. "Together. The best way forward together."

I nodded. "I assume Adrestia will no longer be a problem."

"That was not the time to bring her up, but yes, she's been removed as an issue."

"Sorry, I just wanted to make sure . . ."

Selene kissed me. "Sometimes you really should shut up."

"True story," I said with a smile.

We left the floor and returned to help the others deal with the wounded. Hades made some calls and had several large buses arrive to take everyone to a military airport just outside of town. Apparently, the calls consisted of getting free use of some exceptionally large aircraft that I didn't know the names of. Remy had dubbed them the BFPs, or big fucking planes, and we all felt that it was probably apt.

I arrived back in Shadow Falls to a fanfare I didn't think I deserved. Apparently, my resurrection was big news to the people who lived there, and I saw more than one old friend who told me that now that I was back, we could really take it to Avalon. No pressure or anything.

I spent the next few days in the palace in Shadow Falls. It had once belonged to my friend Galahad, but his murder had been one of the catalysts that had put me on my current path and was still something that felt very raw to me. Everyone brought me up to speed on what I'd missed, a lot of which was good news, although the news of the death of my dear friend Nabu brought it all crashing back down around me.

After the first day of not being left alone, I was pretty much allowed to do whatever I wanted until they were ready for me to undergo the Harbinger trials. I mostly saw old friends and spent time reinforcing the belief that we could actually win this when it came down to it. I stayed away from the Earth realm, simply because I was content to take a break. Also, because there weren't twenty-four-hour news channels in Shadow Falls, and that was never a bad thing.

"You ready?" Selene said as she sat beside me on the steps at the front of the palace, overlooking the city of Solomon below.

"I am," I said. "Who's doing it?"

"We have a few people here who can use mind magic," she said. "And Irkalla is going to help; she thinks having her maintain your spirit might stop you from . . . well, dying horribly. Her words, not mine."

"Ah, that's nice," I said, making Selene laugh. Irkalla was a necromancer, one of the most powerful I'd ever met. She'd been considered the Mesopotamian god of death, Ereshkigal, but preferred the name Irkalla.

"The last few days I've spent with you here have been amazing," Selene said.

I took her hand in mine. "I love you, Selene. When I come out and we've finally defeated Arthur, I want to go to a realm far from all this. Not forever but just to spend some time alone."

"That sounds nice," she said. "Tommy would get jealous, though."

I laughed. "Tommy can bring Olivia, and they can stay on one half of the realm and us on the other, and we'll arrange a big Star Wars convention in the middle."

"He'd never bloody leave," Selene said. "I think he might actually be happier than I am that you're back."

I stood and stretched. "Okay, before I get second thoughts, let's go put me under and do weird things to my brain."

"You make it sound stupid," Selene said.

"I know you don't like the idea," I said to her as we climbed the steps back into the palace. "But it's not like our options were unlimited."

Selene sighed. "I know. Doesn't mean I have to be thrilled about it."

"Point taken."

We took the huge ornate staircase up to the floor above and followed the hallway to a room overlooking the rear of the castle as well as the enormous forest that stretched as far as the eye could see. Irkalla, Mordred, Hades, and two women I'd never met before sat in the room.

"I trust them with my life," Hades said. "They won't want you to know their names. Apparently, if you do, it might interfere with the process and cause some sort of feedback."

"Feedback sounds bad when it comes to this," I said.

"Brain-meltingly bad," Mordred said with a frankly terrifying smile. He gave me the thumbs-up. It didn't help.

I lay down on the bed and waited to be hooked up to several machines that would monitor my heart rate and blood pressure. The blood curse marks on the floor ensured that I didn't need food or drink for the duration and were periodically replaced as the power inside them wore out. Six months was going to be a long time for anyone in the real world, but for me inside my subconscious, it would be years of training. I couldn't say it was something I was looking forward to, but it needed to be done.

Selene kissed me on the lips. "I'll see you in six months," she said.

We professed our love to each other, and she left the room, opening up a hollow feeling in my chest.

"She'll be fine," Irkalla said. "She'll stay busy, and she'll be waiting when you come back."

"I know," I said. "It's just hard to say goodbye when we only just found one another again. This whole thing sucks."

"In an ideal world we wouldn't need to do it," Hades said. "In an ideal world, Arthur would be dead, and Avalon would be a force for good."

"Wow," Mordred said, looking at Hades. "Way to keep the mood up, my man."

Hades sighed. "Sorry. This is all beginning to become a strain. And with Medusa and her people having joined, it's logistically testing." He paused for a second. "Have any of you seen the news in the last few days?"

Mordred, Irkalla, and I exchanged glances and shook our heads.

"You remember I said that there was a possibility that you'd be on film?" Hades asked. "Well, turns out I was right."

"How much film?" Irkalla asked.

"Nate saving the lives of dozens of people when the Harbingers opened fire. Nate creating a gust of wind that knocked down a few dozen people like they were made of paper. You know, that sort of thing. Also Remy giving one of them the middle finger. They had to beep out his words."

"Because Remy," I said with a smile.

Mordred laughed. "I wish I'd seen it now. Remy will want his own show if he gets famous."

"*Swearing with Remy*," I said, which made everyone laugh. Even the two nameless mind-magic users smiled.

"That's a show that has legs," Irkalla said. "It could be educational like *Sesame Street*, but all the puppets are animals that tell people to fuck off."

"Remy has an entertainment empire on his hands," I said. "So, Hades, how bad is it now that we're on the news?"

"Right now, I'm not hearing anything beyond Arthur and his allies being furious that you're alive. A few of our people in their organization had to get out of Dodge quickly, as they were meant to have been involved in your death, so we've lost some resources on that front, but everyone appears to have gotten out without any trouble. Which is probably the best outcome we could ask for."

"Long term, though," Irkalla said, "Hera and Arthur are going to come for him."

Hades nodded. "We're safe here, but yes, they're going to go looking. Hopefully Nate's lack of visible presence will work in his favor, and they'll find very little. We'll run interference until you're back. But once you are back, we're going to need to work quickly."

"I figured burning down everything they built would be a good start," I said. I sighed and looked over at Mordred. "Ready when you are."

Mordred placed a hand on my shoulder. "See you in six months."

"Do you ever wish you'd gone through this?" I asked.

Mordred shook his head. "You're better with power than I am. I'm not the man I was only a few decades ago, but that doesn't mean I don't feel the effects of being him. I'm happy where I am. I'm in a good place."

I squeezed his hand. "I'm glad to hear it, old friend." I closed my eyes as tiredness hit me hard, and in a moment I was asleep.

I opened my eyes to find myself in a large field that appeared to stretch forever. I squinted and could almost make out a mountain range in the far distance.

"So," Hades said from beside me. "You ready to begin?"

Chapter Thirty-Two

LAYLA CASSIDY

Realm of Shadow Falls

The team was back in Jotunheim before nightfall, but after they explained to Tarron what had happened, they had to deal with his and Zamek's need for vengeance. It took several of them a few hours to talk them both down from rushing off to Asgard to wage war against Surtr.

Hel had sent several dozen soldiers through the elven realm gate to help the giants deal with the now-calm volcano, but there were still a lot of fires to extinguish, and several houses had lava pouring out of them, so it became a full-time relief effort.

Layla traveled back to Shadow Falls to talk to Hel and the others in charge of the effort to actually beat Avalon, but she was told Nate Garrett had risen from the grave, and she discovered that everyone was freaking out because he was Odin's son and some kind of living weapon. Layla had spent time with Nate when she'd first become an umbra and had been saddened to hear of his death. To discover that he was alive was a wonderful thing, although it raised more questions in her head than it answered.

With so much going on, it took a few days for the information regarding Avalon's progress in Asgard to reach them.

"Again?" Layla asked.

"Apparently so," Hel told her.

"It's been under attack for the better part of a thousand years," Layla said. "I doubt it's going to fall anytime soon."

"No," Hel agreed. "But we still need to send people there to aid them. The flame giants are going to be a problem, and Odin has asked for our help."

"And you'd like me to go?" Layla asked.

"You and your team, yes," Hel said.

They were sitting outside the realm gate temple in Shadow Falls, eating a bowl of fruit and watching the efforts to rebuild the city of Solomon, which was inhabited for the first time in a few years since Avalon had tried to turn it to rubble.

"I assume that a lot of my team are waiting for us to head to Asgard and help out?"

Hel nodded. "Some are eager."

"I bet they are," Layla said. "The dwarves and shadow elves must be with Surtr. He won't let his slave labor go easily."

"No, he won't. Too many people buy into this Ragnarok bullshit; it makes it dangerous."

"You think a ragtag bunch of half a dozen of us will really swing the war?"

"No, that's why two thousand dwarves are going with you. They're already entering the main city at Asgard; I think they'll help. They asked for you because they've worked with you before and their leader trusts you. Otherwise, I'd be ordering you to get some rest."

Layla knew the dwarves and liked several of them, so she wasn't exactly upset that she'd be working with them again.

"Tarron, Zamek, and Hyperion are already in Asgard. Jidor too. You've assembled quite the diverse team."

"It's my second power. Harry and Kase?" Layla asked.

"Both expressed a need to help, and I assume your cat will be joining you. She's very handy at keeping several of the larger rodents who live in the forest at bay."

"I'm sure she'll be able to help do that when we return."

Hel laughed. "I've sent a few more people to help you. I wish I could give you more, but this won't be easy. If Asgard falls, everything we fought for in the other Norse realms will be for nothing. Avalon has close to half a million supporters fighting in Asgard, and while Odin and his people have managed to hold them off, they can't do that indefinitely."

"Who's the woman in the bed?" Layla asked. She'd seen her taken through the realm gate earlier in the day, along with a dozen heavily armed guards.

"Frigg," Hel said. "Odin's wife. It's a long story, but we felt it safest to move her there."

"To a war zone?"

Hel chuckled. "Yep, pretty much. Shows how fucked we're going to be here, doesn't it?"

"They were close to using realm gates as weapons," Layla said. "I don't think anywhere is safe if they get it to work as well as they think it will. I think they just used an elven realm gate to get from Muspelheim to Asgard. Which means that everything they had Fuvos do was to cause a distraction and have us spend time running around after him. But what if it really works? What if you can take a whole realm and put it into another?"

"I have people working on it. Hades and Persephone also. Basically, what you discovered scared the shit out of everyone, and we're trying to find ways to ensure they can't do it again."

Layla stood and stretched. "How's Mordred?"

Hel's smile was one of warmth. "He's good, thanks. Can I ask you something?"

Layla nodded.

"When this is all over, when the war is finished and Avalon, Arthur, and their minions are no longer a threat, what are you going to do?"

Layla shrugged. "Not thought about it. It feels like a long way off. You?"

"I'm going to rule Helheim. I'm going to do everything in my power to make sure that this realm is secure and safe and that those living here are free from tyranny and oppression. And then I'm going to take Mordred somewhere secluded, and I'm going to see if what we have works in peace as well as war."

"I think it will," Layla said. "I've seen you both together. You complement one another's personalities too much for it to just be a heat-of-the-moment, while-we're-at-war thing."

"I hope you're right. You really never thought about what you'll do?"

"I didn't know when I was at university, I didn't know when I first became an umbra, and I still don't know now. I'm only in my twenties but feel about thirty years older. I'm going to take the world's longest holiday—somewhere that serves really strong cocktails—and I'm going to sleep for about a year, and then I'm going to help people. Somehow. I'm good at it. No boasting—just being honest."

"You are," Hel said. "That and fighting."

"Yeah, the fighting is a necessity but not exactly my choice of how to live my life. I'm living for the moment and haven't really thought about the future. Maybe I need to. To have an exit plan. To do something I love. You've given me something to think on."

"I didn't mean for it to be such an existential question," Hel said with a chuckle.

Layla smiled. "I'm going to go fight a war now. We'll continue this when I return."

Hel hugged Layla goodbye, and she walked into the temple, stepping through the dwarven realm gate, which finally had a full-time guardian operating it.

Asgard smelled fresh. Layla left the dwarven temple and stepped out onto the street beyond. It was full of tall pale buildings and large open spaces. The path was paved with silver stones, and the majority of those who passed her were wearing armor of one kind or another. Mostly leather, some plate or chain mail, but everyone carried a weapon, and everyone looked ready for a fight.

A large man walked toward Layla, all barrel chest and flowing silver hair. He had an eye patch made of black leather and offered her his hand.

"Layla, here to fight a war for Odin," Layla said.

"Odin," the man said with a smile. "Here to watch you kick the shit out of everyone in your way."

Odin took Layla through the streets, where several people bowed to him, and he waved them away and smiled. They used an elevator to go up the side of a wall that stretched hundreds of feet high and got out at the top on the ramparts.

"So this is Asgard?" Layla asked. "You know your son is alive."

Odin nodded. "People keep telling me. I have locked all of the realm gates back down now, so no one else can come or go until I unlock them. Our reunion will have to wait." He pointed across the realm, full of rolling hills, fields, beautiful plains, and not a hint of war anywhere.

"Asgard is one of the largest realms," Odin said. "My scouts say that on foot, it will take the enemy six months to arrive. We've weathered a storm from their kind before, and we will again. We have six months to make this city ready for the giants, for Surtr, for Avalon's machine of war. It will be different than before. This will be the test of us."

"We will endure," Layla said. "We will win."

"You sound so sure of it."

"I have to be," Layla said. "Anything else means the death of everyone in this city. In this realm. It means the death of those in realms we've fought so hard to save. This is where Avalon learns the true measure of those who stand against them. This is where the war truly begins."

Epilogue

NATE GARRETT

Six Months Later

I opened my eyes and blinked at the real light inside the room. Someone had placed blinds on the windows since I'd been taken in there, so thankfully, I wasn't blinded the second I woke up.

I tried to speak, but my throat hurt. They could do a lot to keep you alive, but not talking for six months took a toll.

Tommy passed me a cup of water, which I drank slowly, allowing my throat to ease back into accepting liquids. It would be a while before I was capable of eating anything, but my stomach grumbled all the same.

"Six months, four days, nineteen hours," Tommy said. "I don't know the minutes and seconds, so don't ask."

"How is everyone?" I asked.

"Okay," he said. "Not a lot has happened, to be honest. Arthur is gearing up for a large-scale attack on Asgard, so we're preparing for that. And once they all knew you were alive, there were a lot of doors being kicked in by jackbooted thugs, but with you having been out of the limelight for six months, I think they believe you're off somewhere preparing. Which is sort of what you were doing. Arthur will know that you'll need to get your powers back; I imagine he believes you're training for a few years in some remote realm."

"No one will think I was stupid enough to go through the trials again," I said with a smile and touched my face. "I have quite the beard."

"And long hair. We couldn't stop them from growing. The two sorcerers who did the lion's share of your time under left a week ago. Apparently, people should be left to wake up from their induced coma at their own pace."

"Right," I said, wincing as I moved. "I ache."

"It'll pass, apparently," Tommy said. "There are several things you *really* need to know. I can tell you a few of them, but some are better left for others. You want to go through it all now?"

I rolled my neck. "Sure, let's get this done."

"Okay, well, I don't know how to tell you this, but I'm a father again." Tommy's smile grew tenfold.

"Holy shit," I almost shouted, attempting to jump to my feet, but my legs went, and Tommy had to catch me midfall.

"That probably wasn't what you had in mind," he said.

"No, but a hug's a hug," I said. "Was she pregnant when I went under?"

"No, she got pregnant about a week later, but the mixture of elemental and werewolf DNA means a shorter gestation time."

"A boy? A girl? How old are they? How are they? How is Olivia?" All of the questions flooded out at once.

"Ten days old. A boy. Olivia is fine," Tommy said, still smiling.

I sat back down on the bed. "So what's his name?"

"We named him Daniel Nathan Carpenter."

I sat there, mouth open, in shock. "You named him after me?"

"You're like my brother, Nate."

I hugged him again and felt my eyes tear up. "Damn, thank you. I'm so happy for you." I sat back on the bed. "That's awesome news. I'm surprised you didn't manage to get Han in there somewhere."

Tommy shook his head. "I wanted Han. Olivia threw something at me."

"A perfectly valid response," I told him.

"I see that now. Remy wanted us to name him Remy Remington the Second, but we went in a different direction."

"That sounds like Remy," I said with a chuckle.

"Olivia threw something at him too. So he suggested Remy the Mighty. I think she was about to throw everything at him at that point."

I laughed until my ribs hurt. "I would have loved to have seen that."

Tommy looked over at the door. "Okay, I think the other pieces of news have arrived. I'm glad you're okay. We'll let you get your legs and then go kick some Avalon arse."

"Sounds like a plan," I told him.

As Tommy left, Selene entered the room. I smiled as I saw her eyes, and then my gaze immediately went to her belly.

"Hello, Nate," she said, placing her hands on her stomach. "You want to feel your daughter kick?"

My mouth dropped open in shock. "You're . . . we're . . . a baby? My—our baby? Girl?"

"Yes. I really hope she gets your way with language," Selene said with a broad smile.

I ran over and picked Selene up in my arms. "How long?" I asked. "Are you okay? Is the baby okay?"

"Six months," she said.

"Did me and Tommy both drink something in the water?" I asked.

Selene chuckled. "Apparently so. She is fine. I am fine. I am a bit fed up of being increasingly large, and my feet hurt. Also, I crave cheese. Like, *crave* cheese. I would literally smother you in it and lick it off, is what I'm saying."

"I don't want you to smother me in cheese," I said.

"Don't get me pregnant, then," she said.

"I've never had a child before," I said. "I didn't know I could."

"Well, you can; don't brag," Selene said, kissing me on the lips. "I missed you."

"I missed you too."

"I know we're going to go to war, but if you miss this baby's birth, it better be because you're literally fighting a horde. Not a figurative horde. A literal horde."

"They won't be able to stop me getting to you," I promised.

"You're going to be busy for a while," she said. "A lot of people have been waiting for you to return so we can go after Arthur."

We sat and chatted for a while, making sure not to discuss Avalon, Arthur, or anything else negative. All the while I came to terms with the idea of being a father.

"She told you?" Tommy asked at the entrance to the palace as Selene and I were leaving.

"No," Selene said. "He just thinks I ate a lot of carbs."

Tommy looked between me and Selene.

"Yes, I told him," Selene said, mumbling to herself and walking off down the steps to the city of Solomon. "Find me later," she shouted back.

I followed Tommy to a nearby fort, being congratulated by people on the way. Once inside the fort, we made our way to a large meeting room in the heart of the stone-and-wood building, where Hades, Persephone, and several others stood around a huge table.

"So," I said. "I guess it's time to figure out our plan."

"We're going to go after Avalon's higher-ups," Hades said. "And their cash flow."

I nodded, looking over a selection of maps and pictures that were spread out over the table. "Right. It's time to take this war to Avalon's doorstep."

ACKNOWLEDGMENTS

The first book in this new series and the return of Nate Garrett was always something I was looking forward to writing. And as always, there are many people to thank for making this book possible.

As always, a big thank-you to my wife for just being her and for always being supportive and helpful, even if it just means listening to my stream of consciousness when I try to explain the plot of a book.

To my three wonderful daughters, who are still one of the reasons I write. They've got a while to go before they're allowed to read my books, and if they ever do, I'm not entirely sure I want to know.

My parents, who are always supportive and have a wall of my covers in their home. At this point, I think I just write books so they'll run out of space.

To all of my friends and family, thank you. Your support and friendship mean the world to me.

A big thanks to my agent, Paul Lucas, who is frankly just an all-around awesome person.

To Julie Crisp, my editor on this book, who took my ramble of words and helped to make it into a cohesive story. This book is better for having you as an editor—thank you.

To my publishing team at 47North, who has been so support-ive and helpful over the years. A huge number of people there helped me get this book, and all the other books I've written, into the hands of readers, and I wouldn't be where I am now without your backing. Thank you.

Lastly, I wanted to say a huge thank-you to a man who is sadly no longer with us. Frank Flynn took time to talk to me about stories he'd heard during his time in the military, and parts of those stories are included in this book. He was happy to help, and I will always be thankful for that.

ABOUT THE AUTHOR

Photo © 2013 Sally Beard

Steve McHugh is the author of the bestselling Hellequin and Avalon Chronicles. He lives in Southampton, on the south coast of England, with his wife and three young daughters. When not writing or spending time with his kids, he enjoys watching movies, reading books and comics, and playing video games.